Charming
BLUE

KRISTINE GRAYSON

sourcebooks
casablanca

Published by Sourcebooks Casablanca, an imprint of Sourcebooks, Inc.
P.O. Box 4410, Naperville, Illinois 60567-4410
(630) 961-3900
FAX: (630) 961-2168
www.sourcebooks.com

Printed and bound in the United States of America
VP 10 9 8 7 6 5 4 3 2 1

For my wonderful husband, as always

Chapter 1

Ninety-five degrees in the shade, and still the magical gathered outside Jodi's office, pacing through the landscaping, huddling under the gigantic palms, pushing past blooming birds of paradise that she spent a small fortune on, and leaning on the fountain she paid some city administrator extra just so she could keep it running in the middle of the day. She needed that damn fountain, not because she liked flaunting water laws, but because any minute now a cell phone would explode, and its owner would throw it in panic.

Usually the magical would have enough presence of mind to throw an exploding cell phone *at* water, although she had learned over her long and storied career that using the words "the magical" and "presence of mind" in the same sentence could be a recipe for disaster.

She pulled her sporty red Mercedes convertible into driveway, waved at her current, potential, and former clients, and parked under the carport, dreading the next few minutes. She would have to thread her way along the curved tile sidewalk that she put in a decade or more ago, before cell phones forced her magical clients to stand outside (she *hated* it when cell phones exploded inside). Back then, she thought the smokers might be a problem, so she installed an antique upright ashtray that she bought at a flea market—one of those ashtrays, she had been assured, that had stood on the MGM lot back when Clark Gable roamed the premises.

The ashtray still got a lot of use, but mostly the cell phone users had pushed the smokers aside. And no matter how much she told her magical clients that the longer they used a phone, the more likely it was to explode, they never listened to her.

Of course, you really couldn't survive in Los Angeles without a phone. She bought hers in bulk. The manager at the phone store finally taught her how to transfer her number to a new phone, so she wasn't stopping in every other day demanding an emergency phone repair.

She grabbed her purse, today's phone, and her briefcase, stuffed to the gills with contracts, memos, and all that junk computers were supposed to replace.

By the time she waggled her car door open, she nearly hit four dwarves (of the Snow White variety), two selkies (clothed, thank heavens), and one troll. He was a sweetie named Gunther whom she used to find regular work for in Abbott and Costello movies, before he returned to the Kingdoms. Now that he had come back to the Greater World, she was having trouble placing him, which she thought was just plain weird, given the popularity of fantasy movies these days. But whenever he went to a casting call, he was told to remove his costume, and he couldn't, since he truly was tall, gray, stone-like, and glowery.

She hadn't figured out a way around that yet, but she would.

"I don't have time, Gunther," she said as she slung her purse over her shoulder and closed the car door with her foot. She hadn't looked, so she hoped she didn't catch one of the small magical in that move. Pixies in particular liked to get between cars and doors.

But no one screamed, so she was probably safe.

"I'm so sorry to bother you, Miss Walters," Gunther said slowly, ever proper. He had nineteenth-century manners, which was another reason she loved him. "But I do need a moment—"

"Can Ramon deal with it?" she asked. "Because I have an emergency."

She wasn't sure what the emergency was, but Ramon, her assistant, had called her out of a meeting with Disney and told her she was needed in the office. The Disney meeting was a bust anyway. For some reason the kid in charge, and he really was a kid (twenty-five if he was a day), thought she worked in animation. She couldn't seem to convince the kid that she *didn't* work in animation, so she was happy to leave.

Still, it was unlike Ramon to interrupt her at all. He was the best assistant she had ever had, which was saying something, considering how many of her assistants went on to manage Fortune 500 companies. Ramon knew how important the meeting was in Hollywood, even if it was a bust-deal with Disney.

"I *hope* Ramon can deal with it," Gunther said slowly. He was trying to keep up with her, which showed just how panicked he was. Trolls didn't like to walk fast. "It's the first of the month…"

She stopped, closed her eyes, and sighed. The first of the month. Of course. The rent was due. And Gunther couldn't get work, even though when he returned to the Greater World she had told him she'd have no trouble placing him. All the *Lord of the Rings* knockoff films, the Syfy Channel, the five fairy tale movies in development in three different studios—she had thought at least one of them would need a troll. A real, honest-to-God troll, not something CGIed. But so far, no takers, and Gunther was reluctant to go home and ask for more gold from his family so that he could pay his rent.

"Okay," she said. "Sit quietly in the waiting room. I'll have something for you after I solve this emergency."

Gunther nodded. It took him nearly a half an hour to smile, and the smile was never worth the wait. (In fact, it was a bit creepy.) So the nod had to do.

At least his bulky presence had dissuaded some of her other clients from approaching her. She smiled at them all, held up a hand, and kept repeating, "Make an appointment, make an appointment," as she headed to the front door.

Her office was in a 1920s Hollywood-style bungalow, which meant that it had been upgraded and expanded far outside of its original floor plan. The house had belonged to some important starlet before the Crash of 1929, and then purchased by an even more important starlet in the 1930s, "improved" by said starlet's second husband (a successful screenwriter) in the 1940s, and suffered a decline along with the studio system in the 1950s. An entire counterculture of hippies lived in it during the 1960s, and it was nearly condemned in the 1970s, until Jodi bought it, restored it, and "improved" it some more.

Now it had air conditioning, a large pool for her mer-clients, a cabana, and four other side buildings. She had kept her office in the main building, the historic bungalow, even though she kept thinking she should move to the very back, away from the crowds.

And she had crowds, every single day. This client, that client, this friend of a client, that enemy of an old flame. They made her head spin. She had hired help, but none of them had the organizational magic that she did. They had all been competent, but none were as good as she was.

She had come from a family of chatelaines, the people who kept the castles and great manor houses of the Kingdoms functioning. Her family had served—and still did serve—some of the greatest rulers the various Kingdoms had ever known.

But Jodi was a modern woman, one who did not want to waste her time managing someone else's household. She had fled the Third Kingdom in the early twentieth century, when it became clear that modernity would cause tensions in the Kingdoms themselves.

Until the late nineteenth century, the Kingdoms were isolated from this place, which folks in the Kingdoms called the Greater World. Sure, there was occasional crossover, mostly from literary types. Shakespeare stole half his oeuvre from his Kingdom visits, and Washington Irving had written down Rip Van Winkle's story damn near verbatim, only changing the name of the poor hapless mortal who had stumbled through a portal between the Greater World and the Fourteenth Kingdom.

The Germans were the worst. Goethe claimed his Faust stories were inspired by legends he had heard in a tavern in Leipzig, when actually he had found yet another portal into a Kingdom and barely escaped with his life. And the Brothers Grimm had gone into the Kingdoms on something like an archeological expedition, there to map the Kingdoms themselves, and returning instead with the stories of people's lives, stories the Brothers Grimm exaggerated and mistold to the point of libel— had libel laws existed between the Greater World and the Kingdoms.

Sometimes Jodi found it ironic that she had escaped her fairy tale existence to come to a place that took the Grimm Brothers' lies and exaggerated them even further.

But she wasn't the only fairy tale refugee in Los Angeles, as her front yard now showed. Hundreds of malcontents fled the Kingdoms over the years to come here and have a real life, only to be disappointed at how plain, monochrome, and *real* the lives actually were.

She pushed open the solid oak door and stepped into what had been the living room of the bungalow, now a gigantic reception area with arched ceilings and lots of comfortable seating areas marked off by large fake plants. The cool air smelled faintly of mint, a scent that soothed most of the magical (and most regular mortals as well).

Ramon had suspended two flat screen television sets from the ceiling, high enough to be out of what he called "the magical vortex," whatever it was that caused magic and electronics to intertwine. Ramon corralled all of the electronics here. He made everyone who entered drop their cell phones, MP3 players, and other gadgets into a basket on his reception desk. If the tech stayed near him, it didn't explode.

Ramon was pure magickless mortal, thirty-something, although he pretended he was twenty-five. He called himself Ramon McQueen, after Steve McQueen, the rugged 1960s icon, and some tragic silent film star whom hardly anyone had ever heard of and whom Jodi barely remembered. This Ramon was neither tragic nor rugged, but he was very pretty in a way that would have made him a movie star in the 1920s. He wore as much makeup as silent film actors did as well, accenting his sensitive mouth and outlining his spectacular brown eyes in kohl.

He was so good at organizing things that three weeks after she hired him, she looked into his aura to see if he had organizational magic. She could see auras—that was how she read magic. She should have trusted her instincts: he didn't have any magic at all. But his organizational skills were so amazing that she couldn't quite believe they had no magical component.

The waiting room chairs were filled with even more clients, potential clients, and former clients, mostly separated by type—human-appearing but magical; minor storybook characters; the enchanted; creatures; half-human creatures; spelled humans; shape-shifters; and little people of all species, races, and creeds. Not all were waiting for her. The creatures primarily went to her best assistant, and the extras (primarily the minor storybook characters and the little people) went to her next best assistant. She had a third assistant whose clients worked for the various theme parks, but they had a separate entrance (with a different receptionist) in one of the outbuildings so that they wouldn't contaminate the so-called Real Actors.

She had no one who worked animation. (Boy, that meeting still irritated her.)

The conversations were muted. She didn't allow discussion of magic or former fights or past conflicts, and the magical didn't like discussing their upcoming work with each other out of fear that someone else might get the job. So what few conversations happened were usually about things like apartment rentals, good deals on costumes, and which vehicles were built solidly enough that their computer components survived long-term exposure to magical fields.

Ramon had muted the two flat screens but had left them on all-news channels—one currently covering the fires in Malibu Canyon, and the other giving the latest lurid details of the case the media was calling the Fairy Tale Stalker case.

Jodi hated the case's name and wished she could get the media to change it, but she had become aware of the story too late to do anything. Usually she would have managed something. Theoretically, she was Hollywood's best magical wrangler (although the mortals simply thought she was a manager with some very strange clientele), but in practice, she had become the fixer for all of Los Angeles County.

If someone magical was in trouble, then Jodi usually got involved. Involvement generally didn't mean more than sending the magical to the organization, but occasionally she had to delve deeper. She didn't mind. She had been fixing things since she arrived here almost a century ago. Fixing had become as natural as breathing.

"What couldn't wait?" she asked softly as she opened the gate to let herself into the area behind the reception desk.

Ramon looked up at her. A black curl had fallen over the center of his forehead, and his makeup was slightly smudged. He had removed his suit coat, revealing a gorgeous purple shirt made of some lightweight material.

Even that hadn't stopped a pool of sweat from forming along his spine.

Very unusual. Ramon was usually the picture of crispness, even in the middle of an LA summer afternoon.

"First of all, let me simply say, it is *not* my fault," he said in that precise way of his. "You made the appointment, and you wrote down the man's name instead of the company, for heaven's sake, and he's a newbie, and I had no idea he was with Disney—"

"That's fine, Ramon," she said. "It wasn't going well anyway. He had no idea who I was."

"—*and*," Ramon said, not to be derailed, "she *threatened* me."

That caught Jodi's attention. "Who threatened you?"

"That cantankerous little fairy. I rue the day you made it possible for me to see her and her kind," Ramon said. "If you could ever reverse that spell, I would appreciate it."

Jodi frowned. She had spelled Ramon so that he could see magical creatures normally invisible to the mortal eye. Only one type of creature fit into his current description. In fact, only one person—if she could be called that—fit.

Cantankerous Belle, better known as Tanker Belle, whom some believed to be Tinker Bell's older, meaner cousin. Whoever Tanker Belle was, she led a group of tiny fairies who had either divorced themselves from the human-sized fairies of Celtic lore or had never belonged to the group in the first place.

The magical weren't all from the Kingdoms. And not all of the magical seemed to have problems with electronics that the Kingdom magical did. One faction of the human-sized fairies, who had been involved in a power struggle for more than a century, had found a home in Las Vegas amidst all that technology, and they seemed to be doing fine.

"Tanker Belle's here?" Jodi asked.

"In your office," Ramon said. "I can't make her leave."

Tanker Belle usually traveled with a posse of twenty or so fairies who flocked around an area like hummingbirds. Jodi didn't see them, which didn't mean anything. They could have been hiding near one of the fake palm trees.

"Where's her entourage?" Jodi asked.

"That's the weird thing," Ramon said. "She's alone."

That couldn't be good. Jodi sighed and headed down the arched hallway, past photos of her with her favorite movers and shakers. Some were just plain handsome like Cary Grant, whom she missed tremendously, and others actually got things done, like Jean Hersholt (whom she also missed), and some were handsome *and* got things done, like Brad Pitt (whom she didn't see often enough). She had photos of women as well, but they were deeper in the hallway, and she didn't have to look at them every minute of every day.

She dipped into the half bath outside her office to check her hair. She kept it shoulder-length so that it was manageable, particularly since she had the top down in the convertible most of the time. She untied the scarf she wore over it, like Tippi Hedren in *The Birds*, only Jodi's hair wasn't a rich blond. It was a stunning auburn that set off her café au lait skin and made her green eyes stand out. She didn't have the redhead's curse of too-fair skin, which made being in the sun easier, but in her early years in Hollywood, her dark skin had kept her regulated to the sidelines.

That was how she got into the management/fixer business in the first place.

She splashed some cool water over her face, touched up her makeup, and made sure her white sheath had no stains from the lunch she'd had in the studio commissary. Then she squared her shoulders, took a deep breath, and headed to her office.

Tanker Belle made her nervous, and not just because the little fairy was well named. It was also because she looked like Tinker Bell, with that lovely blond hair, those big blue eyes, and that perfect female form (with gossamer wings, of course). When Tanker Belle wanted, she could even add a little twinkle to her smile, complete with a soft *ting* of a tiny bell.

Jodi was surrounded by beautiful women all day, and usually they didn't make her feel insecure. But Tanker Belle did, and Jodi had no idea why.

The door to her office was big and sturdy, carved mahogany, and original to the house. She had no idea what this room was originally used for, although she had suspicions that it was something illicit. The room was big with great views of the back garden—which she had walled off when it became clear that her clients would be standing outside, texting, and ignoring her request to leave the cell phones at home.

Normally just stepping inside the coolness of her office calmed her, but she could sense Tanker Belle's presence. Even though Tank wasn't immediately visible, something about her or her magic screwed up the office's carefully designed comfortable energy.

"Josephine Diana," Tank said from somewhere near the arched windows. Tank had a voice on her that made her sound huge and tough, like a chain-smoking middle-aged mortal woman. A friend once described the voice as Bette Davis crossed with James Earl Jones. The description was so accurate that Jodi thought of it every time Tank spoke.

"Not fair," Jodi said as she quickly shut the door. "You know my real name, and you won't tell me yours."

Real names had magical power that nicknames and self-chosen monikers did not. Sometimes knowing a person's real name conferred that person's power on the person who knew the name. It often gave the speaker a control that she wouldn't otherwise have.

Jodi hadn't used the name Josephine Diana since she left the Kingdom. She had gone through several names in her Los Angeles life because mortals didn't believe that other people could live for centuries and still look like they were in their thirties, but she had found that names which sounded like hers were the best. "Jodi" was her favorite, even better than the Jo she had used in the twenties. It felt like her name without being her real name.

"I won't misuse it," Tank said. "I promise."

She floated down from the ceiling, wings out like a parasail. She wore a glittery black top tucked into a ripped black skirt, making her look like Tinker Bell in mourning. Tank landed on the back of the antique leather upholstered chair that Jodi had set in front of her desk for clients.

Jodi sighed, set her briefcase beside the door, and walked to the desk. It was an old partner's desk she had bought when Keystone Studio closed. Big, solid, made from redwood back before the days when the trees were protected. She kept the desk polished so that the wood's rings showed rich and fine. She also had a protective magical cover over it so that nothing would mar its surface.

Her phone vibrated in her hand; she had forgotten she'd been carrying it. *Need me to get you out of there?* the message read. Ramon, being efficient.

She didn't answer him—she didn't have to, unless she really did need rescuing—and set the phone beside the small pot of violets on the side of her desk. She put her purse on the floor and sat down, wishing she had just a few more minutes to settle in.

"You called me from an important meeting, Tank," Jodi lied. "This better be good."

Tank sat on top of the chair, lovely legs crossed. On her feet, she wore tiny black shoes that looked like they were made of gossamer, like her wings.

"You've been following the Fairy Tale Stalker, right?" Tank asked.

That question could mean many things in Jodi's line of work, from watching the case unfold to actually stalking the stalker. Rather than risk a misunderstanding, she gave a simple one-word answer. "No."

"Good gods," Tank said, "I would think it would be right up your alley. Fairy tales being slandered in the media, quashing the reference, all that."

So that was what she meant by "following" the Fairy Tale Stalker.

"I tried to quash it," Jodi said. "By the time I realized what was going on, it was too late. The moniker had stuck. When these things don't involve our people, I don't care as much as I would have."

Tank snorted. "You're not following this then."

Jodi sighed. She hated it when folks played the I-know-more-than-you game.

"Enlighten me," she said, because if she didn't, she might be here all day. And judging by the crowd outside, she didn't have all day.

"This stalker who just appears in women's rooms?" Tank said. "They're calling him Bluebeard."

Jodi's stomach clenched. She'd met Bluebeard at several parties, most of them held at the Archetype Place. The Archetype Place was a kind of home away from home for folks from the Kingdoms and had been around for more than sixty years. Jodi had gotten a lot of work through that organization and more than a little comfort.

She never understood why the Archetype Place tolerated Bluebeard. From what she had heard, all the fairy tales about him were true—he had killed his wives and stored their heads in a room in his castle. How he came to the Greater World was beyond her, and why he stayed made no sense either.

Unless he was starting all over here, in a place where serial killers were more common.

She couldn't quite make sense of what Tank was telling her. "What do you want me to do, correct the press because it's not him? Or *is* it Bluebeard just doing his creepy shtick?"

"It's not him," Tank said.

Jodi gave her an odd look. Tank almost sounded defensive. "How do you know that?"

"C'mon, *Jo-Dee*." Tank put the emphasis on Jodi's

name so that they would both know she was avoiding
the real name. "You've met Bluebeard. The descriptions
of this stalker sound nothing like him."

Jodi frowned. Bluebeard was distinctive. His hair
was Smurf-blue, including his signature blue beard. He
had a ragged, hollow appearance. Usually she couldn't
get close enough to talk to him (even if she had wanted
to, which she never had) because he smelled so bad. Not
only did he never wash his clothes or himself, but he
tried to cover the stench with Aqua Velva.

Plus she had never seen him sober. He was a fall-
down drunk who stumbled into the Archetype Place
parties, grabbed the free booze from the bar, and vol-
unteered for work as if someone would consider him
for it.

"Are you sure it's not him cleaned up?" Jodi asked.

Tank raised her perfectly formed eyebrows. "Have
you ever seen him clean?"

"No," Jodi said. "Not in all the years he's been here."

"That's point one," Tank said. "Point two is this."

She waved her tiny hand, making a circle of sparkling
fairy dust in front of her. The fairy dust coalesced into
a news report from KTLA. The ticker underneath had
this day's date. The female midday announcer was saying, "...drawing based on victims' description. He's an
average-size man, maybe five-eight, thin, with black hair
and brown eyes. He introduces himself as Bluebeard,
then tells his victims to beware, because the next time
he will 'marry' them, and the next time after that he will
cut off their heads."

Jodi winced. She should have been paying attention
to this. It wasn't quite fairy tale slander—Bluebeard did

do a lot of horrible things, no denying it—but it wasn't the kind of publicity she wanted for her community.

Then she looked at the artist's rendering of the stalker. Angular face, young, dark eyes, clean-shaven, conservative above-the-ears haircut. It looked nothing like Bluebeard. Even if he had shaved off his scraggly beard, cut his hair, bathed, and dressed in a nice suit (instead of that bright blue velvet thing he usually wore), he still wouldn't have looked like this. For one thing, his face was too square. For another, he was too tall.

There was no way a half-dozen women would think that Bluebeard was of average height. One of the problems he had (one of the many problems) was that he was tall and muscular, six-two, with broad shoulders. He looked strong and menacing, even when his eyes didn't focus. All of that was missing from the KTLA description.

"Okay, fine, it's not him," Jodi said. "Why should I care?"

Tank glared, opened her tiny, perfectly formed mouth, and then closed it, as if she just couldn't bring herself to respond. Her mouth formed words three more times before she finally got some out.

"This stalker?" she said. "This 'not' Bluebeard stalker?"

Jodi waited. She had never seen Tank like this.

"He appears and disappears 'like magic,' they say."

Jodi shrugged. "So?"

"Into locked rooms, with locked windows, into rooms with only one door and no window. There is no way in or out. And the women always say he glowed, as if he was backlit or something. One of them even said it was like he was covered in fairy dust."

"So that's what's bothering you?" Jodi asked. "The fairy dust?"

"No!" Tank slammed her hand on the top of the chair. It looked like a forceful action, although it was rather hard for something that tiny to make a real impression. "Don't you understand? This fake Bluebeard is one of us."

Chapter 2

JODI SAT PERFECTLY STILL AS SHE TRIED TO PROCESS that information. The Fairy Tale Stalker was really one of the magical? She looked at the stalker's image, still floating above her desk just a few feet from Tank.

He wasn't anyone Jodi knew, and she knew most of the magical in Los Angeles. At least most of the magical tied to fairy tales. There was another grouping of magical whose stories got retold as myths and legends, including all of the Greek and Norse gods. Some of them lived in LA as well, but most of them chose to remain in their own worlds (which they didn't call Kingdoms, although her people did). She didn't know them, nor did she know more than one or two people in the Celtic fairy circles, although she had met the King of the Fairies in Las Vegas once upon a time.

"What do you think I can do about this?" Jodi asked.

Tank crossed her arms over that sparkly black top. "You can fix it. You *are* a fixer, right?"

"I'm a fixer," Jodi said, "but not a detective. All of the detectives I know are either humans who don't believe in magic or they're magical and working in their own realms. This is one area where no one crosses between the Kingdoms and the Greater World."

Tank tilted her head sideways, her perfect blue eyes glittering with anger. "Gosh, gee. I didn't know that, Boss. Thanks for enlightening me. Now maybe you can get me a job in a Disney movie or something."

Tank thought Disney and Disney movies the lowest of the low. If any of her little tribe worked for the Big D, as she usually called that corporation, she disowned them.

"No need to be vicious," Jodi said, "and I still don't understand why this is my problem."

Tank uncrossed her arms and put her hands on the top of the chair. "So it's not your problem even if he starts fulfilling his threats?"

"You think I can stop some violent killer?" Jodi asked. "Since you know my name, you also know that I have organizational magic and nothing else. That little trick you're doing with the image there? Way beyond my capacity."

"Actually, it's outside your capacity," Tank said. "Not *beyond* your capacity. You're quite capable within the boundaries of your magic. How do you think you've managed in this tough environment all this time?"

Jodi's eyes widened. Tank had just given her a compliment. Tank never gave anyone compliments.

"Why don't *you* find him?" Jodi asked. "You have a powerful magic. You can figure out who he is and report him to the police."

"The Los Angeles Police Department?" Tank asked. "Seriously? *If* I could appear to them, which I can't—"

"Use your magic," Jodi said. "You can come up with a plausible disguise."

"I don't debase myself like that," Tank said. "And even if I did, how do I make them catch a guy who can appear and disappear in various rooms? He'll be as slippery as fog, and you know it."

"I can't do anything," Jodi said. "I can't catch him."

Tank sighed and rolled her eyes. Then she leaned

forward and almost fell off the chair. She caught herself deftly. If Jodi hadn't been watching her so closely, she wouldn't have seen the move at all.

Tank was rarely clumsy. She really had to be upset.

"You can figure out the basis of someone's magic," Tank said. "That's how you get them into the right job or the right house or make them comfortable or whatever the hell it is you do. So figure out what his magic is. Because it doesn't sound like any I'm familiar with."

Jodi picked up a pen and tapped it on the desk calendar she had scribbled all her appointments on. The thing was covered with circles and lines and crossed-out meetings.

Tank didn't look down at the calendar. She just kept staring at Jodi. Jodi had never seen Tank passionate about anything. Tank was an impish little fairy, a gadfly (almost literally), a troublemaker. But she didn't seem to be making trouble here.

"You're lying to me, Tank. You don't care about this stalker guy."

Tank straightened. She snapped her fingers and the artist's sketch disappeared. The fairy dust holding it up fell to the floor like a cluster of tiny stars.

"That's right," Tank said softly. "I care about Blue."

"Blue?" Jodi frowned.

"Bluebeard." Tank actually looked vulnerable. "He's being unjustly accused."

"Bluebeard?" Jodi asked. "You're kidding me, right?"

"No," Tank said. "I'm not. He didn't do this. He's not going after these women."

"So?" Jodi said. "Why should I care? He murdered his wives."

"Are you sure?"

"Of course I'm sure," Jodi said. "Everyone knows it. It's not one of those Grimm Brother lies."

"Centuries ago," Tank said.

Jodi's mouth opened. She couldn't believe Tank had just said that. "So?" Jodi said. "He *killed* people. I don't care if it was yesterday or a million yesterdays ago. He's not someone I want to help."

"So do it for me," Tank said.

Jodi dropped the pen. It rolled across the desktop and fell onto the floor. She didn't bother to catch it. "For you?"

Tank nodded, looking vulnerable. Tank never looked vulnerable.

"Because you want to help Bluebeard?"

Tank nodded again.

"So you *care* about him? Really? You *like* him?"

Tank bowed her head for a minute. Her body lost all of its tension, and her wings fell against her back.

"Yeah," she said. "I care about him."

"God," Jodi said. "They said he could make anyone fall in love with him, but I didn't believe it."

Tank straightened. "I am not in love with him."

"But," Jodi said, undeterred, "he was a Charming once. One of those Prince Charmings, which means he has the power to charm."

"I am *not* in love with him," Tank said.

"And," Jodi said, more to herself than to Tank, "he would've needed the power to charm to get the second through fifteenth wife to fall in love with him, especially after the beheading rumors started."

"*I am not in love with him!*" Tank said. "I just like him. He's… broken."

That caught Jodi's attention, more than Tank's denials. "Broken?"

"He doesn't go near people, and he makes sure they stay away from him. I've taken him to rehab I don't know how many times, and the day he gets out he starts drinking again. It's really sad."

Jodi had never seen Tank like this. She seemed sincere. No anger, no sarcasm, no need to control.

"I'm not helping Bluebeard," Jodi said. "I don't care what you say about him. I don't care if he feels bad that he killed his wives and it's driving him to drink. I don't care that he can't get sober. I really don't. I don't even care that his reputation is being—well, I was going to say ruined, but how do you ruin a serial killer's reputation anyway? I guess by only stalking the women and not touching them. So far, I don't see any reason to get involved, Tank. It is what it is."

"And if this stalker guy starts killing?" Tank asked. "Will you care then?"

Jodi threaded her fingers together and rested her hands on the calendar. She didn't want Tank to see that the question got her attention.

But Tank noticed. Tank noticed everything.

"He's threatened them. The police say it's only a matter of time before he carries through, and I believe them. I talked to one of the victims. She said it was like he was holding himself back, rubbing his hands together, pushing them against his own chest like he was afraid he would lose control of them. What if he is one of us, Jodi? What if he's lost it somehow, if his magic is starting to go awry? What if he can't stop this much longer?"

Tank was leaning forward again, balancing

precariously on the top of the chair. Jodi blinked twice and focused her vision. She looked briefly at Tank's aura. Tank's aura was bright white, so bright that it hurt Jodi's magical eye, so Jodi looked away quickly, trying to see if there were magical lines between Tank and Jodi.

If there were lines, it would mean that Tank was casting a spell on Jodi. Tank would be furious that Jodi looked at her aura, but Jodi had never seen Tank act like this. Not ever.

Tank wasn't trying to fool her or charm her or make fun of her.

Tank was serious.

And Tank was never this kind of serious.

Jodi blinked away the aura, returning to her normal sight. "I still don't know what I can do."

"Go talk to Blue," Tank said. "He might have some insight into what's going on."

Jodi shuddered. "You mean consult one serial killer about his probably successor?"

"I mean," Tank said, "that maybe Blue will recognize the guy or the pattern or something."

"Why don't you talk to him?" Jodi asked.

"I can't," Tank said. "Someone put wards around rehab center."

"If there are magical wards, I can't get in either," Jodi said.

"Wards against fairies," Tank said in exasperation. "Last I checked, you weren't a fairy."

"Thank heavens," Jodi said.

Tank's wings started fluttering. "So you'll go?"

"I don't want to," Jodi said.

"Think of it as a favor," Tank said. "For me."

That was the second time Tank had said it was for her. Only this time, by invoking the word "favor," she was making it real. Now Jodi was truly shocked. Favors were debts, and fairies avoided going into debt.

"You're serious," Jodi said. "That's really putting yourself out, Tank, for people you don't know."

"I know Blue," she said, still rising.

"And he's worth all of this?" Jodi asked.

"I think so. I know you don't, but I do." Tank shrugged, then grabbed onto the leather seat top to maintain her balance. "You should think those women are worth your time, right? So you'll do it, okay?"

She didn't wait for an answer. She flew upward, then backward, away from Jodi, as if the conversation upset her. As Tank flew, she opened her palm. A wand appeared in it, glistening with gold fairy dust. She tapped one of the windowpanes, coating it in dust, and then flew through it.

Jodi got up and hurried to the window just in time to see the pane reappear. Tank hadn't had to go through reception when she arrived. She could have just opened the window like she had done a moment ago.

But she had made this formal, and she had offered payment in the form of a favor. A favor from someone like Tank was very valuable.

"Crap," Jodi said. She hated things like this. But she was involved now. She hadn't officially accepted the job, but both she and Tank knew she would do what she could.

Even if that meant sitting in the same room as the most loathsome, smelly man she had ever met.

Even if that meant she had to talk to Bluebeard.

Chapter 3

JODI REALLY DIDN'T WANT TO GO TO REHAB—NO, NO, no—so she put the Amy Winehouse song on repeat and blared the damn thing through her car's stereo system. The song had been going through Jodi's head ever since Tank left her office, and it was actually the song that convinced Jodi to go.

Winehouse had died badly, partly because of her intransigence, and these women—these Fairy Tale Stalker victims—might die badly as well if Jodi didn't go to rehab to see Bluebeard.

At least the drive was nice. She always liked the drive to Malibu, particularly as some of the worst of the city fell away and the air lost its tinge of smog. She thought once she was ten miles out of the smog that she could smell the ocean, although that probably wasn't true.

Most people complained about driving in Los Angeles, and while traffic *was* hell, Jodi didn't mind. She bought the best car she could, realizing that to the mortals she worked with, a car was more than a transportation device; it was a statement. So she owned a convertible, extremely expensive, but not so expensive that she would risk both it and her life if she parked it in certain parts of the city. Red, because red was a power color (not because she liked it), and a Mercedes so that it had all the bells and whistles and rode like a dream.

As a result, the last stage of the drive to the coast

felt like it should—hair whipping back, scarf keeping it out of her face, gigantic sunglasses protecting her eyes, music blaring, the sun making everything glisten. Moments like this kept her in Los Angeles even though a good part of her industry had moved to Vancouver, BC. She didn't like the gray or the rain or the trees for that matter. They reminded her too much of the Kingdoms, and made her feel more like a housekeeper and less like the master of her own fate.

Her own fate and the fate of several others. Before she left, she slipped Gunther two thousand in cash from her wall safe, which would keep him for a few months. He would use a lot of the money for essentials besides rent. Gunther worried. The least she could do was ease some of that. She hadn't promised him work this time, just told him she would do her best. Maybe then he would tell her why he didn't want to go back to the Kingdoms.

Maybe the reason he didn't want to leave was as simple as the gray and the rain and the trees. Or maybe something bad had happened there, and he needed to get away. Gunther was particularly close-lipped, even for a troll, and he seemed incredibly sad. He had wrapped his chubby stone-like fingers around her heart and made her feel responsible for him, even though she knew she wasn't.

Maybe that was how Tank felt about Bluebeard.

Jodi had done some checking. Tank took Bluebeard to rehab ten times, twice in the past year. She would wrap him in fairy dust and get her tribe to fly him to the rehab center, dumping him on the grounds. Odd that she couldn't get inside anymore. Jodi would have to investigate those wards. They had to be a recent change.

She had heard about the last rehab flight: It had happened after an altercation at a book release party at The Charming Way in Westwood. Bluebeard had shown up drunk, disturbed the mortals, and the magical had to get him into a back room before Tank could take control of him and send him on his way. That had been about thirty days ago. Tank clearly had access to the rehab center then.

The rehab center was quiet and exclusive, not the most famous one in the world, but one most celebrities used now when the paparazzi staked out the Betty Ford Clinic. The center was on some very expensive land in Malibu, on the hillside overlooking the city.

Jodi had been there a few times to visit clients. This place could handle the magical and over the years had some magical healers on staff. She didn't know if there were any healers now, or if anyone magical worked there at all, although the wards against fairies suggested that someone magical other than Bluebeard was near the center.

Once she got to Malibu, she had to take back roads to get to the center. It was deliberately hard to find because so many patients were celebrities or exceedingly rich, which passed for celebrity in modern culture. She had to go through three different checkpoints. Fortunately, she knew to call ahead.

She had even known who to talk to, thanks to Tank. Tank had scrawled the name of the center and the name of the counselor in charge of Bluebeard in fairy dust on the top of Jodi's desk. Jodi had no idea if it would just fade or if she had to clean it off, something she supposed she, the daughter of chatelaines, should know.

Still, she had left the problem to Ramon. She had

called the counselor, a man named Jamison Hargrove. He had sounded amused when she said she needed to talk with Blue. Fortunately, the counselor thought Bluebeard's Greater World nickname was Blue, because the one thing Tank had neglected to tell her was the name Bluebeard used in the Greater World.

Tank understood the power of real names for the magical, but she didn't understand the importance of fake names in the mortal world.

Hargrove had asked Jodi her relationship to Blue. She said, quite truthfully, that she didn't have one, but that she needed information from him on a life-or-death matter. Hargrove didn't question that.

He even promised she could see Blue, but he said he couldn't guarantee that Blue would talk.

"He has an aversion to women," Hargrove said. "It would probably be best if I sat in on your conversation."

No kidding he had an aversion to women, Jodi barely stopped herself from saying.

"Does he get violent?" she asked. Because if he got violent, then the deal with Tank was off. Jodi knew that Bluebeard wasn't a violent drunk, but she had no idea what kind of man he was when he was sober.

"No," Hargrove said. "He's not violent at all. I'm not worried about your physical safety, Ms. Walters. I just believe I might be able to coax him into a conversation."

"Sorry," Jodi said and mentally added that she was sorry in more ways than Hargrove realized. "I need to talk with him alone. Confidentiality and all of that."

She didn't say confidentiality for whom, figuring she didn't have to. Hargrove was a therapist after all. His life's blood was confidentiality.

"I must at least insist on observing," Hargrove said. "We will watch the video and make sure there is no audio to protect your privacy."

"How do I know that you'll have the audio off?" Jodi said.

"You may check our layout," Hargrove said. "I'll send it to you. We have three rooms outside of the doctors' offices that we call confidentiality rooms. We run our groups in those rooms, as well as allow meetings with other doctors there. If you give me your email address, I'll send you the URL."

She did that and called it up on her computer while talking to him. The rooms were as he presented: they had security cameras but no audio.

"If you don't believe he's violent," she had said as she was poking around the layout of the center, "then I don't understand why you need to observe."

"Well, um, honestly," Hargrove said, sounding a bit less confident than he had a moment earlier, "I've never seen Blue interact one-on-one with a woman. I'm curious."

"About what?" Jodi had asked.

"Whether he can even look at you," Hargrove said. "He doesn't look at the women here."

She thought that was odd. "Not at all?"

"Not at all," Hargrove said.

She shuddered and almost canceled right there. But there were those women to think about. Besides, Jodi didn't entirely trust Tank's judgment. Tank *liked* Bluebeard. Tank might be willing to believe that Bluebeard didn't do anything. But it wasn't unheard of for some of the magical to have more than one type of magic at their disposal. If Bluebeard had charm and the ability to appear and disappear at will, that would explain a lot about the deaths he caused in the Kingdoms.

And it would implicate him in the so-called stalking incidents here.

Jodi thought of all of this as she made the final turns into the rehab center. She had reached the road that branched off into driveways for visitors, staff, and patients. The patient road was larger because it had to accommodate buses. No patient could leave his car parked up here and had to travel down to patient parking five miles away by bus.

Visitor parking, on the other hand, was relatively close at hand. No one had bothered with landscaping here; this part of the complex was deliberately unattractive. The center discouraged visitors and used the visitor area to warn off potential patients who didn't realize that they faced years of hard work.

The parking lot was flat, open, and small. It had no cars other than hers, so she parked next to the guardhouse near the sidewalk. Every time she came here, she frowned at that guardhouse. If that didn't make inhabitants feel like prisoners, nothing would.

Then again, studios had guardhouses leading into them, so maybe the guardhouse just made the Hollywood types feel at home.

Before she got out of her car, she finger-combed her windblown hair.

As she opened the car door, the guard came out of the guardhouse, smiled at her, and gave her a laminated badge with her name on it. She had talked to him on her previous visits.

"I'm not supposed to say welcome back," he said, "but it is nice to see you again."

"You too," she said with her warmest smile. People remembered her. It was part of her magic, and it sometimes caused problems, particularly when they realized how long-lived she was. The magical lived for hundreds of years, aging slowly.

Someone once explained to her that the difference in lifespan between the magical and the mortal had something to do with the lack of magic in the Greater World, but she didn't entirely believe it. What she did know was that the long lifespan felt natural in the Kingdoms (because everyone had it) and quite strange here.

She clipped the badge onto her shirt's collar, grabbed her phone and her purse, and headed into the building.

This part was a flat Southern California design, lots of windows and angles, built to blend into the hillside. The problem was that lots of windows and angles made it easy for paparazzi to snap photographs from a significant distance away, so the main building, back behind this one and available only to patients, was built in a New England saltbox style. The residents who had recovered sufficiently to move to the second stage of treatment moved to small bungalows on the grounds and were not given any cooking or cleaning assistance. They were to learn how to fend for themselves, something that some of the famous found quite novel.

It cost a lot of money for Bluebeard to stay here. It wasn't that unusual for the magical who lived in the Greater World for a long time to have money, but it did strike Jodi as odd that a falling-down drunk would have kept enough money to afford anything, particularly a place like this.

An employee opened the main door for her and, as she expected, Jamison Hargrove was waiting for her.

Hargrove looked like a therapist out of central casting. He had a weathered face that settled into an expression of compassion, warm brown eyes, and dark hair silvered at the temples. He wore a light cotton shirt, white pants, and expensive sandals.

When he saw her, he extended his hand. "Ms. Walters."

She shook it. "Mr. Hargrove."

"I thought you might want a tour of the facilities before you saw Blue," he said. "In particular, I thought you might want to see the area I'll be observing from."

She shook her head. "I'm on a tight schedule. I hadn't planned to make this trip in the first place."

Hargrove's lips tightened just a bit, probably an expression his patients didn't even notice.

"Is there some problem with Blue?" she asked.

Hargrove blinked once, clearly trying to decide what to tell her, maybe trying to decide what he *could* tell her. "He—um—doesn't want to see you."

She bit back anger. She had driven a long way for this.

"But you believe you can get him to talk with me," she said. Otherwise, she suspected Hargrove would have called.

"Yes, I do. Let me take you to the meeting room. He'll join you in just a few minutes."

She pointedly glanced at her phone, both so Hargrove thought she was checking the time and also looking for messages.

"I promise you," Hargrove said. "It won't be a problem."

"I hope not," she said as she followed him to the meeting area. And she didn't add the rest of that thought. The last thing she needed was some kind of problem when the man she was meeting was Bluebeard.

Chapter 4

THE YOGA CLASS NEAR THE POOL HAD ENDED. NORMALLY this was Blue's time; he swam for nearly an hour, alone, in the heat of the day when no one wanted to be outside, not even sunbathing. He was of the private opinion that the midafternoon yoga class was an endurance event, even though he had no firsthand knowledge of it. He simply watched from a distance, waiting for everyone to quit so that he could swim.

He didn't sign up for group activities. He only interacted with people when the interaction was required as a term of his incarceration here. Not that he was really and truly a prisoner; he could leave at any time. But he always felt a bit stifled when he followed the rules—any rules—even though this rehab center was the safest place he had ever known.

He rather liked that people watched him 24-7. He rather liked that they were there to protect him from his darkest self.

Of course, they had no idea how dark that self really was.

The pool water glistened and he wished he could dive into it. The pool was Olympic-sized and well maintained. The cabana to the left was open on both ends and had what the staff called a bar in the center. Even though it wasn't really a bar. A bar would serve alcohol, and that would defeat the purpose.

Still, he could go in there and order a drink with ice in a cool tall refreshing glass as practice for that day in the future when he would be on his own again. As if this kind of nonsense ever worked. When he got out of here two months from now, he would go on a bender that would last at least three days.

He'd found it took at least three days of solid drinking to make his clothes truly foul. It also took three days of solid drinking to ruin all the "good work," as Dr. Hargrove called it, and make Blue look like a die-hard alcoholic.

He wished he was. He wished he liked the taste of booze. He didn't. He hated the stuff and the way it made him feel.

It was only the alternative that kept him drinking.

The fact that he was thinking about a drink was telling: he almost never thought about alcohol while he was here. He stopped pacing near the door of the guest facility and realized his hands were shaking. Not hard like he had the DTs, but as if he was terrified.

And maybe he was. It had been a long, long time since he let himself feel any emotions about anything.

He glanced at the glistening water, saw the bottom shining in the sun, the center's healing hands logo in multi-colored tiles on the bottom. He stared at those hands when he swam above them, thought about those hands as he did his laps, wished that hands could truly be healed, particularly hands that had done horrible, awful, terrible things.

Like his hands.

He shoved them in the pocket of his khaki pants, then squared his shoulders. He had to go through with this or leave the center.

Dr. Hargrove had told him that someone would be watching the interaction with this Jodi Walters at all times. Someone would monitor, security would be outside, nothing would go wrong.

Right. As if Blue believed that. He hadn't spent any time with a woman alone in decades, maybe a century or two. And never had he done so sober.

He was terrified. He tried to tell Dr. Hargrove that he was making a mistake, but Dr. Hargrove wouldn't listen. He blathered on about change and fear and conquering fears, not really knowing who he was talking to about what.

Then Blue pulled out the center's regulations: No visitors in the first sixty days of incarceration. (He actually used the word "incarceration" to annoy Dr. Hargrove; Dr. Hargrove made mistakes when he was annoyed.)

Dr. Hargrove had nodded sagely and said, "I'm aware of that, Blue, but we've had you here several times before and our normal methods haven't worked. Perhaps trying something out of the ordinary will make a difference."

Dr. Hargrove had an answer for everything.

Which meant that Blue had a choice. Either he could do what Dr. Hargrove wanted, or he could leave the center. If he left, he wasn't sure he would ever be allowed back. Not that they had threatened him; they hadn't. He just had a sense that at some point, they might tell him to try somewhere else.

He rather liked it here. It was one of the few places where he felt like he could be himself (or rather, the part of himself that was tolerable) and not worry about the effect he was having on others. The center itself kept him organized, and because of the adamancy of his own requests, the center protected vulnerable people from him—women and children (not that he had ever hurt a child, but he had never thought himself capable of hurting a woman either, and he had done so, repeatedly).

The center also set up a schedule for him and helped him follow it. An early morning run (on the grounds, with security near him), breakfast, therapy session, lunch, rest, swim, dinner, group session, entertainment (movies, books, music—anything solitary, since that was what he chose), lights-out. Then it would all start over again. The rhythm of it was predictable, soothing, and there was always someone to protect him from himself.

Except right now. It would be so simple to walk away, so simple to give up. But he wasn't the kind of man to give up. If he had been, he would have killed himself a long time ago.

He just had to find a way to comply with Dr. Hargrove's admonition and yet somehow stay away from that woman.

He had to go back to who he had been a long, long time ago, before the name-calling, before the murders, before *Bluebeard*.

He had to go back to the days when he was a Charming. More than that, he had to go back to the days when he was a prince and used to getting his way.

It felt like putting on a costume. He stood a bit straighter. He felt a little taller.

Then he grabbed the glass door handle and stepped inside.

Chapter 5

THE MEETING ROOM THAT HARGROVE LED JODI INTO didn't look like a standard meeting room. Instead of a conference table with uncomfortable chairs, there were couches with soft cushions and standalone upholstered chairs that were built for comfort. The brown rug was so plush that she wanted to take her shoes off and rub her feet into it. Big square multicolored pillows, the size of the chairs, were piled in one corner of the room. That section of the room had no furniture at all, and she knew from what she had seen from the center's welcome video years ago that that part of the room was used for group meetings.

Someone had put fresh coffee and healthy snacks on a sideboard. Before he left, Hargrove told her to help herself.

She wouldn't be staying long enough to consume anything. She didn't want to sit down either. She wasn't quite sure what to do with herself. The room had no windows (so the paparazzi can't see you, my dear) and no art on the walls. The walls themselves were a soft beige, which someone somewhere had probably decreed a soothing color.

She hated the lack of diversity in the room itself.

Then the door banged open. She whirled. The man who stepped in was no one she knew. Tall, well built, with clothes so perfectly tailored they looked like they had been designed for him. He wore khaki pants, but they didn't seem casual, perhaps because of the sharp crease running along the center. Even his shirt—a short-sleeved cotton thing that most men would wear wrinkled—looked like it had been freshly ironed.

He was clean-shaven with perfectly cut black hair. He was, bar none, the most handsome man she had ever seen.

And she had seen a lot of handsome men. She worked in a city, in an industry, that attracted the most handsome men in the Greater World and some of the handsomest men from the Kingdoms.

She knew handsome men.

And this guy, this guy beat them all without a contest. This guy was *stunning*.

"I was supposed to see you," he said, his gaze not quite meeting hers. In fact, it took her a moment to realize he wasn't looking at her at all. "I've done that. I'm going."

Her breath caught. *This* was Bluebeard? This man? This unbelievably gorgeous specimen of a man was *the* Bluebeard? Really?

Well, then, she finally understood—on a very deep visceral level—how he had had fifteen wives.

And she saw where the nickname came from. As the light caught his hair, it filled with dark blue highlights.

He was backing out of the room when she found her voice.

"You haven't watched the news, have you? The Fairy Tale Stalker? He identifies himself as Bluebeard."

He closed his eyes and bowed his head. "It's not me. I can't get out of here, even if I wanted to."

And it sounded like he didn't want to.

"That's what Tanker Belle says, and I didn't believe her until now."

He looked up, his gaze finally meeting hers. He had the most electric blue eyes she had ever seen. Stunning, adding to that amazing face, making him almost irresistible. How the hell was that possible? Was this what the full power of magical charm felt like?

"Tank sent you?" he asked, then looked down as quickly as he looked up. Suddenly Jodi had the sense that he was afraid of her. Why would the most notorious man in all of fairy tale history be afraid of her?

"Yes, Tank sent me," Jodi said. "She can't get in here anymore. There are wards against fairies around this place."

"What?" He seemed genuinely shocked. "No there aren't. She dropped me inside just over a month ago."

"There are now. She can't talk to you."

"I didn't put up any wards," he said, threading his fingers together. "I can't do that kind of thing."

He spoke so softly that she could barely hear him, almost as if he was speaking to himself. Yet he was being defensive. This was not at all what she had expected.

Nor had she expected him to have such beautiful hair, rich and thick and glistening with that hint of blue in the artificial light.

"I know you can't," Jodi said. "You can't do anything except Charm."

He looked up at her again, those blue eyes connecting with hers so strongly that it took all of her strength to keep from stepping backward. Or forward.

He literally took her breath away. No man had ever done that.

"What makes you so sure?" he asked. The question wasn't menacing; it was almost needy.

"I knew it from the moment you walked in the room. You have only one kind of magic, although you have that in abundance." Somehow she had managed to tear her concentration away from his physical beauty long enough to glance at his magical aura. Blue, which was expected, but the blue belonged to his charm magic. And he had no other kind of magic. None, not a thread of anything else. Although he had more charm than anyone she had ever met, and that included a man named Charming, who ran The Charming Way Bookstore in Westwood, but who in reality had married Cinderella a long, long time ago and was known to many as *the* Prince Charming.

"What are you?" Bluebeard asked.

Which wasn't really, when you got down to it, a charming question. It was, in fact, somewhat rude. But she understood what he meant.

"I'm the daughter of chatelaines," she said. "I can see magic, mostly so I can accommodate it and make the person near me more comfortable. I have a strong domestic magic."

"And Tank sent you?" He sounded confused. She didn't blame him. She would never put the words "Tank" and "domestic" together either.

"She did," Jodi said, "because she knows what I do here in the Greater World. I'm what's called a fixer. I make things happen, or unhappen as the case may be."

He frowned. It just creased a small portion of his unlined forehead, making him look intellectual and oh-so-delicious. (And she was freaking herself out, being attracted to *Bluebeard*, of all people.)

"How is that related to domestic magic?"

"Ah," she said, feeling a bit more comfortable. She had given this speech a million times in her long life. "Domestic magic is all about fixing things so that people enjoy their lives, so that problems go away. Home should be a comfortable, easy place, outside the troubles of the world. So the troubles of the world need to be solved or at least placed at bay. If you take that concept and apply it to work, you get me—a wrangler of the magic by day, fixer by night."

Most people smiled when she told them that. He just looked down, as if her words made him uncomfortable.

"We've met," he said, and it wasn't a question.

"More than once," she said. "And I must say, I didn't recognize you either."

He nodded and bit his lower lip, still not meeting her gaze. "So, Tank sent you to see if I was behind this stalker thing."

"No," Jodi said. "Tank believes you had nothing to do with it. I'm not sure Tank thinks you did anything wrong ever."

He shook his head, just a little.

"She believes you might have some insight into what's going on." Jodi took a step toward him. "Do you?"

He took a step back and hit the door, putting his hand on the knob. "I didn't even know there was a stalker until you mentioned it."

"No television? No radio?"

"No contact with the outside world for sixty days," he said. "That includes news. If we watch a movie or a TV show, we watch on DVD."

"Hm." That revelation made her task a little harder. "I don't even know how to start on this then. The guy appears in women's bedrooms, declares that he's Bluebeard and is going to harm them the next time he sees them, and then he disappears. They get terrified, contact the police, and so far, the police haven't got a clue what to do about it."

He swallowed, shook his head again, almost as if he was trying to clear it. His head was low enough to avoid eye contact, but she had the sense he was watching her just the same.

"How did Tank get involved?" he asked.

"She wants to prove that it's not you."

He bobbed his head—another nod? If so, it was a private one, meant for him alone. "And how did you get involved?"

"Tank believes that the entire scenario harms our people here. And she's afraid that the guy will escalate. She thinks you might have some ideas on how to stop him."

He let out a bitter chuckle, then ran a hand through his thick hair. It fell back into place, looking perfect. "Me. That's rich. I have no idea how to stop anything."

"She wants you to help," Jodi said, not sure what she wanted. All she knew was that she couldn't leave until he did. He was still blocking the door.

He brought his head up just a little. "Me."

"*Yes*," Jodi said, starting to get irritated. Clearly he wasn't trying to charm her. But she still found him annoyingly attractive—even as he was irritating her.

He made a soft sound, lowered his head again, then moved it sideways, as if he was arguing with himself. "I doubt I can provide any assistance at all."

"Okay then," Jodi said. She was about to ask him to move when he spoke again.

"But Tank thinks I can do something." It was almost a question.

"Yes," Jodi said, trying not to let her irritation show again.

His broad shoulders went up and down as he took a deep breath. It was almost as if he was bracing himself. "I'll give it a shot then. I owe her. She's been helping me."

Jodi waited. It was a bit like talking to Gunther, only Blue wasn't physically slow. But he clearly wasn't used to dealing with people.

He kept his head down. "Can you give me what information you have?"

"Do you have an email address?" Jodi asked. "I'll send you links and video clips. There's one from KTLA that has a police sketch, which, I must say, looks nothing like you."

"Like me now," he said.

"In any incarnation," she said.

He winced, ran a hand through his hair again, and once again, it fell back into place as if he had never ruffled it. How far gone had this man been to look as horrible as he had all those years?

"I don't have an email address," he said. "No smart phone, no computer, no nothing, not for the duration. Nothing that smacks of outside world. Just bring me some paper."

He raised his head slightly, looking at her for a brief moment—a heart-stopping moment in which he looked like he might break. Then he bowed his head, turned the knob on the door, and backed out of the room, closing the door swiftly.

She stared at it, her heart pounding. He was attractive. He was beyond attractive. He couldn't meet her eyes. He was nervous or afraid or just plain off his game, and she still found him attractive.

Which had to be what happened to all those other women. Attractive, blindingly attractive, and then bam, *off with their heads*, as one of those *Alice In Wonderland* queens used to say. Of course, Jodi was mixing her literary references. No *Alice In Wonderland* here, although she did feel as if she had fallen through a rabbit hole.

She let out a breath and headed for the door. What if he had locked her in here? What if he had trapped her?

Not that it mattered. She was in a rehab center with people watching, cameras everywhere, someone who could get her out if she needed it.

He frightened her. Of course, he frightened her. He was *Bluebeard*, and yet she had felt just a half second of compassion for him.

Worse, if that was the right word, she had agreed to come back. With paper on the crimes. She had agreed to see him again.

And somehow, the very idea unnerved her.

It's just charm magic, she told herself. The most powerful charm magic she had ever seen. She hadn't seen magic that strong in anyone's aura in years. Charm magic... charmed. That was all.

Next time, she would have her defenses up.

Next time, she would be prepared.

Next time, he wouldn't affect her at all.

Chapter 6

BLUE WENT BACK TO THE POOL AREA AND SANK INTO one of the lounge chairs under the shade provided by a gigantic umbrella. His legs could barely hold him up. His heart was pounding.

He had looked at her. He had broken every rule he had and he had looked at her, and God, she was beautiful, and he hadn't expected it. He should have. He should have recognized her name. He had *met* her, for God's sake, a number of times, she said, and he could almost remember it.

Stumbling into those parties he always went to when he got beyond drunk and lonely for others of his kind, looking for the bar, scanning the room, gaze falling on the willowy woman with auburn hair, light coffee-colored skin, and stunning green eyes. High cheekbones, perfect lips, features that meant she should have been in a movie, but he hadn't seen her in a movie, right?

And at that party, he had forced himself to look away, berating himself, then he had gone around the room, past the overdressed, too-skinny things that passed for celebrities these days—how they winced at his appearance, his smell, and they were supposed to. Everyone was supposed to wince and stay away from him. People didn't always stay away though, so he finally dyed his hair Smurf blue as a big neon warning sign.

That usually worked.

But on this day, in this place, he didn't have his guard up. His guard was completely shut off here, no bright blue hair dye, no scraggly beard, and no Aqua Velva. It was a great babe-repulser, especially in large doses. The staff wouldn't buy him any bottles of it; they had done so during his first tour here, and then made him shower after he dumped an entire bottle of the vile stuff all over himself.

After that incident, they didn't let him wear any cologne here, not even the expensive kind like Ralph Lauren's Polo or something that someone else (not him) would think twice about dumping all over themselves. He just figured any artificial scent in sufficiently large doses kept people away from him, and usually it worked.

They'd learned. Even his soap and shampoo was unscented. And early on in his rehab, they forced him to take showers. Now he took them voluntarily, sometimes two or three a day, depending on his workouts.

He did have to admit that it was a joy just to be clean. And he thought he could indulge in that luxury here.

He hadn't expected a beautiful woman. He hadn't expected to be alone with her. In the same room.

Looking at her.

How many times had he done that? Once? Twice? Three times?

Too many, that was for sure.

He had vowed he would never look at another woman again, because he didn't want her in his mind. Not even slightly. Because his mind couldn't be trusted. It would see a woman, fixate on her, and then take over, without leaving him any memory at all.

It would force him to do horrible things, things he never ever wanted to do again.

He looked at his hands. Still shaking. He was lying to himself, of course. Again. He was lying to himself again. Because he did have a memory of each one, his hands around her beautiful neck, the fear on her face, the blood. Oh dear God, the blood.

That's what he would remember.

And the heads. In that room in his father's castle—now his castle—now someone else's castle, because he hadn't been in it in quite literally centuries. All those beautiful women, women he had loved, or at least liked, women he had thought he had respected. Reduced to heads in a room, skin pale, eyes closed, their beauty intact.

"God," he said and buried his face in his hands. Then he realized what he had done and pulled his hands away.

And he had told her to come back. With papers.

She would just have to leave them at the desk. He couldn't take the risk of seeing her again.

She was in his brain, and that was dangerous.

No woman had been in his brain for a long, long time. He hadn't allowed it.

He stood up, shoved his hands in his pockets, and stared at the pool. The water was completely smooth, the hot sun falling on it and making it very bright. He needed a drink. He needed something to separate himself from his brain, to forget.

Maybe he should leave here. Maybe he should go back into his defense. It had worked for centuries, in one way or another.

But if he left here, he wouldn't be monitored. No one would keep an eye on him.

And she was in his brain.

Where the pain began.

If he allowed it. If he didn't have help preventing it.

He didn't know how to forget her, but he had to. Somehow. He had to pretend this afternoon hadn't happened at all.

Chapter 7

EARLY THE FOLLOWING MORNING, BLUE STOPPED NEAR the bottom of the stairs in the main building. Many patients were just coming back from breakfast, and some were heading to a group therapy session. When he had first come here years ago, he found it fascinating how many familiar faces he saw, faces from billboards or album covers or movie posters.

Now he was more or less used to it, and he was unfazed by it. Most of the famous looked as normal as everyone else when they weren't wearing piles of makeup or had someone doing their hair. Their skin was blotchy, their hair ragged, and their clothing sometimes as ratty as the stuff he wore when he was drunk. Only they wore it as a fashion statement; he wore it as a people repellent.

He didn't nod to anyone. He never socialized, and he almost never talked to anyone outside of a group session. (Hell, he never talked to them in group either.) Some people thought he was famous because of the charisma that went with his charm powers, and they simply figured he was aloof so that he wouldn't be recognized.

He didn't disabuse them of that. And, if the truth be told, he *was* famous, just not in the way that they thought.

This morning he had dressed with even more care than usual. He had gotten up with the sun, done an extra two miles on his run, and showered, discovering that he was still too early for his usual breakfast. He had shaved and picked out a shirt that brought out the blue in his eyes before he realized what he was doing.

He wanted to impress Jodi Walters. It was a natural human response, one that he hadn't had in years (decades, no, centuries) and one that scared him more than her arrival had.

He changed into a comfortable pair of threadbare blue jeans and a mustard-colored shirt that made him seem sallow, a shirt that he had arrived in and some brave soul in the center's laundry had cleaned for him. Then he had mussed up his hair, wished he hadn't shaved, and ate something with onions for breakfast.

That was the best he could do.

Until he figured out how to solve this problem.

He crossed the main floor to the administration desk. The person behind the desk was female, which made his palms sweat. He wiped them on his thighs, then made himself focus.

Charm. He needed to be charming, which shouldn't be hard, but he was so out of practice that he wasn't quite sure how to do it.

He put his elbows on the desk, partly to keep his hands from shaking, regretting the onions now. He made himself smile.

"Hey," he said softly.

"Mr. Franklin," the woman behind the desk said with more warmth than he'd ever heard her use with other patients. John Franklin was the name he had chosen years ago because it wasn't memorable, but it wasn't an obvious fake name like Carter or Smith might be. "What can I do for you?"

"Um," he said, trying not to meet her gaze, but also

trying not to be conspicuous about it. It wasn't that he found her attractive—far from it; she was one of those doughy women who had given up long ago. But he didn't know if every woman he paid attention to was at risk from him or just the ones he found interesting. "I, um, wondered if it would be possible to send someone to the guest building. Someone is supposed to drop off something for me and I didn't tell her where and—"

"Never mind, he'll get it himself." Dr. Hargrove took Blue's arm and pulled him away from the desk. "Thanks."

"S-s-sure," the woman said.

Blue let Dr. Hargrove pull him to the center of the room, and then planted his feet. "I'm not going to see her."

Dr. Hargrove looked like a man who had just arrived at work. His cheeks still had razor-scrape, and his hair looked newly combed. He had on a bit too much cologne which, Blue knew from experience, would fade as the day went on.

"Yes, you are going to see her," Dr. Hargrove said. "Look at the beneficial effect she has already had on you. You voluntarily spoke to another woman."

Blue closed his eyes, feeling frustration well. If only he could explain to Dr. Hargrove what the real problem was. Then imagine what would happen: screaming, mayhem, lockdown (*"You're insane. Bluebeard is fiction"*), or arrest (*"Officer, he's admitted to murdering women for years"*). Blue could probably get out of both, but he didn't want to go through the steps in between.

Dr. Hargrove shook him slightly. "Come on. She's already here."

Great, Blue thought. *Just great*.

He opened his eyes. "Please, don't make me."

"We all have to do things we don't like," Dr. Hargrove said. "Although for the life of me, I can't understand why you don't want to spend a few minutes in the company of a beautiful woman."

"You wouldn't understand," Blue muttered.

"Try me," Dr. Hargrove said.

Blue shook his head.

"Well, then we're going to the other building," Dr. Hargrove said.

"You're coming with me?"

"Not to see her," Dr. Hargrove said. "She wants to keep what you're discussing private. Any reason for that?"

Magic, fairy tales, the existence of whole other worlds. "Not that I know of," Blue said.

"Still," Dr. Hargrove said, "she made the request and I'm going to honor it, so let's go."

And with that, he dragged Blue out the back exit, toward the pool, and to the guest building. Blue stumbled along, trying to figure out how he could keep the meeting short.

Chapter 8

PAPER. HE SAID HE WANTED PAPER.

Jodi had been irritated at that request since she left the rehab center the day before. She was no happier now. She was standing in the visitor area of the rehab center at an ungodly hour of the morning. Everything started late in Hollywood, and she'd gotten in the habit of arriving places at a reasonable hour—like ten.

But she had needed time to drive out to Malibu and drive back, and still manage to have her normal day. Which meant starting hours earlier than usual.

Not even coffee had helped.

And then the fact that she was lugging paper didn't improve her mood much either.

Paper was a foreign concept to Jodi. She had bunches of it, mostly tied up in contracts with the studios' legal departments. Legal always wanted paper—reams and reams of it—because they believed that paper showed things better, things like signatures. Mortal lawyers believed that signatures needed to be solid things, things you could run your fingers across.

Never mind that the magical had known for years that paper was susceptible to corruption. Signatures could be copied with the right magic (she had it—it was part of the domestic skills that she needed to get things right in a household), and the words on the page could be changed with a touch.

So she had turned over the entire process to Ramon the day before, after she got back from the center. She had told him to give her everything he could find on the subject in hard copy—and she meant *everything*. He had given her one of his patented are-you-kidding-me looks but had jumped right in.

Which was a good thing, because she had had that day's messes to clean up, some of which happened because of her trip to Malibu.

A trip she was repeating this morning.

She stood in the entry, tapping her heavy purse against her leg, feeling irritated. She had planned to drop this stuff off and leave. She certainly wasn't going to spend much time talking to Bluebeard.

He had unnerved her the day before—and not in the way she had expected. All night long she thought about how handsome he was and how different he was from the smelly drunk she had met.

At first she blamed her reaction on his charm, but then—deep into the night—she began to wonder: Was she that lonely? It had been years since she'd had a serious relationship. (Make that decades.) She'd dated a bit a year or two ago, but none of the men she'd met had interested her.

She hadn't really sworn off men, but she hadn't pursued any either. Having relationships in the Greater World was just too hard.

So maybe, she figured, her reaction to Bluebeard was simply a hormone thing: she'd been too long without a man, and he cleaned up well.

Still, the fact that she was obsessing about him worried her, so she planned to keep everything short, to the point, and professional this morning.

That was, if she saw him at all. If Hargrove showed up first, Jodi was going to shove the papers at him. And then she was going to leave.

Jodi hadn't been in the main entrance for five minutes when the guard stuck his head in the door and told her someone would be right with her. She thanked him. Then she set her purse near one of the empty Eames chairs and walked around the room.

All 1960s California modern with the angles and light, which made it look different in the early morning than it did in the late afternoon, almost like she was in a completely different place.

The moments alone gave her a chance to look for the wards that Tank had told her about. It took some searching, but Jodi found six wards along the top of the door she had entered through. There were five matching wards on the door that led to the back, the door marked "Private." She wondered how many other wards she would find.

The six were somewhat crude, and it took her a minute to figure out why. They hadn't been assembled on the spot, the way that wards should have been. Instead, they had been made elsewhere and then put up near the door. Which meant that the wards had two features: one to keep fairies away, and one to help the wards stay in place.

The two features diminished the power of the wards and gave them limited effectiveness. In fact, they were starting to curl around the edges as if they were drying up.

She didn't dare move them for three reasons: she hadn't made them, she hadn't purchased them, and she didn't live here. If she lived here, then she would be able to put them up or take them down at will.

She would tell Blue about them and have him remove the wards. Then she would tell him how to safely neutralize them.

She wondered if he would do it or if he had been the one to purchase the wards.

A commotion in the hallway made her step back. She picked up her purse and turned toward the noise. Two men came down a long corridor. She recognized the tall one instantly. It was Bluebeard, moving like an athlete, quickly, gracefully, and with ease—so unlike the Bluebeard that she used to know. At his side was Jamison Hargrove, and unless Jodi missed her guess, Hargrove had his hand on the flat of Bluebeard's back, propelling him forward.

So Bluebeard hadn't wanted to come. Interesting. She wondered why. He had been awfully nervous the day before.

Maybe he *was* involved in these stalkings, although she didn't see how. His magic showed that he couldn't transport himself out of this facility, and she didn't see the point of working with a partner, not on something like this. There were other ways to terrorize women without appearing in their bedrooms at night.

The two men stopped in front of her. Sweat beaded on Hargrove's forehead, but Bluebeard didn't look as if he had exercised at all. He was looking down, his gaze not meeting hers, again.

That was unnerving all by itself.

"Ms. Walters," Hargrove said.

"Dr. Hargrove," Jodi said, feeling awkward. She didn't know what to call Bluebeard. "Blue."

He didn't answer her.

"Why don't you take Mr. Franklin to the same room you met in yesterday," Hargrove said. "I'm sure you have a lot to discuss."

Franklin, huh? Awfully close to Frankenstein. But of course, she didn't say that. She wondered why Hargrove was being so formal this morning, when the day before he had called Bluebeard "Blue." Perhaps because Hargrove was irritated with Bluebeard? To make a point?

She didn't know, and she didn't want to know. Instead she smiled at Hargrove—since he was the only person looking at her.

"Lead the way, Doctor."

He did. He steered Bluebeard as if the man were on a string, sending him toward that room like he had no choice. Maybe he didn't. Hargrove opened the door, and as he did so, he seemed to push Bluebeard inside.

Jodi followed a little slowly.

"I'm afraid we'll still be observing," Hargrove said, "but with the sound off as we agreed."

She wasn't sure if he was talking to her or to Bluebeard or to both of them.

"I won't be staying long," she said. "I just have a few things to drop off."

"I understand," Hargrove said, although there was no way that he could. He gave her a smile, then peered into the room. He nodded once, the way a parent nodded to direct a recalcitrant child, and then hurried down the hall.

Jodi took a deep breath and stepped inside the room. She pulled the door closed but didn't let it latch. As she stepped away from it, the door latched anyway. Apparently it was one of those heavier doors on some kind of spring, designed to close once it was in a particular position—probably for confidentiality.

Bluebeard had gone deep into the room near the pillows. He stood with his back to her, hands clasped behind him.

"I brought you the files you requested," Jodi said.

"Thank you," he said without turning around. All that did was make her realize that he had a beautiful voice with just a bit of an accent. It almost sounded British, but it wasn't. It came from one of the Kingdoms, from the old language. He had probably been raised speaking that.

"I'm not going to explain them to you," Jodi said. "Just look them over, then have Hargrove contact me when you've finished. I'm sure you'll have something to say about them."

"I'm not," Bluebeard said softly.

"Still," Jodi said, "I want to hear your ideas. Or rather, Tank does."

He nodded, then shoved his hands in his pockets. He no longer stood straight. He was hunched slightly, as if the very idea of going over the papers unnerved him.

"Speaking of Tank," Jodi said, "I had a chance to look at some of the wards in this building. They're weakening. They weren't made by someone living in this facility. They were brought in from the outside."

He turned slightly. His head was tilted downward but at an angle so he could see her now. He sounded surprised. She had finally caught his attention.

"You can tell this how?" he asked.

"Domestic magic specializes in warding," she said. "Each ward is made differently, and each ward has a different purpose. These wards aren't native to the building, meaning they have no connection to someone who lives here, and they have two different purposes—to keep fairies out and to stay on the walls. Which means that someone from the outside made them, and someone connected to this place bought them."

He ran a hand over his mouth. She could almost hear that defensiveness he had had the day before: *I didn't put up any wards. I can't do that kind of thing.*

He didn't say anything. She couldn't tell if he was at a loss for words or if he was being purposefully silent, so she said, "I can tell you how to take them down."

He threaded his hands together. This time he turned all the way, but again, he kept his head down. "Why do I have to take them down?"

He didn't sound surly; he sounded worried. He understood magic, then, and all of its good and bad attributes.

"Because I can't," she said. "I didn't make them or buy them. And I don't live here."

He nodded, then licked his lower lip. He ran a hand over his face again and looked at the wall just past her. It made her feel better that he had raised his head slightly. She could see his eyes now, even though he still wasn't looking at her directly.

She hadn't imagined it yesterday; he *was* the most gorgeous man she had ever seen. She had no idea how that was possible, given how many amazing men she'd met, drop-dead beautiful men who got paid to share their beauty on film.

But there was something else to him—a sparkle, a shine, a gloss—something that made him seem even more handsome, even with the weird behavior.

She would have to do some reading on charm magic.

She had avoided it until now. The charming ones usually didn't need her services to get work in this town. Either they had enough money, or someone approached them à la Lana Turner in a drugstore.

"So someone who lives here put them up?" he asked.

"Not necessarily," she said. "It has to be someone with a legitimate connection to this place. An employee could do it. An absentee owner, an heir of that absentee owner, a relative of yours—"

He actually shuddered as she said that and shook his head. The movements were small but noticeable.

"—even someone who supplies the place with food on a regular basis," she said. "Anyone could do it with the right connection."

"So why can't you?" he asked. "You're here."

"I'm here as a favor to someone else," she said. "I have no real connection here. Besides, these went up before I got here."

"Did they go up before I got here?" he asked, clearly looking for an out.

"No," she said.

His eyes flicked toward hers for just a moment, and then his eyes moved away quickly, like a child who had been told not to look at something but couldn't restrain himself.

She had had enough weirdness. "Why don't you look at me?"

"Personal quirk," he said too quickly.

"No, it's not," she said. "You looked at Dr. Hargrove when he spoke to you. You don't want to look at me. I want to know why."

He shook his head. "Really, it's nothing."

"If it was nothing, then you should look at me," she said.

He swallowed and closed his eyes. Then he turned his back on her. "You know who I am, right?"

"Of course I do," she said. "That's why I'm here."

"No, you're here because Tank asked you. If she had asked you to see some homicide cop to see if there were murders that were similar to the stalkings, you would have done that, right?"

Her heart raced. "There are murders similar to the stalkings?"

"No, no. I didn't say that." Then he bowed his head and paused for a long moment. "I don't know anything about these events or anything else that's been happening in the Greater World since I got here."

"But you know what's going on in the Kingdoms?"

He let out a small sigh. "Hell, I haven't been there in a century or more. No, I don't know anything."

He seemed defeated somehow, as if this very conversation hurt him. She didn't have a lot of experience with criminals. She didn't know if they could all affect this vulnerable stance or if only the ones with magical charm could pull it off.

"All right then," she said. "For a brief moment, you managed to deflect my question, but now I want to return to it. Why won't you look at me?"

He shook his head. "Please. There's nothing I can say."

She crossed her arms. He had been making her uncomfortable. Now she was making him uncomfortable, and she rather enjoyed it. She hated behavior she didn't entirely understand.

"Say it anyway," she said. "I know who you are.

I know what you've done. You can't say anything to make me think less of you."

He bent his head even more, as if her words were a blow. "I'm not trying to curry favor—"

"Good," she said. "You're not going to get it."

He nodded. "So long as we're clear."

Then he took a deep, visible breath and turned around. This time his gaze met hers, for just a second. Eyes wide, clear, a small frown line creasing his forehead. After a moment he blinked and looked down.

"I know what I've done," he said softly. "I know I don't deserve your respect or even your attention. It's just that, for the most part, I don't remember doing any of those things in my past. I did them, there's no doubt about that, but except for a few random images, I can't remember anything."

She waited, her stomach twisting. She had asked him to explain, and so he was. But she didn't have to like what he was saying.

"The women who died were… well, one was my wife." His voice was very soft. "The others were my fiancées, and then toward the end just women I had conversations with. It got twisted in the retelling that they were all wives. Maybe it would have been easier if they had been."

"Easier?" Jodi asked in spite of herself.

"Yeah," he said. "I would have known how to stop my behavior. I wouldn't have married anyone."

Her breath caught. He sounded so smart, so calm, so *rational*. No wonder Tank believed him. The charm combined with the way he took responsibility was attractive.

This was how cult leaders did it—they made the unreasonable sound reasonable.

Her silence seemed to bother him. He shrugged, still not looking at her. "No one has died at my hand in several centuries. No one has died in the Greater World."

What, do you want a medal? she almost asked but didn't. She resorted to sarcasm when she was uncomfortable. And right now, she was so uncomfortable she was ready to back out of this room.

"Since the last death, I haven't looked at a woman. I haven't talked to a woman, except in passing, and I never ever touch one. I try to avoid people as much as possible. I'm afraid if I get to know a woman's face, the image will get in my brain, and then…"

He closed his eyes. She waited.

"Then it'll start all over again," he whispered.

He opened his eyes and looked at her. She had an odd sense that she was seeing down to the very core of him.

"I don't want it to start again, can't you see that? I'm doing everything I can to prevent it. You're the first woman I've talked to in at least a century—"

"That's not true," Jodi said. "I've seen you talk to women at parties."

He shook his head. "They talk to me. Mostly they tell me how much they despise me or how badly they want me to leave. Sometimes they yell at me. I might talk back, I don't know, but when I'm drunk, nothing stays in my head."

Her eyes narrowed. This sounded plausible. She hadn't seen him have actual conversations. She'd seen people talking to him, and then the situation devolving into fights or upset. But an actual conversation, no.

"Is that why you come to parties? To talk to women?"

He shook his head. "I never plan to come. Then I

get drunk, and I think I can lurk in a corner, maybe cage a free drink. I never really look at anyone, and then I get tossed out." He shrugged. "Weirdly, I'm an optimistic drunk."

Jodi didn't want to think about that.

"What about Tank?" she said. "She's female."

"Tank." He smiled and the smile was clearly a fond one. He seemed to like her as much as she liked him. "Tank isn't like us. She's something else. There's never going to be an attraction because she's a different species. We had this discussion, she and I, a long, long time ago. And she proved over decades that I don't have to worry about hurting her."

"She likes you," Jodi said, as if that was a character flaw.

He nodded. "I like her too. And so far, that hasn't come back to haunt either of us."

Jodi sighed. "So you can't talk to women because if you do, you might kill them."

"Yeah," he said. "To put it bluntly."

"And you have no control over that?" Jodi said. At least, she had meant that as a question. Instead, it was more of a statement. A statement filled with sarcasm.

"I have control," he said. "I stay drunk. I stay away from people. I don't interact. But see, here's the problem. I am talking to you, and I remember you, and I'm sober, and frankly, that scares the hell out of me."

She just realized that her heart rate had increased as well. Apparently it scared the hell out of her too.

"What can you do to me?" she asked. "We're being watched on security cameras, and your magic won't let you fly out of here on a wing and a prayer. If I drive away, you can't follow me. If I go home and lock my doors, you can't get in. If I put up wards against you, you can't break them. So tell me, *Bluebeard*, why the hell should I be scared of you?"

He looked at her. The color had left his face. His mouth was open slightly. Clearly no one had talked to him this way in a very long time.

"Fifteen women," he said quietly. "Fifteen women that I *liked*, or worse, that I *loved*. What happened to them…" He shook his head, almost as if he couldn't contemplate it. Then he took another of those visible deep breaths. "What happened to them shouldn't have happened to anyone. It was brutal, more brutal than the fairy tales described, and the one thing the fairy tales got right, the one thing, was those heads…"

He bowed his head and put his hand over his mouth as if trying to prevent himself from talking more. Either what happened really did disturb him, or he was the best actor she had ever seen.

But she knew that murderers often felt remorse for their crimes.

"You haven't told anyone here who you are, have you?" she said softly.

He swallowed hard, let his hand drop, and said, "No. What am I supposed to say? Hey, I'm a fairy tale creature? The worst bogeyman from the very worst fairy tale?"

"No," she said, "but you could tell them about all the women you killed."

"To what end?" he said. "Tank brings me here. They guard me. They keep me segregated at my request—at least, until yesterday—and then I get clean. This is—was—the only place where I was reasonably certain people—*women*—could be safe from me. I'd finish my little stint here, and they'd release me, and I'd be drunk two hours later. It worked. Probably better than putting me in prison for life where they couldn't figure out why I don't age like everyone else. Besides, Tank would probably bust me out of there. She seems to believe I'm redeemable."

"What does that mean?" Jodi asked.

He shrugged one shoulder. "You'd have to ask her."

Jodi frowned. She never would have expected Tank to be susceptible to charm magic. Or at least, not for very long.

So Tank brought him here hoping he'd stay clean, but he never would. Yet he stayed for the entire program each time. There had to be only one reason.

"This is your safe haven, then," Jodi said. "And I just ruined it for you. You can't come here anymore."

"I can stay here if you don't come back," he said. "If you stay away, we'll be fine."

She nodded once. He didn't have to ask her twice. She reached into her purse, removed the thick file of printouts that Ramon had made, and tossed them on the coffee table.

"Tell you what," she said. "You read this stuff. I'll tell you how to take the wards down, and then you and Tank can discuss how similar this guy is to you. I don't have to come back, and you don't ever have to see me again. Does that sound good?"

"Yes," he said. "Will what you tell me work on all wards?"

"Why?" she asked. "You want to break into my house?"

"No." He sounded sad. "But I don't want to know how to break all wards. I don't want to have that power, you understand?"

Oddly enough, she did.

But she didn't want to sound in any way sympathetic to him. She didn't want to give this guy the wrong idea about anything.

"Here's how wards work, Romeo," she said.

"Don't," he said. "Don't call me that, not even in jest. Please."

She frowned at him and continued.

"You can't touch a ward that's made to protect some-one from you. If you do, depending on the power of the ward, you could get hurt or maybe even killed. You can't even spectrally cross a threshold that has a ward against you."

"Ever?" he asked, looking confused.

"Ever," she said.

"Has that changed over the years?" he asked.

"No," she said. "That's the nature of wards. They've always been like that."

"That's not possible," he said. "The village, at the end, the entire village had wards against me. Still, one of the girls who died, she was in a house with wards against me."

Jodi looked at him. His gaze was meeting hers and she had the sense that he didn't even know he was doing that. She could see deep into those beautiful blue eyes, and she saw no deception in them.

Maybe she was really, really susceptible to his magic.

"That's why my parents sent me away," he said, "be-cause even the most powerful wards designed to keep me away didn't work against my twisted magic. No one was safe. So I left. I did. I stayed as far from people as I could. That's why the Greater World was so appealing. America. Back then, it didn't have a lot of people, and I could be by myself for a long time."

The idea of wards that hadn't worked disturbed him. But it didn't disturb her as much as the beauty of his eyes did.

"Clearly," she said, "whoever made the wards did it wrong. That happens. It's not a common skill. Not all domestics have it."

"But you do," he said.

"Yes," she said.

"And you know you're good," he said.

"Yes," she said.

He nodded, and finally his gaze left hers. She felt his gaze move away, as if he had been touching her and stopped.

"Look," he said, "it's too risky. I don't want to know how to disable those wards. Either you do it, or we wait until they decay."

"Tank wants to settle this Fairy Tale Stalker thing," Jodi said, not sure exactly what she was trying to convince him of.

"Yeah," he said. "I understand that. Tell her that— well, hell, don't tell her anything. I'll look at this stuff tonight, and if I have nothing, I'll have Hargrove call you. Otherwise, I'll get permission to call you and give you the update, okay? He already got to see me interact with you twice."

"He wanted to see you interact with me?" she asked.

Bluebeard smiled. It was a rueful look. "Yeah. He

seems to believe that something about my relationship with women causes me to drink."

"And he thinks he can solve that?" she asked.

Bluebeard's smile became real for just a brief second. His eyes actually twinkled.

"Well," he said, "sometimes we all have delusions of grandeur."

Chapter 9

NO MATTER WHAT HAPPENED, THAT MAN LEFT HER terribly unnerved. Jodi left the rehab center with her head spinning. She believed that he didn't remember much about the murders, just enough to convince him that he did it. She also believed that he was doing whatever he could to prevent another, at least consciously.

The idea that his subconscious wanted to kill women who interested him... well, that was more upsetting than she wanted to acknowledge. Because she didn't get a sense of evil from this man, and she usually got a sense of evil from evil people/creatures.

She wondered if the attraction and the charm overwhelmed her own sense of danger. She didn't know if that awareness-of-evil sense came from her domestic magic or if it was just a part of her. If it came from her magic—and she had never seen anything to convince her that it did or did not—then something he had done had overwhelmed it.

And it would imply that he had done something to overwhelm those wards all those years ago.

She drove back to her office with the top down and songs blaring, although once she got to work, she had no sense of what she listened to. A group of gnomes huddled in her front yard like a defeated army. After she got out of the car, she discovered that they didn't want to be classified as "little people" on a movie set, and they were tossed off for being unnecessarily political.

It took three phone calls to settle that mess, and another to deal with shape-shifter revolt on the set of the latest *Twilight* knockoff. Mostly her job was either about finesse (the gnome crisis) or about plausible lies (the shape-shifter issue). And her lies weren't even that plausible. No one really listened in Hollywood, so long as the problem got taken care of.

She half expected to see Tank, but Tank didn't show. Jodi left a message at the Archetype Place because that was the only way she knew how to reach Tank. But no one there had seen Tank for a week, which wasn't that unusual. Tank did what Tank did, and usually without letting anyone know about it.

Jodi got her dinner at In-n-Out Burger—simple cheeseburger, fries, and a vanilla shake. She'd planned to eat better for years, really, and she did exercise (didn't everyone in LA?), but on days like this, days when she couldn't quite deal with all the various stresses, she ate badly. On purpose.

Still, she didn't eat the burger in her car or at one of those never-quite-clean tables. She got takeout and brought it home.

Home was a 1924 Spanish-style bungalow in Hancock Park. Jodi had bought the house new, although it had taken work. Back then, people who looked like her couldn't buy homes in Hancock Park which was, at the time, the most upscale part of the budding city of Los Angeles. Jodi had a friend from the Kingdoms who did an appearance spell, so Jodi's looks matched the neighborhood's desires—only for her dealings with the bank. Once she purchased the house, she went back to her usual look. At the time, the neighbors thought she was the help and didn't pay attention to her. But others did. Nat King Cole bought a house in the area in 1948, partly because he thought the neighborhood was friendly, since he'd been to parties at Jodi's house. Instead, he was the one credited (correctly) with breaking the color barrier—since he was the first one to challenge it.

Jodi just went around it, like she did so many other goofy and inexplicable things in the Greater World.

She was feeling the weight of those things as she let herself into the house, balancing her purse, her phone, the bag of greasy food, and her briefcase. She put the phone in its recharging cradle on the occasional table beside the door—she was damned if she was going to talk to anyone tonight—then she kicked off her shoes, walked stocking-footed across the polished hardwood floor, and dropped her purse and briefcase along the way.

She was tired, grumpy, and hungry. Normally, she would have set herself a plate at the breakfast nook in the kitchen, but she didn't. She went straight to the family room off the pool, dropped the burger bag on the ratty coffee table she kept for just that purpose, turned on the big-screen TV on the wall, and set it to show her sixteen channels at the same time. She didn't care which sixteen channels she watched; she just wanted faces and noise and something to think about besides hiring the magical and just how disturbing her conversation with Bluebeard had been.

Of course, the TV found three local news channels and all of them were running stories on the Fairy Tale Stalker. No new photos, no new sketches, nothing except that there'd been another sighting or visitation or whatever the hell you wanted to call it, this time in Echo Park, an area of the city he hadn't worked before.

If indeed what the stalker was doing was work. She wasn't so sure. It seemed to her it was someone magical getting his rocks off by scaring mortal women.

She gave up, clicked on KTLA, and watched their coverage, feeling slightly dirty as she did so. She couldn't quite get it out of her mind that she had talked with a man just that morning who was as sick (sicker) than the Fairy Tale Stalker.

And she knew, had she met him under other circumstances without any idea about his past, that she would have liked him—if, of course, he had looked her in the eye when he was talking to her. Otherwise, she would have thought him attractive but strange. (And maybe not even human; she'd known some feline shape-shifters who couldn't handle direct eye contact on first meeting because in the feline world direct eye contact was considered threatening.)

She shuddered at the thought. She finished her vanilla shake, packed up her mess, and patted her too-full stomach. She didn't usually overeat like that. But she did feel better.

She had a long night ahead of her. In addition to the work she had brought home, she also had to make about a dozen wards. Despite what she had seen in Bluebeard's magic, despite Tank's belief that the man had nothing to do with the current stalking cases, Jodi would be remiss if she didn't protect herself from Bluebeard and from people like him.

Someone had warded the rehab center against fairies, which meant that someone either wanted to keep

Bluebeard's only friend away from him or that someone had another agenda, one that had nothing to do with Bluebeard or with Tank or with anyone that Jodi knew.

She would have to ask Tank if she had any dealings with the staff at the center. But she had a hunch Tank would say no. Tank didn't like to deal with mortals any more than she had to. Jodi doubted anyone at the center wanted to keep Tank out.

Still, those wards at the rehab center had given Jodi the idea. She needed to make sure her house was protected, at least for the short term. Especially if Bluebeard had told her the truth—if he had no control over what he did to a woman who came to his attention. And he was right: Jodi had come to his attention.

Tank had put her in an impossible position, and Jodi needed to deal with it in all ways—not just intellectually, but practically and magically.

She needed to make sure she was safe.

Chapter 10

BLUE SAT ALONE IN THE READING ROOM, A SINGLE light on the table focused on the printouts before him. Jodi had given him nearly five hundred pages of material, organized by date, with notes on the top. She clearly hadn't compiled this. He found on the top of the first sheet a Post-it signed by someone named Ramon (who had very flowery handwriting, and who used a scented purple pen). Ramon's handwriting covered the notes, and the deeper Blue dug, the more grateful he became to this mystery Ramon.

Ramon was quite the organizer, and he made wading through this material very easy. Not that Blue was wading. He was reading with increasing horror.

The reading room was on the far end of the main building. He liked to think that no one else came here because it was named "the reading room," as opposed to the library. But the reading room was the only place in the center that had books.

They covered the walls, with newer battered paperbacks scattered on various racks throughout the room. Every time he came to the center he saw new books, so he figured that patients left them when they checked out.

Sometimes he just spent the entire night in here reading fiction. He had trouble sleeping because of all the nightmares, so he tried to do as little of it as possible.

On this night in particular, he had a hunch he would

have trouble sleeping, even if he hadn't had the excuse of the documents to keep him up.

He had told Jodi more about himself than he had told anyone except Tank. And Tank had pried some of this out of him when he was drunk. He didn't remember telling her, but she knew.

Shortly after he sat down, one of the staff brought him some bottled water and some fresh fruit.

"Another late night?" he'd asked Blue sympathetically.

Blue had shrugged. "Is there anything else?"

The people here were kind to him, and they did do the best they could to accommodate him, given their mission to "heal" him. He always supposed that they did so because of his charm and because they had no idea who he was.

He rubbed a hand over his eyes. The Fairy Tale Stalker was a misnomer. This guy, whoever he was, terrorized these women. The entire mess had started several months ago and got a short column in the local papers, primarily because the whole thing sounded so LA and ridiculous.

A man appeared in a woman's bedroom claiming to be Bluebeard. He told her, in a "watery" voice (her term), that he would visit her again, and the next time he would make her "his." Then his voice changed, sounding panicked. He spoke rapidly, as if he was trying to get the words out before they failed him. (Again, this was her description, in a longer piece written later.)

He said, "After you're mine, I will cut off your head and keep it forever."

And then he disappeared. Again, that was her word. He appeared, and then he disappeared.

She called 911, and the police did respond rather quickly (she was in an upscale neighborhood), but they couldn't find anything. No sign of forced entry, and her alarms were still activated—she had to deactivate them to let the police in. No footprints outside the house, and she had never given her key to anyone, not even a neighbor.

The cops initially wrote it up as a "bad dream" call and laughed about it, but it was so bizarre that one of them told the beat reporter who handled local crime. That was how the story initially broke.

The man "appeared" two more times to the woman, freaking her out but never touching her, and not talking to her. The cops would have thought (maybe did think) the woman was a nut, until another woman reported the same thing.

Then another, and another, and finally, the cops got a clue that this stalker was a problem. There were dozens of theories, all of them about "special effects" and "Hollywood magic," as if the guy was some kind of projection sent from another building. But the cops couldn't figure out where that projection came from.

Blue knew. It wasn't Hollywood magic. It was real magic, and the projection came from a man's mind.

If he wasn't caught, this guy would do the same thing Blue did—he would kill dozens of women all in the name of love.

Blue stood, walking to the window and clasping his hands behind his back. He hadn't been able to stop himself. How could he help anyone stop some other guy? He didn't even know what caused all of this. It certainly wasn't intent. He had never meant to hurt anyone. His mother used to say in bewilderment that he was the most kindhearted child she had ever known.

And that hadn't turned out well.

He ran a hand over his face. He was tired, deep down bone-tired. He wished the rehab center allowed energy drinks, but the folks here thought of them as a drug. Even though they did allow coffee. He could go to the kitchen and get some. It would make him jittery and tired instead of just tired, but that might be good enough.

The last thing he wanted to do was fall asleep, particularly with the Fairy Tale Stalker on his brain. And Jodi.

Jodi. She was beautiful and determined, and properly disgusted by him. He appreciated that. She seemed sensible.

He wasn't quite sure why Tank had roped her into all of this. He had known Tank long enough to know she often had motives that no one understood.

He always wished Tank would stop helping him, because he thought it would get her in trouble. And now she was helping this other guy—or the women this other guy was victimizing.

He clenched a fist. Maybe it was someone he'd been drinking with, someone who had heard of Bluebeard. Maybe the media was right and there was some kind of way to do a Hollywood magic projection. Maybe there was a simple explanation for all of this.

But he doubted it.

And he didn't know what he could do about any of this. He wasn't the heroic type.

The only thing he could do—besides stay awake—was share his insight into what was happening. And he had insight, although probably not the type Tank wanted.

He knew what this guy was doing. He knew how it

would escalate. And he knew if someone couldn't figure out a way to stop it, a lot of women would die.

Chapter 11

JODI WOKE OUT OF A SOUND SLEEP, HER HEART POUNDING.
Someone was in the room.

She didn't move except to open her eyes. An odd amber light came through the sliding glass doors. The light over the pool went out at midnight, although she did have lamps scattered through her garden—little one-foot-high things that some dumb marketing executive called "fairy lights." If he'd ever seen a true fairy light, he would have called them something else.

If the pool light was off, all she should have seen was the edges of the patio around the pool. If the light was on, she would have seen the pool itself.

Then she woke up enough to realize that she shouldn't have seen any of it. She had pulled the blackout curtains. She ordered new blackout curtains every few years from the same organization that made them for Vegas casinos. When she was in her bedroom, she wanted to sleep, not worry about light creeping in at dawn.

Carefully she looked around the room, trying not to move so that she wouldn't make any noise.

Her bedroom was square and large, dwarfing her California king-size bed. A door opened in from the hallway, and she had converted a smaller second bedroom into a completely luxurious bathroom. That door was open, as it always was, just like the door to the hallway. She lived alone, so she didn't have to close doors. She didn't need the privacy.

A large wood-burning fireplace dominated the remaining wall. She only used the fireplace on the cool rainy nights of deep winter—nights that people elsewhere in the country would believe temperate or even mild. She had lived here long enough that such nights seemed frigid to her.

And even when a fire burned in that fireplace, the light in this room was never amber.

She eased herself up and finally looked toward that light. It took all of her strength not to gasp at what she saw.

Bluebeard stood in the center of the light. His gaze met hers, his spectacular blue eyes unmistakable. They twinkled. Then he smiled at her, slow and easy.

The smile was sensual, and it transformed him from an incredibly good-looking man into a seductive one. She almost—almost—smiled back.

Then she realized what she had done. She shuddered, threaded her hands through her sheets, and whispered a small phrase that activated a protective spell embedded in it, shielding herself.

He looked powerful, the king's son, the man he had been born to be, not the broken, half-frightened man he had become. She understood even more the lure of his charm—he could crook a finger and a more susceptible woman would be heading straight for his arms or inviting him into her bed.

He warned her about this: he had said that he would get her into his brain, and then he would come after her.

And here he was in her room. Just smiling at her.

"Get out," she said, wondering why her wards had failed. They should have protected her against him and anything he sent directly. "Get the hell out."

His smile grew, and now it was less charming and more sinister. She didn't get frightened very often, but she was frightened now. This man had killed fifteen women that she knew of. Fifteen women in the Kingdoms. He could have killed dozens in the Greater World and never gotten caught. Once serial killers crossed state lines, Americans had no real way to track them.

He could have killed women in every single decade he was here, so long as he did so in different towns, different places.

"Get out," she said again, wondering what she could use against him. Comfort magic was not offensive magic. It didn't kill by definition. It didn't harm. It didn't maim. It eased. It soothed.

She wondered if that would work—some kind of soothe spell. But she didn't want to raise her hands, didn't want to let go of the sheets just in case he launched himself at her.

He wasn't holding a weapon, so she didn't know how he could hurt her.

Except, at the rehab center, he had looked down at those hands of his as if they had done very bad things. Had he killed those women without the aid of a knife? Had he done it with brute strength alone?

He wasn't moving toward her. He was just watching her.

She had one other power: she could get rid of something that disrupted. And he was clearly disrupting.

She sent a bolt of energy toward him, banning him from the house.

His smile faded, and he looked oddly disappointed. Then he turned around and headed through the door. The amber light faded as if it had never been.

But she didn't hear the front door open. Nor had her alarm gone off.

Her heart was still pounding, and she wasn't sure if he was still in the house.

So she grabbed the backup cell phone that she kept in a recharging cradle beside the bed, grabbed her robe, and slipped it on. Then she put her feet over the side of the bed, careful not to step into her slippers, which had heels and would make a sound on the hardwood floor.

She was heading out to the pool. If the warded house couldn't protect her, then she saw no point in staying here, particularly if he was still inside.

She wished she knew how to reach Tank, but she didn't. And she didn't want to call the police. They couldn't do anything.

Instead, she dialed 411 as she quietly let herself out the sliding glass doors. She needed to call the rehab center.

She needed to know what Bluebeard was doing right now.

Chapter 12

"MA'AM," SAID THE ANNOYED VOICE ON THE OTHER end of the phone. "We do a bed check. All our residents are accounted for."

Jodi paced around the pool. The tile was cool under her feet. The fairy lights illuminated her plants, making everything beautiful, and not creating shadows. So far, she saw no amber light, and no Bluebeard. But she spoke softly just in case.

"Is he asleep?" she asked.

"Ma'am, he's not required to be asleep. He's just required to be inside when we lock the facility at night."

"Please," she said. "Check for me."

The person on the other end of the phone sighed. "Ma'am, look. He can't come to the phone. Our rules say no outside contact for weeks, and he's not on the contact list."

"I know that," she snapped. "I just got a call from someone claiming to be him, and I'm hoping to hell it was a prank."

Working in Hollywood all these years made it easy for her to tell a plausible lie.

"Oh," the voice on the other end of the phone said, as if he (she? Jodi couldn't quite tell) finally understood why Jodi was calling. "Let me check."

She paced, swallowing hard, keeping an eye on the house and all the entrances to the pool area. She had gated this off when Hancock Park got more popular. Her land abutted the Wilshire Country Club, but she had at least two lots between her and the nearest fairway. Two overgrown lots where someone could hide.

She had put a gate in the trees years ago, but she had disabled the alarm system she placed on it when she realized that the stupid duffer golfers would shank the ball into the gate and set off the alarm. Then she deemed it more trouble than it was worth.

Now she wished it was on.

She felt surrounded by danger on all sides—and she was scared to go back into her house, which pissed her off.

Then she heard the phone on the other end rattle.

"He's here, ma'am," the voice said. "He's been awake the entire time, in our reading room, studying some computer printouts."

"You're sure he's been awake?" she asked.

"I looked at our security footage, ma'am. Making a phone call during your no-contact period here is a major violation of our policies."

"Did you talk to him?" Jodi asked a bit breathlessly. He was a Charming. He could convince anyone of anything.

"No, ma'am. But I did check with our other staffers. He's been awake the entire time, ma'am."

So the voice—whoever this was—had also thought that he had tampered with the security feed and had checked with the other employees to make sure he hadn't.

"And no phones nearby?" Jodi asked.

"We keep our phones under lock and key," the voice said without irony. "It would take a miracle for him to find an unattended phone. And it would be even more of a miracle if he made a call to you and the call didn't get caught on our security feed."

Jodi let out a small breath. She wasn't quite sure how to process this information, but she did know one thing: It made her brain hurt. How could he send a projection of himself without being unconscious or unaware of it?

And if he was on the security feed, then he hadn't left the facility, which meant he hadn't been in her house. Besides, he couldn't have messed with the security feed. The Kingdom magical couldn't manipulate electronics. They could use the electronics—thank God, she wouldn't survive in this modern age without her computer—but they couldn't tamper with them. The electronics got frizzed out. If a magical being could be filmed (and not all of them could), then their image on film was actually their image—and what they were doing at the time.

Someone else had done this. Somehow. But she didn't know who could have.

She thanked the nameless voice on the other end of the line, hung up, and then speed-dialed the Archetype Place. She knew no one would be monitoring the phone at this hour, but she also knew she could leave a message.

When she heard the voice of Griselda, the woman who had run the Archetype Place successfully for more than sixty years, Jodi let out a small sigh of relief, even though she knew Selda wasn't there. Jodi was relieved by the sound of Selda's voice mail message.

"Hey, Selda," Jodi said, "I need to talk to Tank ASAP. Can you find her for me? And I also need to talk with you when you get in. Thanks."

She hung up and stared at her house. She hated all those countless Hollywood movies where the heroine (or the dumb half-naked chick in the nightgown) went into the place where the Big Evil was, completely un-defended. At least Jodi wasn't wearing high heels and a miniskirt.

But she couldn't quite convince herself to go back inside. She didn't see herself as a dumb half-naked chick. Or the heroine, for that matter.

"You rang?"

Jodi eeped, tossed her phone into the air in surprise, and nearly fell backward into the pool. She didn't see where the voice came from, until the phone stopped its descent about two feet above her head.

She looked up, saw motion, and realized that she was looking at gossamer wings in the pale light, wings fluttering really, really, really hard to deal with the weight of the phone.

"Tank," Jodi said. "Thank God."

"I don't believe in God," Tank said. "I believe in gods, and mostly I avoid them. They have a different kind of magic, it annoys me, and they listen to those god-awful Fates all the time, which really pisses me off."

Jodi wasn't going to talk politics with Tank. Jodi especially was not going to talk politics mixed with religion with Tank. Jodi didn't know what Tank believed in, and she didn't want to know.

Jodi held out her hand. "I'll take the phone. It looks like it's weighing you down."

Tank lowered herself slowly, her wings still working overtime. As she got closer to Jodi, Jodi realized that Tank's face was red with effort.

"I may have killed it," Tank said. "It made a zapping noise."

Jodi tried not to sigh. That would be the third phone in three days. But she didn't have the luxury of being annoyed. She was still scared, and her heart was beating so hard that it made Tank's wings look like they weren't beating at all.

She took the phone away from Tank and set it on a glass poolside table. Then she took a deep breath, trying to calm herself.

"Something was in my house," she said.

Tank lowered until she landed on the table. Then she gave the phone the evil eye, as if it had disabled her. She stomped to the edge of the table and peered up at Jodi.

"What kinda something?" she asked.

"I thought it was Bluebeard," Jodi said.

"He doesn't do that," Tank said so fast that Jodi got annoyed.

"I didn't say that it *was* Bluebeard, I said I *thought* it was Bluebeard."

"And that's why you're out here wearing that?" Tank raised an eyebrow. As if she had the right to comment. Tank was wearing a black dress made of some kind of gauze. Its hem was uneven, like a disco dress from the 1970s modified for a funeral garment.

"I wasn't going to stay inside with... whatever it was," Jodi said. She glanced at her bedroom and didn't like the feeling of fear that rose inside her. In fact, she hated that. No one should be afraid of her own house.

"You think it was the stalker guy?"

"I don't know what it was," Jodi said, realizing she was raising her voice. "And I don't even know if it's still in there."

Tank frowned at her, then glanced at the house. Clearly Tank wasn't ready to go in either.

Jodi made herself take another deep breath. "Okay, look, I don't think it was the stalker guy, but I don't know. I do know that it looked just like Bluebeard, and you'd think if those women saw him, they wouldn't have called him average. They would have said—"

"Tall, dark, and handsome?"

Jodi looked down at Tank, who was still staring at the house. Had she even realized she had spoken out loud? Probably. Jodi had the sense that Tank never did anything involuntarily.

"No. But yes. But no. You never think of your stalker as handsome," Jodi said. "But taller, and those blue eyes, they would've noticed those. I did."

Tank nodded. "So it looked like Blue. Did he say anything?"

"No," Jodi said. "He just smiled at me."

"Smiled," Tank said. "So he didn't threaten you."

"He was in my bedroom uninvited, after I talked to him about a stalker who did the same thing. Wouldn't you call that threatening?" Her voice was going up again.

"No," Tank said. "I wouldn't."

She floated upward as if a draft caught her. Then she headed to the sliding glass doors and peered upward. "You warded the house."

"Yes," Jodi said. "And I just called the rehab center. They said that he hasn't left. He's been on their security feed the whole time. And he's not asleep either."

"You warded the house against Blue?" Tank asked, as if she hadn't heard Jodi at all.

"*Yes*," Jodi said, using her how-dumb-are-you tone. "He killed fifteen women."

"Allegedly," Tank said, sounding distracted.

"*He* says so," Jodi said. "That's not so alleged. I know people who've seen the heads."

"Yeah, me too," Tank said.

"You *saw* the heads or you know people who have?" Jodi asked.

"Yes," Tank said, flying even farther upward. God, she was annoying. How did anyone have a conversation with her? "These wards look perfect. In fact, they look better than perfect. They should've worked."

"Unless he's figured out some other kind of magic," Jodi said.

Tank floated down and stopped right in front of Jodi's face. Jodi backed up, felt her heel hang over the edge of the pool, and damn near fell in a second time.

She ducked and stepped onto the patio. "Stop that. It's rude."

"You warded against Blue and his magic, right?" Tank asked, again as if Jodi hadn't spoken.

Jodi moved away from the pool edge. "Yes."

"Not against Charmings or against anyone else, right?" Tank asked.

"If I did that, I wouldn't be able to have clients in here," Jodi said. "Sometimes I do work from home, you know."

Tank flew back to the doors. "Can you let me in?"

"Why?" Jodi asked.

"Because I want to attack the bad guy in your defense," Tank said.

Jodi looked at her. Tank wasn't serious, was she?

"Oh, by the Powers," Tank said. "If the bad guy was still in there, he would have come out to the pool and drowned you with his bare hands, which I might just do myself. You asked for my help. Now take it."

"Technically, I didn't ask you for your help," Jodi said. "I asked Selda to contact you."

"So you could have my help," Tank said, floating in front of the door.

"Did you ever think it might be because you hired me to look into something for you?"

"You wouldn't call about work in the middle of the night," Tank said. "You've lived around mortals too long to do that."

Damn, that little fairy was pissing her off. Jodi stomped across the patio and pulled the slider open. But she wasn't going to go in first.

Tank threw in a handful of fairy dust. It flew brightly across the air, like the edges of a Fourth of July sparkler, and then it wrapped itself around an image.

If Jodi hadn't been watching the fairy dust, she would have retreated all over again.

The dust formed around the image of Bluebeard as he had appeared at the edge of her bed, smiling at her. Only it didn't look real. It looked like a faded snapshot.

Tank had used magic to reveal someone else's magic.

"Tell me what's wrong with that," Tank said from just inside the door.

"It's in my bedroom," Jodi snapped.

"Besides that," Tank said. "*Look* at him."

So Jodi did. She wasn't facing him any longer. She couldn't see his eyes. Instead, she saw his entire form.

And he was wearing some kind of costume. It was blue, with big sleeves belled above the elbow—Tudor period, if she missed her guess—and tights.

No self-respecting heterosexual man in the Greater World of the twenty-first century wore tights when he snuck into a woman's bedroom.

"What the hell is that?" Jodi asked.

"I don't know," Tank said as she flew deeper into the room. "But I mean to find out."

Chapter 13

JODI FOLLOWED TANK INSIDE THE DARKENED BEDROOM. The fairy dust–illuminated image didn't give off a lot of light, not like that amber light Jodi had seen before. And this Bluebeard didn't move. He really did look like a fading, three-dimensional Polaroid.

She walked around the image, her heart pounding. As she did, she realized that fairy dust smelled faintly like baby powder. She didn't mention it to Tank, because that would make Tank defensive. But the thought was just enough to calm Jodi down.

In fact, it almost made her smile.

At least it took her mind off her pounding heart.

The image was the right height, but in addition to the weird clothes, it was about twenty pounds heavier than the Bluebeard she had met. Not fat. Muscular. Broad shoulders, narrow hips, great legs, if those tights were any indication. And the face was more filled out, rounder and—dare she think it?—younger, or at least not as beat up by time and drink and general unhappy living.

This Bluebeard looked almost cheerful. Then she decided to drop the "almost." He did look cheerful.

"This can't be the stalker," Jodi said, more to herself than to Tank.

"It's *not*," Tank said. "Jeez, don't you recognize Blue?"

Jodi gave her a withering look but doubted Tank could see it. Tank was flying in front of the image, just six inches from its face. Just like she had done to Jodi near the pool. Only the image wasn't backing away from her.

"It's not quite your friend Bluebeard, though," Jodi said. "The clothes are off, his face is too round, and he's too young."

"No," Tank said. "This is Blue. This is the Blue I met hundreds of years ago."

Jodi peered around him at Tank. Tank was hovering and staring at him. Was she looking besotted? Really?

"You *do* have a thing for him," Jodi said.

"I keep telling you," Tank said. "I like him. I've always liked him."

"Boyfriend-girlfriend liking?" Jodi asked. "Or friend-friend?"

Tank flew straight up, like a missile, and then she came down in front of Jodi. Tank's eyes flashed.

"You are unrelenting," Tank said. "And it is not possible for me and Blue to have a relationship. Think about it."

Jodi didn't want to imagine that relationship. "Nothing's impossible with magic."

Tank threw her arms into the air. "Friend-friend!" she shouted. "Is that good enough for you? Or do I look that much like Tinker Bell to you?"

Tinker Bell's obsession with Peter Pan had become so extreme that some mortal actually wrote a book about it—getting it wrong, of course. Mortals always got the details wrong.

Then Tank put her hands on her hips, still hovering in front of Jodi.

"Why do you care so much anyway?" Tank asked. "You think the guy is a serial killer."

Jodi frowned. She had never thought Peter Pan was a serial killer. She had thought him a lot of things, but never anything so bad as all that.

"I do not," Jodi said.

"You do!" Tank said. "You just said so outside."

"About Bluebeard," Jodi said.

"Yes, about Bluebeard," Tank said. "Who did you think I was talking about?"

"Tinker Bell," Jodi said. "And Peter Pan."

"Tinker Bell is a lot of things, but she would never kill anyone voluntarily," Tank said. "She leaves that kind of crap to me."

"You've killed someone?" Jodi asked.

Tank flew around the image and hovered over Jodi's right shoulder. "You know, this partnership is not going to work if you keep accusing me of weird things."

Jodi opened her mouth and then closed it. The conversation had already taken so many tangents that she wasn't sure she could properly follow it.

"Sorry," she said. "I'm still a little shaken up."

"Clearly," Tank said angrily.

Jodi took a deep breath and wished Tank would too. Then Jodi nodded at the image—which still hadn't moved.

"So, what do you think this is?" Jodi asked. She wanted to change the subject quickly or, to be more accurate, bring the subject back to where it belonged. "The stalker?"

"That Fairy Tale Stalker?" Tank asked. "I *told* you. That's not Blue."

It was Jodi's turn to sigh in irritation. "I *know* that. I just—I was hoping I didn't screw up my wards. I thought I protected myself against him."

"The Fairy Tale Stalker?" Tank asked. Was she being deliberately obtuse?

"Bluebeard."

"You did," Tank said. "This isn't him."

"It looks like him," Jodi said. "And if it isn't him, then what is it?"

Tank landed on her shoulder, startling her. Tank's wings brushed against her ear as they stopped fluttering.

Jodi wanted to brush her off. But she didn't dare.

"It's what I've always suspected," Tank said softly, so softly that if someone else had been in the room, they wouldn't have been able to hear her. "It's a curse."

Jodi leaned forward. A curse. Of course. The amber light should have been a tip-off. Curses brought their own illumination. And unlike evil spells, curses lasted forever. Or, at least as long as the cursed thing (or person) still existed.

Jodi poked at the fairy dust image with her forefinger, and the image crumbled, falling to the floor.

"Great," Tank said. "Thanks for that. I was studying that."

"Do it again," Jodi said. "You can bring the image back."

"*Do it again*," Tank said in a mocking tone. "Like I answer your every command. *Just do it again*. Like it's easy. *Do it again…*"

But she did. She lifted a handful of fairy dust into the air. It fell around them, illuminating not just the original image, but one a few feet away. This was the image of Bluebeard leaving. Still smiling. Looking a little seductive.

"Keep going," Jodi said.

"You keep going," Tank said, and at first Jodi thought it

was another verbal put-down. Instead, it was a command. Tank clearly didn't want to fly. Maybe she couldn't. She had put out a great deal of effort this evening.

Jodi complied, taking a few more steps toward the door. Tank tossed more fairy dust and got two more images of Bluebeard walking away. Theoretically.

"Again," Tank said.

Jodi walked around the images into the hallway. Tank tossed more fairy dust. This time it caught the edge of the previous image, but nothing else.

"Should I keep going?" Jodi asked.

"One more," Tank said.

Jodi took a few more steps. Tank tossed one more handful of fairy dust, but it, too, failed to catch anything. It just fell to the floor like sparks from a Fourth of July sparkler.

"So he *did* vanish," Jodi said, feeling a little ridiculous. The entire time she had stood on the patio, shivering and lying to herself that it was because of the cold, she had been hiding from no one.

"Appeared and disappeared," Tank said thoughtfully. "You didn't see him arrive, did you?"

"I was asleep."

"And what did he say to wake you up?" Tank asked.

"He didn't say anything. It was the amber light."

"You didn't tell me about the amber light," Tank said.

"I know," Jodi said. "I forgot until we were inside, and then you were talking about the image, and I couldn't get a word in edgewise—"

"Don't make this my fault," Tank said.

"I'm not," Jodi said. "So you think it's a curse."

"An elaborate one," Tank said. "And you activated it."

"*I* did?" Jodi said. "How could I have activated it?"

"Something happened between you and Blue, something that started the whole damn process up again." Tank stood up, her little feet pressing hard on a nerve on the top of Jodi's shoulder. "Boy, are we in trouble."

"You will be if you don't move your feet," Jodi said.

"My feet? What's wrong with my feet?"

"You have sharp little pointy feet, and they dig into the wrong places," Jodi said. "So let's move away from nerve endings, shall we?"

"Like that's possible," Tank said. "Where to, Your Highness?"

Jodi extended her hand palm side up. "Stand here."

"I'm sure there's nerve endings on that big fat palm of yours." It felt like Tank was digging her feet in harder.

"But they're not on the surface, because, as you pointed out, my palm is fat."

"Touché," Tank said as she flew down to Jodi's palm. She landed hard, almost like she was trying to find the nerve endings. "Sharp little pointy feet. That's the first time I've heard that accusation."

"How often do you stand on people?" Jodi asked.

"Not often enough it seems," Tank said. She sounded distracted. Indeed, she had her hands on her hips with her wings folded against her back. She was staring at all of those fairy dust images. Echoes of Bluebeard in different poses, like fading statues in a holographic museum.

"I'm still confused," Jodi said. "The wards should have protected me against Bluebeard."

"They did," Tank said, still staring at the images.

"They did not," Jodi said. "His curse got in here."

"No," Tank said. "The curse has nothing to do with him."

"Really?" Jodi said. "Because there he is in my bedroom, smiling at me."

"He's not here, and no part of him is here," Tank said. "His curse is here."

"That's right," Tank said. "*The* curse is here. It's not Blue's spell, it's not a spell Blue created. Blue had nothing to do with the curse. Someone else created the curse and placed it *on* Blue."

"I'm not sure I entirely understand the difference," Jodi said.

"That's because you're one of the good guys," Tank said. "You've probably never cursed someone in your entire life."

She was heavier than Jodi expected, and awkward as well. Jodi's arm was feeling the strain of keeping her hand palm-side up so that Tank could continue to stand on it.

"I have cursed a million people," Jodi said, thinking that she was annoyed enough at Tank to curse at her right now. "But not with magic, no. Of course not. That way lies madness."

"Exactly," Tank said. "And Blue might be a drunk, but he's not insane."

Jodi almost disagreed automatically, and then she thought about it. That was true. Bluebeard had struck her as strange but rational. And if he had been placing curses on people, then he would be more than slightly crazy.

Of course, no one put a curse on himself.

"My presence activated the curse," Jodi said thoughtfully. What had Bluebeard said to her that morning?

Since the last death, I haven't looked at a woman. I haven't talked to a woman, except in passing, and I never ever touch one. I try to avoid people as much as possible. I'm afraid if I get to know a woman's face, the image will get in my brain, and then... then it'll start all over again.

He had finished with a whisper as if it had all been too much to contemplate.

He had looked at her, *seen* her, talked to her, and brushed against her. And then his image—his younger image, the image from the Kingdom, the image fifteen women had seen before their deaths—had shown up in her bedroom.

"Holy crap," Jodi said softly, letting her arm down.

Tank slid, then threw herself flat against Jodi's arm, grabbing onto her wrist. Tank swore in the old language. Her grip was surprisingly strong.

"Sorry," Jodi said and eased her to the top of the dresser near the door.

"Holy crap what?" Tank asked as if she hadn't panicked, as if she hadn't swore. She brushed herself off. Her gauzy black dress was covered in fairy dust.

"This poor man thinks he's been killing women," Jodi said, more to herself than Tank. "And he hasn't harmed a soul."

"Finally! Someone who understands!" Tank said and clapped her little hands together, releasing more fairy dust sparkles.

Jodi glared at Tank. "You knew this all along, and you let him suffer?"

"No, I didn't know it," Tank said. "I suspected it, though. It was the only thing that made sense. I've been around evil. He's not evil. He never has been."

Jodi had had that same sense. She had discounted it because of the charm. How many other people had done so?

"He's been punishing himself for no reason," Jodi said, still thinking out loud.

"Oh, there's a reason," Tank said. "Those women died."

Then she floated up just enough to get in Jodi's face. Again. This time Jodi brushed her away.

"That's a bad habit," Jodi snapped.

"It gets your attention," Tank said.

"You already had my attention," Jodi said.

"Did not," Tank said. "You were thinking out loud."

Jodi did not like how accurate Tank's assessment was. "Fine. What do you want?"

"*Those women died*," Tank said, as if that was enough to get through to Jodi.

"Yes, I know," Jodi said. "And how does that affect me…?"

Her breath caught. It affected her because of the curse. The curse had activated again. The women died because Bluebeard had noticed them. Then his curse turned on them, somehow killing them. Which was why he couldn't remember killing them himself.

"Oh, great," Jodi said. "Now I'm a target."

"Yep," Tank said. "There's only one thing we can do."

"And what's that?" Jodi asked.

"Figure out how to lift the curse."

Chapter 14

LIFTING A CURSE WASN'T AS EASY AS IT SOUNDED. TANK couldn't just wave her tiny arms, say "Hocus Pocus!" and lift the curse. Nor could Jodi throw some comfort magic against it.

Jodi and Tank had to figure out the nature of the curse, then they had to find the cursecaster. If the cursecaster was still alive, then he could lift the curse — or be forced to. (Jodi did not have offensive magic, so she wasn't sure how you'd force anyone to do anything. She'd never forced someone to cast a spell in her life.)

But if the cursecaster was dead — which this one might have been — then they had a whole other issue. Jodi wasn't sure what they would do then.

Jodi thought of all of that as she left Tank on the dresser. Jodi walked to the side of her bed, keeping an eye on the images of Bluebeard. The images were slowly fading, like a Polaroid development in reverse. They were getting muddier, and darker, and slowly dropping away.

She turned on one of the lamps on the bedside table. A soft glow illuminated the room. She usually liked that softness. It eased her into relaxation; it eased her into sleep.

But she didn't feel like relaxing or like sleep.

Still, she sat on the edge of the bed. "I didn't see this curse in his aura. It was the proper blue for charm magic, and it had no other magic woven into it."

Tank flew from the bureau top to the bedside table. The light from the lamp fell across her as if it was her own private spotlight. She looked exhausted.

Jodi had never seen Tank look exhausted before.

She sat on the edge of the table, then rubbed her tiny hand over her face. After a moment, she said, "When did you check the aura?"

Jodi frowned. She didn't know why that was important. "The moment I met him. I was worried, Tank. You sent me to a guy I thought was a killer—"

"Think about it," Tank said. "You hadn't reactivated the curse yet."

Jodi's breath caught. She thought the encounter through, ran the memory through her brain. She had checked him the moment she walked through the door—after she could tear her gaze away from his stunning handsomeness.

And she hadn't glanced at his aura after he had looked at her. It took special vision, and she hadn't used it again.

"So the curse activates," she said, "and he has no idea?"

Tank shrugged. "Every curse is different."

"But he didn't kill those women," Jodi said. "The curse did."

"Something did," Tank said.

"And gave him a memory of it."

"But not a good one," Tank said. "Just enough to convince him."

Jodi shuddered. This was one nasty curse. "Isn't this complicated for a curse? I thought curses were simple."

Tank shrugged. "They can be extremely powerful, depending on who casts them. Experienced cursecasters can be very elaborate."

"Still," Jodi said.

Tank didn't say any more. She leaned against the lamp, her wings wrapping around its base, almost as if she was using it to hold herself up.

"It's gotta be a curse," Tank said. "What else would last that long without the person who cast it present?"

Jodi didn't know. There was so much about evil that she had never ever contemplated. She had no need to. Up until now, it really hadn't been a part of her world.

"I assume it would take time for the curse to play out against me," Jodi said.

"I don't know the timetable," Tank said. "We're going to have to ask Blue."

Like they were asking him about the Fairy Tale Stalker. Jodi's breath caught.

"My God," she said. "It's happening again."

"Duh," Tank said.

"No, think, Tank. If this curse takes time to play out against the victims, if it happens event by event—first a visitation, then another, and finally the murder, all those women are still in danger. This new guy, this new Bluebeard, he saw them, he remembers them, and now they're at risk from him. They've had the first vision. Some have even had the second. And—"

"This thing will escalate. Crap," Tank said. "How many times has this creepy cursecaster done this?"

"And what does he get out of it?" Jodi said. "It would take a lot of magic to establish a curse like this one for so very long."

"It's almost enough to send me to the Fates," Tank said.

Jodi looked up. The Fates were three women who governed the rules of magic. They were the final arbiters for the Powers That Be, who were in charge of all magic. But the Kingdoms rarely dealt with the Fates. Many of the Kingdom magical didn't have enough power to even get themselves to the Fates unless there was an emergency, and the Kingdom folk had learned long ago that getting the Fates to solve a dispute might take centuries, at which point the dispute had faded into unimportance.

"So go," Jodi said. "They might know who is doing this."

"I'm sure they know," Tank said. "But getting them to tell me is another matter. Have you ever talked to the Fates?"

"No," Jodi said.

"More rules than a fairy tale princess," Tank said. "And to say that they speak elliptically is an understatement. I've gone to them before, and their advice then boiled down to *Solve it yourself*."

"Greee-at," Jodi said.

"We'll work on this one," Tank said, "and if we need them, we'll send Blue."

"Blue?" Jodi said.

Tank shrugged. "I always look at it this way: let the person with the most at stake deal with those women."

"So you don't have to." Jodi smiled tiredly. She had that philosophy about her own business. "Has he gone to them before?"

"Are you kidding?" Tank asked. "He thought he was a mass murderer. Do you think he'd go to the law?"

"Good point," Jodi said. Then she fell backward on the bed. "What's going to make him believe us now?"

"I don't know," Tank said. "But he's got to. There are a lot of lives at stake."

Jodi propped herself up on her elbows so that she could see Tank. "Gee, Tank, you sound like you actually care."

"I'm not the heartless fairy," Tank snapped. "Her name is spelled differently."

"What is this with you and Tink?" Jodi asked.

"None of your damn business," Tank said and flew away.

Chapter 15

Tank came back ten minutes later. By that time, Jodi had all the lights on and had changed into a pair of jeans and a white blouse. She was still barefoot, but she felt a bit more in control now.

Except that she knew she couldn't sleep.

She went into her in-home office because she wasn't comfortable anywhere else. She loved her kitchen, but there was no quick exit out of it. The dining room was too formal, and the front door in the living room made her nervous.

The office, like her bedroom, opened onto the pool. In fact, when she bought the house, the office had been the master suite—not that 1920s houses had master suites. It had been the biggest bedroom, and it had had a small window that looked out over the pool. She had replaced the window with sliding glass doors so that she had a good view of the pool and the backyard.

A soothing view—one that still managed to soothe.

"There's no one outside," Tank said, as if that was news, as if she hadn't left because Jodi pissed her off.

Tank was sitting on the edge of Jodi's desk. The desk here was glass with steel legs. Tank had walked across the glass to get to the edge, leaving tiny footprints on the polished surface.

"It's okay, Tank," Jodi said tiredly. She was sitting in her desk chair, but she wasn't getting any work done.

She wasn't even sure what work there was to do, which made her realize just how rattled she was. "You don't have to stick with me. I'll be fine."

"No, you won't," Tank said. "Right now, all we have to go on are those Fairy Tale Stalker reports and all the versions of the Bluebeard fairy tale. And while that doesn't give us a lot, it does give us one thing: we know that these women were always alone when they were attacked."

"They were alone except for that image or projection or whatever that thing was in my bedroom." Jodi shuddered. She was still creeped out by this. She wondered if she would always be.

"Well, it depends on your definition of alone, doesn't it?" Tank snapped. "I'm not even sure that thing is alive."

"But it can kill."

Tank made a loud exasperated noise. "We don't know what kills the women. We just know that this thing—this image—is the first sign. And we know it shows up when women, the *victims*, are alone."

Jodi narrowed her eyes. She was not a victim. Or, at least she wasn't going to be. Victims screamed and cried and ran helplessly through dark streets.

She hadn't screamed or cried, but she had run out of her bedroom, somewhat helplessly.

She banished that thought from her brain. She had *escaped*, that was all.

"My point," Tank was saying, "was that these women were ripe for the pickings. Easy targets. Vulnerable."

She rolled the words through her mouth as if they were specially designed to irritate Jodi.

"I'm not an easy target," Jodi said.

"I think anyone would be an easy target if they were alone," Tank said.

Jodi looked at her for a long moment. For once, Tank wasn't trying annoy her. Tank was worried about her.

"Thanks," Jodi said. "I really appreciate it."

Tank nodded, then waved a hand. "Do whatever it is you do. I'll keep an eye out."

And then she wove a circle of fairy dust around the room, slipped down onto one of the easy chairs, and fell sound asleep.

Chapter 16

THEY LEFT THE HOUSE A FEW HOURS LATER.

Jodi called Ramon's office line and got his voice mail. (She had a tiny hope that he would come in early, but this was *really* early.) She said that she had an unexpected meeting that morning, and he should reschedule everything she had for that day to later in the week. Then she drove to the rehab center with Tank so that they could arrive by the beginning of visitor's hours.

Jodi had called ahead, just to let Dr. Hargrove and Bluebeard know she was on her way. They were halfway there when she remembered the anti-Tank wards.

Tank waved a hand, which was clearly her don't-sweat-it gesture. "I'll just wait for you outside."

And after Jodi parked, Tank sat on the dash as if the car had been designed for her. True to form, the guard didn't even notice. He just gave Jodi her name badge as if they had become old friends and escorted her inside.

Bluebeard was already in the meeting room. As she walked toward it, Jodi's stomach did one lazy flip. Since Tank had accompanied her the entire way, Jodi hadn't given these next moments any thought. For some reason, she thought Tank would have her back, and of course, Tank wasn't even here.

Jodi straightened, tugged her purse over her shoulder, and headed toward the room. Before she had left the house, she had taken a long, hot shower and changed

into an all-black business suit. She found that clothes—
particularly dress clothes—made her feel stronger. And
she had a hunch that she would need to feel strong
today. But she felt grimy just the same. Part of it was
the exhaustion, which was stalking her like a tiny but
relentless demon.

She resisted the urge to touch her hair or check her
makeup. This Bluebeard problem was a job she was
doing for Tank—even though she wasn't quite sure how
or even if Tank would pay her.

It was hard to keep her professional attitude, though.
The bottom line was that someone had hated Bluebeard
enough to put this horrible, horrible curse on him, and
now somehow, she had been sucked into it as well.

She pushed the door to the meeting room open and
stopped, surprised to see him sitting down. His hair was
wet, like he had just gotten out of the shower, and it
dripped along the back of his white shirt. The shirt was
untucked, and he wore a ripped pair of blue jeans. His
feet were bare, and the room smelled faintly of chlorine.

"Hey," he said, still not looking at her. Instead,
he had the papers she had brought him spread out
over the coffee table. They were in little bundles. "I
thought you were going to call. I didn't expect to see
you here. When Dr. Hargrove told me you were coming, I was surprised."

She didn't respond right away. Instead, she remained
beside the door, purse in hand, and looked at his aura.

It was blue, like it had been the day she met him,
but the blue had faded. It was diluted with disorganized
magic that snaked and sparked around the edges, almost
like heat lightning in a clear sky.

Unlike heat lightning, though, an amber light surrounded and contained his aura, puncturing it and damaging it.

She wondered if he could feel the change.

"Everything all right?" he asked, looking up. His gaze met hers so briefly that if she hadn't been watching for it, she wouldn't have noticed it.

"Actually, no," she said.

He blinked, looked down, then moved his head to the other side, as if he didn't quite know where to let his eyes settle.

"It's okay," she said as she came farther into the room. "You can look at me."

"No, I explained—"

"I know," she said, "and you were right."

This time he did bring his head up, and on his face was an expression of such naked pain that it almost hurt to see it. "What happened?"

She could hear the panic in his voice, so she smiled at him. This was what she did: she fixed distress.

"Tank and I," she said, "we figured out what's going on."

"Oh," he said and immediately looked away. He clearly thought she meant with the Fairy Tale Stalker.

"With you," she said.

He frowned, then shook his head. "I've know that for centuries," he said.

"No, you haven't," she said. "What happened to you isn't what you think. It's a curse."

"No kidding," he said.

"A *real* curse," she said. "And it's destroyed countless lives. And now it's starting again."

"With this guy," he said softly, his hand moving across the papers.

"No, Blue," she said, deciding to use his nickname. "With you."

Chapter 17

BLUE PROPELLED HIMSELF OUT OF THE COUCH AND backed away from Jodi as quickly as he could. He scrambled around the couch, putting it between them.

"I didn't do anything, did I? I was awake all night. I was *here*. I couldn't have done anything, could I?"

He sounded like an ass. He *was* an ass, but that was the least of his worries. He had hurt someone, damaged someone, maybe had been hurting or damaging all along.

Or killing them. God, what if he had been killing people without realizing it?

Again.

What if he had been doing it again?

But Jodi hadn't run away. She hadn't fled to the door; she hadn't done anything.

Except sit down.

She set her purse on the floor beside her chair and folded her hands in her lap.

Like a counselor would, waiting for the patient to calm down enough to talk to.

But she wasn't a counselor. She was a chatelaine or the daughter of chatelaines, and she'd transferred that to Hollywood somehow. She had called herself a fixer. She fixed things. That was why Tank had gone to her.

At least, that was what she had said.

"How come you're not scared?" he asked. "Yesterday

you were scared of me. You were disgusted by me. Today you're not."

She sat straight, hands clasped together. She was wearing black, and it accented her auburn hair. She looked perfect. She looked calm.

She looked beautiful.

He couldn't notice how beautiful she was. He didn't dare.

"I'm not scared or disgusted," she said, "because I know what's going on now."

His heart was racing. He gripped the back of the couch so hard that his fingers were digging into the fabric. "You're what, psychic now? How can you know?"

"You're not going to like what I tell you," she said. "Why don't you sit down?"

He was too panicked to sit down. Too frightened. Not of her. But of himself.

"Just tell me," he said.

So she did.

And it was hard for him to listen to her. He had gone to her house, to her bedroom, he had woken her up like he had done every other woman he ever hurt, and he hadn't spoken. His fiancée—his first one—she had thought it seductive, seeing him, thought he was teasing her, and she had joked about it the following day. And it had gone on for a few more days before... before...

"Are you listening?" Jodi asked.

He nodded. "That last part," he said. "I was in the room, right?"

"That's what I thought," she said, "and truthfully, I ran. I was afraid of you, Blue."

He nodded. He could barely breathe. Dammit, it was

happening again. To this woman. He *liked* her. He didn't want to hurt her.

He didn't want to hurt anyone.

"You should be afraid of me," he said sadly. "Everyone should."

He was.

Then the door opened. Dr. Hargrove peeked in. His curly hair was mussed, and he had a fresh coffee stain on his shirt. He'd clearly hurried here from somewhere else.

"What's going on?" he asked.

Blue had forgotten: the staff had been watching everything on a security feed. They saw his panic, saw Jodi act calm, saw how distressed he was.

Blue didn't even have a plausible lie.

"I had some news for him that surprised him," Jodi said calmly. "Nothing more."

"It looks like more," Dr. Hargrove said from the door.

"I know, and I'm sorry," Jodi said. "I—"

"It's my fault," Blue said. "I'm sorry. It's my fault. I overreacted. I'm still not used to this kind of conversation. I'm—you know—fragile."

Normally he hated that word, but today it fit. He *was* fragile, and terrified. But he couldn't let Dr. Hargrove see that or Dr. Hargrove would find himself deep in a magical universe he didn't understand.

Or he would turn it into some mundane serial killer thing that would fit perfectly into some Greater World box but wouldn't work with the magic and the Kingdoms and... a curse?

Did she really mean a curse?

"All right then," Dr. Hargrove said. "But let's stay calm, shall we?"

You try to stay calm in this circumstance, Blue wanted to say. *You just try it. You'd be a gibbering idiot in a week. You couldn't have stood up to half of what I lived through.*

But he didn't say it. He was rather astonished that he had thought it. He tried not to think of himself or his circumstance at all, and suddenly it was at the forefront of his mind.

"Blue?" Dr. Hargrove said. "All right?"

All right what? Was he all right? He was so upset that he couldn't follow the conversation. He was trying to think about all of this, and he couldn't.

"Are you all right?" Dr. Hargrove asked. "Can you stay calm?"

Oh, that was what he meant.

"Everything's fine, Doc," Blue said. "Really. I just got startled, that's all."

Jodi smiled at Dr. Hargrove. "I appreciate the fact that you checked in. Thank you."

Her tone was both grateful and dismissive, a real trick. One that Blue used to know. He used to be able to do that and make the person feel like they'd just received the biggest compliment of their entire life.

Doctor Hargrove frowned at both of them, then pulled the door closed.

Jodi stared at it for a moment, as if she was making sure he was gone, then she sighed and looked at Blue. "Are you really okay?"

"No," he said, and he couldn't keep that panic from his voice. "I was in your room."

"*You* weren't," Jodi said. "You didn't let me finish. I called here to check, and they tracked you down. You were reading this stuff."

"They saw me?"

"In person and on video," she said. "The person who answered the phones even checked the security log."

"I was here," he said in wonderment. And yet he had been in her bedroom. "So I—what? Sent some kind of projection of myself?"

"You didn't lose any time, did you?" Jodi asked.

He shook his head. "I don't think so."

"You didn't," she said confidently. "I'm sure you didn't, and even if you did, it wouldn't matter."

"It would," he said. "God, I don't want to hurt you, and now you're in real danger—"

"I am in danger," she said calmly—how could she be calm about that? "But not from you."

"What?" he said. "How could that be?"

"Let me finish," she said.

"Okay," he said and braced himself for the worst.

Chapter 18

JODI TOLD HIM ABOUT TANK FINDING HER, ABOUT THE fairy dust, about the images, about what was wrong with the images. She told him everything in great detail, including their conclusion—hers and Tank's—that this wasn't his magic at all.

All the while he watched her warily, flinching sometimes, as if he didn't quite believe her or as if memory was taking him elsewhere. He had grown very pale. His hands gripped the back of the couch so tightly that she thought his fingers were going to poke holes in it.

"So when I came in here," she said, "I checked your aura. It looks different today. It has all kinds of disorganized magic surrounding it."

He swallowed visibly. "And that means what?"

"I think it means Tank is right. I activated the curse."

He shook his head. "*I* activated it. I noticed you. I thought about you. And now you're in danger, aren't you?"

She took a deep breath. That was the crux of the problem. Whether caused by Blue or by someone else, the fact didn't change that fifteen women had died.

"Yes," she said.

"Tank wouldn't leave you alone," he said. "That means she's scared for you."

"Yes," she said.

"And she's not in here, so there's still something preventing her from getting in," he said.

"Yes," she said. She was beginning to sound like a broken record.

He leaned over the couch. She wondered for a moment if he was going to be ill.

She had never seen anyone so shaken before. Of course, she had never changed someone's perspective this much before, altered his worldview, made him look at everything—including himself—differently.

It took all of her strength to sit calmly. She wanted to go over to him and put her arms around him.

She wanted to comfort him, and that surprised her. Usually she tried to keep her distance, but this man was in such distress…

And he had charm magic. She had to remember that.

"Teach me how to take down the wards," he said. "I need to talk to Tank."

"Why don't we just go outside?" Jodi asked.

He shook his head. "We'll have our own security guard following us, and I don't want him to hear this."

"All right." She stood up and brushed her skirt over her knees. She was shaking just a bit herself. "It's not that hard, really. It's like taking down a spiderweb, only you have to crumble the pieces and say the right words over it."

"You'll teach me the words, right?" he asked.

She nodded.

"Before I do, can you look at them and figure out who put them up?"

"No," she said. "The person who put them up is not the person who made them, so the wards can't tell me much."

He glanced at the security cameras on the ceiling. "The staff is going to be wondering what I'm doing."

She shrugged. "Tell them you don't like spiderwebs."

He smiled at her absently. She was amazed he could smile right now.

"You know," he said, "I don't."

Chapter 19

THE WORDS THAT JODI TAUGHT HIM MADE NO SENSE to him, but that was the way of magic spells. They used an old language, older than some of the Kingdom languages. Besides, she must have come from a Kingdom different from his (or she really would have been terrified of him), and the language must have been vastly different.

She helped him pull over a chair. Then he climbed on it, crumbled the first ward, and said the words. Apparently he had said them right, because she smiled at him and ducked outside.

He watched her walk to the only car in the visitor lot, a red Mercedes convertible that somehow suited her. Beautiful, powerful, flashy, but not too flashy.

He swallowed hard, then concentrated, taking the next ward in his hands. The things felt like spiderwebs too, old spiderwebs, crumbly, sticky, and forgotten.

He said the words, and the ward poofed out of existence. Like the first one had done.

Magic. He didn't really understand it. His magic was a part of him, like his nose. Charm wasn't something he consciously did—not until his father taught him how to enhance the charm. His father had been a Charming too. Blue looked like his father—or he had as a young man. His father had loved his charm magic and loved to use it.

He had probably overused it when the killings started.

The murders.

And Blue hadn't done them.

He was a little dizzy, a lot stressed, and very, very confused. Those memories, they had been partial, but they had been real. And yet, these wards were real. He felt them beneath his fingertips, but once he disarmed them, they vanished.

A curse. Could it be that simple?

Why hadn't his parents seen it?

Why hadn't anyone?

He so wanted to believe this, but he didn't want to at the same time. If Jodi and Tank were wrong, then he was going to do a lot more damage.

He took the next ward, crumbled it, and said the words over it. It vanished with a little puff of magic.

Jodi had her back to him. She had a beautiful figure, and she dressed well. She was one of the most stunning women he had ever seen.

And he couldn't think that. He thought it because she was one of the few women he had seen—actually *seen*—in years. Decades. Centuries.

That was all.

If he could disconnect the attraction somehow, maybe he could negate the curse.

If it was a curse.

He worked on the next ward.

He would talk to Tank. Tank would give him answers. He would believe Tank.

Kinda.

He closed his eyes for just a moment. He was terrified. He hadn't been this afraid since the first accusation all those years ago. Since the images came. The "memories."

What if Jodi was wrong?
What if she was right?
What then?

Chapter 20

BLUE LOOKED SHELL-SHOCKED AND FRIGHTENED. OR stunned and alarmed. Jodi wasn't quite sure what the right words were. But she knew she had to give him time, and taking down the wards was easy.

He needed a minute alone. So she went outside to tell Tank that she could join them in the conference room, provided she did not alight anywhere for long. She usually wasn't visible on film because she moved too fast, but if someone wanted to see what she was, they could slow the images down.

Usually Tank just threw fairy dust at a camera, but Jodi didn't want her to do that either. Given how fast Hargrove had entered the room when he saw Blue upset, she figured Hargrove would teleport there if the camera cut out.

Tank was dive-bombing some seagulls, screaming at them and pulling their feathers out. She had dropped a small collection of feathers around the guard station.

The guard himself, glittering a bit with fairy dust, was watching the birds with a frown on his face.

"I've never seen them do that," he said to Jodi.

"Me either," she said. "You'd think someone was torturing them or something."

"I am not torturing them," Tank said as she dropped another feather beside the guard. He didn't seem to hear her. She had magicked him well, then. "You were in there a long time."

Jodi nodded. She spoke to the guard. "I'm still not done with my meeting. Can you make sure those birds don't poop on my car for the next half hour or so?"

"I'll do what I can," he said, "but they're acting crazy."

"Everything's topsy-turvy today," Jodi said. "I wish I knew some magic that would make the gulls settle down."

"Yeah, me too," the guard said. "It sure is bothering me."

"He's got too much time on his hands," Tank said, grinning. She was enjoying this.

Jodi narrowed her eyes. Tank had been particularly difficult this morning. It was probably stress, but it made things hard for Jodi.

"You," Jodi said in the softest voice she had. "With me. Now."

She hoped Tank understood that message was for her. Tank rolled her eyes and flew right next to the door. Then she stopped and peered above the mantel. She was clearly looking for the wards.

She clapped her tiny hands together and spun in a circle for a moment. She looked like a little tornado.

She stopped and ended up facing Jodi. "They're gone."

"Yes," Jodi said softly. She knew that because Blue had moved the chair back to its original spot. He wouldn't have done that if the wards were still up.

He was nowhere to be seen. Either he was in the meeting room or he was cleaning up. She had told him to wash his hands thoroughly and to change clothes, just in case part of the wards had fallen on him.

Then she frowned. She had trusted him to remove the wards correctly. She usually trusted no one to act properly with magic.

Charm or practicality? Or exhaustion?

She wasn't sure what it was.

She pulled the door open and said quietly to Tank, "You can come in now."

"Oh, goodie." Tank bobbed up and down on the air currents that came from inside. She actually seemed pleased to go into the rehab center.

Jodi still hated the place.

"Keep moving. There are cameras," Jodi said as she headed toward the meeting room door.

Blue's paperwork was inside, but he wasn't.

She sat down in her chair. Tank flew around her. Jodi kept her head down so that no one could see her lips move on the security footage.

"Are you sure you're safe in here?" she asked Tank. "We still don't know who put up those wards."

"Oh, I figured that out yesterday," Tank said.

"It would've been nice of you to share," Jodi said.

Tank flew past her, headed up toward the camera, and Jodi said, "Don't do it. They'll come in here if the cameras cut out."

"Great," Tank said and flew down toward the papers. "I'd really like to stop moving."

"Your only choice is to hide in my purse," Jodi said.

"That is not a choice," Tank said. She flew over to the pillows, then dove in and out of them, as if she was inspecting them for hiding places. Then she flew back to the couch, moving low across its surface.

"So who set up the wards?" Jodi asked.

"Oh, guess," Tank said.

"I don't know," Jodi said.

"They're store-bought. They were made general because store-bought wards can't be specific. But most people don't hate small fairies. Well, all except one. People only know about one. And she's a featured icon of Disneyland, the little—"

"Are you saying that this was for Tink? Who would do that?" Jodi asked.

Tank flew to the other chairs, inspecting them. She was clearly looking for a place to land. But she was visible against all of the chairs. If she landed, the staff would be able to see her.

"Peter's in here. Again," Tank said.

"You're saying Peter put up the wards? I thought Peter and Tinker Bell got along."

"Nooooo," Tank said. "The relationship ended years ago, but she won't admit it. He became a Lost Boy out of necessity, not because it's a cool name."

"I don't want to hear this," Jodi said. "I rather like that story."

"You read the Greater World story?" Tank said as if Jodi had grown fangs.

"I read all of them, Tank. I like to know what's being said about us."

The door opened, and Tank dove into Jodi's purse. The purse rattled, and from its depths, Jodi heard a faint "Ow."

She tried not to smile.

Then she looked at the door. Blue came in, his hair wet again—he must have showered—and this time he was wearing a light blue shirt and khaki pants. He wore sandals. The entire outfit looked comfortable and suited him.

He gave her a tentative smile. "Dr. Hargrove thinks you're good for me. He says I would never have noticed the spiderwebs if it weren't for you."

"He's right," she said with a smile. "About the spiderwebs, that is."

"The rest of it too," Blue said. "If you're right, I mean, and this is a curse. If it is a curse, then it's really old."

"Do you have any idea who could have cast it?" Jodi asked.

He shook his head. "I killed a lot of brain cells. I don't remember as much as I probably should."

He sat back down into his old spot on the couch. Then he moved the papers around. "I'm still not sure I believe you. But—"

"Oh, believe her." Tank's head appeared over the edge of the purse.

"The staff can see you," Jodi said.

"They're not going to be looking at your purse," Tank said. "Besides, I can make it invisible."

"Then they'll wonder what happened to it," Jodi said.

"Just don't move much," Blue said to Tank. "They're going to be watching me anyway."

He was looking down at the papers, shuffling them back and forth. He smiled, though, and added quietly, "It's good to see you, Tank."

"It's good to see you too," Tank said. "You look better when you're sober. Smell better too."

"Thank you, I think," he said. Then his smile faded. "Is what Jodi says true? Is this a curse?"

"Yep," Tank said, "and you seem to be sharing it with this unfortunate bastard."

She waved a tiny hand at the papers on the table, and the purse rocked.

"Tank," Jodi said, trying hard not to look directly at the purse. "Don't move at all."

"Spoilsport," Tank said.

"The curse has started again, though, right? I mean, if that's the right language. It always happens, but sometimes it gets worse, right?" Blue said, as if Jodi and Tank hadn't spoken. "It's ensnared Jodi and she's in danger from me. I mean, that's what we know, right?"

"She's not in danger from you, Blue," Tank said. "She's in danger from the magic. And she's not ensnared. She's a target. The one ensnared is you."

He sighed, then shook his head. "That can't be possible. I remember killing. I remember…"

His voice trailed off, but he raised his hands as if they were still stained with blood.

Jodi's heart started to pound. The way she understood curses, they couldn't force someone to do something he wasn't inclined to do in the first place. Of course, technically, he didn't do anything. An illusion of him did.

But she didn't know this man, and she didn't know what he was inclined to do. She only knew what his magic said he could do—magically. And that was charm. But if there was a violence already in him…

"You remember what, exactly?" Tank asked.

"Not a lot," he said. "Images. My hands—"

"Strangling those women?" Tank asked. "Cutting off their heads? Putting their heads on a pike? Ever wonder why those heads never decayed?"

"By the Powers, Tank, no, God, stop," he said.

"Not beheading them?"

"I blocked it," he said.

"There would've been a lot of blood," Tank said with a little too much relish. She was making Jodi nervous. More nervous, if that was possible. And Jodi was trying to concentrate on Blue. "Do you remember being covered with a lot of blood?"

"*Tank*," Blue said, and he sounded distressed.

"Or what you did with the bodies? Did you chop them up?"

"Tank!" he said. "Stop."

"You're awfully squeamish for a mass murderer," Tank said.

Tank was right. He *was* squeamish. And Jodi found that interesting.

"Those heads belonged to women I cared about," Blue said primly. He was still looking down at the papers. It was almost as if he had reverted from the man Jodi had spoken to this morning to the man she had met two days before.

But his comment about the women didn't sound like a bid for sympathy to Jodi. It sounded honest. And if she wasn't so sure of what she saw in his aura, she would be wondering how deep his ability to charm went.

"You didn't answer me," Tank said softly to Blue.

"I did too," Blue said. "I told you I blocked the killings."

"You said you blocked the beheading," Tank said. "But that other stuff, that would be hard to block. Besides, there would've been a murder room somewhere close to you. Did you have one? It would have been—"

"Tank, really," he said and stood up. He moved to his position behind the couch again. "I can't listen to this. I did it, okay? The curse forced me to. And then I blocked it."

"Or you never did it in the first place," Jodi said. She leaned back in her chair. She was calming down again. Tank had asked a lot of logical, if gruesome, questions.

And while Blue's reaction to them seemed convincing enough, there was something else that bothered Jodi.

Blue had his head down. He had the couch between him and Tank or him and Jodi or him and both of the women, depending on how paranoid Jodi wanted to be. He was digging his fingers into the back of the couch again.

"I did it," he said. "I remember it."

"You remember an image," Tank said with sarcasm that only Tank could wield.

"It's vivid," he said. "I know what it's like to have a patch-hole memory. When I drink—"

"Were you drinking then?" Tank asked.

"Of course I drank," Blue said. "Everybody drank."

"To excess?" Tank asked. She climbed to the edge of the purse.

"Get back down," Jodi said to Tank.

Tank ducked down just a little. "This is impossible," she muttered.

Jodi ignored that. Instead, she said, "You're both missing one important piece. Why didn't anyone question the survivability of those heads? Blue, you don't have the kind of magic that would keep them fresh. Someone kept them fresh and visible. That's a spell. That's something separate."

He winced, then raised his head just enough so that he could see her.

"Did anyone check to see where that spell had come from?" Jodi asked.

"I don't know," he whispered.

"The fairy tale says the heads were in your castle. Is that true?"

"Yes, it's true," he said. "But only I could see them."

"Oh," Jodi said. Which made the fresh heads part of the curse, not a spell. That curse was powerful; it made Blue see all kinds of things that never happened.

"And you *told* people about seeing the heads?" Tank flew out of the purse and hovered in front of Blue. "Blue, that's just plain dumb."

"No," he said, still looking at Jodi. "I didn't tell anyone. Whenever any woman I was interested in came into the castle, she saw them too."

Tank cursed, then did a backflip and flew upside down around the room for a few minutes, as if what she heard infuriated her.

"And no one tried to find out where the heads came from?" Jodi asked.

He hadn't looked away from her at all. "I don't know. I don't think so. They thought I did it."

"But you don't have the magic to keep the heads fresh. So they would have had to know someone had cast a spell on the heads," Jodi said.

"It was a curse," Tank said.

"But they didn't know that, and the heads were fresh," Jodi said. "Someone had to wonder about that. If I were chatelaine, I would have wondered how those heads kept appearing in the castle I was responsible for. And I would have wondered why the damn things didn't decay."

"I have no idea," Blue said. "Everyone was so shocked that I murdered women that I don't think anyone thought about it. It's all confused. No one talked to me. I was the villain, remember? Plus, my dad ruled the Kingdom, so he could—and did—decline to prosecute me. I could have run amok forever. As it was, I ran amok for years before I decided I couldn't take it anymore. Not that it mattered. No one sent their daughters to the castle."

"And no one else saw the heads?" Jodi asked again.

"I thought they did, but I don't know. Half a dozen women ran screaming from that place. I don't blame them."

Jodi didn't either. She wouldn't have gone up there in the first place, had she known what he had done.

Although that was a silly thought, considering she had come here at Tank's request, knowing exactly who Blue was.

Or who everyone thought he was.

"Didn't your castle have a chatelaine?" Jodi asked.

Blue frowned, clearly trying to remember. "Sure. She, she had been there for a while. She didn't like children—"

"What does that mean?" Jodi asked. It was her experience—hell, it was her training—that chatelaines had to make life comfortable for everyone in the castle.

"She said children were better seen, not heard. You know, that old thing. And she wouldn't deal with the children's areas. She brought in someone else for that. My mother wanted to get rid of her, but my father wouldn't."

"Why?" Jodi asked. "It sounds like she couldn't do her job."

Blue shrugged. "It's a very long time ago."

"An important long time," Jodi said. "She should have found the magic around you. She should have cleared those awful images of the heads. And she should never have passed off any of her duties overseeing any part of the house."

Tank dove into the purse again, and puffs of fairy dust rose around it like talcum powder. This time there was no "ow." Then she popped her head out of the purse.

"You think she's the one who cursed him?" Tank asked.

"I don't know," Jodi said. "The timeline doesn't fit. She'd been around him since he was a child."

"Curses are more powerful when they grow from childhood," Tank said.

Both Jodi and Blue looked down at the purse. Tank shrugged, raised her tiny hands, and said, "Just sayin'," like the goth teen she was dressed as.

"Why would she do that?" Blue asked. He was looking at Jodi and for a minute, she thought he meant Tank. Then she realized he meant the chatelaine.

"Curse you from childhood?" Jodi frowned. "That's not how we're trained. Chatelaines are trained in good magic. We don't touch dark magic. We shouldn't, anyway."

"Why didn't your dad fire her?" Tank asked.

"I don't know, Tank," Blue said. He was sounding tired. "It was a long time ago."

"I think it's important, Blue," Tank said.

"It's all important," Jodi said. She peered down at the table. Blue's memories were important and those printouts were important. Something was very wrong. Something had been very wrong for a very long time.

"My father left the household to my mother," Blue said softly. He had a faraway look in his eyes. "She— she was shy. She hated dealing with people. It was almost as if they frightened her."

"So she didn't deal with the chatelaine," Tank said. "Even though the woman didn't do her job."

"What kind of magic did your mother have?" Jodi asked.

"I don't know." Blue brought a hand to his face. "I honestly don't remember. I worked so hard at putting all of this out of my mind. I have no idea."

His voice was shaking. He sounded fragile.

Tank said, "Well, Blue, you gotta remember—"

"Shush, Tank," Jodi said. "We're overwhelming him."

At that moment, the door opened again. Dr. Hargrove came inside the room. "I think this has gone on long enough," he said. "Clearly Blue is tired."

"I'm fine," Blue said curtly.

Hargrove came deeper into the room. He glanced at Jodi's purse, and she cursed silently.

"What's in there?" he asked.

Tank dove deeply into the purse.

"My dog," Jodi said. "She's a miniature Chihuahua."

"Hey!" Tank said from inside the purse.

Hargrove looked over his shoulder, as if he had heard that but thought it came from outside the room. Both Jodi and Blue were careful not to react.

Then Hargrove glanced at the purse again. "They call those pocket dogs, right?"

"Yes," Jodi said.

"You do realize pets aren't allowed here."

"She never leaves the purse," Jodi said with emphasis.

Hargrove nodded, then frowned. "Still, you should have told us."

"Sorry," Jodi said. "Next time."

"Doctor Hargrove." Blue spoke, his voice deep and assured. He startled Jodi, and Hargrove looked at him like he hadn't expected Blue to talk at all.

"Yes, Blue?" Hargrove had a tone of voice that he seemed to use with patients. Jodi hadn't noticed it until now. It was… not quite patronizing, but just a fraction off. You had to listen to hear it, but this time Jodi heard it.

"Ms. Walters has brought me bad news," Blue said. He was using that strange deep confident voice again. "It's something I'm going to have to take care of."

"What is going on, Ms. Walters?" Hargrove asked. He stopped in front of her, looming over her. She hated it when people did that.

"It's confidential, Dr. Hargrove," Jodi said. "I'm sure you can understand that."

"Let's talk to me, Dr. Hargrove," Blue said, and Jodi had to suppress a smile. Blue managed to replicate Dr. Hargrove's almost-patronizing tone exactly.

Hargrove looked at Blue in surprise. Had Blue never spoken to him like that before?

"Forgive me, Blue," he said, and now his tone was patronizing. "It's just that—"

"Here's what's going on, Dr. Hargrove," Blue began. He looked taller. Suddenly he looked powerful. Not dangerously powerful, but like a man who was groomed to rule a kingdom. A man who knew that he controlled his small patch of the world, and no one could shake him from that.

Tank poked her head out of the purse and folded her arms on the edge, resting her chin on her wrists. She had a Kleenex over her head. Someone could see that she was a live creature but not really tell what kind unless she made some kind of move.

Jodi hoped Tank wouldn't make a move.

Blue continued, "I need to finish my discussion with Ms. Walters. It's important. I prepared all day yesterday and most of last night for it."

"Yes," Hargrove said in that same patronizing tone. "We discussed it already, and how important sleep is to your healing. This is not acceptable—"

"And when I am done talking with Ms. Walters," Blue said as if Hargrove hadn't spoken at all, "I will talk with you about my treatment. But not until then. Is that clear?"

"Right now, Mr. Franklin, you are in no position to give orders," Hargrove said.

"All right then," Blue said. "Let's put me in a position to do so."

He turned slightly and bowed just a little to Jodi. The courtly manners suited him. She felt a smile starting in spite of herself.

"Excuse me for a moment, ladies," he said. "I'll be back. I'm going to talk with Dr. Hargrove."

Jodi didn't quite wince when Blue said "ladies," but she wanted to. And of course, Hargrove caught it.

"Ladies?" he said. "See, this is why I believe you need to take better care of yourself, Blue. There's only one woman here—"

"Ladies," Blue said firmly. "Ms. Walters's pocket dog, Tank, is female as well. I'm quite fond of her."

Tank growled from Jodi's purse. Jodi wanted to hit the purse to silence Tank, but she was afraid of knocking the Kleenex off her head.

Hargrove narrowed his gaze. "Something's not right here."

"Yes, I know," Blue said. "Let's go outside."

Hargrove glanced at Jodi as if he expected her help. "But—"

"No buts," Blue said. "Let's go."

He crossed around from the back of the couch and headed toward Hargrove. For the first time, Jodi realized how much bigger Blue was than the doctor. It seemed like Hargrove just realized it as well. Panic crossed his face and then disappeared as if it never was.

Suddenly Hargrove was afraid of Blue. Or had he always been afraid of Blue? Jodi didn't know. And she wanted to find out, but she didn't know how to ask.

Blue put his hand on Hargrove's shoulder and propelled him from the room.

Jodi let out a small sigh. Tank pulled the Kleenex off her head.

"That was weird," Tank said as she crawled out of the purse. "Did Blue really just call me a bitch?"

Chapter 21

THE MOMENT THEY STEPPED OUT OF THE MEETING room, Blue took his hand off Dr. Hargrove's shoulder. Blue had started shaking; he didn't want Dr. Hargrove to feel that.

Everything that Jodi had told Blue, everything that Tank had confirmed, made him queasy. Maybe he should have felt joyful—they were telling him that none of this was his fault—but he had lived with the image of himself as some kind of horrible involuntary killer for so long that he didn't trust this transformation now.

When he was young, he had thought himself invulnerable. He had planned to be a better ruler than his father, who wasn't a bad man, just a bit oblivious at times. His father had used that obliviousness to his own advantage when Blue got accused of killing young women. His father pretended the news wasn't relevant at all, which had disturbed Blue.

Blue started traveling when he realized how bad it could get. He grew a beard so he wouldn't be recognized, but that didn't work. He was well known as the Prince Charming whose family called him "Blue" because of the highlights in his hair. Those highlights dominated his beard. He couldn't hide. But when he got recognized, people weren't willing to call him Prince. They called him Bluebeard.

So he traveled even more. He stayed away from

women, stayed away from people for the most part, trying other Kingdoms, and then finally coming to the Greater World, thinking that nothing could happen here.

And as far as he knew, nothing had.

Until this Fairy Tale Stalker. And for a few minutes when Jodi had told him about it, Blue actually worried that he could have done it. (More than a few minutes, if truth be told. A lot more.)

"Let's go to my office," Dr. Hargrove said in that voice he used when he expected to be listened to.

Blue looked down at him, this man who had worked so hard to keep Blue sane all these years. Doctor Hargrove was starting to get a bald spot on top of his curly head. His hair was mussed and he still had the coffee stain on his shirt. He wasn't as young as he used to be.

But Dr. Hargrove had done a good job, better than he knew. The compassion he had shown was just enough of a lifeline to keep Blue from giving up on everything.

Because, as he had once said to Dr. Hargrove in complete despair, what was the point of a long life if a man couldn't enjoy it? Doctor Hargrove had thought that Blue was talking about drinking, and how much he enjoyed drinking, but Blue hadn't been. It took Blue a while to convince Dr. Hargrove that he was talking about obliviousness, and not remembering anything, and how difficult that was. Blue then said he came from a long-lived family, and he didn't understand why, if he was going to spend this life in a worthless state of semi-consciousness, he should go on.

Doctor Hargrove understood that and tried to convince Blue his life would be better without the alcohol.

But Blue hadn't been talking about the alcohol. And even though Dr. Hargrove repeatedly asked Blue about the pain behind his addiction, Blue refused to talk about it.

He also refused to lie.

Now, Dr. Hargrove was looking at him expectantly, waiting for him to lead the way to the office. The office was the place where Dr. Hargrove had complete control, where he ruled supreme. He also had easy access to security and lockdown procedures.

Blue had always come to this place as an addict seeking treatment, not as a psychiatric patient, but he was suddenly worried about California law on this subject. Because state-to-state committal laws were different, and sometimes someone who had voluntarily gone into a clinic couldn't check himself out.

Blue knew that much. In the past, he hadn't cared.

But today, he did.

"No," he said. "I don't want to go to the office. I'd like to talk here."

Doctor Hargrove was frowning. He clearly hadn't seen this side of Blue before. Blue was channeling his father, searching for the commanding part of his nature, a part that had been long buried. His father hadn't always used charm when being regal. And Blue wasn't using it now.

"There is no privacy here in the entry area," Dr. Hargrove said. "We have no guarantee of confidentiality."

He sounded concerned. He glanced at the meeting room door, then at the front doors. He pointedly did not look at the Eames chairs, because they would provide a place to talk.

Blue didn't look at the chairs either. He glanced into the meeting room. Jodi was still in her chair. Her head was down. She was probably talking to Tank. Outside, Blue could see the mostly empty parking lot and a flock of seagulls swarming over the security guard's station.

"I don't expect privacy," Blue said.

Doctor Hargrove stood as tall as he could. He didn't look as put together as usual. But then, he wasn't used to Blue rebelling.

Other patients rebelled. Blue never had. Not once in all the years he'd been coming here.

"Privacy is necessary," Dr. Hargrove said. "If this goes into your record—"

"Doctor Hargrove," Blue said in a tone he hadn't used in centuries, if ever. Commanding, a bit too strong, but warm. He was somehow managing warmth. Or at least he hoped he was. "As I said, I had some difficult news from Ms. Walters. I'm going to need to check out of the facility to deal with it."

He didn't realize that had been his plan until he spoke it out loud. But he had to leave, if only for the short term. He couldn't keep having meetings here, and he couldn't deal with all the rules right now. He had to help Jodi and Tank get on the right track to stop the Fairy Tale Stalker, and more importantly, he had to figure out exactly what was wrong with him—who had cursed him and how. He had to get rid of that curse.

Before it killed Jodi.

"I'm sorry," Dr. Hargrove said. "You can't leave. It's too early in your treatment."

"Nonetheless," Blue said, "I have to. I'll pay for the entire month in fees."

"It's not the fees I'm worried about, Blue," Dr. Hargrove said. "You've been our guest almost a dozen times—"

Blue hated the use of the word "guest" in this context. He always had, but this time he let himself feel it. It was patronizing and incorrect. He wasn't a guest. He was a patient.

"—and while we've made progress, it hasn't been as much as I would like. I worry that if you leave to work on a crisis, you will stress your own recovery to the breaking point."

In other words, he'd start drinking almost immediately.

It was a good concern, an accurate one for the Blue of the past who relied on the alcohol to protect him from himself—or from the curse, if what Jodi and Tank had said was true. It was also an accurate concern for the real addicts in this place, who used any excuse to return to the source of their addiction and often did not have the personal inner strength to deal with any kind of crisis.

But Blue had a different problem. He couldn't even quite imagine telling Dr. Hargrove about it:

Excuse me, Doctor. I'm not concerned about the drinking. I only drink to prevent myself from murdering women that I love. Only now I've discovered that I didn't kill those women. It was a curse all along.

Yeah. He was supposed to believe that. He didn't quite believe it, although Tank did. And Tank was a hardheaded old soul. And Jodi, she said she could see his aura, that it was different today.

Last night, he hadn't left the facility. Not physically, not mentally. He hadn't blacked out, and they'd actually had him on surveillance video. He had been here. So something magical was up.

And that was what he couldn't tell Dr. Hargrove.

"I promise," Blue said, "once this crisis is resolved, I will check myself back in."

Doctor Hargrove tilted his head, and Blue braced himself. This time, the response would be patronizing. And Blue wasn't sure he blamed Dr. Hargrove. As Blue had spoken those words, he had heard how stupid they had sounded. Who checked themselves back in after fleeing a place like this?

Except for him, of course. He had done it a dozen times, mostly because Tank forced him.

He could probably stay here, but it didn't feel right. He needed to see what was going on for himself.

"Blue," Dr. Hargrove said in his most patronizing tone, "that hasn't worked in the past."

"Well, there's always a first time," Blue said. "I'm checking myself out, no matter what you say."

Doctor Hargrove crossed his arms. "Are you leaving with Ms. Walters?"

"Yes," Blue said, even though he hadn't asked her. He hadn't told her any of his plan. Maybe he *was* acting like an impulsive alcoholic.

"Are you sure that's wise?" Dr. Hargrove asked.

Blue felt a surge of panic. Had he told Dr. Hargrove about his dark side when he was drunk? He never thought he had.

"After all," Dr. Hargrove continued, "she's not trained to handle a recovering alcoholic."

Doctor Hargrove was making an assumption. He had no idea who the real Jodi was. Blue let out a small sigh, forcing some of the panic to escape with it.

"She's just going to take me to a place in Anaheim," Blue said. "It's that recovery house I've used before."

He had listed the Archetype Place as his recovery home on at least three occasions. The first time, the rehab center had checked the Archetype Place out, and someone had to magick the center's representative so he didn't see the dwarves and fairies and griffins and other so-called mythical creatures that visited the place every day.

In the end, the center had approved the Archetype Place as a recovery facility. And even though the rehab center called to update its files every now and then, it hadn't tried to prevent him from going there in the past.

"Can you guarantee that you're going there?" Dr. Hargrove asked.

"Yes," Blue said.

"Then here's what I want you to do," Dr. Hargrove said. "I want you to check in with me on a regular basis, and I need to see you at least once a week."

"All right," Blue said. This was easier than he had expected.

"I'll release you on an outpatient basis, and I'll give you a list of local meetings. You must attend at least one per day."

Or what? Blue wanted to ask. But he didn't, because he didn't want to complicate this any further.

"Thank you," Blue said. "You won't regret this."

"Oh," Dr. Hargrove said, "I'm regretting it already. But you've made some progress. You're talking with a woman. You're caring about things outside of yourself. Maybe you need someone to trust you just a little. I'm going to do that."

But Blue could hear the words that Dr. Hargrove left unspoken. *I'm going to do that, even though it goes against my own best judgment.*

"I appreciate it," Blue said. "I'm going to let Ms. Walters know what I'm up to, and then I'm going to get my things."

"I'll have the release documents waiting for you at the front desk," Dr. Hargrove said, "along with a date and time for your first appointment. Do you want me to call ahead to the Archetype Place and let them know you're coming?"

"That's not necessary," Blue said. "Ms. Walters has already been in touch with them."

And strangely enough, that wasn't a lie.

"I wish you the best with this, Blue," Dr. Hargrove said. "You're an unorthodox man. Perhaps an unorthodox method of treatment might just work."

He extended his hand. It took Blue just a second to realize that Dr. Hargrove wanted to shake on this. So Blue took his hand and shook.

Then Dr. Hargrove nodded and headed down the hall.

Blue felt a pang as he watched the man go. For all his quirks and his mistaken judgments, Dr. Hargrove had done his best by Blue.

Blue owed it to him to resolve this.

Blue owed it to himself as well.

Chapter 22

Jodi hadn't moved from her chair, but she kept glancing through the glass at Blue and Hargrove. They stood just outside the door. Hargrove looked upset. He kept gesturing, but Blue looked immobile. His back was straight, and he looked strong.

Until this morning, she had never seen him look strong.

Tank climbed out of the purse. "Should we do something?"

"You should get back in that purse," Jodi said.

Tank stuck her tongue out. "No one is looking at me," she said as she flew upward.

For a minute, Jodi thought Tank was going to fly right in front of one of the cameras, but she didn't. Tank just zoomed around the room as if staying in that purse had seriously cramped her style. (It probably had.)

Then she stopped in front of the glass, staying up high so that Hargrove wouldn't notice her. (Or might not notice her. Jodi wasn't sure which. Not that it mattered. What mattered was Blue, the Fairy Tale Stalker, and that damn curse, which was starting to freak her out the longer she had to think about it.)

"That doctor guy, he looks mad," Tank said.

Jodi resisted the urge to stand up. But Hargrove's body language had tension in it. He seemed upset. Blue had crossed his arms. He kept nodding his head just a little, the way people did when they were emphasizing something.

The power relationship between the two men was changing, and Hargrove didn't know how to deal with it.

Then he nodded once and spoke to Blue. Blue looked determined. Hargrove extended his hand. Blue shook it. Then Hargrove walked away.

Jodi exhaled. She hadn't realized that she had been holding her breath, but she had. She was nervous. For Blue? For Tank? Or for herself?

Probably all of the above.

Blue watched Hargrove walk away. Then Blue moved once toward the corridor and seemed to decide against it, pushing open the door.

Tank fluttered down toward him.

"You should be in the purse," he said as he walked across the room.

Tank stuck her tongue out at him too, but he clearly couldn't see it. His back was to her, and his gaze was on Jodi.

He looked... different. Stronger. Straighter. Handsomer, if that was possible. His blue eyes blazed, and she got a very real sense of power from him.

But she got no sense of danger.

Her heart started to pound. She stood up, mostly because she couldn't continue sitting any longer.

"What was that?" she asked.

"I have a favor to ask of you." His voice was shaking just a little. That confidence she had seen vanished with the very first word. "Would you mind driving me out of here? I told Dr. Hargrove you would, but I'll arrange something else if you need me to—"

Tank whooped. Then she pumped her tiny fists and whooped again. "Finally!" she said.

Blue's mouth opened, and he frowned at Tank. Then he must have realized he was looking at her, and that the cameras would find her as well, because he turned his head toward Jodi. But he wasn't looking at her. He was clearly watching Tank out of the corner of his eyes.

"You're the one who kept bringing me here, Tank," he said with just a touch of annoyance.

Good point, Jodi thought. But she wasn't going to get into the middle of this.

"Yes, I did," Tank said. "But you've never decided to leave before. You waited until they kicked you out."

She whooped again, and then flew in dizzying circles, leaving little glowy swirls in the air.

Jodi hoped the cameras wouldn't pick that up. She tried to ignore Tank's euphoria.

"Where would I take you?" Jodi asked Blue. Her heart was still pounding so hard that she could almost hear it. Did she really want to be alone with this man? Would she be alone or would Tank be with her? Could Tank defend her? Could she defend herself?

And what was she so frightened of?

"I told Dr. Hargrove you'd take me to the Archetype Place," Blue said. "But they're not real fond of me there. Still, I'm sure they'd help me find an apartment—"

"I thought you had a place," Tank said.

Blue shook his head.

"You *said* you had a place," Tank said, her voice rising.

Blue shook his head again. He was not looking at her, which was a good thing, because Tank was getting visibly angry. She had stopped flying and she was hovering near him.

"Tank," Jodi said. "The cameras."

"You *told me* you had a place to live," Tank said again, so firmly that she sounded like she was much larger. "You lied to me."

Blue closed his eyes. "Let it go, Tank."

"I hate it when people lie to me," Tank said.

"Purse," Jodi repeated.

Tank shot her a furious glance and then flew to the ceiling. She stuck close to it and moved to a far corner, probably out of camera range.

At least Jodi hoped it was out of camera range.

"It doesn't matter right now, Tank," Blue said.

"It does right now," Tank said, her words echoing with fury. "We have nowhere to take you. Selda won't help you get another apartment. Not after what happened to the last one."

"What happened to the last one?" Jodi asked in spite of herself.

Blue closed his eyes. "I—you don't want to know."

"I do, actually," Jodi said. But she wouldn't tell him why. She wasn't about to tell him she had access to some apartments.

"He says he trashed the place," Tank said. "I don't believe it. He'd never trashed a place in his life. I think he let some of his homeless friends in there, and they trashed the place after I brought him here a couple of trips ago. But he says no."

"Tank," Blue said, "it's irrelevant. What matters is this: we need to continue our discussion, and we can't do it here. I worked a long time last night on those clippings Jodi gave me and I want to talk about them."

He paused. Jodi could see him thinking about how much more he wanted to say. And then he stopped.

The man kept a lot of things close to the chest. Normally she respected that, but in this case it worried her.

Everything about him worried her.

And intrigued her at the same time.

"You also want to talk about the curse," Jodi said. "About what's been happening to you."

He shrugged one shoulder and bowed his head. "I didn't mean to get you involved in this."

"And you didn't get me involved," Jodi said. "Tank did. So any time you feel like taking responsibility for the fact that the curse is on me too, blame Tank."

"Hey!" Tank said.

Blue frowned. He moved his head toward Tank, then stopped himself again, keeping those amazing blue eyes on Jodi.

She made sure he was focusing on her before she spoke again.

"Realize this," she said. "If Tank and I are right, then Tank has done you a favor. Maybe the biggest favor anyone can do for another person."

Blue blinked, as if he didn't quite understand. Or maybe he was having trouble processing. After all, he had thought of himself as an out-of-control psychopath, when really he just suffered under one major curse.

"I do him a favor," Tank muttered. "The biggest favor anyone can do for another person, and then he calls me a bitch."

"What?" Blue asked. "I didn't call you anything."

"'*Ms. Walters's pocket dog, Tank, is female as well*,'" Tank said, mimicking Blue's voice exactly. "What is that if not a bitch?"

Blue blinked again, then looked at Jodi, who couldn't

help herself. She smiled. He smiled too, and it seemed to soften him.

Not to mention what it did to those marvelous blue eyes.

Wow. He hadn't even turned on the charm, and she could feel it. She was going to have to watch herself.

"I'll drive you out of here," Jodi said, partly so he wouldn't have to answer Tank on the bitch comment. "And I'll help you figure out what to do next."

He let out a small breath. All of that power, all of that confidence, seemed to fade with the breath.

"Thank you," he said. "I just have to grab a few things and then I'm ready to go."

"I'll take these papers to the car," Jodi said.

He nodded and hurried toward the door. When he reached it, he turned.

"Thank you again. You don't have to do this, you know."

"I know," she said. "Believe me, I know."

Chapter 23

IT TOOK THEM ABOUT A HALF AN HOUR TO GET OUT OF the rehab center, and most of that was Blue. Jodi was surprised when he showed up with only one small duffel—an old leather one that looked well used.

"He has to get new clothes every time," Tank said from her perch on Jodi's shoulder. Earlier, Tank had spelled the security guard so that he couldn't see her, but apparently the spell didn't apply to everything she said. So she annoyingly settled on Jodi's shoulder ("*Trying to avoid those nerve endings with my sharp little pointy feet*," Tank said as she climbed on, also apparently never forgetting a negative comment) and gave a play-by-play.

Jodi was leaning on her car, watching the door. The guard was standing in his guard booth, looking worried. The booth had turned white with bird crap—probably gull crap—and there were feathers everywhere. It looked like the aftermath of an epic bird battle, one that Tank had clearly started.

She had smiled when they came outside, so she had enjoyed the evidence of her chaos as well.

"Why does he get new clothes?" Jodi asked quietly.

The guard was watching the door as well. She didn't know if he had been told that Blue was coming out or if he had deduced it. Or if he was still worried about the birds.

"Well," Tank said in Jodi's ear, "first, he always wore those blue velour fake velvet things when he was drinking, and second, he never washed them."

Then Tank shuddered so hard that Jodi's shoulder vibrated. Jodi wanted to grab her and move her but didn't dare with the guard this close.

"So," Tank said, "I drop off his empty duffel outside when I drop him off, and the staff fills it with real clothes."

"Good heavens, this place must be expensive," Jodi said.

"He can afford it," Tank said.

"How can he afford it if he's been drinking it away?" Jodi asked.

Tank sighed but didn't answer. Apparently, Jodi wasn't cleared to know. Or maybe Tank was making assumptions.

Either way, the duffel looked like it was filled to capacity. Jodi expected Blue to carry it to her convertible and put it in the backseat. Instead, he walked over to the guard and handed him some paperwork.

The guard frowned at it, then tapped it with his fingertips. "You sure you want to do this, buddy?"

Jodi let out a small sound of surprise. Did everyone here know Blue? And more importantly, did they all care about him?

"They don't know who he is, do they?" she asked Tank softly.

"Oh, yeah, like he tells them in a drunken rage— *Don't bug me. I've beheaded women.* He drinks to forget, and to not engage, and jeez, do you tell all of the mortals that you work with how long you've lived or where you were born? Of course not." Tank slapped a tiny hand against the back of Jodi's head.

"Do that again," Jodi said in that same soft voice, "and I'll feed you to the seagulls."

The seagulls still circled in the distance. Jodi had the distinct impression that they were waiting for Tank. Clearly, seagulls did not forget a slight. The seagulls she attacked and their little seagull friends had formed a posse and they were searching for her.

Fortunately, she had hidden herself from them too.

Every five minutes or so, one seagull would fly over the parking lot. Every ten minutes or so, that gull would release a bird dropping nearly as big as Tank. Jodi wasn't sure if that was deliberate—if the gulls actually knew what Tank was and were trying to find her by coating the area in white bird crap—or if the birds were just that messy.

So far, the droppings had missed the convertible, and Jodi was hoping that Tank had spelled that too. Although some of the shielding came from Jodi's own protect spell, one she put on everything she owned. She had doubled down on that spell with her car, given that she was in Los Angeles, drove everywhere, and knew the odds were against her using normal methods to avoid a fender-bender or some other kind of LA-car-related problem.

She didn't hear what Blue had said to the guard, if he had said anything. Blue was walking toward the convertible now, and he stopped at the passenger door, as if he was trying to decide.

"You don't have to leave," Jodi said softly. "We can work this out inside. You can stay protected."

His gaze moved from the car to her face. It was a deliberate movement, as if he had to work on making eye contact. Maybe he did, after decades (centuries?) of refusing to look at anyone he might possibly care about.

Her heart hammered again. She wished she could will it to go back to normal. What was she thinking? He hadn't said "care about" earlier.

Except that he did.

When Tank was describing what happened to the other women, he'd said, *Those heads belonged to women I cared about*. Not *women I'd noticed* or *women I thought were attractive*. He had said, *women I cared about*.

And that meant he cared about Jodi, right?

She moved her head slightly, as if she could shake the thought from it. She didn't want to think about him caring about her. She really didn't want to care about him.

Although she did.

She felt very real compassion for him. If this curse thing was true (and it was, she could see it in his aura), then he had suffered like no one she had ever met before.

It made her wonder about his so-called victims. Had they died as horribly as the fairy tale said, or did the curse simply wipe them out, cancel their existence?

And who had that kind of power? She had never met anyone with that much magic before. It took a lot of magical ability to take a life; that was why the fairy tales were full of weird tortures (birds plucking out the step-sisters' eyeballs at Cinderella's wedding, for example) and not filled with weird deaths.

Blue didn't answer her. She had given him an out. He didn't have to leave. But he didn't acknowledge it. If he hadn't looked at her, she would have thought that he hadn't heard her at all.

But he had.

He took a deep breath, as if he was steeling himself, and then he slowly, carefully, put the duffel in the backseat.

"I need to do this," he said. "And I need to do it properly."

He was frightened. That impressed Jodi as well. He should be frightened. He was about to step into his life, not drink it away and try to hide from people, and that was going to be tough enough.

But eventually, he would have to confront the curse-caster, and the cursecaster clearly had real magic. Not only that, but if the cursecaster had been doing this for centuries, then the cursecaster was, by now, certifiably crazy.

Which meant that the cursecaster was dangerous and powerful and unpredictable. Blue didn't have the skills to go up against someone like that. Charm clearly hadn't worked against the cursecaster before.

Jodi didn't have the skills either, or at least, she thought she didn't. Sometimes chatelaine magic shifted to deal with a crisis. But Blue wasn't in her household, so her magic wouldn't shift to protect him.

However, she was a fixer. She could find people who had the magic to help him — or at least, she thought she could.

Blue was still staring at the passenger seat of the car.

"It's leather," Jodi said. "And comfortable. I can put the top up if you want."

He shook his head, then pulled the door open. He got inside as if he was afraid someone would yank him out, then he slid down in the seat.

Jodi climbed in and started the car. "It doesn't matter if people see you," she said.

"Yeah, it does," he said quietly. "You have no idea what people think of me."

Actually, she did, but she wasn't going to tell him that. At the moment, she didn't give a rip about what they thought, and she wasn't going to tell him that either.

He needed to figure these things out on his own.

Tank flew off Jodi's shoulder and sat on the dashboard, under the windshield.

Jodi frowned at her, then realized that Tank was protecting herself from gulls.

"They will follow you, you know," Jodi said.

Tank shook her head.

"Why did you pick on them?" Jodi asked.

"They're mean bastards," Tank said. "Do you know how many of my people they've eaten?"

Jodi raised her eyebrows. How could a gull eat a fairy? She wasn't going to ask.

"Can we just go?" Blue asked.

"Yeah," Jodi said, backing the car up, turning around, and heading across the parking lot. "We've got a lot of stuff to figure out."

Chapter 24

BLUE DIDN'T FEEL FREE. HE WAS RIDING IN AN EXPENSIVE convertible along the Pacific Coast Highway in Malibu, the glistening blue ocean to his left, a beautiful woman beside him, and he didn't feel free at all.

He felt terrified.

He was sitting up because Jodi had shamed him into sitting up, the wind whipping his hair. Hers was hidden under a scarf, her chin tilted up, large sunglasses on her face—typical Southern California beauty, the kind they made movies about. The kind of women he had always avoided—or he would have avoided, if he had tried to talk to any women at all, which he hadn't.

Not in a long, long, *long* time. Centuries, in fact.

A man could forget a lot over centuries.

If he had known anything at all.

The last time he had spent more than a moment with a woman, he had been a young man. Marriageable, still living with Mom and Dad, being groomed to take over the family business. He had his education—stellar for the time, woefully lacking for now—and no expectations on him whatsoever. He could have been the worst king in the history of kings, and no one would have cared.

Not true.

The accurate thing was that no one would have stopped him from being a bad king.

And he had been on track to be the worst king ever. If he, like his father, had ignored all those dead women…

Blue shuddered, even though he wasn't cold. Tank was huddled on the dashboard, her wings pasted against her sides. She looked miserable.

For years, Blue had asked Tank what she saw in him, and she had always smiled at him, telling him that he had misunderstood his own life.

And now, apparently, she had been right.

Jodi turned the car onto Sunset Boulevard, which wound its way through the canyon. He had no idea exactly where she was taking him, but he found it metaphorically appropriate that she took him down a road linked to a movie about lost opportunities and faded glory.

He didn't know if she wanted to talk, but he knew he didn't. As they drove along the foot of the Santa Monica mountains, he watched the scenery go by. Ahead, he could see the smog layer over Los Angeles, and it made his stomach twist.

He wasn't sure what he was doing. He had been impulsive, and that wasn't good. Impulsive had never worked for him.

Or rather, it hadn't worked since he impulsively left the Kingdom and moved into the Greater World. Where he decided to stay drunk to protect everyone around him.

He leaned an arm on the window and looked out, the warm wind whipping his face. What could he do, really? Break a curse he hadn't even known existed? And then what?

Those women, all those women, would still be dead.

But Jodi wouldn't.

He snuck another glance at her. She had a small smile on her face as she drove. She had been frightened of him a few days before, and now she seemed comfortable with him, able to spend time with him, willing to help him, even though it was going to cost her.

It had already cost her.

That visit in the middle of the night by someone— something—that looked like him. He tapped his fingers on the outside of the car. That was how it all began. And she thought she could defeat it.

Tank and Jodi believed the curse could be beaten.

But at what cost? And what would happen afterward? What kind of life could a man like him have? If indeed there was a curse, and the curse got broken, and he was now free.

He had no idea who he would be, what he could be, what opportunities he would have, if any. His past was gone, the Kingdom gone, not that he wanted to go back there. Even if the magical images of the heads were gone, he would probably always see them.

He rubbed his thumb and forefinger over his eyes.

One day at a time. That was what Dr. Hargrove and the others had preached during rehab. One day at a time. Sometimes it was one hour at a time. Sometimes one minute at a time.

Live in the present. Don't look at the regrets of the past—you can't change them. Move forward, some- times by inches, counting each sober moment a victory.

He would have to count sober moments as a victory as well, even though he wasn't an alcoholic. Alcohol had been his defense, and it had finally collapsed around him. Now he needed to confront the problem head-on.

He smiled, just a little, his face still turned away from Jodi so she couldn't see that smile.

Because it was an ironic smile. He might not be a traditional alcoholic with the genetic disposition and the symptoms of disease. But he had acted like a traditional alcoholic in all ways, including the most important.

He had used alcohol as a crutch so that he wouldn't have to deal with the problems in his life. Never mind that he had had no idea how to deal with those problems, and there had been no real help for them when they first appeared. What mattered was that he had used alcohol to cope.

And now, he was taking away the crutch. Now he had to be himself, whoever that was, and dig to the root of the problem.

Doctor Hargrove had been so worried about Blue as Blue left this morning. Doctor Hargrove thought Blue was abandoning his treatment.

But Blue was actually putting it into practice for the very first time.

He was confronting his past, making his amends, fixing the problems that he could fix—whatever it took.

He had help—he had always had help. He just hadn't realized it. Tank had supported him as best she could.

And now Jodi was going to help him find a solution to the curse. Or so she said. And he had to remember that she had self-interest here. If they didn't solve this, she would probably suffer the same fate as all those other women.

And the women of the Fairy Tale Stalker might as well. He shuddered.

This wasn't just about him. This was about them too.

He had to remember that. It might give him the strength
he needed.

And in his back pocket, he had the list of meetings
that Dr. Hargrove gave him. Blue might not ever tell
anyone there what he was dealing with, but just sitting
there, with people struggling to maintain their sobriety—
their *presence* in the world—might be enough for him.

He hoped.

Because somehow he had to find the strength to get
through this.

Not for himself.

But for everyone he came in contact with, now and
in the future.

He owed it to them.

And he owed it to all those women who had died in
his past, deaths he could have prevented, if he had only
understood what exactly had been going on.

Chapter 25

BLUE WAS BEING VERY QUIET, AND JODI WASN'T SURE she minded. She probably should have raised the car's top so that she could talk with him, but she wanted the time to think. She liked the way the warm wind fluttered her scarf, the smell of exhaust, the sun on her arms.

She wished she could turn up the music, but she knew that would bother Tank, who looked just plain miserable on the dash.

Jodi was trying to ignore that too.

She couldn't take him to the Archetype Place, at least not yet, given what both he and Tank said. Jodi couldn't imagine Selda giving them a private place to talk, not without a lot of effort.

Right now, it seemed, Jodi didn't have time for effort. Blue was doing his best to shrink into the passenger seat, his face turned away from her as he studied the passing cars.

She wondered if he had any regrets. She hoped he would have enough courage to tell her to turn around if he wanted her to.

So far he hadn't. He'd been amazingly quiet, not that it was easy to talk in a convertible with the top down. Tank was being quiet too, huddled against the windshield as if she was afraid of something.

And considering the posse of seagulls behind them, she had something to be afraid of.

Tank and the seagull wars. Jodi hoped those wouldn't escalate into something awful.

Because of Tank, they couldn't just stop in a park or near the Santa Monica Pier. Those gulls would be all over them in a minute.

Jodi didn't want to take Blue to her office. She couldn't face the questions, let alone how many clients she might lose just by being in his presence. She wasn't sure how many would recognize him or how many knew him centuries ago. She didn't want to risk it. In these early stages, she wasn't sure how to defend him to the magical without revealing his curse.

And she wasn't ready to do that. Because she might be warning off the very person they all were trying to catch.

She frowned just a little as she turned south off Sunset onto the 405. It was still early in the day. Traffic actually moved on the 405, so it was the shortest route. In another hour, she'd have to avoid the freeways altogether.

Blue didn't seem to notice, and Tank had probably never understood the road system in Los Angeles in the first place. Jodi didn't like the thought she'd had.

What if one of her clients was the person who had cursed Blue? What if that same person had created the Fairy Tale Stalker?

Shouldn't she have been able to tell? She tried to avoid evil wherever possible. She thought she had weeded it out of her clients (even though she still had to contend with it on a daily basis with the studios).

She turned off the 405 less than five minutes after getting on it. She rounded several corners, suddenly realizing what she was doing.

Her subconscious had known what to do all along. She had always been that way, trusting her gut.

She was taking him to Century City.

Back when ALCOA started building Century City in the late 1950s, she had hated it. The aluminum company had purchased the old 20th Century Fox lot and had "developed" it into the skyscrapers that were now iconic in LA. But back then, she hated the destruction of history, not realizing quite yet that that's what LA did—destroy its own history.

Now she spent a lot of time in and among those skyscrapers, just like everyone else who worked in "the Industry," as those inside the entertainment called it. She even had a favorite restaurant.

Blue sat up. "Where are we going?"

His voice sounded calm, but his lower lip trembled, as if he couldn't control it.

"I know a place we can talk," she said.

"Here?" he asked.

She nodded.

Tank was sitting up now too. They slowed as they went into a parking structure underneath one of the high-rises. The sudden darkness made Jodi's eyes hurt. She pulled off her sunglasses with a practiced movement and almost tossed them on the passenger seat like she usually did.

She managed to catch herself just in time.

"All steel," Tank said. "I hate that."

"You got a better suggestion, Miss Seagull Enemy?"

Tank glanced up, as if seagulls lurked on the ceiling of the parking structure. "Not at the moment," she said.

"You have an office here?" Blue asked.

"No," Jodi said. "Just come with me."

She put the top up on the car as she pulled into her favorite parking space. Then she got out. Tank flew out tentatively, as if she really did expect to be attacked by a seagull in here. After a moment, Blue got out too.

Jodi got the papers he had worked so hard on out of the backseat, along with her briefcase, then locked the car.

"Let's go," she said. She walked ahead of both of them to the elevator. As they stepped inside the lavish gold and mirror structure, she typed in a floor number.

"I'll meet you," Tank said and flew to the already closed door. She put her hands on it in despair as the elevator started up. She flew around in circles, clearly upset.

"This is just as fast," Jodi said. She was lying, but not by much. The elevator was an express that opened onto the entrance of Echoes, one of the hottest restaurants in the business.

As soon as the doors opened, Tank flew out so fast that Jodi had only seen a blur. If Tank had said something, Jodi hadn't heard it because of the music. The music wasn't blaring—it was at an afternoon level—but it wasn't soft either.

It was technofusion, probably composed specifically for the restaurant, and it filled the entry. The entry was black and silver, with the harsh sunlight-like lighting that Echoes used in the daytime. At twilight, the lighting grew darker, and by evening the place had more shadows than a haunted house, but right now it strove for bright and gorgeous and relevant.

She didn't know about the relevant or even the gorgeous, but it did manage the bright.

"We can't stay here," Blue said. "We're not dressed for it."

"Doesn't matter," Jodi said.

"We can't talk about what's going on," he said, sounding panicked now. "I mean, all that mayhem and everything?"

He was already using coded language. He didn't mean "mayhem." He meant "murders."

"Where do you think people discuss their next film? I've heard people talking about everything from natural disasters to poisoning the water supply," Jodi said. "Trust me. This is the perfect place."

Tank was no longer with them. Jodi hadn't seen her fly off. She figured Tank would join them once they settled.

"Seriously," Blue said, "can't we find somewhere else? I don't think this is a good idea."

"Does anyone in the Industry know you?" Jodi asked without looking at him.

"The Industry?" he asked. "You mean the movies?"

"And network and cable and music? Do they know you?"

He looked confused. "I-I-I hope not."

"Good," she said. "Then we'll be fine."

The maître d' came over, clutching two menus and nearly bowing in his eagerness to see her. "Ms. Walters. Would you like your table?"

She shook her head. "I need one of your private rooms, Carlos. Do you have one on such short notice?"

The question was a formality. Echoes always kept a few rooms in reserve in case someone famous or important wanted them. Jodi wasn't famous, but in Hollywood terms, she was important, so she got what she wanted in a place like this.

"But of course," he said and snapped his fingers discreetly at one of the staff behind him. That poor person—a thin man who looked scared to death—hurried ahead of them.

"I'll need a third setting," Jodi said. "A friend might join us through the back entrance."

"Should I keep an eye out for this friend?" the maître d' asked a bit too eagerly. He was supposed to stay calm in the face of celebrity, but usually someone who snuck in the back would be famous enough to impress the most jaded maître d'.

"She'll find us," Jodi said. "No need to worry."

Blue was looking at Jodi as if she had grown a third head. He tugged on his shirt and ran a hand through his hair, trying to make himself seem presentable.

Jodi wanted to reassure him, but she couldn't. They were already threading their way through male and female diners all in Armani suits or something equally black, equally conservative, and equally expensive.

"See," Blue hissed at her. "I'm underdressed."

"Only the plebs dress up, Blue," she said. "They're all on expense accounts, and right now they're all wondering who you are."

His cheeks grew red. People were watching him.

"Oh, that's not wise," he said. "Really, that's—"

"Don't worry," she said. "Handsome men are a dime a dozen in this town. Strikingly handsome men are too. These folks'll remember that you're pretty and they'll remember that they don't know you, but they won't remember your face unless it becomes famous."

"I hope you're right," he said.

Of course she was. She had been doing this kind of thing forever. They were in her world now, and she felt a lot more comfortable than she had in that rehab center.

The maître d' took them up a small flight of stairs to what looked like a wall of smoked glass. He grabbed a nearly hidden doorknob and pushed open a door. Then he took menus from a female member of the waitstaff who had snuck in from one side, and he cradled them to his chest as Jodi and Blue walked inside.

The room was already set up for three. The smoked glass was a one-way mirror, with a view of the corridor and of the restaurant. On the other side was real glass that opened onto a private terrace which, Jodi knew from experience, was walled off from the other private terraces connected to the other private rooms. Through the half-open door, she could see red and pink flowers, some orange that she couldn't identify, and a lot of green.

"We can set you up on the terrace if you like," the maître d' said as he pulled out her chair, "but you had said the meal was private."

"It is, thank you, Carlos." Jodi sat down in the offered chair, took the menu, and nodded toward the seat next to her.

Blue bit his lower lip, then pulled his own chair back and sat quickly, as if his entire body might decide against it. The maître d' handed him a menu, but sideways, as if Blue's presence offended him slightly.

Jodi knew that Blue would sense the attitude and would attribute it to his real past, when actually, the maître d' was ignoring him because he believed Blue to be a nobody in the entertainment world.

"We'd like a bell, please," Jodi said as the maître d' set the remaining menu on the empty place. Blue's frown got deeper. He didn't know what she meant.

But the maître d' did. He reached into his pocket and pulled out a small paging device. In the past, Echoes had used an actual bell, but that meant that the waitstaff had to listen to see what was happening. This worked better; she could summon a waiter when they were ready for one so that no one hovered.

"Do you like meat?" she asked Blue.

"Yes, but—"

"Good, then we will order now," Jodi said. "Two prime rib sliders, one large watermelon salad, lots of bread, and ice tea."

"And for your third party?" the maître d' asked as if he was used to taking orders—which he was, in this circumstance. His hand hovered over the menu on Tank's place.

"We'll figure that out if she gets here," Jodi said in her most dismissive tone.

"Thank you," the maître d' said, then he picked up the menu and left, closing the interior door behind him.

"What the hell was that?" Blue asked.

She took a deep breath. She hadn't realized that she had been nervous too. "You wanted discretion. This is discrete."

"But the people out there, they saw us," he said.

"And immediately dismissed you. This is the most mortal of mortal worlds," she said. "It's a place where if you haven't done something last week, then you're not important. And importance is all that matters—their kind of importance. Right now, you're an unknown."

"But you aren't," he said.

"I'm not known to the paparazzi, and I can guarantee there were some paparazzi ringers out there letting their employers know who was having lunch with whom in this place. They don't care about me because I'm a talent wrangler. If I had come in with a studio head, then maybe they'd pay attention, but probably not. Because I'm a problem-solver of a kind they don't care about. But the studios do, which means that I have a lot of clout in this town. Carlos and guys like him know that, so they stay on my good side. And part of staying on my good side is not talking about my lunch partners or the deals that I'm working on."

She held up the pager, and Blue followed her fingers.

"This thing works both ways. They'll let me know when they're bringing food, and I'll let them know if I need them."

"Wow," he said, "I thought the rules in my father's Kingdom were strict."

She shrugged one shoulder. "It's a different kind of royalty in Tinseltown, and fortunately, you're not part of it. Which means that we won't get interrupted at all."

Famous last words. Because at that moment, Tank flew in from the terrace and landed on the back of the empty chair. She had changed from her black dress into something pink and gauzy that matched her wings. It also made her less conspicuous. She could actually stand in the middle of the table, and the unobservant would think her part of the floral arrangement.

"I *love* this place," she said. "Do you mind if I sit on the table?"

"Only if you stay inside your place setting," Jodi said.

"Then how's a girl supposed to eat?" Tank asked.

"Don't worry," Jodi said. "I've taken care of it."

Tank rubbed her little hands together and hopped from the back of the chair to the table. "Okay," she said. "Where do we start?"

"I don't know," Jodi said. "Maybe at the beginning?"

Chapter 26

STARTING AT THE BEGINNING PUT IT ALL ON HIM. BLUE was nervous enough. He hadn't been to a restaurant like this in years, except to cause a scene. He didn't believe he had caused one here, or they never would have let him back in, but he wasn't sure. He did look different when he was sober. And Jodi seemed to have a lot of pull, which surprised him.

It shouldn't have surprised him, but it did.

He wondered if she had enough pull to get him past the maître d' if indeed he had trashed the place and didn't remember. Probably. And he probably had done something wrong here, given the coldness the maître d' had shown him. There was probably some kind of gossip network among maître d's at places like this, spreading the word about people who were trouble.

And he had been trouble.

He adjusted the silverware, noting how heavy it was. Real silver. And he supposed the water glass was real crystal and the tablecloth real linen. He hadn't even looked at the prices here, but he imagined they were high.

He could afford it. He'd brought a lot of gold with him from the Kingdom, and he never spent it, not even during the worst of his drinking. But he didn't have any money on him. He only had one credit card and he doubted a place like this would take it.

"What do you remember about your chatelaine?" Jodi asked.

Blue shook his head. He was nervous enough, unsettled enough, that going back to his past right now would upset him further. He needed to grab on to something, and this restaurant wasn't it. This restaurant made him more uncomfortable than staying at the rehab center had.

"Do you have—did you bring—do you have the papers?" he asked.

Jodi gave him an odd look, then said, "Yes. In my briefcase."

She stood and picked it up, and then opened it on the unused edge of the table. Her movements were smooth and graceful. He could watch them forever.

Then he made himself look away, caught himself at it, and sighed. His heart was pounding. He didn't know how to be. He didn't know *who* to be. He'd never experienced anything like this before.

Tank was sitting cross-legged in front of the linen napkin. Someone had folded it in a cap-like shape, and she was leaning against it. Apparently the fabric was sturdy enough to keep her up.

She was watching him like she had never seen him before.

"Why don't you want to figure this out?" she asked.

Jodi sat down, the papers in her hand. She set them in front of him. "Leave him alone, Tank."

"Well, seriously," Tank said, her little face turned toward him. The pink in her cheeks matched the pink in her dress. If her blue eyes weren't so full of mischievous intelligence, she would look like Tink. "The only way to figure out what's going on is to know how it started. You both know that's how the magic works. We can't unravel it without knowing the cause."

"You assume I can remember," Blue said. His voice was shaking. *He* was shaking, inside and out.

"Yeah, I am," Tank said.

He was starting to panic, and for the first time since he got out, he wanted a drink. Maybe he did have a problem, since he wanted a drink to quell the panic. Normal people didn't drink for that reason. Or at least, that's what Dr. Hargrove told him.

Doctor Hargrove wouldn't lie.

Would he?

Did they?

"Tank," Jodi said in that voice the brooked no disagreement. "We're going to take our time on this. If you don't like it, I can brief you on our conversation later."

Tank made a little face and crossed her arms, as if that made a difference.

Then Jodi smiled at him. The look made his breath catch. He wasn't going to turn away. He wasn't. He needed to make changes, and looking at a beautiful woman was one way to do it.

"Blue," Jodi said with real warmth. "Let's just go over the work you did last night. I'm sure it'll be useful."

He nodded and reached for the papers just as Jodi started to hand them to him. Their fingers brushed, and something so electric shot between them that Blue thought for an instant there should have been sparks.

His heart was pounding, and his breath caught. Jodi looked at him in surprise. She had felt it too.

Or maybe she had just been startled that they touched.

Surely she had just been startled.

There was no way a woman like her could be attracted to a broken-down ruin like him. Not unless he had turned on the charm, which he most decidedly hadn't.

He wasn't sure he was ever going to try to charm a woman again.

He held her gaze, though, then nodded just a bit, as if acknowledging her. Then he slipped the papers out of her hand.

He was shaking violently, but he managed to control it enough so that the papers didn't vibrate. He set them on the table quickly.

"You kept them in order," he said with surprise.

She smiled. "Of course I did. You worked hard on it."

Somehow that sentence didn't sound patronizing. It should have sounded patronizing. Doctor Hargrove would have made it sound patronizing.

She made it sound like the most logical thing in the world.

"Thank you." Blue separated them back into their piles, and as he did, the pager buzzed.

Tank cursed and flew upward without uncrossing her legs. "What the hell?"

Jodi glanced at the pager. "Our drinks and some bread," she said. She tapped it, apparently letting them know it was all right to bring everything in. "Just turn over the top pages for a moment."

He nodded, his heart pounding. But differently now, a fear-based pounding rather than one based on a surprise connection.

Only it hadn't been a connection. He couldn't presume to have a connection. Once they figured out what was going on, he would probably never see Jodi again. The thought made him sad but relieved at the same time.

He didn't want to hurt her, but all he had ever done with women was hurt them. Whether he meant to or not, whether it was a curse or not.

He was the kind of man that women shouldn't trust. Because he didn't even really trust himself.

Chapter 27

THE WAITER SET DOWN TWO GLASSES OF ICED TEA, A pitcher, and an extra empty glass for the person who (supposedly) hadn't yet arrived. He also gave them some bread and a complimentary hors d'oeuvres just because Jodi was a valued customer.

She was glad for the interruption. She hadn't been able to catch her breath since her fingers brushed against Blue's. His touch had sent shivers through her.

The man radiated charm even when he wasn't trying.

She didn't want to be attracted to him. Intellectually, she knew what a disaster that would be. But her body wasn't listening. She wanted to brush against him more often (she wasn't even sure that touch was a complete accident), and she wanted to sit much closer to him, maybe lean against him.

It took most of her self-control to prevent herself from putting a comforting (yeah, right) hand over his or patting him slightly on the shoulder (to see if those muscles were real).

She felt her cheeks heat. She didn't want to think about this, so she smiled at the waiter as he set down the empty glass right near Tank and nearly put an appetizer plate on top of her.

Tank didn't move. She was used to this. Instead she huddled against her napkin as if she was part of it.

Apparently the waiter thought she was.

Blue had moved the paperwork slightly to the side so that the waiter wouldn't set anything on it. Blue kept his head down, as if he didn't want to be recognized. So far as Jodi knew, no one had recognized him, so she wasn't entirely sure what the problem was.

The waiter left, and instantly Tank grabbed a roll nearly as big as she was. She staggered a little and set it on her bread plate. Jodi wasn't sure if Tank was actually going to use the gigantic butter knife or not. Jodi shouldn't have wondered about it. Tank was already tearing the roll into tiny bits.

"I *love* this place," Tank said, her mouth full.

Blue actually smiled. A real, amused smile. His eyes twinkled and he looked at Jodi, and then the smile faded. He looked down, adjusting the papers.

"I, um, organized everything last night," he said.

Jodi nodded, pretending that he hadn't made her breath catch yet again. She grabbed one of the rolls, and she used the butter knife to cut it in half and spread some butter on it.

"I noticed." She sounded absurdly formal. "It looks like you found something."

He nodded. "I recognized the pattern, even before you two mentioned a curse."

He thumbed through the papers, then set the ones with yellow Post-its on top. They had been paper-clipped together.

"See, the first thing, what happened here, it's what happened before." Then he glanced up, his gaze meeting Jodi's, before he looked down again. "It's what happened to you."

His voice was soft, almost hesitant, definitely

apologetic. Jodi set the butter knife down, feeling odd since he was so upset.

"Except I think there might have been one difference."

"Just get to it." Tank sprayed crumbs as she spoke. She had actually tunneled into the roll and was pulling out the soft yeasty center.

Blue smiled a little, but the smile was distracted, as if he hadn't been able to control it. The smile was just a bit sad.

"This guy," Blue said, "this guy introduces himself. He says he's Bluebeard and he'll cut off her head."

Jodi frowned. "My visitor didn't say that."

"On the first meeting, that never happened with my—the women—in the past." Blue rubbed a hand over his face. "Sorry."

Jodi put out her hand, almost touched him, and then thought the better of it. The last thing she wanted to do was feel that spark again. She needed to concentrate.

"But the Fairy Tale Stalker identifies himself," Jodi said.

Tank shoved aside the roll and grabbed some of the appetizer. It was some kind of caviar, and she just put her hands in it.

Jodi almost chastised her, then thought the better of it. Tank wasn't going to listen anyway.

"In a strange voice," Blue said. "He spoke faster and with a higher pitch. And the first victim said he sounded almost panicked."

Tank's arms were black with caviar. She stood up, dripping on the linen tablecloth. "Like he was breaking through the curse."

"How could he do that?" Jodi turned to Blue. He was

watching Tank with disgust on his face. "You had no idea this was happening to you, right?"

Blue set his bread plate aside, as if Tank had just put him off food forever. "That's right," he said. "I had no idea what was happening. But I didn't have a fairy tale to go on. I mean, everyone knows the story of Bluebeard, right? And if I had known—"

"I thought you couldn't feel the curse," Tank said.

"There were the odd memories I told you about," Blue said, "and dreams. Nightmares. I had never heard of dedicated dreaming, but maybe this guy has."

"Dedicated dreaming?" Tank asked.

"It's a learned skill where you take control of your dreams," Jodi said, trying to ignore the dripping caviar.

"You can do that?" Tank asked.

"Some people can," Blue said. "It's one of the techniques they teach you in rehab."

"Maybe that's it," Jodi said, hoping her doubts weren't coming through. "Or maybe the curse isn't as powerful with him. Tank mentioned that a curse made in childhood was stronger than one made in adulthood."

Tank tilted her head back and let caviar drip off her fingers into her mouth. Then she used the edge of her shirt to wipe off her face, leaving little caviar prints on the fabric.

"There could be a million reasons for curses to have different strengths," Tank said, the words a bit mushy because her mouth was still full. She chewed for a moment, swallowed, and added, "This stalker dude is a different guy. He probably has different magic, and it might interfere with the curse, or give him some insight or something."

"Or this has happened to him before," Blue said. "Just because it's the first mention in the paper doesn't mean it's the first time it has happened to him."

Jodi looked at him. Blue's mouth was a thin line. She wasn't sure she had ever seen anyone look so tense before.

At that moment, the pager went off.

Tank cursed and dove into her napkin, leaving a caviar trail from the bowl to her hiding spot.

"Is there a reason you're such a slob, Tank?" Jodi asked as she accepted the page.

Tank didn't answer. Jodi knew she wouldn't. Jodi had half expected to see Blue's smile again, but he didn't even seem to hear her. He was thumbing through the stack of paper, as if he was looking for something.

He didn't even attempt to cover it all up when the waiter came back in with their meals. First the waiter removed the appetizer dish. Then he took out a small cleaning tool and scraped off the top of the table onto a tray, scraping the caviar-covered napkin hiding Tank with it.

Blue started to say something, but Jodi put a hand on his arm, silencing him. The warmth of his skin made her palm tingle. He looked at her, arm twitching as if he wanted to move it away.

She shook her head slightly, but if pressed, she wasn't sure if she could tell him that she wanted him to remain quiet or to keep his arm in the same place.

Or both.

Probably both.

The waiter set their plates down with a flourish, asked them if they wanted anything else, and they both shook their heads. The napkin on the dirty tray didn't move.

The waiter picked it all up and carried it out of the room, closing the door behind him.

"Do you think he hurt Tank?" Blue asked. He still hadn't moved his arm.

"No," Jodi said. She'd seen Tank do similar things, particularly when she encountered food she liked. This gave Tank a direct route into the kitchen. "I think she'll be just fine."

"Should I wait for her to come back?"

"It's Tank," Jodi said. "Who knows when she'll be back."

"Good point," he said.

He hadn't moved his arm. She hadn't moved her hand. He gave her an awkward look, then set the paperwork to one side, narrowly missing the damp caviar stain that the waiter's scraping tool couldn't remove.

Then Blue grabbed his own napkin and slowly, gingerly, started to move his arm.

Jodi caught the hint and lifted her hand. She almost spoke, but she wasn't sure what she could say. *Did you feel that too?* seemed trite and a bit needy. *Wow, that was interesting* could cover anything but was either an understatement or a bit dismissive, depending on her tone. And *I'm sorry, I know there's a spark but you're a little too dangerous for me* was, well, too honest for her tastes.

So she said nothing. Instead she handed him the large salad bowl with the watermelon salad. It was one of her favorites, filled with watermelon, watercress, mint, cilantro, pine nuts, and something else. Normally, she would tell him to leave some for Tank, but she had a hunch Tank was making a pig of herself in the kitchen.

Jodi could only hope that the city health inspector

didn't show up today, or if he did, she hoped that Echoes was willing to pay the city a huge bribe to overlook whatever Tank was doing.

Blue put the salad next to his three small prime rib sliders. Jodi took one of the sliders off her plate and set it on her bread plate in case Tank returned and wanted more food.

Then Jodi said, "You were looking for something a moment ago. What was it?"

Blue had taken a bite of the salad. He swallowed, then said, "I was trying to get a picture of the time frame. This has been going on for a while."

Jodi nodded. She hadn't looked closely, but she was certain the stalker had been in the news for at least a few weeks. "Did it take a while with you?"

He frowned, then shook his head. "It was a long time ago."

She would have thought that he would remember how long it took from the first sighting until the women ended up dead. He had sounded almost cavalier, and that bothered her.

He still wasn't looking at her either. Then he set his fork down and rubbed a hand over his face.

"I'm sorry," he said. "I don't know if I can be much help."

You're the original Bluebeard, she almost said. *Of course you'll be of help.*

Instead, she waited. She had learned through her clients that it was better to let them talk rather than jump in immediately. Often the first sentence that they uttered had little to do with the real problem.

"I—It—" He sighed, kept his head down, and then

shook it slowly. "I spent most of my life putting everything out of my mind. It was a long time ago, but it's more than that. I really tried not to think about it. I worked at forgetting, and what I couldn't forget I tried to destroy with drink. When they came out with that study that alcohol destroyed brain cells, I prayed that the study was right. Because I didn't have enough courage to do those drugs, you know the ones that really do destroy your brain. They also put your inhibitions down in unpredictable ways, and I was unpredictable enough. Alcohol, at least, deadened you, and if you drank enough, it just made you pass out. The other stuff—it was too scary for me. But I would have used it if I thought I could control myself and it would have destroyed my brain. I would have."

Her breath caught. She had never heard anyone be so very honest. She wasn't sure what to say to it.

He raised his head, blinked those beautiful blue eyes at her, and smiled ruefully. "T.M.I., right, as one of the teenagers in my group therapy session would say. I know. I'm sorry. I'm usually not an oversharer. I just wanted you to understand why I can't just trip this stuff off my tongue. I really honestly never talked with anyone about it before."

"Except Tank," she said.

"I don't talk to Tank," he said. "She talks to me."

"She has a thing for you," Jodi said.

"No. She's a rescuer, haven't you noticed? She likes damaged creatures. She likes rehabilitating them. She often called me her greatest challenge." Then he let out a small ironic laugh. "Which is exactly what Dr. Hargrove called me too."

"For different reasons," Jodi said. "Imagine what he would think if you were honest with him."

Blue shook his head. "Dr. Hargrove lives in the world we're sitting in. The rich, the famous, the troubled. He thrives on it. But he would never work with the really difficult people, the psychopaths, the criminally insane. He even passes off the sociopaths to some of the other therapists there."

"So he doesn't consider you a psychopath or a sociopath," Jodi said. She found that interesting. She knew what both were—who didn't, working in Hollywood?—and she usually avoided them. Although it wasn't always possible to avoid the sociopath in Hollywood. The sociopath could charm and work the system but had no real respect for the rules, no real ethics. The Hollywood environment—the quick rewards for a lot of talk and a lot of game—attracted a lot of sociopaths.

It attracted a few psychopaths as well, but those guys usually went out with a bang, often taking people with them. Psychopaths were truly nuts, while sociopaths could function in society. And she had found, in her not-so-limited experience (she had actually met Charles Manson back in the day), that psychopaths were easy to recognize, whether they were on or off drugs.

She hadn't pegged Blue as either when she met him, which seemed odd to her now, because had he really been the killer everyone claimed, then she would have noticed something off besides his eye contact. And technically, she should have been wary of anyone who was as charming as he was, particularly with his history, since charm was often such a large part of the sociopath.

Still, she found it fascinating that Dr. Hargrove, who sounded like he had a hefty survival instinct, didn't consider Blue a sociopath or a psychopath, even after repeated encounters with him. Fascinating and a bit of a relief.

"I guess I hadn't thought of Dr. Hargrove's reluctance to treat people he didn't like in relation to me," Blue said. "I guess—sometimes, you know, it's reflexive. The charm. You think people will get along with you no matter what. But sociopaths can be charming."

"Charming but empty," Jodi said.

Blue nodded. He pushed one of the sliders around but didn't pick it up.

"Don't you find it important that your therapist thought you were just a normal guy with a huge problem long before we discovered the curse?" Jodi asked.

Blue shrugged. "I was lying to him."

She gave him a small smile, but he didn't see it. He still wasn't looking at her. "All patients in rehab lie. And besides, sociopaths and psychopaths are really obvious if you spend a lot of time with them."

"You know this?" Blue asked, bringing his head up.

She nodded. "I've met a few in my day. How come you don't know this?"

"I only know about them from books," he said. "Dr. Hargrove sends the real crazies to other facilities if he can."

"Books?" Jodi repeated.

"When I'm sober, I can't sleep," Blue said. "So I read. And guess what the center has. Lots of psychology texts and manuals. If I was truly paranoid, and maybe I am, I would have diagnosed myself long ago."

Jodi tilted her head just a little. "Everyone who reads those books diagnoses themselves. You did, right?"

He picked up one of the sliders as if he thought about eating it, then he set it down again. "I didn't fit into the categories. I figured that the diagnostic stuff written for the Greater World didn't know how to take into account the magical ones."

"That's probably true," Jodi said. "But don't you think we're enhanced humans?"

He frowned at her. "Meaning what?"

"Meaning we're just like them but with magic," she said.

"How can you be just like normal people when you have a major difference like magic?" he asked.

"I don't think there are normal people," Jodi said. "I think we're all different from each other."

"And Tank? Is she normal people?"

"Well, she's not entirely human, now is she?" Jodi said. "So I'm only talking about us. Those of us who can pass, to use an old-fashioned phrase."

"Pass," he muttered. "I guess that's what I've been doing."

"Yet believing yourself to be secretly different," Jodi said.

"They say that's one of the signs of alcoholism," he said. "Believing in your own difference even in the face of evidence to the contrary."

"But you *are* different from the mortals," Jodi said. "The charm magic, the curse, they don't have those things."

He looked up. That sad look extended to his eyes. He had a somewhat doomed quality, as if he knew himself better than anyone else. "Charm magic and a curse," he said. "In mortal terms, charisma and bad luck. They're not real, Jodi. It's what you do with what you have that makes you real."

Her breath caught. His honesty astounded her, and so did his willingness to see the worst in himself. Maybe that was part of it; if she had thought she had done such horrible things without much memory of them, she would think the worst of herself too.

"What you do with what you have," she repeated. "Well, you figured out that you had charm and it attracted women, and in attracting women, you put them in danger, so you made yourself as unattractive as possible, did what you could to avoid them, and tried hard not to hurt anyone, am I right?"

He nodded.

"So," she said, "not realizing it was a curse, thinking it part of you, you did the best you could to neutralize all of those things that harmed people. Seems to me that you did really well."

He let out a small sigh. "If I had done really well, I would have figured out the curse on my own."

"Really?" Jodi said. She hated this kind of revisionist history. *If I had done this, then I would be that.* Yeah, right. So not true. "How old were you when this started?"

"I don't know," he said. "Marriage age."

"Which back then was barely a teenager, right? You looked like a man so you were one. That's how we thought in those days."

"It's not an excuse."

"You lived in a magic world where people didn't

confront you, they covered up for you. You had no guidance. You did what you could."

His gaze met hers. "You forget. Fifteen women are dead. I did not do what I could. If I had, then they'd be alive."

She closed her eyes for just a minute, not sure how to answer him. She couldn't fix him, and that was what she was trying to do. It was the downside of her magic, trying to make everyone feel better, and sometimes there was no feeling better. Sometimes there was just living with the past.

He touched her hand, his fingertips warm. That electric charge ran through her, strong and powerful. It was an attraction pure and simple, and it took her breath away.

She opened her eyes to find him looking at her. He didn't look at all like the man who had appeared in her bedroom the night before. That man had an innocence in his face. This man had care lines around his eyes, a tiredness to his features. He was handsome, yes, but handsome in the way of a man who had lived a long time and had the trials of his life etched on his face.

The image she had seen in her bedroom hadn't been a man but a boy, a boy at the cusp of his life, thinking all things possible.

This man knew that all things were not possible, and that some things actually harmed.

He squeezed her hand, then let go, almost ruefully.

"Look," he said. "I left the rehab center because I believe you and Tank. I believe I'm suffering from a curse, and I believe whoever cast the curse has done it again. What I'm afraid of is that the cursecaster has been doing this for centuries, to a lot of people, and that we're just seeing the beginning of it. We have to stop it, and I can't do that from inside the rehab center."

He nodded once, as if he wanted to give emphasis to his words.

"I have to stop him," Blue said. "You can't. Tank can't. I have to. Not as revenge or anything, but because of what you said. This curse is wrapped in my aura, which means that I carry his magic with me. That means we can find him, through me."

"It's not that simple," Jodi said. "I can't just touch you and unravel the curse and have it bring me to the cursecaster."

"I know that," Blue said. "It sounds like the curse has an automatic component to it—he sets it up, and then it runs until he shuts it down, without him having to touch it."

Jodi nodded. That made sense, given the fact that the curse had started up again when Blue had noticed her. The cursecaster had to have his attention focused on the Fairy Tale Stalker, not Blue, so the appearance of the image had to be automatic.

That idea made something ping in her brain. A thought, a realization, but she couldn't quite grasp it.

It would come to her.

"When the time comes," Blue said, "when we find this guy, then I'll shut him down. Not you, not Tank. Okay?"

Jodi frowned. "Why?"

"Because, to do this for so long, he has to be powerful, and dangerous," Blue said, "and there isn't a guarantee of success."

Jodi shuddered. "You think he might kill you."

"No," Blue said. "Magic on this level isn't common. And to destroy it sometimes takes more power than an individual usually has."

"That's why we'll bring in a specialist," Jodi said. "Someone who deals with this all the time."

"No one deals at this level all the time," Blue said. "You know it and so do I."

She pursed her lips, finally understanding him. "Suicide is not an option."

"I'm not talking about suicide," he said. "But I do remember some of my princely training. When you have a dangerous mission that might not succeed, you don't send in the irreplaceable expert. You send in someone who can do the job and won't be missed."

Jodi frowned. "You'd be missed."

He shook his head. "By Tank maybe," he said. "But no one else."

"Me," she said. "You'd be missed by me."

He touched her hand again, lightly, with a bit of a smile. "You'd remember me, maybe, but we don't know each other well enough to really miss me. And you're not going to really miss me. We have to make sure of that."

Chapter 28

"WHAT DO YOU MEAN WE HAVE TO MAKE SURE THAT I don't miss you?" Jodi said.

Blue took a silent half breath. Damn. He had been thinking out loud, being honest, and that sentence had gotten out. He didn't know how to explain himself without sounding arrogant.

And without lying.

He didn't want to lie anymore, particularly to this woman.

The prime rib sliders still steamed. It felt like he had been in this conversation forever, and it hadn't been very long at all. The ice hadn't even melted in the iced tea. And none of those observations gave him any way to approach this subject, now that he had (accidentally) brought it up.

"I—ah, hell." He gave her a small smile. A frown creased her forehead. He wanted to smooth it away. Maybe he had been talking to himself more than her. And maybe that was the tack he needed to take.

"I haven't talked to a woman in a long, long time," he said, "and I find you attractive."

Then he shook his head. He had promised himself he would be honest.

"No, strike that," he said. "I think you're beautiful."

Her cheeks flushed, but she didn't look away. He had half expected her to look away. He wanted her to look away.

If she had looked away, she would have shut down this part of the conversation.

But she was *interested*. Dammit.

"I'm already attracted, and I don't know, maybe you always touch people when you talk to them and smile like that, but if I—"

"I think you're very handsome," she said softly. "And I'm well aware of your charm."

Which made him even more nervous, since he hadn't been actively trying to charm her. He'd been trying *not* to charm her.

"Then, then, then…" He took a deep breath, trying to stop himself from stuttering. He did not need to know that this woman found him attractive. He wished she hadn't admitted that. "Then it's good we're talking about this, because we can't."

He blurted the words out, keeping his gaze on her face. Her frown had grown deeper.

"Can't what?" she asked.

"Ever be more than colleagues," he said. "If we can even be that. I'm not even sure how friendship will work."

"Work?" she asked. She sounded confused.

He was making a real mess of this. "This curse. It activates when I notice a woman. We haven't figured out the time frame. Does it just escalate on its own, or does it change as my feelings change?"

She let out a small "oh," as if she could see where he was heading. "That seems awfully complex."

"The whole thing seems complex to me," he said.

"Spells aren't usually complex," Jodi said. "The more complex they are, the easier they are to collapse."

"Even evil spells?" he asked. He really didn't know. "Even curses?"

"I don't know," she said. "This is outside my area of expertise."

He nodded, then gave her a small smile. He had smiled more today than he had smiled in a long time. Relief at learning about the curse? Or being out of the rehab center? Or Jodi's presence?

He hoped it wasn't Jodi's presence, because if it was, they were in trouble. He didn't want to be attracted. He didn't want to think about her. He didn't want the burden of yet another woman's life on his conscience.

"Yeah," he said. "I hadn't given curses a second thought until today."

She sighed.

"You did a lot of work last night," she said. "Why don't you boil it down for me."

He grabbed the paperwork like it was a lifeline. "There are at least three phases," he said. "And then the phases have at least three components to them."

"That makes sense." She picked up one of her sliders. "Magic likes unity."

She took a bite. At that moment, he realized she hadn't responded to what he had said earlier. She hadn't agreed to keep this professional, even though she probably would. Except for that blush, he hadn't even been sure she was listening.

"From what I can tell here," he said, "this Fairy Tale Stalker, as the papers call him, his curse seems to be in the first phase."

Maybe he had misread her. Maybe that admission of attraction was just a fact, something she was aware of and determined to fight. After all, he had been aware earlier that she had disapproved of him, and then that feeling had changed. Maybe he was the one who had overreacted.

"First phase meaning that no harm occurred?" Jodi asked.

So they were going to pretend he hadn't said anything? He wasn't sure they should do that, but he also wasn't sure he should say anything more.

At least he had gotten it out. At least he had mentioned the elephant in the room. He would discuss it more later if he had to. But at least she knew his concerns.

"The first phase, a seemingly innocent visit," he said.

She started to speak up, but he continued before she could interrupt him.

"I know," he said, "in today's world, popping into someone's bedroom uninvited is not innocent. But think back to the world we grew up in. Sometimes that was seen as romantic."

She took another bite of her slider and chewed as she thought. He took that moment to take a bite of his. The sandwich was good, the prime rib rich and well-cooked. He was hungry. And he hadn't had something this good in a long time.

It took a lot of effort not to just wolf it down.

"Romantic visions," Jodi said after a moment. "All those small spells even mortals could do by tapping into loose magic, like looking into a mirror backwards on a significant birthday to see your future beloved."

"Yes, exactly," he said. "At first, my wife thought that what she saw that night was a romantic vision."

And so did his second fiancée. By the third, people had started to get suspicious, and that whole idea of the romantic vision was turning sour. But at first, that was how both women had misunderstood his arrival—well, not his, but that image's arrival (the curse's arrival?)—in the middle of the night.

"So in some ways," Jodi said, musing, "this curse is a romance that goes deliberately wrong."

"Only it's old-fashioned," Blue said. "So in today's world it seems threatening from the first."

She looked at him. His heart did a small internal flip. He wondered if she could see it, that little bit of excitement he felt whenever their eyes met.

Probably not. He hoped not. Because his life—and because of him, her life—was complicated enough.

"I know that you're having trouble remembering the timeline," she said, "but with you this happened to one woman at a time, right?"

"I haven't forgotten that," he said. "Yes. One woman at a time."

She tapped the printouts. "But not to the Fairy Tale Stalker. Several women over the space of months."

"Either he's several guys," Blue said.

"Or something is different," she said.

He ate another slider as he thought about the differences. "It might be cultural. I met women, but I had to concentrate on one at a time. And many weren't suitable, so I wasn't even allowed to think of them."

Jodi snorted. "C'mon. Surely there was a village girl or two in your past. Maybe a tavern wench?"

He shook his head. It was hard to believe now, but he had been a conservative young man. More than that, he hadn't wanted to disappoint his parents. Of course, he had become the biggest disappointment of all.

"No," he said softly. "My first victim was the first girl I was ever serious about. My wife."

So long ago. He hadn't permitted himself to think about her. He had actually been in love. So young, so eager. So lost.

Jodi put her hand on his arm. "Not your first victim. The curse's first victim. You have to make that distinction now."

"I suppose," he said. But it seemed like such a minor one to him. His wife was dead, long dead, but dead because of him. Whether or not he had actually harmed her seemed beside the point.

"The fact is," Jodi said, "this other man, this so-called Fairy Tale Stalker, is either seeing and being attracted to several women, or the spell is different. Maybe the curse is more sophisticated."

"Or maybe it's not as strong," Blue said. "Because remember, this is supposed to be a seduction. He shouldn't use the name 'Bluebeard,' and he shouldn't be telling them he's going to kill them. He says that in a different tone of voice."

"He's warning them," Jodi said.

Blue nodded. "Which means he knows that something is wrong."

"I wonder if he knows what it is," Jodi said.

"We have to find him," Blue said. "Because the next stages for these women are sheer terror, followed by death."

"What about the heads?" Jodi asked.

He winced. He hated thinking about that. "What about them?"

"It seems a major part of the Bluebeard fairy tale is

the fact that the young wife sees the heads of her predecessors. Did that happen?"

"Aside from the fact I only married once," Blue said. "Yes. When each woman came to the castle, she could see the heads."

"And you could see them," Jodi mused.

"But no one else could," Blue said.

She frowned. "That seems so strange. I'm going to have to do some research here. I mentioned before that it bothered me, and it still does. It bothers me a lot."

She cut her last slider in half and ate one part of it.

Blue finished his last one.

"But it doesn't matter," she said. "These modern women, they should see the heads too."

"If it's the same curse," Blue said.

"Or the same cursecaster," Jodi said.

"Unless he refined the curse." Blue shuddered and suddenly regretted that last tiny sandwich. It sat like a lump in his stomach. "Unless he's been practicing that curse for centuries."

"On other people," Jodi said softly. "You're not the mass murderer, Blue. Whoever this cursecaster is, he's the mass murderer. And he's getting other men, innocent men, to take responsibility for his crimes."

She was right. It didn't stop Blue from feeling responsible, but she was right. They were talking about a mass murderer here, and the murderer wasn't Blue.

He had been using Blue. And the Fairy Tale Stalker. And probably countless other men. The cursecaster had used all of them to commit his crimes.

Blue felt the first threads of a fury he had long buried.

"Let's figure out how to stop this," he said. "I'll do whatever it takes."

Chapter 29

WHATEVER IT TAKES MEANT THE FIRST STOP WAS THE Archetype Place. Blue had said he was persona non grata there, but Jodi was going to change that. She was a fixer, after all, and she needed the expertise that the Archetype Place represented.

She didn't call ahead, though. She didn't want anyone to prepare for her or to muster up arguments against Blue. He sat beside her now as she turned on the side streets leading to the Archetype Place. He had gotten more and more tense as they drove the hour plus to get from Century City to Anaheim.

The Archetype Place had been built by two so-called evil stepmothers—Mellie, who was Snow White's stepmother, and Griselda, who was Hansel and Gretel's. Both got maligned terribly in the fairy tales as retold by the Brothers Grimm. Mellie had lost her magic trying to save Snow's life, and Griselda had rescued Hansel and Gretel on the night their father had tried to kill them with an ax.

But the Brothers Grimm apparently had a thing against women, or they deliberately misunderstood most of the stories they had heard, but whatever it was, they had mistold almost every story they had heard.

And that thought made Jodi give Blue a sideways glance. He was looking out the window, so tense that his fingers were threaded together and his knuckles had turned white.

Had the Brothers Grimm misheard the stories about Bluebeard? Did the fairy tale about Bluebeard even come from them? She wasn't sure. She hadn't re-searched him—hadn't even thought to research him.

But given the terrible accuracy track record of the Brothers Grimm, maybe they had screwed up Blue's tale too. Although he did confirm a lot of it.

She frowned, wondering if she should hire someone to check him out in the Kingdoms, wondering if she had time, wondering if she dared.

She almost asked him but then decided against it. He was still looking out the window, but now he was wav-ing a hand in front of his face. She smiled. The air from the backseat was purple—again.

When Tank rejoined them in the parking garage be-neath Echoes, Jodi decided to put up the car's top. She thought it would make the long drive easier on Tank. Jodi wasn't sure if the wind would blow Tank out of the car. If Tank blew out, Jodi worried that she wouldn't wake up right away and sail into a windshield or bounce under a wheel. Tank would die with a splat before any-one could stop it, and all that would remain would be little gossamer wings.

Jodi hadn't foreseen the problem having the car's top up would cause. Apparently, Tank had eaten her way through Echoes's kitchen. Tank belched loudly when she got into the car. Then she climbed into the backseat and fell asleep. Ever since, she'd been letting out little fairy farts. The smell wasn't bad, but the purple vapor trail coming out of the backseat had twice interfered with Jodi's view of the road. She and Blue had come up with a system where they just rolled down the windows in tandem to clear the purple haze before it became impossible to see through.

Jodi pulled into the parking lot behind the Archetype Place. From the back, it looked like a gigantic warehouse. In the front, someone had painted a series of delightful murals that made the warehouse look like a series of Disney storefronts. But the back was just painted white, and Jodi preferred it.

There weren't a lot of cars back here. Most of the folks who frequented the Archetype Place either flew there, magically appeared inside it, or walked over from Disneyland where a bunch of them worked. Jodi brought a lot of her clients to the Archetype Place because they got very discouraged working in the Industry. The Archetype Place did a lot to combat the myths about the magical perpetrated by the Industry. The Archetype Place had a wing devoted to the founding branch of PETA—People for the Ethical Treatment of Archetypes. Jodi was a member, but mostly she just paid her dues and kept silent. Until recent years, PETA had been too radical for her.

She rolled one window down a fraction, then got out of the car. Blue looked a bit disoriented, but he got out too.

"Should we wake Tank?" he asked.

Jodi shook her head. "She'll join us if she wants to."

Jodi really didn't want Tank to join them inside the Archetype Place, but she didn't want to say so, because for all she knew, Tank wasn't really sleeping and might actually hear her. At the moment, Jodi wasn't willing to seem ungrateful to Tank in any way or form.

Jodi waited for Blue in front of the car, then slipped

her arm through his. He stepped back as if she had pinched him. Then he gave her a wary look.

"We have to go in together," Jodi said. "It's better if we look relaxed."

"We can look relaxed without… that," he said. He sounded nervous.

She was nervous but decided not to show it. "You have to stay at my side. It's easier to keep you there when I have your arm."

He nodded, then shook his head. "No. No, I… Just no. Okay?"

"Okay," she said. She hadn't meant to set off quite that reaction. After all, she had touched him in the restaurant. But not quite in that way. Even though she had gone into the Archetype Place a million times with a client on her arm just like that, none of the clients felt quite the same way. None of them had such firm biceps (how did a heavy drinker get such firm biceps?), and none of them made her feel tingly with just the slightest brush.

It probably was better not to have her arm threaded through his. She could concentrate better if she wasn't touching him.

"At least stay by my side," she said. "I don't want to lose track of you."

He nodded distractedly, a small frown creasing his forehead. His nerves were affecting her.

Jodi and Blue walked to the smoked glass doors in the front of the building. Jodi pulled them open and stepped inside the coolness. Something about the Archetype Place smelled like home. She'd discussed it with others of the magical, and they all described the smell differently.

For her, it smelled faintly of hot chocolate on a cold winter day mixed with a trace of wood smoke, and just a hint of cinnamon. When she was growing up, both chocolate and cinnamon were luxuries that very few people had access to. She had indulged only rarely, and only on the most special of occasions.

Still, the smell always soothed her, and she always smelled it when she came into the Archetype Place. She knew it was a domestic comfort spell—it was one of the earliest spells she had ever learned—but that didn't make her appreciate it less.

Beside her, Blue didn't seem to be soothed. He seemed so tense that she felt like she could shatter him with the flick of a fingernail.

No guests sat in the reception area. The Frog Prince had reception, again. He'd been working it a lot lately.

Froggy was probably the most handsome man that Jodi had ever met (until she met Blue, that is), but he preferred to remain in his frog form. His beloved wife had died a few years back, and ever since, he had stopped taking care of himself. Selda had given him a job in the Archetype Place so that she could keep an eye on him and dump him into a pool of water when she felt he needed it.

He looked like he had been in some water recently. His skin was a shiny forest green, and the ridges on his back looked healthy, not bony. His feet were splayed across a lily pad that doubled as a desk blotter, and Jodi thought she saw a dead fly in one corner.

It made her shudder. She had heard of people who took on the characteristics of their other form, but she tried not to think about what that meant.

Froggy's golden eyes had met Blue's, and for the first time since she met him, Froggy actually looked cold.

"We're here to see Selda," Jodi said.

"Not him," Froggy said without taking his gaze off Blue.

"I'll just wait in the car," Blue said. "I probably shouldn't be here anyway."

Jodi caught his arm and held it, even though she knew he didn't want her to. She also realized, as she felt the developed muscles that went all the way down, that she wouldn't be able to keep him here if he didn't want to stay.

"You can be here," Froggy said, "or have you forgotten that you signed the *I'm Not Evil* pledge to get in here? Or should I say, have you forgotten *again*?"

Blue's muscles had tightened, not because he was going to hit someone, but because he'd been surprised. He shook his head, then frowned, then looked at Jodi.

"See? I shouldn't—"

"*We* need to see Selda," she said to Froggy, "and I'm not taking no for an answer."

"*He's* not allowed to see Selda ever again," Froggy said, "and you will take no for an answer because *I* work for her."

"Then get her for me and we'll change this," Jodi said.

"No, really," Blue said. "I don't mind. I can—"

"You be quiet," Jodi said without looking at him. She held his forearm, effectively preventing him from moving. Then she said to Froggy, "You tell Selda we're here. Tell her we need to talk about the Fairy Tale Stalker, a curse, and Bluebeard."

Froggy tilted his head so he looked at her from one bulging eye. "This job means a lot to me."

"Selda won't fire you," Jodi said.

"She might," Blue said softly. "You don't know what I did last time I was here—"

Jodi held up her free hand, effectively silencing him. "You're right. I don't. And I don't want to know. Froggy, if she fires you, I'll hire you, all right?"

"I don't like Hollywood," Froggy said. "I won't work for some studio. They'll make me sing that Muppet Green song. I don't like to be green. I like emerald."

Which is green, Jodi thought but didn't say. Her irritation level was high enough without aggravating Froggy further.

"I won't get you a Hollywood job," she said.

"Good, because I don't sing and I don't do commercials and I don't do cute." Froggy slapped one long toe onto the intercom button and leaned forward so he could talk into it. "Selda, it's me, Froggy."

"Who else would it be?" Jodi muttered to herself. Blue put a hand on top of hers and looked at her. He shook his head and mouthed, *This is a bad idea.*

She ignored him while Froggy explained who was at his desk and why they were here.

"…something about a stalker, a curse, and this disreputable Bluebeard."

The intercom crackled with static. "Is Blue drunk?"

Jodi thought that a good sign: Selda actually didn't dismiss him out of hand.

"No," Froggy said with a bit of surprise. "And he's showered too."

"Aqua Velva?" Selda asked through the intercom.

Blue was cringing. Jodi suppressed a smile.

"Thank the Powers, no," Froggy said. "You can actually breathe around him."

Blue made a sound of distress. Jodi clamped harder on his arm.

"Then send him back," Selda said.

"Alone?" Froggy sounded alarmed.

"With Jodi, who is probably listening and better have a good reason for this."

The intercom clunked off. Froggy stood at his full height—which was about as high as the mug of pens on the far side of the desk.

"You heard her," he said. "Enter at your own risk."

Blue shot Jodi a panicked glance. She gave him a re-assuring smile, then slid her hand up his arm and tucked her hand through his elbow, as if they were on their way to a ball.

He was actually trembling, and his cheeks red. She hadn't really thought before about all of those times she had seen him drunk and rude and out of control. She had always thought that was the man. But the real man was embarrassed by what he had done, and now she was forcing him to face that.

But wasn't that part of recovery?

Although she doubted he had planned to enter this stage of recovery today. She doubted he had planned to enter it at all. He had only done his recovery at the rehab center and then, when he left, had deliberately fallen off the wagon.

She led him down the narrow hallway, past a few closed doors, to the open door at the end. Jodi had never seen Selda's door closed, not even on the worst days.

Selda's office was huge, bigger than Jodi's office. Only Selda's office didn't feel as big. Part of it was the gigantic fireplace on one side of the room, part of it was all of the comfortable upholstered furniture scattered about. Some of the chairs already had cats on them, one had a dog sprawled across its entire length, and only two were empty, the two closest to the desk.

Jodi didn't know if that was by design. Selda had one of those offices where nothing seemed like it was by design, and yet it had to be, from the spider plants hanging off all the surfaces to the macramé plant hangers filled with climbing ivy in front of the windows to the constantly percolating pot of coffee in the very back.

In the center of it all was Selda, a woman as large and comfortable as the furniture. She had been gorgeous once—Jodi had seen the images—but she had let that slide as her reputation disappeared. She had saved two children on a very harrowing night in the woods and had gotten excoriated for it for decades. Branded an evil witch, she was actually shunned by people who had once cared for her, and eventually she had come here where her reputation preceded her.

She transformed herself with Jodi's help, landing the gig as "Mother Nature" on a series of commercials in the 1970s. She had almost balked at the tagline—*It's Not Nice To Fool Mother Nature*—because it was followed by a peal of thunder and a crack of lightning, but Jodi convinced her to do it, and ever since, people (mortals) had reacted well to Selda.

The commercials had captured her warmth and her power. Jodi had liked that. Selda had felt exposed and had left the business shortly thereafter to continue her work here at the Archetype Place.

She stood behind the desk as they came in, a tall square woman wearing a brown and orange caftan. The caftan suited her. It matched her curly brown hair and should have made her eyes sparkle.

But she wasn't sparkling anywhere. In fact, Jodi had never seen Selda stand when someone came into her office. Selda had her hands behind her back and she was watching Blue warily.

If Jodi didn't know better, she would have thought that Selda was frightened.

"I'm letting him in here because of your phone message last night," Selda said. "You sounded distressed, and Tank leads me to believe it had something to do with that stalker. Now you come here, dragging the real Bluebeard, and I'm worried."

Jodi hadn't expected Selda to start. "When did you see Tank?"

"Before she went to see you. She said she had it under control," Selda said. "Where is she now?"

She asked this last question of Blue as if he had done something with her.

He glanced at Jodi, who kept her hand clamped on his arm. "I—um—"

"She's in my car," Jodi said. "I made the mistake of taking her to Echoes. She's sleeping off her food coma."

Selda grunted.

"Look," Blue said. "I know you don't want me here. Let me just apologize for everything I've done, and all the things I've said, and then Jodi can talk to you. I'll wait with Tank—"

"Jodi wants you here," Selda said. "So you stay. Sit. And I don't want to hear some twelve-step apology."

She waved her hand at the two open chairs near the desk.

This time Blue didn't argue. He glanced at Jodi. Together they went to the chairs and sat down. Jodi had to let go of his arm to do so and felt it as a real loss.

He didn't look at her. Instead, he looked directly at Selda, his hands gripping the arms of the chair as if it was about to levitate.

"I owe you an apology," he said. "And it would be real."

"I don't care," Selda said.

Selda sat down too, but she didn't lean back like she usually did. Instead she leaned forward, elbows on her cluttered desk.

She looked directly at Jodi. "Curse? Fairy Tale Stalker? And now Blue in my office. This had better be worthwhile. I trust you plan to tell me everything?"

And so Jodi did.

Chapter 30

OR AT LEAST, JODI TOLD SELDA EVERYTHING SHE knew. There was a lot of information, but as Jodi told the tale, she realized there were a lot of gaps as well. And Blue wasn't doing anything to fill them in.

He sat quietly, not moving, as if he expected Selda to banish him immediately.

Jodi had never seen someone with such a large presence recede into the background the way Blue had. It was as if he had shut off his charm, as if he had taken his personality and shoved it into a corner of himself. He was trying to fade away, and he was doing a very good job.

Or so it seemed to her. But she was trying to focus on Selda, who was listening intently. Selda's gaze never left Jodi's.

"You're certain this is a curse?" Selda asked as Jodi finished.

"I've never seen a curse before, but this seems to follow all the signs," Jodi said. "The magic is threaded through his. You can see it in his aura."

"I can't," Selda said. "I don't have that kind of magic. But you're excellent at what you do, Jodi. I don't need a second opinion for this. I'm just amazed no one has noticed it before."

She still didn't look at Blue as she spoke, and he remained relatively motionless. It had to take a lot of concentration to keep himself that still. But Jodi didn't look directly at him either. She didn't want to make him more uncomfortable than he already was.

"There's a reasonable explanation for that," Jodi said. "It's only visible once the curse activates. Otherwise it's dormant. All you can see in his aura is charm magic."

"And now it's different?" Selda asked.

Jodi nodded. "Just since yesterday."

Selda let out a long sigh. "We're dealing with someone quite powerful then, someone with magic that can span centuries. And work on multiple people at once. That's rather terrifying. I would think the Fates would shut him down."

"Not without a complaint," Jodi said.

"And curses are too subtle for a complaint before the Fates," Selda said. "You'd have to know who placed the curse to stop the curse."

She turned her head, looking at Blue for the first time. Jodi looked sideways at him. He swallowed visibly.

"Well?" Selda said. "Do you know who did this?"

He shook his head. "I didn't know it was a curse until this morning."

"And now you're out, but not drunk." Selda folded her hands together. "Tell me, is this the first time you've been loose in the Greater World without some alcohol in your system?"

"Outside of a rehab center?" Blue asked.

Selda nodded.

"Yes," he said.

"Well," Selda said. "I'm beginning to understand the fairy tale now."

Blue looked confused. Jodi smiled. Selda was

referring to Blue's handsomeness. Jodi had had the same reaction. Her gaze met Selda's and they had one of those woman-to-woman moments of understanding.

"What does that mean?" Blue asked.

The edges of Selda's lips turned up, but she didn't quite smile. Jodi knew the look. Selda wasn't going to answer him directly.

"You know," Selda said to Jodi, "I always wondered why the story of Bluebeard was included in a group of fairy tales. Didn't you?"

Jodi started to answer, but Selda cut her off.

"I mean, at its heart, it's not a *fairy* tale at all, but a horror story about something rather mundane. What do they call them now here in the Greater World? A serial killer, right? Someone who murders for pleasure."

Blue said, "I didn't—"

"There's no magic in that, no fairies, no bargain with a magical being." Selda didn't even seem to notice that he had spoken. "But if you look at the story as the story of a curse, then it belongs in the oeuvre of fairy tales. So those Grimm Brothers screwed up again, taking a tale they knew had magic and removing all the magic from it."

Selda said that last with a touch of bitterness. Maybe more than a touch. Jodi was getting the impression that if Selda ever ran into the Brothers Grimm (were they still alive? She didn't know. But assuming they were), then the Brothers Grimm would have a lot to answer for.

It's not nice to fool Mother Nature, Jodi thought and smiled to herself.

"Do you think the Brothers Grimm knew it was a curse?" Jodi asked.

"Do you think they knew that I would never harm a

child?" Selda asked. "Of course they knew. Those boys had agendas I still don't understand."

She turned toward Blue.

"And you," she said to him, tapping the desktop with her free hand. "You did something to anger them."

"I wasn't even in the Kingdoms when they arrived," Blue said.

Selda made a soft noise, as if that was a missing piece to a puzzle. Jodi didn't pretend to understand. And honestly, she didn't really care about the Brothers Grimm. She cared about the curse—all versions of it.

"I know there are people who are good at curse removal," Jodi said. "Do you know any we can contact?"

"I know several," Selda said. "Unfortunately, they're all on other jobs. Rather big ones too."

"Since when is the death of a lot of women not big?" Jodi asked, a bit snidely. She knew that in the not-so-distant past the death of women was always considered no big deal.

Another thought made her frown. That must have factored into Blue's father's decisions not to deal with his "murderer" son.

"Those deaths are big," Selda said. "It's just—I can't tell you what they're working on, but trust me, if they solve those things, well, look at it this way. Remember the zero-year curse?"

"No," Jodi said.

"Presidents elected in a year ending in zero died in office, until Ronald Reagan. Remember that?"

"Vaguely," Jodi said.

"That's one of ours. We solved it. We stopped the curse. It's that kind of big."

"Of course, solving that one had all kinds of other unintended consequences," Blue muttered.

Jodi glanced at him, but Selda didn't seem to notice. Jodi bit her lower lip, reminding herself—no politics. No religion. Not even Greater World politics and Greater World religion.

"We could use some kind of support here," Jodi said. "I mean, it's just me and Tank and Blue, and we didn't even know it was a curse until today."

"Tank did," Blue said.

"She wasn't sure," Jodi said. "The thing is, we don't have the skill to combat this thing."

Selda frowned. "I'm not sure that's true. I'll see what I can find out. There are special rules for curses and long-lasting spells. I might even consult with the Fates."

"Better you than me," Blue said.

Both Selda and Jodi looked at him. He raised his head so that his gaze met theirs. He wasn't trying to disappear now, but he wasn't using the full force of his charm either.

"You went to the Fates with this?" Selda asked.

"Tank says you didn't," Jodi said.

"Tank doesn't know everything," Blue said. "It was before I came to the Greater World. Centuries ago. I asked the Fates to help me stop. They said no."

Jodi let out a small breath. She had been hoping, deep down, that the Fates could be their ace in the hole, that with some manipulation—and yes, charm—the Fates would tell them how to get out of this mess.

"Well, that makes sense in Fate-land," Selda said, again with the bitterness.

"It does?" Blue asked. There was a touch of color in

his cheeks and an edge in his voice. Did Selda's comment make him angry? Jodi hadn't seen him angry. Despite everything, he hadn't gotten mad—or at least not obviously mad. Which, she had to admit to herself, was a bit odd.

If she found out she had been cursed for centuries and that curse had destroyed her life, she'd be furious.

"You have to understand the Fates," Selda said. "Or understand them as best as possible."

That flush in Blue's cheeks had gotten deeper. Jodi didn't want him angry at Selda. Clearly these two rubbed each other the wrong way. Jodi wanted him and Selda to work together.

So Jodi stepped in. "Understand the Fates how?"

"Blue went to the Fates and asked them to help him stop killing people, right?" Selda was looking at him. Jodi got the distinct impression that she was poking at him, that she was trying to make him angry. Jodi wasn't sure why.

"Yes," Blue said tightly.

"Well, you weren't killing people," Selda said. "So the Fates couldn't help you."

"They could have told me what was going on," Blue said. And now Jodi was certain. He *was* angry.

Here was the fury that she had expected, and it worried her, because it was directed at Selda, whom they needed on their side.

"Technically, no, they couldn't," Selda said. "They're not supposed to interfere with our lives unless we do something terrible."

"Like curse someone for all eternity and cause the deaths of innocent people," Blue snapped.

His eyes were a dark, dangerous blue. Jodi put her hand on his arm. She wasn't going to tell him to calm down, but she didn't want an incident. Not here.

"They can't even intervene in that unless they're asked to," Selda said.

"I asked them." Blue had raised his voice. "I asked them for help."

Jodi had to use a bit of force to hold him in his chair. But oddly—or maybe not so oddly—she wasn't afraid of his anger. If he was dangerous, she should have been afraid of him.

But he wasn't. He was just angry. Justifiably, understandably angry.

"You asked them to help you stop killing people," Selda said, and she had lowered her voice. Apparently she was starting to understand what was going on with him too. "They could only act on what you knew."

"That's crap and you know it," Blue said.

Selda nodded. "Yeah, I know it's crap. But it's the Fates. That kind of crap is why Mellie and I started this place. We weren't getting any help from the Powers That Be, except admonitions to leave the Greater World. We were told we didn't belong here."

Blue was breathing hard. Jodi watched both of them. She hadn't realized how much pain Selda felt. All those years of being accused of things she had never done.

Like Blue.

"Their rules are arcane," Selda said so softly that Jodi had to strain to hear her. "They haven't been updated in a millennia, and they really don't apply to us anymore."

Blue shook his head. He looked down, his body trembling. Then he burst out of the chair with such power that the chair scuttered away. Jodi's hand fell uselessly against the side of her chair, and Selda leaned back as if she expected Blue to attack her.

But Blue didn't head for the desk. Instead he paced around the gigantic room, as if he was filled with so much energy that he couldn't contain it.

"I can't go back and undo the damage," he said. "If I had known it was a curse, I could have stopped it. But I can't reverse any of it."

Jodi glanced at Selda. She was watching him as if she had never seen any of it before. And she clearly wasn't going to step in.

"We have to stop it now," Jodi said. "You and I, Blue, we know what's going on. But those women in the Valley don't know, and neither does the so-called Fairy Tale Stalker. We can put an end to it right now."

"If that woman"—and he pointed at Selda—"would get us some help. But your hands are tied too, aren't they, Griselda? You can't help us either because your people have something better to do."

"It's not like that," she said. "You can't stop a magical intervention in the middle. Our anticurse specialists are already engaged. We have to wait weeks for them to free up. And from what you say, I'm not sure we have weeks."

"So what are we supposed to do?" he asked, approaching the chair, putting those big powerful hands on the back of it and sliding it back into place. He didn't sit in it. Instead, he just stood there, tall and powerful, like the king he should have been. "Watch as this curse destroys other lives?"

"I believe there are things that the cursed can do to

stop their tormentor," Selda said, "but again, I'm not an expert, so I'm going to have to look all this stuff up. While I do, see if you can find this so-called stalker. He would benefit in hearing from you."

"And what am I supposed to say?" Blue asked. "Look, kid, listen to us or you're going to end up a broken wreck like me? With everyone you love dead and the world you know destroyed?"

Jodi's breath caught. Selda's mouth thinned, and for a moment, Jodi thought Selda was going to yell back. Instead, she tilted her head, closed her eyes, and sighed.

"I'm sorry," she said after a moment, opening her eyes so that they met his. "I'm having trouble thinking of you in this new light."

"Yeah," Blue said bitterly, "me too. I have trouble thinking of me that way too."

Chapter 31

To everyone's surprise, Selda offered Blue an apartment, but he turned her down. He didn't want to be beholden to her, he said, but it was clear that he didn't want the risk of another repeat of his bad behavior the last time she had given him an apartment. Apparently he didn't trust himself either.

But Jodi trusted him. And she found that odd, yet natural. It felt right.

Which was why, as they left the Archetype Place, she offered him a place to stay. *Not* with her, much as she wanted to. It wasn't that she didn't trust him or she hadn't known him long, although those were good enough excuses. She had just learned long ago, after some bad relationships, that she didn't share her home with anyone for any reason.

No. The place to stay that she had offered him was one of the apartments that she usually put some of her clients in.

Blue shook his head. They were walking back to the car. "I'll just go to a hotel."

But he said that in a way that made her wonder if he was going to find a place to rest his head at all.

"I have furnished units," Jodi said. "I use them for folk who work for me. It'll give you a quiet place to think."

He gave her a sideways glance. "I'm not sure I want

to think. And I certainly don't want charity. I can afford a hotel room."

"Good," Jodi said. "Then you can afford that apartment."

Her car was still the only one in the parking lot. She opened the door, and purple air floated out. Apparently Tank was still inside.

Jodi left the door open to air out the car.

"Besides," she said to Blue, "your neighbors will be from the Kingdoms and will be able to help if you need it."

His lips turned up in a half smile. "No one'll help me. No one will even talk to me. It would be better if my neighbors weren't from the Kingdoms."

She let out a small laugh. Selda and Blue were having trouble forgetting his old identity and believing the new one. Jodi had already moved past that old identity, so far past it, in fact, that she hadn't thought about it when she made the offer.

She leaned on the car door and peered at him. Tall, well-dressed, unbelievably handsome. So handsome her eyes almost hurt when contemplating him, even with his black hair mussed and a bit of a sunburn along his nose, probably from the ride into Century City.

"If you don't tell anyone who you are," she said, "I doubt anyone will recognize you. Not unless they've been around a long time, and most of the folks in the apartments haven't been here for a long time. Maybe you should use the name you used in the rehab center."

"John Franklin?" He sighed. "Won't everyone wonder why I'm in your little Kingdom housing project then?"

Little Kingdom housing project stung just a bit, as if he dismissed what she did. To be fair, however, she hadn't really told him what she did, not in depth. And he might have been trying to push back. He still seemed off-balance from his discussion with Selda.

"No," Jodi said. "Not everyone from the Kingdoms is famous. You never heard of me until a few days ago, right?"

"For all I know, you're the sorcerer's apprentice," he said with just a bit of a smile, "and Disney got it wrong casting Mickey Mouse. It wouldn't be so far-fetched, considering how much Disney gets wrong."

Jodi laughed for real this time. "I'm no one's apprentice, and no one has ever written a fairy tale about me. And I'm pretty common. Most of us who came here from the Kingdoms are people no one has ever heard of. Some of us like it like that, and everyone else wants to be famous in one way or another."

"So they end up in LA," he said.

She nodded. "So they end up in LA. But I think my little Kingdom housing project, as you called it, is perfect for you. If something goes wrong, that something will be magical, and we won't have to explain ourselves to mortal authorities."

He grunted. "I hadn't thought of it like that."

He walked around the car and opened the passenger door. More purple air wafted out. Tank really overate.

"I'm still going to pay you," Blue said.

"Notice I haven't argued with that," Jodi said. Then she slipped inside the car. Tank hadn't moved. She was surrounded by a small bubble, with clear air inside.

So she had awakened herself at one point, then put herself in a little protective shell, and had gone back to sleep.

Jodi had had enough. There was a thin purple haze inside the car.

"Tank," she said, "go get yourself the magical equivalent of an antacid, will you?"

Tank blinked, then sat up, piercing the bubble. She made a face at the purple air and said, "Caviar. Does it every time."

Then she flew out of the car on a somewhat wobbly path, still under the influence of whatever else it was she had gorged on.

Jodi waited until Tank took the back entrance into the Archetype Place, then put the top down.

"C'mon in," she said to Blue. "Let's take you to your new home."

Chapter 32

Blue's new home was a small bungalow in what had once been a roadside motel. Someone had remodeled the entire motel complex creatively, combining rooms, adding windows and a lot of greenery, but it was hard to hide the footprint of that 1940s complex. Blue remembered when those motels were new and fashionable, long before the interstate highway system. The motels were romantic, like the open road itself, an upscale place to lay your head after a long day driving America's back roads, looking for adventure.

Of course, he hadn't stayed in a place like that until the 1970s, when the motels had gone to seed, and most of them rented by the hour.

This one still had its original kidney-shaped pool, kept up with sparkling water and little blue dolphins painted along the bottom. The original office remained as well, only now it was the stand-alone manager's apartment, a little house complete with swing set in the backyard.

Jodi knew everyone here and greeted them all by name. The moment he came in here, he knew why she wanted him here. She wanted him here because any problems he caused—magical problems—would seem normal. This was like a bit of the Kingdoms in Los Angeles.

In addition to the selkie swimming in the pool, there

were mermaids lounging in the deep end and water sprites playing tag along the surface. Dwarves pretended to be lawn gnomes when the car pulled in. It wasn't until Jodi got out that they actually moved.

In fact, Blue realized more than half the lawn decorations, from the tiny leprechauns to the fauns to the crouching lion in the back, weren't statues at all, but living, breathing creatures.

His room was next to that of a troll named Gunther, a big glowery creature that smelled faintly of molten iron and stagnant water. Jodi asked Gunther to keep an eye on Blue—whom she remembered to call John— and Gunther had accepted the assignment as if Jodi had told him that he was guarding the president of the United States.

Gunther had looked at Jodi with that melty look Blue recognized. The troll was smitten. And Blue didn't like that.

Jodi deserved better. Not that Blue was going to get a say in anything. He wouldn't. Jodi was her own woman, and besides, he was damaged goods.

(And "damaged goods" was such an understatement.)

Besides, while she was friendly with Gunther, she didn't give Gunther a melty look. Still, she touched him casually too.

Apparently she touched everyone.

Blue tried not to feel disappointed about that.

She left him and his leather bag outside number forty-two, a pale blue bungalow with white lattice work covered in fragrant peach-colored blossoms. It was pretty, and it made him nervous.

So nervous that when she told him she wouldn't see

him until the following day, he asked her where she was going.

He had sounded like a needy kid.

Maybe he was needy. And maybe Jodi had heard that, because she looked at him oddly.

"I have a job, you know," she had said. "I haven't done any work all day. I doubt Tank will pay me for this one with you, even though she said she was hiring me. Tank has weird ideas about what constitutes payment."

He had smiled and nodded, as if he understood, and to be fair, he did understand. He was just a job to Jodi. A job she was doing reluctantly for someone she didn't quite trust.

Nothing more.

She hadn't even waited until he went into the apartment. He had unlocked the door to his new home, and she had taken off for her car.

Apparently, she couldn't wait to get rid of him.

Not that he blamed her. He was beyond damaged goods. He was a man who had spent centuries believing the worst of himself and destroying himself to make sure that he wouldn't behave badly again.

Such euphemisms he had learned to use. "Behave badly." "Damaged goods." He had done his best to destroy himself so that he wouldn't kill anyone, because he believed himself capable of it, and not just that, but doing horrible things to the bodies.

He had believed the worst of himself, and then when he had found out that he was under the influence of a curse, he fled from the place that had provided him a modicum of comfort, a bit of help.

Of course, it had been the wrong kind of help, the

wrong kind of comfort, given who he thought he was. He was a man who had made terrible, terrible mistakes, even when looked at through the prism of the curse. He hadn't defended himself. He had let himself sink into the morass that his life had become, and then he hadn't even done the honorable thing and ended it all.

Because if he truly believed he could hurt people like that, he should have prevented it by ending himself.

He had known that for a long time, and even tried to act upon it a few times, but something had stopped him.

And he was never quite sure what that something was. Of course, he wouldn't let himself reflect backward. He had tried to live in the moment and do some of the sobriety things that the rehab center had taught him, taking each day at a time, rewarding himself for getting through yet another difficult situation.

Only he hadn't applied it to alcohol. He had applied those sobriety rules to murder. If he hadn't harmed anyone that day, if he hadn't put someone in harm's way that day, then he had had a good day.

And technically, by his old rules, he had had two very bad days. Jodi was now in danger.

But the rules had changed.

He used the key she had handed him—an old-fashioned one, with an old-fashioned blue plastic fob and a number, just like old motel keys—and let himself into the apartment.

It was pleasant, which he hadn't expected although he should have, given the exterior. The living room was small but furnished, with comfortable couches and chairs, and a flat screen television on the wall. Directly across from the door was the door to the kitchen, and through it he saw another big window which opened into the garden. Clearly someone had put two motel rooms together to create this one.

He set his bag down and stepped inside, closing the door behind him. Good light, comfortable. So different from any place he had stayed for decades. Even his favorite room at the rehab center didn't have this kind of light.

Then he remembered: Jodi was a descendent of chatelaines. She specialized in comfort, especially in a home.

He smiled a little, and even though he knew she hadn't designed this for him, it felt like she had. Part of the magic, of course, but a nice part.

He wandered through the living room to the bedroom—a third former hotel room, with another large window. But it didn't look like an old hotel room, and the bathroom—with its double sinks, standalone rainwater shower, and large claw-foot tub—didn't look like an old hotel bathroom.

He was lucky to be here, in more ways than one.

He went into the kitchen and to his surprise saw a computer on one of the counters. The computer was running, with a Post-it note on the screen saying it was all right to use it.

Such a risk, given the way that the Kingdom magical destroyed electronics. But computers were cheap now. The Post-it did not have his name on it, so he knew this was a feature of all of the apartments, probably to help the folks who lived here find work.

He moved the mouse, and the screen came up onto a series of rules for the magical and computer use.

He smiled, then turned away feeling his smile fade.

He was disappointed that nothing here was personal, and he shouldn't have been. But he was. Because of Jodi. He should have realized how he felt this morning when Jodi told him that the curse had started to have an effect on her. He should have thought it through.

It wasn't just that he had noticed her or looked at her or talked with her.

He found her really attractive, but more than that, he liked her.

He wanted to be with her.

He put his hands on the edge of the sink and looked into the garden. Some pixie children were playing tag around a sapling, occasionally sparking when one of them rubbed against something clearly spelled as untouchable.

He was so needy. That was it. No real warmth, no real contact for centuries. The talks with Dr. Hargrove didn't count, because Blue had paid the man to listen. Blue never thought of Dr. Hargrove or the others of his ilk as anything more than resources. And Blue could never let himself think that anyone cared for him.

He blamed any good reaction he got—sober or not—on his charm magic, not on anything to do with him.

So he had to remember that Jodi's kindness came from the fact that Tank had hired her. Although Jodi could have left, probably would have left, if she hadn't discovered the curse.

But even then, the hiring had less to do with him than the Fairy Tale Stalker. And Blue was supposed to help her find that guy, stop that guy from hurting others, and maybe that would lead to this damn cursecaster, whoever he was.

They hadn't been able to finish the conversation at

the restaurant. Too many distractions, what with Tank and the caviar and the waiters. By the time Blue realized he hadn't finished telling Jodi what he had learned from the material she had given him, they had already moved to another topic, which was finding him some place to stay.

The job Blue had to do now was both simple and hard. He had to look backward, all the way back to those horrible days when he thought that he was killing people and not remembering it. He had to look at a part of his life he had shut off, and as he did, he had to reassess it, realize that everything he thought was true wasn't.

Tall order for a man to do with the help of a counselor. Even taller for a man to do on his own.

But Jodi was taking a risk with him. Tank had taken an even bigger risk: she had believed from the beginning.

And if Blue could find some of the secrets in his own past, he would be able to help this so-called Fairy Tale Stalker.

One day at a time. One moment at a time.

Because he didn't want to think about what would happen if finding the Fairy Tale Stalker led to the cursecaster.

Blue wasn't sure what he would do to that cursecaster when he found him. For generations, Blue had believed himself capable of horrible, awful murders.

He didn't want to think about how, if he found the cursecaster, he might learn that the image of himself as killer was true after all.

Chapter 33

TEN MINUTES. THAT WAS ALL JODI PROMISED HERSELF. Just ten minutes.

She had come home for an hour only, which was stupid in LA because driving took so damn much time, but she needed to decompress, and she couldn't, not with Ramon asking a ton of questions, the phone ringing like crazy, the reception area full, and all of the meetings she had pushed back from that morning crammed into the late afternoon.

She needed a shower, a glass of wine, a nice dinner, and some Jodi-time. But most of all, she needed to stretch out on the bed and close her eyes for ten minutes.

The lack of sleep from the night before had caught up to her, along with the stress, and just the general confusion.

The confusion concerning Blue.

She didn't want to think about him. She had been a bit dismissive of him at the apartment, but she needed to get back to work. Besides, she didn't want to see him in the place. She would have felt the need to add a few more spells to make him even more comfortable.

She didn't dare do that, not when he had asked that they remain the magical equivalent of professional.

She went into her bedroom, ignoring the fairy dust from the night before—in fact, pretending the night before hadn't happened at all—and kicked off her shoes, then stretched out, still in her business suit, feet tucked under the thin duvet she had on top of the bed. The bed (the room itself?) smelled faintly of baby powder.

She didn't care. She just needed to close her eyes.

She didn't even set an alarm, figuring the phone would wake her, or the sun itself as it lowered over the Wilshire golf course and came streaming into the sliding glass doors overlooking the pool.

Besides, in her entire life she'd never been able to nap longer than ten minutes, not even when she was sick (which was rarely).

She had barely closed her eyes when she heard something rustle. Her heart started to pound, and she wanted to leap out of the bed, but she didn't. She had to get used to being in her own room again. Just because she had been frightened out of it by a vision the night before didn't mean she needed to be frightened whenever the house creaked.

She opened her eyes, and there he was, again. Blue. Or Not-Blue. Bluebeard, with his young face and innocent eyes, oozing charm, wearing that light blue top with the big sleeves, and those tights.

The tights fit him well, showing muscular legs.

He smiled at her and she smiled back before she realized what she was doing.

She let out a small "eep," and rolled off the bed on the opposite side. He walked around the bed toward her, hand extended, and damn if she didn't want to take that hand. It took all of her strength to stay on her side of the bed.

Eye contact. She had to sever eye contact, and she did, going for the sliding glass doors again, running onto the patio, and this time, she hadn't remembered to grab her phone.

Not that it mattered. He was reaching for the patio door—how the hell could he do that? Was he corporeal? Could he pull the doors open? Or was he about to step through the glass like a ghost? She couldn't tell. She ran along the stone path she had built on the far side of the house, stopping when she reached the front, and she rummaged in her car (thank heavens she had left the top down) and grabbed one of her extra phones.

With her thumb, she dialed Selda's direct line. Jodi backed toward the street so that she could see the entire house, but she kept looking over her shoulder to make sure he hadn't come up from behind her somehow.

Her heart was still racing, but she was beginning to get her breathing under control.

Finally, Selda answered. "Jodi?"

"He's back," Jodi said. "*It's* back. That vision-curse thing. It's here."

"Here is…?"

"My house," she said.

"And Blue?"

"I put him in an apartment hours ago," she said.

"Alone?"

"Yes, alone," Jodi said. "But there are monitors. He doesn't have a car. I don't know how he could get here if he wanted to. I need Tank. Do you know where she is?"

"Right here," Tank said from beside her.

Jodi eeped again and almost dropped the phone.

"Last I saw her," Selda said, "she was mixing some potion to calm her upset stomach. I'll send someone looking for her."

"Never mind," Jodi said. "She just showed up."

Selda started to say something, but Jodi didn't wait to hear what it was. She hung up and stuffed the phone in the pocket of her skirt.

She looked up at Tank, who was wearing a purple gossamer dress that matched her wings—and was the color of the air she had been creating in the car earlier in the afternoon.

"It's back," Jodi said.

"I gathered from your call to Selda," Tank said.

Jodi blinked. "You heard it?"

"I was at the Archetype Place when the call came in," Tank said with a bit of annoyance. Maybe she had a right to be annoyed. Jodi hadn't noticed until now how hard Tank was breathing or how rapidly her little wings were moving. "I got here as fast as I could."

"That *was* fast," Jodi said. "Thank you."

"Don't thank me," Tank said. "We have to figure out what's going on."

If Tank could get here that quickly, could Blue? Jodi didn't understand everyone else's magic. And if there was a way besides teleportation to get here that quickly, then she wanted to know what it was.

She dialed the cell she had left on Blue's kitchen table.

Tank flew over the house toward the back.

Jodi followed, the bottom of her feet sensitive to the rocks and the uneven concrete of her driveway. She hadn't noticed any of that when she had run out from the bedroom, but she noticed all of it now, including the way that her heart wouldn't stop pounding.

The phone kept ringing. Either he hadn't noticed or he didn't have the phone with him or he was here.

She hoped he wasn't here.

Then the ringing stopped. Someone answered.

"Um… hello?"

It was Blue. She knew it was Blue. Her heart lifted, and she let out a small sigh.

"This is Jodi. Where are you?"

"The apartment," he said as if she were a bit deranged. "Why?"

"Because you're here too," she said.

"Here…?"

"My house," she said. "Wait there."

"But—"

She hung up and walked around the house. Tank was flying over the pool, hands on her little hips, wings working extra hard. She looked unnerved.

Jodi had never seen Tank look unnerved before.

"What is it?" Jodi asked as she hurried along the path. "Is he gone?"

"Stay there," Tank said, holding up her little hand.

Jodi didn't stay, though. She came the rest of the way around until she saw what Tank was looking at.

Something—someone—that Bluebeard vision-thing—had shattered the sliding doors. Glass littered the back patio.

Jodi hadn't even heard that. She should have heard that, right? She looked up at Tank.

"He—it—what did that?" Jodi asked.

Tank shook her head. "If it's just an image, it shouldn't have been able to do that. It shouldn't have been solid enough to do that."

Jodi clutched her phone so hard that her hand hurt. She looked at the shards of glass, glittering in the late afternoon sun.

"I don't like this," Tank said.

"I don't either," Jodi said. Of course she didn't. This was her house. How come someone had destroyed her house?

Then her breath caught. It could have been her. He could have destroyed her.

The phone rang, startling her. She nearly tossed it away from herself and stopped herself just in time.

She didn't recognize the number displayed on the screen, but she answered anyway.

"Yes?" she said in her most dismissive tone. If this was business, whoever it was would have to wait.

"Jodi?" It was Blue. He had called her back. "What's going on? What happened? Are you okay?"

She let out a small sigh. "We're fine. I'll talk to you soon, okay?"

Then she hung up. She cradled the phone against her chest and looked at Tank who was still floating over the pool.

"Aren't you going to do that fairy dust thing?" Jodi asked. "Shouldn't we see what he—it—that thing did?"

"We can see what he did," Tank said. "And I don't think I should use dust at all. I'm not sure what we have here, but whatever it is, it's powerful."

Jodi let out a small breath. She needed to get a grip on herself. "This happened awfully fast, didn't it? I mean, the Fairy Tale Stalker women talk about weeks between visits."

"Yeah. Wow. I hadn't thought of that." Tank rubbed a hand over her mouth. Her wings kept fluttering hard. "What happened exactly?"

"I took a nap," Jodi said.

Tank looked at her, frowning. At least, Jodi thought she was frowning. It was hard to tell from this distance.

"You fell asleep," Tank said. "Alone?"

Jodi nodded.

"Crap," Tank said. "Crap, crap, crap. You said you weren't going to be alone."

"I didn't think a nap would hurt," Jodi said. "It's daytime."

But as she said that, she realized she'd been rationalizing. She didn't like to have people around her all the time. She needed to be alone, so she stole some time—and it had caused this.

"We need to find out what Blue was doing," Tank said.

"Well, if we can get back into my house, we can do that," Jodi said.

"I don't know if it's safe," Tank said, and that was when Jodi realized Tank was terrified. "We need to get someone here before we do anything. We need to investigate the magic, and I'm not going to do it."

Jodi sighed. Of course, Tank was right. The magic needed investigation, and more than what Tank had done the night before. Jodi redialed Selda. This was beyond all of them now.

They needed to figure out what was going wrong, and they had to do it fast.

Chapter 34

BLUE STOOD IN THE KITCHEN OF THE NEW PLACE, staring at the cell phone in his hands. It was square and complex and confusing. He had never really mastered these things—he'd had no reason to. He had never owned one and had used them only rarely.

When this one had started to ring, at first he had thought it had come from outside. But it was also vibrating, and it vibrated its way off the table. When it tumbled on the floor, he realized what was going on.

He spoke to Jodi, who sounded terrified. He hadn't ever expected her to sound terrified, and that unnerved him. She hung up after she told him to stay put, and he had studied the damn thing for nearly a minute before he figured out how to call her back.

And then she had hung up again.

Something had gone wrong. Something had gone horribly wrong.

Where are you?

The apartment. Why?

Because you're here too.

His stomach was churning. Just like in the past. His mind hadn't been playing tricks on him. He hadn't misremembered anything. This curse had activated much quicker for him than it was for this Fairy Tale Stalker. Blue didn't know if that was because the cursecaster was more experienced now or less powerful or more cautious, and he didn't want to give it much thought.

He just had to make sure Jodi was all right. Because if this went the way it had in the past, she had less than a week.

He couldn't just stand here stupidly holding a phone. He needed to get to her. All of the other women had died alone. And Jodi was alone.

He didn't know how to get there. He didn't have a car, and a cab would take forever. He wasn't even sure there were cabs in LA anymore.

Plus he didn't know where her house was.

He held the phone for a minute, then stared at it, trying to figure out how to work it. He didn't dial "0" any longer for information. There was a number. It was one that had become slang, a number people used instead of the word "information." "Give me the… 4-1-1." That was it. 411.

He had to punch the screen a couple of times to find the keypad, which irritated him. But he found it. And then he called the Archetype Place. He needed Jodi's address.

They had to give it to him.

Froggy answered. His voice, deep and raspy, was recognizable just from hello.

"It's Blue," Blue said, knowing he would have to fight to get through. "Put me through to Selda."

The direct route first. Because if he didn't go direct, then he wouldn't have a chance with anything else.

But Froggy didn't answer him, and Blue's breath caught. Had Froggy hung up on him? The little bastard.

Blue was about to hang up when someone answered.

"Blue? It's Selda. Where are you?"

It irritated him that they wanted to know where he was, even though he should expect it. They had to change their thinking, just like he had. But still, these questions wasted time.

"Jodi brought me to one of her apartments. I don't know exactly where it is," he said. "Selda, she's in trouble."

"I know," Selda said. "She already contacted me. Sit tight, and we'll deal with you in a bit."

"No!" he said. "Please, don't hang up. Please. I'm the only one who has seen this before. Please."

Silence. He let out a breath. Dammit. She had hung up.

Only then she said, "You're right. Of course. I'll send a car."

"That'll take forever," Blue said. "Can't someone teleport me?"

"I don't know," Selda said. "Most people want nothing to do with you."

Of course they didn't. Of course. He hadn't thought of that. "What about Tank? She can get some fairies to move me."

"She's already with Jodi," Selda said. "Let me see what I can do—"

"Just tell me her address," Blue said. "I'll figure out a way to get there. Just tell me where she lives."

"You don't know where she lives?" Selda asked.

"No," Blue said. "How would I know?"

"What about where she works?"

"I thought she has her own business," Blue said. "Is the office somewhere other than her house? I thought she was at her house when she called me."

"She was," Selda said. "You really don't know where she lives?"

"How could I?" Blue asked. "Selda, please. She's in trouble. This is escalating."

"Yes, it is," Selda said. Then she sighed audibly. "We'll send someone for you."

"But I thought you said that no one will work with me."

"Oh, they probably won't," Selda said. "But I have some pull with folk. I'll get someone to find you."

"Just give me the address," Blue said. "Please."

There was another moment of silence, then Selda said, "I'm going to regret this."

And she told him where Jodi lived.

Chapter 35

BLUE STAGGERED OUTSIDE, STILL CLUTCHING THE phone. That troll that Jodi had assigned to keep track of him, Gunther, was sitting in the middle of the grass, or maybe he was squatting. Blue didn't know the variations of troll posture. And it didn't matter, because Gunther had been there since Jodi asked him to keep an eye on Blue.

Gunther had done his job.

"Does anyone here have a car?" Blue asked.

"Why?" Gunther asked. He spoke slowly, like all trolls, and in this state, that irritated Blue.

"Because Jodi's in trouble. I need to get to her house."

"Yeah. Sure," Gunther said. "Uh-huh. I'm sure that's okay. Not."

Blue looked at him, not expecting a troll to use Valley speak.

"Call Selda if you don't believe me," Blue said and tossed Gunther the phone.

For a moment, Blue thought that Gunther wouldn't catch it. But at the last minute, the troll's gigantic hand came up and wrapped itself around the phone.

The troll's eyes glittered as he studied Blue. "I know you," Gunther said.

"Yes, you probably do. Most people know me, and not in a good way." Blue wanted to add that Jodi knew him. Jodi trusted him. She had given him a home, for heaven's sake. But he didn't. He had long ago stopped apologizing for himself, not out of respect for himself, but because in the face of everything, what could he say?

Gunther picked up the phone and punched a number into the keypad, watching Blue the entire time. Blue knew at that moment that Gunther was not calling Selda.

"I'm putting it on speaker," Gunther said as he tapped the screen a final time.

A faint ring sounded over the yard. Then another. Then Jodi spoke, her voice small.

"Really, Blue," she said, "I don't have time."

"It's not... 'Blue,'" Gunther said with a particular emphasis on Blue's name. The troll's eyes had narrowed as he looked at Blue.

"Gunther?" Jodi still sounded odd—panicked, tense, Blue couldn't quite tell which. "Where are you? I've been trying to reach you. You're not answering your phone."

"It's inside. I'm outside. Watching John, like you told me to."

"Yes, of course, and...?" Jodi asked.

Blue started. She had been calling Gunther to find out what Blue had been doing? But she was the one who told him about the curse, she was the one who believed in it. She was the one who had convinced him.

Had she lied about that?

"And he's been inside his apartment the entire time, looking at the computer," Gunther said, still watching Blue.

"Good. I *knew* it. Thank you, Gunther. Thank you." She sounded relieved. Blue didn't like that she was relieved. That meant a small part of her still thought Blue would do something to her.

But didn't a small part of him (maybe not so small) still

believe that he could harm her without knowing it? It was impossible to hold one belief for such a long time and not have it creep back in at the most inopportune moments.

Then Jodi, sounding panicked again: "Gunther, where did you get this phone?"

"John handed it to me and told me you're in trouble. Are you in trouble?" Gunther was still watching Blue, as if he expected Blue to lie.

"I've had better days," Jodi said, "but I'm fine, really. Tell… John… that I'll talk to him soon."

And then she hung up. Again.

Gunther frowned and looked at the phone as if he couldn't believe that she had hung up on him. Blue had had trouble with that same thing earlier.

"She doesn't sound fine," Gunther said.

"She's not," Blue said.

"She calls you Blue," Gunther said.

Blue nodded. He didn't want to explain this, not now. "I need a car, Gunther. Or a way to get to her. Can you help me with that?"

"Yes," Gunther said. "I know someone who drives. He can get us to Jodi's house quickly."

Blue didn't like the "us," but he didn't argue. He couldn't argue, not really. He needed to get there, and he needed to get there now.

Chapter 36

THE "SOMEONE WHO DRIVES" WHOM GUNTHER KNEW turned out to be the selkie in the kidney-shaped swimming pool. And the selkie didn't even own a car. He acted as driver for one of the mermaids who didn't like transforming her tail into feet to get across town. Apparently, she found touching the accelerator painful, but she said that pushing on the brake was excruciating, and she preferred not to do it at all.

Which meant she had more accidents on her record than allowed. Which meant that her license got revoked.

Now she made the selkie drive her everywhere, and since it was her car, she insisted on coming along.

They all did. Blue wished he could drive, but he hadn't been behind the wheel of a car since the 1940s, and that hadn't ended well. The whole drinking and driving thing was true: one shouldn't do them together.

The group had trouble just getting to the car. The selkie—whose name was Bosco—had peeled off his pelt as soon as he got out of the pool, transforming into a naked man. Then he claimed it was too hot for clothes and started to lead them all toward the parking area.

"At least drape your pelt over your privates," Blue snapped, but the selkie looked at him as if he was crazy.

"If I do that, dude," the selkie said, "I go back to my seal form. It's not good for driving."

They had an argument—a too-long argument—about

clothes, until the mermaid tossed the selkie a Hawaiian shirt and shorts so loose that the selkie might as well not have been wearing pants.

Then the mermaid decided to come along. She transformed too, but put on clothing (some kind of sarong) and tiptoed toward the car, a blue 1950s convertible so long that it looked like a boat. The mermaid kept the keys until the group got to the parking lot. Then she handed the keys over reluctantly.

She was a stunningly beautiful woman, the kind any man would have been attracted to, and she knew it. She was blond and blue-eyed, and muscled in the way of mermaids and modern women, and she had a cute little upturned nose that made her look more innocent than she probably was.

She shoved Gunther out of the way so that she could sit next to Blue in the backseat, then she leaned toward him, smelling of fish, chlorine, and Chanel No. 5 and said, "My name is Marilyn" in a wispy little voice that he knew wasn't her normal tone.

He gave her a dismissive smile. "John," he said, then he leaned forward, giving the selkie the address.

Gunther sat in the front seat with his cell phone (Blue's cell phone, really) open to a screen with a map and two blinking icons showing where they were. The selkie drove fast, and the mermaid complained, mostly to get Blue's attention, which he wasn't giving.

He had forgotten that part of his life, the part where women, influenced by his charm magic, tried to interest him. They usually failed. There was always an air of desperation about them.

But then there was an air of desperation about this

mermaid with her fake name, bubble-top convertible, wispy voice, and 1960s sarong. He had seen men who were better Marilyn Monroe impersonators, but of course he didn't tell her that.

He just wanted out of this car. He wanted to get to Jodi's.

And then, in a blink of an eye, he was.

Jodi's house was three miles from the apartment complex, but only because they had to drive around Hancock Park. If Blue had walked across the park, the house was only a mile or so away, and he wouldn't have wasted all that time getting the car, making sure the selkie was dressed, and putting up with the gropey mermaid.

As the car pulled in front of the little green hedgerow that separated the driveway from the street, Blue vaulted over the car door and landed on the street. He ran around the car while Gunther, the mermaid, and the selkie yelled at him. He headed into the driveway, searching for Jodi.

He didn't see her, but there were a lot of people milling about, most dressed in Kingdom clothing—breeches, blousy shirts, and long skirts. The air smelled of sulphur, and a small cloud of something floated up from behind the Spanish-style house.

He ran around cables and steaming caldrons and jars of various magical ingredients. He saw at least two eyes of newt and a pickled dragon heart. He also saw a row of colored bottles, probably filled with potions.

The house's front door was blocked by two gremlins and a Minotaur arguing about something, so he decided to go around.

It worried him that no one had noticed him. Shouldn't they have noticed him by now?

The only path he saw went around the house's south side, so he took it and nearly ran into Jodi's back. She was standing on the edge of a patio, Tank fluttering near her, a woman that Blue didn't recognize explaining something about the pool.

Blue was so relieved to see Jodi that he nearly grabbed her and enveloped her in his arms. At the last minute he stopped, raised his hands as if he was being arrested, and stepped backward.

He had never done that before, never spontaneously touched anyone. Or at least, hadn't done it in centuries. The very impulse worried him.

"Jodi," he said softly.

She turned, smiled in relief, and then she hugged him, her body warm against his, her head coming up to his shoulder just perfectly.

She smelled of sunshine and lavender. He wanted to close his eyes and inhale. He wanted to wrap his arms around her and never let her go.

Instead, he kept his hands up, looking at Tank over Jodi's shoulder in a silent plea to be rescued. He couldn't let Jodi treat him like this. It was too warm, too personal, too intimate.

After a moment, Jodi stepped back. She was smiling at him. She didn't seem to notice that he hadn't hugged her back.

"I am so relieved to see you," she said. "You have no idea."

Apparently she hadn't noticed his odd reaction at all. No one had ever been relieved to see him.

He let his hands drop, and as they did, they brushed her shoulders. He wanted to tell himself that touching her was an accident, but it wasn't. He wanted to touch her, to acknowledge her in some way.

Then he let his hands fall to his side, but he didn't step back. He should have stepped back so she couldn't touch him again, but he didn't. He couldn't quite bring himself to do that either.

"Tell me what happened," he said.

And so she did.

Chapter 37

THE THING THAT STRUCK HER WAS HOW LITTLE BLUE looked like that image that she had seen in her bedroom. She had noticed the difference before, but it was clearer now. Blue was big and solid and handsome and strong, and putting her head against his shoulder seemed like the most natural thing in the world.

Hugging him had been a spontaneous reaction: she had been so relieved to see him, so relieved that he looked different from the thing that had been inside her house, so relieved that he was clearly *him* that she felt an odd joy when she saw him.

Then she turned around and saw his face, the surprise on it, the vulnerable look, a window right down into him, and she realized that he probably couldn't remember the last time someone hugged him.

So she told him the truth, that she had been *relieved* to see him, although she hadn't told him the whole truth, which was that she was happy to see him too, that she had actually needed him beside her for this—and that word "need," that word startled her a bit too.

He had blinked twice, then taken a deep breath, all the while clearly struggling for control of his face. He got it, but he didn't have control of his hands. They had fallen to her shoulders, brushing them lightly, before he let them drop to his side.

His hands wanted to touch her—gently—and he

hadn't wanted to let them, so he had clearly compromised. He had touched her just so briefly that he probably hoped she hadn't noticed.

She had noticed. How could she not when the slightest brush against his skin sent a tingle through her?

He wanted to know what happened, and she turned toward the sliding glass doors, explaining everything, but she refused to move away from him. She almost wanted to lean against him as she spoke. She needed the reassurance.

That thing—that creature—had frightened her. The fact that it had actual substance frightened her more. And the fact that it had somehow crashed through her sliding glass window soundlessly terrified her.

Blue put a hand against the small of her back, sending another of those tingles through her. Then he gently moved her to one side as he stepped past her.

He didn't make it to the pool. One of the techs Selda had sent had installed an invisible crime scene barrier around the pool, the sliding glass doors—hell, probably the entire house. Jodi didn't know, and she tried to pretend she wasn't angry about that. It was her house after all.

But her house had been violated.

Still, the crime scene barrier was see-through, and Blue, after he bumped against it, peered through it like a kid looking at a carnival ride that his parents had forbidden him to go on.

Then he came back to her, his gaze on hers as he walked. She could still feel the light pressure of his hand against her back, the impression of his muscular chest against her cheek. She wanted to touch her face like a giddy schoolgirl, but she didn't.

It's relief, she told herself. *Just relief.*

But she didn't believe it. She was falling for him. Whether it was the mythical charm or the fact that he had been so hurt for so long and he had stood up so well against it, or maybe she was just plain lonely or— heaven forbid—maybe there was something about him.

If it was something about him, the real him, that deep down man that he had kept hidden, then she was doomed. Not doomed to die like his other fiancées had, but doomed to love him, and she didn't want to love him.

She didn't want to love anyone.

She liked her independence. The relationships she had tried in the past had never worked because she had been too independent, too disengaged. Too strong.

And up until this moment, she had been the strong one with Blue too.

"You didn't hear the glass breaking," Blue repeated, as if he was trying to get that fact in his head.

"I ran out front," she said. "I didn't hear the glass shattering. You'd think I should have heard the glass shattering."

"You'd think." He looked over his shoulder, a frown on his face. This time he didn't clarify that the creature/ image/thingie had looked like him. Apparently he saw that as a given now. "You came out through the door, and you closed the door behind you."

"I didn't close it," Jodi said. "That implies a careful movement. I pulled it open and then pushed it shut, a movement I had done—slower—countless times before."

In fact, in her memory, she could actually hear the sound of the door whooshing open and then closed along its slider, then the slight bang as it shut.

Blue sighed and looked over his shoulder, as if he could get more answers from that door itself.

"Well, that solves one thing," Blue said.

"What's that?" Jodi asked.

He didn't look at her right away. The setting sun caught his jaw and illuminated his face, and she suddenly saw just how classically handsome he was. Like a painting, not a painting of a young man, not a fashionable image of someone starting out. A painting of a man in power, a man making a decision, a true man, an adult who knew how the world worked and had an idea how to make it work for him.

Then that moment passed, and he looked at her.

His eyes were sad, and the corners of his mouth tightened.

"How all those women died," he said softly, and then turned back toward the door.

Jodi almost asked what he meant, and then she realized exactly what he meant. The women hadn't died from some vision that somehow erased them or caused their hearts to stop. They'd been murdered. Horribly murdered, with pain and loss and violence.

The magic had become real, just like it had in her room, and that was something awful.

"This is moving incredibly fast though, don't you think?" she asked him.

He frowned slightly, as if her question surprised him. Then the frown cleared. She wondered what he had thought: Was he thinking she had meant the hug? She hadn't, although her feelings for him were stronger than she wanted them to be, and they had become strong faster than she wanted them to.

"I mean," she said, because she suddenly felt the need

to clarify, "if we can believe the news reports, it takes the Fairy Tale Stalker weeks to visit his victims again."

"Victims," Blue repeated, as if the word bothered him.

She supposed it did, on some level, because she was wrong: the Fairy Tale Stalker himself didn't have victims. The curse did.

"Yes," he said. "If you compare this to the Fairy Tale Stalker case, this is moving a lot faster. But if you look at what happened in my past, it's right on pace."

Her stomach clenched. If it was right on pace, then she was in even more trouble than she thought. Because those women ended up dead.

"You remember now?" she asked.

"I thought I had misremembered," he said. "When you drink as much as I did, you have to figure—*I* have to figure—that I did a lot of damage to my memory. But apparently I didn't do as much as I thought. So, yes, that's a long way of saying I'm beginning to trust my memories more and more."

"And what do you remember?" Jodi asked softly.

But apparently not softly enough. Because suddenly Tank was hovering over them, as if she had a right to this information. Maybe she did.

What maybe? Of course she did. She was, theoretically, Jodi's client.

Blue glanced at Tank, gave her a small smile of welcome, then returned his attention to Jodi.

"It took about five days," he said. "But that's from my perspective. Five days from a conversation about some inappropriate flirtation in her bedroom to my finding her… head… in that room."

His voice wobbled at the end of that. Tank flew lower

and peered at him. Jodi recognized that look. Tank wanted to ask a question.

But so did Jodi, and she butted in first.

"A room?" she asked.

"Oh, yeah," he said. "That part of the fairy tale is true. All of the—oh God, you know. They were in a room, on frickin' pedestals, with scarves beneath them, like a display of marble sculptures. Only these weren't marble."

"Scarves?" Jodi asked as Tank asked, "Was there blood?"

"Yes, scarves," Blue said to Jodi, and then he looked at Tank. "And no, there was no blood in the room. In my memory, though…"

He let his voice trail off.

That seemed odd to Jodi. "Not even dried blood?"

There would have to be. Given the technology at the time, it would have been impossible to sever a head without sawing it off, leaving a lot of mess and blood. It would have taken magic to make those heads look like sculptures.

Tank had moved down far enough to peer at Jodi. Clearly this had Tank's attention as well.

"No blood that I could see," Blue said, "but as I said, there were scarves."

"So where were you an hour ago?" That was a new voice.

Jodi turned. Selda was striding across the far side of the pool, clearly going around the invisible crime scene barrier. She was wearing sweats, which Jodi had never seen her in before, and her hair was pulled away from her face. It took Jodi a minute to realize that Selda probably thought this was crime scene attire.

Selda hadn't been speaking to Jodi. She was speaking to Blue.

He turned, slowly, reluctantly (unless Jodi missed her guess), and said, "I was in my new apartment. If you don't believe me, ask Gunther. Or look at the video Jodi made of my every move."

Her breath caught. How had he known?

He gave her a sideways smile, as if she had asked the question out loud. "You didn't think I'd miss the cameras, did you?"

"Yes," she said. "I did. No one else knows about them."

Not that she spied on everyone who lived in the complex. Most of the apartments had no tech at all. But that one did. It was the place she put potential clients who might cause some kind of trouble.

She didn't think Blue would cause problems, but she wanted a record of where he was if that creature/image/thing had showed up again. Which it had.

He let out a small chuckle, quiet, as if it was just for her. "I didn't see them either. But they make sense."

She wanted to whack him on the arm playfully, the way that friends did when something happened between them. But she restrained herself.

Selda saw the interchange, however. Selda didn't miss much.

"Well, good," Selda said, still speaking to Blue. "Because I really didn't want this to be something you caused."

"Technically," he said. "It wouldn't have happened if I hadn't noticed Jodi—"

"Save it," Selda said impatiently. "This is beyond goo-goo-eyed looks and hints of attraction. This is something big. Curses shouldn't become corporeal, and this one has. I had hoped, when Jodi told me that she thought this was a curse, that everything existed in your imagination, Blue. But it doesn't."

Blue stood up straighter, putting his shoulders back. "My imagination?"

His voice had grown softer, but it held a bit of anger. Of course, Selda didn't seem to notice.

"Yes, your imagination," Selda said. "That's how most curses work. They manipulate the reality of the cursed, but everyone else is left alone."

"Those women died," Blue said, his voice even softer.

"Oh, that's the first thing I checked," Selda said. "And yes, they're gone, and you're not the only one who saw their remains."

Blue nodded. "I told you that."

"And you're the one who is at the center of this," Selda said. "So forgive me if I didn't believe the entire story without doing a little digging."

She had an edge to her voice now as well. She and Blue really didn't like each other.

"Forgive you," Blue repeated softly, with just a hint of sarcasm. "Yeah, I suppose I could forgive you."

Jodi's stomach twisted. She didn't want these two to fight. She couldn't have them fight and help Blue. Or herself, for that matter.

"This curse, Blue's curse," she said to Selda, "it seems to be on a faster track than the Fairy Tale Stalker's curse."

"Yes, I've noticed that," Selda said. "I'm thinking that perhaps it's a different cursecaster."

"No," Blue said with confidence. "It's the same one."

Jodi looked at him. His jaw was set. "How do you know?"

"I spent the afternoon on this," he said to her, not looking at Selda at all. "And I found a couple of things.

First, as far as I can tell, the new curse isn't that much different from mine."

"It's happening slower," Jodi said.

"Which is the sign of a cursecaster in control of his magic," Blue said. "Early curses are often too strong."

Selda made a small sound. Jodi looked over at her. Selda nodded slightly. "I hadn't thought of that," she said.

"And secondly, the curse is still focused on me," Blue said. "It's personal against me."

"And you are, of course, the center of the universe," Selda said.

Jodi felt a surge of anger, but she tamped it down. She had never seen Selda like this.

"No, he has a point," Jodi said. "The image, it mentioned Bluebeard more than once."

"So?" Selda said.

"So," Blue said softly. "I'm in LA. I never advertise my presence anywhere, and no one bothered me for a long time. I disappeared. But in the last decade or so, I got lonely and I got drunk, so I went to parties when I was drunk—"

"I know," Selda muttered.

"—and people noticed me. I suppose the word would have gotten back to the Kingdoms that I was still alive. But from this cursecaster's point of view, I had circumvented the curse somehow. He wanted me to get in trouble again. He sent someone out to be me so I would get arrested, or something worse."

"Put to death," Selda said.

Jodi shook her head. "It takes years for mortals to catch someone and at least a decade after that to execute anyone."

"And I'm supposed to know that how?" Selda said. Which was a good point. If Selda, who had lived here for decades, didn't know it, then how was some curse-caster who had one foot still in the Kingdoms supposed to know? Most of the magical who came here from the Kingdoms never really did understand how mortals conducted their business and, more to the point, never really tried.

"But if he wanted to kill you," Selda said, "why didn't he just get it over with? He has the magic power to kill the women."

Blue shrugged. "You understand magic better than I do."

Selda frowned and looked at Jodi. Jodi opened her hands. "I specialize in white magic."

"So do I," Selda said, as if they were blaming her for the bad stuff. Which they weren't.

Jodi didn't know how to avoid the toxic relationship between Blue and Selda. In fact, she wanted to fix it, but she also knew that wasn't something she could focus on right now.

Sometimes that fixer part of her got in the way.

"All of this arguing, of course, is ridiculous," Selda said as if she wasn't a part of it. She must have seen the expression on Jodi's face. "Our concern is this curse or whatever it is. It's dangerous, and its next victim is clearly going to be Jodi, unless we figure out what to do next."

"Is that why you brought out the big guns?" Blue asked, nodding toward all the activity around Jodi's sliding glass doors.

"Those aren't a protection detail," Selda said as if Blue was stupid. "That's the magical crime scene folks."

"I know," Blue said in that soft sarcastic tone again.

"Magic leaves evidence—traces, if you will," Selda said. "Those traces will take us back to the cursecaster. But it'll take time."

"How much time?" Jodi asked.

Selda shrugged, looking over her shoulder at the increasing number of workers, all of them consulting about each small detail.

"A while," she said.

"We don't have a while," Blue said. "This part of the curse, my part, will be over in days."

Fortunately, he didn't say Jodi would be dead in days, because that would sound bad, particularly considering the mood Selda was in. Selda might take it as a threat.

"I have no idea how long this will take," Selda said, looking at Jodi. Did Jodi see an apology in her eyes? Worry? Jodi wasn't sure. "But I thought it was our best bet."

"It'll help you catch this cursecaster," Jodi said.

"But it won't help Jodi," Blue said.

"Well, then, it's settled," Tank said, lowering herself so that she was between the three of them. Tank's wings were beating so hard that she actually had achieved that buzz that hummingbirds had.

Jodi had actually forgotten that Tank was hovering near the conversation. But now that Tank had inserted herself in it, Jodi wouldn't have been surprised if Tank just contributed a bit of sarcasm: *Settled that Jodi must sacrifice herself to keep your stupid schedule, Selda*.

Of course, that wasn't Tank's thought. That was Jodi's. She tried to keep the bitterness off her face. Apparently she was on her own on this one.

"What's settled?" Jodi asked.

"You'll just have to stay with Blue," Tank said, and it took Jodi a moment to realize that Tank was talking to her.

"What?" Jodi asked.

"Well, you can't go back in the house, right? Because it's a crime scene." Tank whirled so that the "right?" was directed at Selda. Then she whirled back to Jodi. "And it's pretty clear that you shouldn't be left alone."

"Yes, but Tank, I'm sure there are people who can actually protect Jodi," Blue said. "People with real magic."

Apparently he didn't think his charm magic was real. Jodi noted that in passing as this conversation continued to spin out of control.

"But others can't protect her as well as you can, Blue," Tank said.

Blue and Selda started to protest, but Tank waved a small hand at them.

"Read the fairy tales, consult your memory, whatever you need to do," Tank said, "because it's pretty clear to me that none of those women died when they were with Blue."

Jodi's breath caught. Tank was right. The women had died away from Blue—away from anyone, if her experience was anything to go by. Alone, asleep, and vulnerable.

"That can't be true," Blue said. "I saw them die."

"Magical memories, remember?" Tank asked. "You have images inserted into your brain of killing them. But you didn't do it."

Blue looked at Jodi. Something in his eyes pleaded with her. It was too much for him; he clearly didn't understand it all.

"Brilliant," Selda said to Tank. "I hadn't thought of that, but it's true. You can protect her best, Blue."

Blue shook his head. Jodi put her hand on his arm.

"The curse wouldn't have worked if you had been with them," she said. "You would have known that you weren't the one hurting them."

His mouth was open slightly, the now-familiar frown between his eyes deeper than it had been before.

"What if I *am* hurting you?" he whispered.

"You're not," Tank said, ruining the moment. "Otherwise there wouldn't be images of you doing something else at the time. I've known you a long time, Blue, and a technical wizard you're not."

His gaze didn't leave Jodi's. She could feel his fear. He didn't trust himself, and why should he? Not after all of those years believing the worst.

Even if Tank's idea was wrong, even if the curse could be activated with Blue in the room, it would still be better to be at his side than to leave him alone with his personal demons. Because he needed to see that the curse had nothing to do with him. Well, it had a lot to do with him, but he wasn't the one harming people.

He needed real confirmation of that.

"I think it's a brilliant idea," Jodi said. "And since I can't go into my house anyway, I need a place to kick off my shoes and relax. Your apartment is perfect for that."

"You don't have any clothes," Blue said, clearly grappling for an excuse to keep her away.

"True enough," Jodi said with a smile. "But that's what stores are for."

Then she turned to Selda, who was watching their interaction with something like disbelief. Or maybe it was disgust. Jodi couldn't tell, and she didn't want to tell.

"Can you do something to get these people to hurry?" Jodi asked. "Because we don't have a lot of time here."

Selda nodded. "I'll do what I can. But magic does what it does.'"

"Then find someone to break the curse," Tank said.

"I'm working on that too," Selda said. The harsh expression left her face. She reached out to Blue almost, but not quite, touching his arm. "Keep her safe."

"Yes, ma'am," he said with a bit of wonder. "You can bet everything that I will."

Chapter 38

Yes, ma'am. He had sounded so sincere. *You can bet everything that I will.* Keep Jodi safe. Him, Bluebeard. The first mass murderer of all time.

The first serial killer, in modern parlance.

Everyone else believed he was cursed. He did too, intellectually. But now Jodi was gambling her life on it, and he didn't want that.

He didn't know how to get out of it, though.

He thought about ways to get out of it the entire time that Jodi drove him around Larchmont Village, stopping frequently to dash in and out of boutiques. First, she picked up shoes, which surprised him. Stores he had gone into barefoot (and drunk) had always used the lack of shoes to kick him out.

Mostly, though, she picked up clothes that were on hold for her, or things in her size that she passed on the way to the checkout. The sales associates all seemed to know her and seemed to be prepared for her arrival.

It wasn't until Jodi hit the third store that Blue realized this was how she always shopped: the associates held clothing for her until her next arrival, and then she sorted through it.

Each stop in each store lasted no longer than ten minutes.

Still, he was flagging by the time she ordered two take-out pizzas at a pizzeria with one of those "Best in LA" stickers on its window. He expected something foo-foo, but the pies in their cardboard boxes smelled of tomato and mozzarella and garlic.

His stomach growled. He was hungry, and he hadn't realized it. He had been thinking too hard, still trying to find a way to stay away from her and yet keep her safe.

He intellectually believed that Tank's conclusion was the correct one: No one would hurt Jodi while she was with him. But he had thought of himself as a monster for so long—untrustworthy, difficult—that he worried he *would* be the one to hurt her.

The back of the convertible was filled with shopping bags, pizza, and some real food from a trendy deli, so that they would have breakfast and lunch for the next day, or so Jodi said.

She seemed to be in her element, shopping and organizing, as if nothing had happened to her at all.

Maybe that was how she coped. But it seemed strange to him. He was still shaken by the strange scene at her house. And then he felt guilty as they pulled up at the apartment complex, parking next to Marilyn's blue convertible.

It surprised him that the motley little group had returned to the complex. He wondered when they had done that. He wondered if they had waited for him at Jodi's house.

"I should have told them I was leaving," Blue said.

Jodi smiled at him. "I took care of it," she said.

She gave him the pizzas and the bags from the deli. She carried her clothing bags, looking lost beneath the piles of stuff.

Somehow she had managed to drive all over one section of Los Angeles, get food, get clothing, and get takeout all in the space of an hour. That had to have something to do with her magic, because he didn't believe it possible without magic.

Even though she had keys, she let him flounder for his in front of the apartment. He set the food bags down, adjusted the pizza boxes, and reached into his pocket—as the door opened.

He let out a yelp. A young man with black curls stood there. He wore a shiny silver suit and, unless Blue missed his guess, eyeliner. (What did they call that? Guyliner? Blue had never ever seen it before. At least not up close. It was hard to avoid such things in LA, after all.)

"Who the hell are you?" Blue snapped, not sounding as fierce as he wanted to. At least he hadn't tossed the pizza boxes into the air in surprise. He probably should set them down, however.

Although, the man with the guyliner didn't look that threatening. In fact, Blue had a hunch he could take the guy with a single shove backward.

"I could ask the same of you, except that I know who you are," the man said. "You're our new tenant, Mr. Franklin."

Then, as Blue was processing "our new tenant," trying to figure out if this guy was part of the rental staff, and if Blue had actually met him and didn't remember (how could he forget someone like this?), the guy looked over Blue's shoulder at Jodi and mouthed *Pretty*.

Blue frowned. What the hell?

Jodi laughed, which surprised Blue, and said, "Stop it, Ramon. Help us with these packages, would you?"

Ramon? The Ramon of the organized papers and the purple pen? Somehow that made sense.

Ramon took the bags off the stoop and carried them into the kitchen, putting everything away without being asked.

Blue set the pizza boxes down on the kitchen table, and immediately Ramon moved them to the kitchen counter, taking down plates (who ate pizza with plates?) and pulling out a bottled water.

Jodi brought her own shopping bags inside and carried them into the bedroom, without asking, making Blue's stomach clench. He hadn't figured on her sleeping in there. In fact, he hadn't thought of the sleeping arrangements at all. The couch didn't look long enough for him.

"I see you brought some clothes," Jodi said, and Blue's frown deepened. Of course he had. She had seen his leather bag. He'd dutifully hung up his belongings at the beginning of his long afternoon, and that had taken all of five minutes.

"I figured you'd need something to wear since they've closed you out of the house," Ramon said from the kitchen. "I didn't expect you to clean out Rodeo Drive."

Jodi laughed. "I didn't go to Rodeo."

Blue let out a small sigh. Jodi had been talking to Ramon, not to Blue. She had used that same familiar tone she used with him. So this was how she treated her friends. Then Blue shook his head slightly. He didn't consider himself a friend.

How she treated people she liked, then. That was how she treated people she liked. And even that thought boggled his mind.

Ramon came into the living room, handed Blue a cold bottle of water, and kept one for himself. Blue felt overrun, and self-conscious, and nervous.

What was he supposed to do? He actually had to fall back on advice from Dr. Hargrove. When in doubt, remember your manners.

"I'm sorry," Blue said, extending his right hand. "We haven't been formally introduced. I'm John Franklin, but my friends call me Blue."

Ramon took his hand and didn't shake it. Instead he held it lightly, his eyes twinkling. "I can see why they call you Blue. Those eyes of yours are something. Aren't they something, Jodi?"

"He's not your type, Ramon," Jodi said from the bedroom.

"Why don't you let him tell me that," Ramon said. Then, softer to Blue, "Please don't tell me that."

No one had flirted this outrageously with Blue in years.

"Sorry," Blue said again, glancing at the bedroom, not sure why he was continually apologizing to this man. "I'm afraid that's true."

"Ah," Ramon said like a man used to rejection. Then he turned his head, looked at Blue out of the corner of his eye, and dramatically turned his head toward the bedroom. His lips pursed just a little, and he said, "Oh. *Really*?"

Blue blushed. He hadn't blushed in years. He couldn't remember the last time. He hadn't meant to reveal his interest in Jodi. He didn't have a right to be interested in Jodi. He didn't have a right to be interested in anyone.

Ramon looked pointedly at the bedroom again, then leaned toward Blue. Ramon still hadn't let go of Blue's hand.

"Our Jodes," Ramon said in a tone so soft that Jodi

couldn't hear, "is terribly picky. So if she gives you trouble, you tell her to talk to me. I won't change her mind, but I will step in on any missed date. I don't mind expensive food and a chance to dress up."

Blue laughed in spite of himself. Ramon patted their clenched hands with his free hand, then let go.

"Seriously," Ramon said, losing the air of flirtatiousness. "I'm a matchmaker from way back and a firm believer in true love. If you're right for Jodi, I'll do everything in my power to make sure the magic happens."

Blue clutched the cool bottle of water like a lifeline. This conversation made no sense to him. He didn't know what, if anything, led Ramon to that true love assumption. Maybe it was just Ramon's own attraction to Blue. Maybe it was the way Ramon always spoke to the men in Jodi's life.

"What are you doing?" Jodi said as she came out of the bedroom. She had changed into a pair of jeans and a light green top. Her feet were bare again, but her toenails were painted a glittery silver. She looked better than she had all day.

"I'm telling Blue how available you are," Ramon said.

Jodi rolled her eyes. "Ramon believes that I should find a nice man and settle down. Maybe then I won't work him as hard."

"I do *not*," Ramon said. "I don't like how lonely you are, that's all. And you shouldn't let this man go. He's a Greek god."

"Actually, I'm not," Blue said with more seriousness than he had planned.

"Oh, that's right," Ramon said, waving a hand. "I

would see sparkles of weird magic if you were. Although I am seeing magic sparkles, aren't I, Jodi?"

Blue swallowed hard. He had no sense that Ramon was one of the magical, so this conversation had taken an even odder turn.

"You are," Jodi said. "Blue has charm magic, which is why you think he's perfect for me."

"Ooooh," Ramon said, raising his eyebrows in mock surprise. "You're one of the Prince Charmings. How marvelous. I've met Cinderella's, you know. He has a bookstore in Westwood."

"I know," Blue said, not willing to say any more.

"So," Ramon said, "which one are you?"

Blue gave him a tight smile, hoping the man wouldn't push anymore. "I'm one of the insignificant ones."

"Really?" Ramon said. "There are insignificant Prince Charmings?"

"Ramon," Jodi said, sliding her arm through his, much as she had done with Blue earlier. "I appreciate the clothes, but what are you doing here, besides mooching our pizza?"

"To mooch, my friend, means we must eat." Ramon put a hand over hers and walked into the kitchen. Blue followed, feeling like the odd man out. "So you get the food, and I will tell you all of my little secrets."

"Not all," Jodi said as she sat at the table. "Please."

Blue sat across from her, and Ramon put pizza slices on plates in front of them, along with some silverware. Even though Blue was trying his best to be polite, he had never in his life eaten pizza with silverware.

He put his water down and stared at the pizza. He had been hungry. Now that hunger was a distant memory.

"*I*," Ramon said with emphasis, as he sat with his own piece of pizza at the head of the table, "have all kinds of news."

"I hope it's important," Jodi said. "It's already been a very long day."

And a confusing one. Blue had had no idea, when he woke up the day before, that he would end up here on this night. It almost made him nervous to go to sleep later—that is, if he and Jodi could work out the issues with the bed.

And he blushed again.

Fortunately, no one was looking at him.

"Of course it's important," Ramon said. "Do you think I'd crash your little love nest if it wasn't important?"

"Ramon," Jodi said tiredly.

"Yes, well," Ramon said, sliding his plate around. "I do hope you're still interested in our friend the Fairy Tale Stalker."

Suddenly Blue snapped awake. So did Jodi. They both stared at Ramon.

"What about him?" Jodi asked.

"I think I know where to find him," Ramon said. "And I did it all without any hocus-pocus. Are you proud of me?"

Chapter 39

"Proud of you?" Jodi exclaimed. "My God, Ramon, I could kiss you."

Blue profoundly hoped that she wouldn't. He still hadn't completely figured out exactly what her relationship with Ramon was, or who this Ramon really was, or even if he had magic. (It didn't seem like he had magic.)

"No need to make the handsome Blue jealous," Ramon said, his eyes twinkling. Blue started. It unnerved him how clearly this man saw him.

"Ramon, you're teasing," Jodi said, setting her plate aside and leaning toward him. "Tell us what's going on."

"Only if you eat," Ramon said. "Good pizza going cold."

Jodi rolled her eyes at him again, then picked up her plate and moved it back in front of her. Blue took a dutiful bite of the pizza, and the burst of tomato, spices, and garlic brought his hunger back. He glanced at Ramon and found himself wondering who really had the domestic/fixer magic, Ramon or Jodi.

Jodi took a very obvious bite of pizza. Ramon nodded, as if he approved, then he said, "You had me look up all of this information on the Fairy Tale Stalker, I assume for Mr. Blue here, because if he's like you, then technology is not his friend."

Blue smiled, just a little. Ramon smiled back. So apparently Ramon was the assistant Jodi had mentioned, the one who did all the scut work for her office. That answered one question.

"Then today," Ramon continued, "you said that you would need to do some research into this stalker just to see if you could find him, but you weren't sure how or when you would have the time."

Jodi put the heel of her hand against her forehead. "I barely remember that. The afternoon was a nightmare."

"Not counting the actual nightmare," Blue said softly.

Ramon looked at both of them, eyebrows raised. "Uh, huh," he said. "Right. No interest at all."

Jodi glared at him.

He smiled at her and said brightly, "So, you know me, I was thinking how do I take that pressure off you? So I looked through all of that material I downloaded for you and I ran an in-kind search to see if I could find the names of the women—"

"I thought news outlets don't use the names of women who've been sexually assault," Jodi said.

"*News outlets* don't," Ramon said, "but police calls do. And since small towns have police blotters, I figured larger towns did as well, the difference being that the larger town police blotters aren't reprinted whole-hog in a cheesy advertising mailer masquerading as a newspaper."

Now Ramon had Blue's full attention.

"You didn't hack into the LAPD, did you?" Jodi asked.

Ramon smiled widely. "Hack? No. I may have misidentified myself, however, just once or twice in my quest for court filings, *not* that there were any court filings, since no one knew who to press charges against. But the news stories had the times of day, and the police blotter had the times of day and the divisions and the addresses that the police went to, and home ownership is a matter of public record, and a surprising number of these women owned their homes, so I was able to get names."

"I can't believe you did this," Jodi said, sounding a little appalled.

Blue was in awe. He would have no idea how to do any of it. He was beginning to understand why Jodi had hired such a strong personality as an assistant.

"And once I had the names, I went to Facebook to see if they had any friends in common, and sadly, they didn't, but they did have work in common."

Both Jodi and Blue were staring at him now. Jodi hadn't had a bite of her pizza since that ostentatious one, but Blue had finished his piece. He was still hungry, but he didn't get up to get another. He was too riveted by this.

"They were all assistants of various levels at several different studios," Ramon said.

"How is that work in common?" Blue asked.

"Ah, the same position, different titles in different places of employment," Ramon said. "Very important. They were, essentially, either working for or in charge of casting—not the high-level Brad Pitt kind of casting, but the extras, the walk-ons, the bit parts. These women carried clipboards and assessed anyone who walked through the door. They had to be attractive women because—hello!—this is Hollywood, but not so stunningly attractive that they would make the talent nervous because—hello!—this is Hollywood."

"Oh my God," Jodi said. "And he's one of us."

Ramon grinned at her. "That's right. Our FTS is one of us."

Blue couldn't sit any longer. He got up to get his next slice of pizza. "And that's important how?"

"I'm the one who handles ninety percent of the hires of the magical in Hollywood," Jodi said. "They might not come to me first, they might have mortal managers or important agents, but those high-powered pricey types come to me whenever things get a bit—well, one of them described it as 'too woo-woo' for him. Things that they can't explain they dump on me. And most of what our people do no one outside of our little world can explain."

Blue picked up the entire pizza box and moved it to the table, mostly to mask his own nerves. Then he sat down again and took two pieces. Ramon took another.

"You know the stalker, then?" Blue asked.

He couldn't understand, if the Fairy Tale Stalker had met Jodi, how come the stalker hadn't targeted her. Then, for a brief second, Blue wondered if the curse problems Jodi had came from the Fairy Tale Stalker. But Blue immediately rejected that. If she had been noticed by the Fairy Tale Stalker, then she would be seeing that guy and not Blue.

"I don't know if I know him," Jodi said. Then she looked at Ramon. "Do I know him?"

"You met him once, shortly after he arrived," Ramon said. "You thought he looked and acted normal enough to follow traditional lines of employment. You hooked him up with one of the major talent agencies in town, super-vised the meet like you always do, and then let everyone know if there was a problem, they should come to you."

"Has anyone come to me?" Jodi asked, sounding just a bit nervous.

"No," Ramon said. "And it was nearly a year ago.

This guy is unbelievably normal, good-looking enough to get cast, and from what I put down in your notes, has a mild amount of charm magic."

Jodi looked at Blue. "That can't be a coincidence," she said.

"How do you know you have the right man?" Blue asked. A lot of people from the Kingdoms had a bit of charm magic combined with other magic. Some of the Prince Charmings had a lot of other magic. Sleeping Beauty's Prince Charming, Alex Blackstone, had oodles and oodles of magic and wasn't above using it—he had, in fact, used it for centuries.

Blue had always wondered what he would have done if his magic had extended beyond charm. He always thought he could have spelled himself to control himself—no alcohol, no outside influence. But of course, he had it wrong. He hadn't known what caused the problem, and even with all of that magic, a self-cast spell wouldn't have worked against a curse.

"I know I have the right man because of police sketches and head shots," Ramon said. "Let me show you."

He got up and went into the living room. Jodi used the break to finish her piece of pizza and take another. Blue finished his pieces as well.

Ramon came back with a manila folder. He went to the side of the table that didn't have pizza or plates and spread some images across the tabletop.

"I searched through our system by description," he said. "And I modified by timeline. So they said that he had dark hair, so I eliminated all of the blonds, you get the idea. Now, come over here."

Blue wiped the grease off his hands with his napkin

as he walked over to that part of the table. Jodi brought
her plate, eating that other piece of pizza. She clearly
had realized how hungry she was.

"These are the police sketches," Ramon said, pushing
three pieces of paper down to the edge of the table.

Blue recognized them. He'd been staring at them for
hours the night before. The dark hair, the narrow mouth.
The man didn't look ordinary, but he wasn't that distinctive either. He was, if Blue had to describe him, very
Hollywood attractive. Square-jawed, high cheekbones,
broad forehead.

"And these," Ramon said with a flourish, "are the
head shots."

Jodi gasped beside Blue, and Blue didn't blame her.
It was almost as if the police artist had used the professional photographs as a template for the sketches. The
photographs were softer—the Fairy Tale Stalker had
been trying to get work, not look menacing—but they
were so similar that there was no doubt.

The black-and-white stills were the most damning.
They looked just like the sketches. The color photographs made the Fairy Tale Stalker a bit more human to
Blue. The man's skin tone was a bit uneven—probably
because like most people from the Kingdoms, he wasn't
used to LA's level of sunshine—and he didn't quite
seem comfortable in his open-collared shirt. His smile
was a bit hesitant, his eyes a little worried, and those
details alone probably made it hard for him to get work,
what with all the other beautiful people descending on
this city each and every day.

Jodi wiped her hand on the leg of her jeans, and then
picked up one of the head shots. She flipped it over.

"Gregory Shea," she said, "and he has a Hollywood address, with a landline. How very not-LA."

"I already called the landline," Ramon said. "It's been disconnected."

"Of course it has," Blue said, peering over Jodi's shoulder at the little white label of information behind the photograph. The man's name, his address, his phone number, and the name of his representation. "Gregory Shea can't be his real name."

"I'm sure it's not," Jodi said.

"It's not," Ramon said, "But I've never heard of him. I've got his real name in the file somewhere. He's like seventieth to the throne in one of the minor Kingdoms."

Blue couldn't take it anymore. He had no idea how someone mortal knew all of this. If, indeed, Ramon was mortal.

"I get no sense of magic from you," Blue said to Ramon.

"And that, my friend, is a tragedy," Ramon said, "because you and I could make beautiful magic together."

"The quote is music," Jodi said, still studying the photograph. "You would make beautiful *music* together. And really, Ramon, he's not your type."

"You know, usually you don't harp on that," Ramon said. "You let me figure it out for myself."

Jodi looked up, a bit of surprise on her face. "I do? Really? Well, I'm distracted."

Her cheeks had grown a bit pink. Or maybe Blue was imagining that. Maybe he wanted to imagine that.

Her gaze met his. The gaze looked steady, which Blue was most decidedly not feeling at the moment, not with her looking at him like that.

"Ramon can see magic," Jodi said, her tone

matter-of-fact, "because I needed him to see magic. He already had a small ability to see auras—there's someone magical in his past, and since what little magic he inherited had been overwhelmed many, many, many generations of mortals ago, I had to dig, find it, and enhanced that little bit."

"You make it sound like I'm so inept," Ramon said, a smile on his face. Then his smile faded, just a bit. "She also added some kind of spell so I can see Cantankerous Belle and all of her obnoxious little friends whom I refuse to call fairies."

"Not to mention that he can now see people like Gunther for what they actually are rather than how they present themselves to mortals," Jodi said, still turning the photograph over and over in her hand. She then leaned forward and compared it to the police sketches. Something was bothering her, but Blue couldn't tell what.

Nor did Blue know how Gunther appeared to mortals. He supposed that the selkie, the mermaid, Gunther, and all the others had to appear slightly differently to mortals, or mortals would know that magic walked among them. But he had never given it any thought before.

"That little magical boost does make me better at my job, which I appreciate," Ramon said. "It also gave me a few nightmares in the beginning when I realized that all of those things I'd seen out of the corner of my eye as a child were actually real and not the product of an overzealous imagination."

And there, most likely, was Blue's answer. But he didn't ask. He felt they were on enough of a sidetrack already. Still, he had one more question.

"I thought it was against the rules to let mortals see us for who we are," Blue said to Jodi.

She shrugged. "Rules within rules. It's hard for a chatelaine to work with other chatelaines, and I needed some kind of help. I thought of hiring someone with magic similar to mine, but it really worried me. I don't get along with other chatelaines. Apparently it's part of our magic. We're quite jealous of our turf."

Blue raised his eyebrows slightly. He couldn't quite imagine Jodi jealous.

"Really, though," she said, "what I needed was organization and street smarts, and mortals have that without the annoying competing magic thing. Ramon has it in spades."

"Thank you, milady," Ramon said, bowing just a little.

"Besides, if I hired someone magical, I couldn't do most of my job, given the prevalence of BlackBerries, iPads, computers, and technical equipment around Hollywood these days. We certainly wouldn't have all of this research right now." Jodi was still staring at the pictures.

"What's bothering you about these?" Blue asked her.

She picked up one of the head shots, studied it for a moment, and shook her head. "I don't remember him at all."

"Is that unusual?" Blue asked.

"I like to pride myself on a great memory," Jodi said as Ramon said, "No, it's not unusual."

Jodi gave him a playful glare, then slapped the head shot against the palm of her other hand. "All right. It's not unusual. Ramon does a lot to make sure I get a client's name right."

"And even then she misses," Ramon said in a stage whisper.

Blue was beginning to like the fondness the two of them seemed to have for each other.

"But this Gregory Shea has charm magic," Jodi said, "and the thing about Charmings, even minor ones, is that they're memorable. It's part of the charm. People don't forget you, do they, Blue?".

"I wish they would," he said, thinking of all the things he had done since coming to LA. Hell, all the things he'd done—or supposedly done—in the Kingdoms as well.

Jodi frowned. "It seems to me, though, that you weren't as memorable when you were drinking."

Blue gave a rueful smile. "I certainly hope not."

"Blue," Ramon said, "Blue, Blue, Blue... Blue! Oh my God! You're the Aqua Velva guy!"

Blue closed his eyes, then made himself smile. It was actually work to open his eyes and smile at that. "Yep. That was me."

"Smurf hair, blue velvet clothes even in the LA heat—you'd get stinko in more ways than one," Ramon said, eyes twinkling. "I had forgotten about you, and I certainly didn't find you charming. But you were—oh my God! Bluebeard, right?"

"Still am," Blue said.

Jodi moved closer to him, as if in comfort.

"Oh, yeah, not charming at all." Ramon said. "Not at *all*."

Then he turned toward Jodi, giving her a strange look. "*Bluebeard?*" he said. "Really?"

"The fairy tale has it wrong," Jodi said.

"Well, that's a relief," Ramon said. "So long as you're certain."

"I am," Jodi said.

Blue wished he was.

"Not memorable, though," Jodi said. "Except as a problem, that's what you're saying, right, Ramon?"

"Well, except in an oh-my-God-who-invited-*that*-guy kinda way," Ramon said. "As a charming, memorable, kiss-me-you-fool kinda way, *noooo*."

Blue gave him a sideways look. The kiss-me-you-fool comment made him uncomfortable. In the long-distant past when people were interested in him, they weren't so blatant about it. But he knew that modern culture had gotten crude.

Not that the culture he had grown up in hadn't been crude—it had in a variety of ways—but no one said such outrageous things to him, maybe because he was the king's son.

In fact, no one had been this outrageous with him ever.

"You know, really," Jodi said, "it shouldn't have been that easy for you to mask your charm. Your charm magic is extremely powerful. More so than most of the Charmings I've met."

Blue wanted to ask her if that was just because she was attracted to him, but he didn't dare, not for her, but because he didn't want to embarrass himself. He didn't want to seem vulnerable.

Or, at least, more vulnerable than he already was.

"And I didn't remember this Gregory." Jodi picked up the rest of the pictures, studying them. "I don't even sense charm coming from the photos and you'd think I would."

Ramon was watching her now, a small frown creasing his forehead.

"What if we have this wrong?" she said. "What if this isn't a curse?"

"Then you need to get the hell out of here," Blue said. He was shaking. He hadn't wanted it to be wrong. He wanted it to be a curse, and not something he did. He *needed* it to be a curse. He couldn't lose the hope that he was redeemable, not now, not after a chance had been dangled in front of him.

Jodi put a hand on his arm. "No, no, that's not what I mean."

Blue stood very still. He wasn't going to move away from her, but he wasn't going to encourage her either. And he was going to have to think of a way out of here, something that would keep them very separate. Something that would somehow protect her.

"I'm wondering if this is some kind of real spell, something that was supposed to neutralize charm."

It took him a moment to understand her. He had been thinking so hard of protecting her, he hadn't followed the tangent.

"Isn't a curse a real spell?" Ramon asked.

"It's different," Jodi said. "Sideways magic. And Selda is right. It shouldn't be able to become corporeal. But real spells have real effects, real power, depending on the caster, and they can get tangled up in an aura…"

She put her hands on Blue's shoulders and turned him toward her. He looked directly at her, his heart pounding. He found himself wishing that the higher powers he had learned about in rehab existed for him, wishing that he hadn't met so many of the minor (and major)

Greek gods, as well as some of the Egyptian deities, and the nutty Norse gods. If he hadn't met them, he would have been more inclined to believe in some of the other gods, the ones that seemed to help those he'd been in rehab with.

Or even if those gods hadn't helped, he might have tried to believe. Because right now, he wanted to be praying. He wanted to pray that Jodi found something, something that didn't blame him.

"Ramon, you look too," she said, letting her hands drop off Blue's shoulders and taking a step back.

Ramon stood beside her. They tilted their heads at him, like women watching a friend at a bridal fitting.

"I've never seen sparking like that," Ramon said. "Didn't I say that before?"

"You know," Jodi said, her head still tilted, "I hadn't either. And that's where I went wrong."

Blue regretted each piece of pizza. Because his stomach was twisting, and he felt queasy. "Wrong how?"

"I shouldn't have listened to Tank," Jodi said. "This is not a curse. This is one honking doozy of a spell, and it's getting all of its power from your magic."

"Great," Blue said wryly, or at least, he hoped it was wryly. Because he didn't feel wry. He felt scared to death. "I thought you said that spells deteriorate and curses don't."

"Well, technically, that's true, but this spell has to be extremely powerful to last centuries. You know, like that sleep spell that snared Emma Lost." Her frown got deeper.

He didn't know Emma Lost, but he'd heard the story. The spell she suffered sounded awful. He felt cold. "How do we neutralize the damn thing?"

Jodi crossed her arms, still clutching those photographs of the hapless Gregory. "I don't know yet," she said, "but I have a few ideas."

"What kind of ideas?" Blue asked.

"The kind that need to be explored through trial and error," Jodi said. "Which is why I need to find Gregory first."

Chapter 40

JODI HADN'T LOOKED AT BLUE'S AURA SINCE THAT morning, and it surprised her how much the aura had changed. He stood near the wall in the kitchen, looking like a neatly dressed model posing for an ad parodying a mug shot. His features were strained, his eyes haunted.

But she wasn't really looking at his face. His aura entranced her. The first time she had seen it, it had been a healthy blue, filled with charm magic. This morning, the blue still dominated, with the amber light reflecting off the edges, like heat lightning.

Now the amber light had made some headway into the blue, threading with it, making it look like someone had attached amber edges to blue thread. The amber still sparked, however, and it made fist-sized gray spots in Blue's aura.

"What *is* that?" Ramon asked.

"Magic being consumed too quickly," Jodi said.

"Can he feel that?" Ramon asked.

"Um, I'm right here," Blue said. "No need to discuss me in the third person."

"Well," Ramon said with a touch of impatience. "Can you?"

"I doubt it," Jodi said, answering for Blue, since he couldn't see his own aura and didn't know what they were talking about.

"If you're asking if I can feel my aura," Blue said, "of course I can't."

"I would think," Jodi said, "that it would feel more like a loss of magical power."

"If I had ever felt like I had magical power, then maybe I would feel it," Blue said. "But I never did, and I don't."

She nodded. She wasn't surprised at his response. This magic was parasitical. It fed off the victim's magic, which explained why the women around Blue saw the effects of the spell quicker than the women around a third-rate Charming from a fifth-rate Kingdom.

"You said you could find this Gregory Shea," Jodi said, turning her attention to Ramon. He had his head tilted too, and he looked as if he couldn't quite believe what he saw.

"Yeah," Blue said. "Then you tell us his landline is disconnected."

"Ah, fear not, pretty one," Ramon said, recovering. He was an outrageous flirt when he was attracted to someone, and usually that didn't bother the subject of his flirtation, but Blue looked a little nonplussed.

Of course, he had hid his extreme good looks under a rather hideous costume, so he hadn't been subjected to this kind of treatment from anyone in a long, long time.

In fact, way back when he last let himself look attractive, it had been illegal and dangerous for another man to express an interest this clearly, and women who talked like Ramon were considered to be little better than trash.

So probably Blue had never heard this kind of talk directed at him before. Jodi smiled in spite of herself.

"I am resourceful," Ramon said. "I looked in our

friend's file, found the name of his agent, and made a phone call."

Jodi's smile grew. This was why she adored Ramon. He made everything interesting, and he was competent.

"His agent did not know where he was, but the agent had the all-important cell phone number, which I have."

"I don't suppose you called it," Jodi said.

"What do I look like, a doofus?" Ramon said. "Of course I didn't call it. This man is feeling hounded and harassed. He wanted to go into the movie business or at least the TV business, so wherever he's holed up, he's watching all of this coverage of him and worried that someone will find him. So I'm sure he's not answering his phone."

"Even if his agent calls?" Jodi asked.

"It doesn't matter how strong his dreams are," Blue said. "He's seeing them disappear, and quickly. He's probably terrified of what he's done. The magic hasn't harmed anyone yet—hasn't *killed* anyone yet."

Jodi could see Blue correcting himself. She like that about him. He tried to use precise language, language that did not cut anyone any slack at all.

"So right now he thinks he's sleepwalking or sleep-driving or something. He's scared, but not that scared. Although he has a sense of how out of control this can be given the mention of me."

"Hmm, yes," Ramon said. "I wonder if he's doing that or if that's programmed in."

"No way to know," Jodi said. "The point is that he's scared and you said you know how to find him."

Ramon smiled. "No, I said I know where he is."

"Enough with the drama," Blue said. "Where is he?"

"He has been ordering takeout and it's been delivered to one of those rent-by-the-week places near LAX," Ramon said.

"How do you know that?" Blue asked. Jodi hadn't wanted to ask that part, because she had a hunch she knew the answer.

"Well, let's just say that cell phone records aren't as private as they should be," Ramon said, with a twinkle in his eye. He knew how uncomfortable his flirting was making Blue, and that only encouraged it.

"Okay," Blue said, sounding a bit confused. Clearly he didn't entirely understand what Ramon meant. But Jodi did.

Still, not understanding didn't stop Blue from asking the next question. "The takeout is important how?"

"Oh, you have to use a credit card if you don't show up in person, so I called about his usual time, ordered him some Chinese—his usual, and put it on the firm's card—sorry, Jodi."

"No, it's a business expense," she said, wondering if it was, and wondering if it really mattered.

"And then I had them double-check the address they had on file with me, and they did. Voila!" He handed a slip of paper to Jodi.

She looked at it. Her hand was shaking only slightly. Ramon was right. One of those rent-by-the-week places near LAX. Anonymous, but not that cheap. Apparently a third-rate Charming from a fifth-rate Kingdom had money, just like a lot of the other Charmings that came to LA. He probably thought he was slumming it. He wasn't as far gone as Blue had been, at least not yet.

"Great," Jodi said. "I have to pay him a visit."

Blue frowned at her. It was a magnificent frown, filled with disapproval and strength and all of that power that he usually didn't use. "*You* have to visit him?"

"Yes," she said, suddenly realizing why he had frowned.

"*We* have to visit him," Blue said. "I'm not leaving you alone."

She gave him her best dismissive smile. "You'll freak him out, Blue, especially when he realizes who you are. He's terrified of becoming you. For you to show up, well, that'll probably push him over whatever edge he's clinging to."

"So I'll go and soften the blow," Ramon said. "I want to see this guy again anyway."

Jodi turned to Ramon. "You remember him, don't you?"

Ramon shrugged. "He was pretty too, just not as pretty as your guy there."

"He's not my guy," Jodi said.

Blue blinked and looked down, as if her words had stung. Had they stung? She hadn't meant them to. She wasn't sure why they would sting. Blue liked her, but right now, any interest he had was just gratitude. When this all cleared up, he would find a woman worthy of him. A woman who was just as beautiful as he was, with just as much charm, who really did want a fairy tale—that happily-ever-after thing that Jodi read about in movie scripts and had never seen in real life.

Jodi wanted to get past this moment quickly.

"And as weird as this might sound, Ramon," she said, "I need you back at the office. I need you to monitor the police scanner to see if there are any more reports of the Fairy Tale Stalker. If there are, you have to call me immediately."

"What are you planning to do?" Blue asked.

"I figure this Shea guy is practice," Jodi said with more bravado than she felt.

"Practice for what?" Blue asked.

Practice for whom, Jodi almost said. But she caught herself. If she told him what she planned, he might try to stop her. And she didn't want him to do that.

"Let's not worry about that right now," she said in her most soothing tone. "Let's see if he is what we think he is."

"I don't like that answer," Blue said.

"How about we'll discuss what I'm about to do when and if I'm about to do it?" Jodi said.

"I don't like that much either," Blue said.

She sighed. "You don't have to like it. But if you're going to come along, you have to let me be in charge."

"Why does one of us have to be in charge?" Blue asked.

"Well, duh," Ramon said to Blue before Jodi could answer. "Because you're going with Jodi, of course."

"Of course," Blue said, his gaze on hers. The look was unsettling, and it wasn't until they were halfway to the car before she realized that he hadn't agreed to anything at all.

Chapter 41

THOSE RENT-BY-THE-WEEK PLACES NEAR THE AIRPORT all looked the same to Jodi. Square, ten-story complexes that looked like hotels that someone had stretched just a bit out of proportion. These places always had a little too much landscaping—a few too many trees, so that the parking lot was hard to see. The windows had that cross-hatching that was supposed to look like Tudor glass but managed to look like a cheap version of bars over the windows.

Gregory Shea had chosen one of the more upscale by-the-week places. It had a little courtyard entry, and the faux wood looked more expensive than the faux-wood at the other places.

Jodi didn't feel uncomfortable parking the convertible near the side of the building—there were good security lights, and a fence hidden by the bushes. There were visible security cameras as well, and a notice that some major security service patrolled the area. It was all designed to reassure, and it did.

It made her wonder if this place was the first step for Gregory in his downhill slide: he wanted a place where someone would observe him leaving to stalk the women, a place where someone would comment on his absence.

Then again, he might be one of those men who couldn't live without some kind of comfort.

She glanced at Blue who seemed very nervous. He

was looking at the security as well; in fact, he was giving the entire building a once-over. She couldn't tell what he was thinking, either. He had essentially stopped talking to her on the trip here, except to ask her plans one last time.

She wasn't exactly sure what those plans were. Some of what she wanted to do would depend on the Fairy Tale Stalker himself, and she told Blue that. He didn't like the answer.

She got out of the car as Blue did. She locked it, put the keys in her purse, and walked to the front entrance. Blue did not walk beside her. Instead he was scanning the building.

"Is this warded?" he asked her.

She shook her head. If this Gregory only had charm magic, he would have had to buy wards or to have been working with someone who could make them.

"Why?" she asked. "Did you think it would be warded the way the rehab center was?"

"Just curious," he said.

She opened the door to the lobby. It had a lot of plants, seating groups of leather furniture set off from each other by more plants, two walls of books that looked like leftovers from previous guests, and across the corridor, a small restaurant that appeared to be empty in the midafternoon.

It was almost impossible to see the reception desk at first glance. Apparently whoever owned this place wanted it to seem as much like a fancy apartment/condo setup as possible.

The reception desk was behind some of the fake trees and was smaller than Jodi expected. The desk was made of a dark wood, shiny with brass, and the man behind it looked like a manager of some kind.

She had hoped for a young assistant, someone who would be free with protocol.

Blue touched her arm as he, too, noted the front desk attendant. "Let me talk to him," he said softly.

"Blue," she said in protest, but he smiled at her ever so gently.

"Charm, remember?" he said just as softly.

He walked ahead of her to the desk. He extended his hand, called the man by name, and said, "Just the person I was hoping to see."

Jodi wasn't even sure how Blue knew the man's name until she caught up to him. Then she saw the man's name on a little gold name badge with the word "manager" underneath it.

She hadn't wanted to see the manager. She didn't like that idea at all. But Blue was smiling with him, joking lightly, something about the discomfort of being this close to LAX, and the man seemed relaxed.

"I have an unorthodox request," Blue said with the kind of confidence that Jodi had only seen in great actors. "My brother is registered here. He expects me tomorrow. I'm supposed to call him when I arrived from Baltimore, but I got here early, and I want to surprise him."

Then he put his arm around Jodi, startling her as he pulled her close. He smiled down at her, eyes warm. She liked this. She smiled back, in spite of herself.

"Actually," Blue said, "*we* want to surprise him. He doesn't know that I just got engaged, and honestly, I didn't want to play out the scene at the airport."

"I can understand that," the manager said. "It's nice

to see Mr. Shea's family. He's been looking a bit forlorn of late."

"He sounded down the last time I spoke with him," Blue said. "I don't want to call his cell, because then he'll know it's me. If you can just give me the number to dial on the house phone…"

"It's 9784," the manager said.

Blue's grip around Jodi tightened, and she smiled again. It wasn't hard to smile, given how savvy Blue was. She wouldn't have thought to ask for the room number that way. All hotels and most places like this put a nine to make phone billing easy.

"But," the manager continued, "why don't you head up there and knock. That way you won't be playing the scene out here, either. It'll give you some privacy."

Blue smiled. Jodi had never seen that smile before. It was one part gratitude, one part surprise, all charm.

"Thank you," Blue said. "That means a lot to us."

He looked over at Jodi, who gave him her best smile. "It sure does," she said, and kept that smile for the manager.

The manager didn't even look at her. He was just smiling at Blue—not in the way that Ramon had, but just like the manager had done something he was proud of as well.

"The room is 784, and the elevators are just down the hall," the manager said, nodding in that direction. "And if you'd like some kind of celebration dinner here—I know this isn't the fanciest of places—but tell Mr. Shea that it'll be on the house."

"I will," Blue said. "Thank you."

He kept his arm around Jodi as he walked in the

direction that the manager had indicated. She didn't mind. In fact, she enjoyed this more than she should have. She made sure her arm was around his back too, so that they looked like a happy couple for the manager.

Blue snuggled her close even as they rounded the corner away from the desk.

"Stay like this until we get upstairs," he said softly. "Cameras."

She nodded, then leaned her head on his shoulder as they waited for the elevator. The thing was slow and big, clearly designed for a lot of luggage and people.

They were able to walk in it side by side, which surprised her. Then they remained close as the door closed. Blue leaned forward just a bit to push the button for the seventh floor, then settled in beside her.

The mirrors that surrounded them revealed a couple that looked comfortable with each other. They fit together physically. She came up to the right part of his shoulder, and he could hold her close without any discomfort.

Odd the way she could analyze this. She'd spent so long in Hollywood that she could see at a glance how a casting director would view them. A casting director would think that Jodi wasn't quite pretty enough for Blue's girlfriend, but if she had enough personality and was a good enough actress, she might overcome that, because they looked so right next to each other.

Not that looking right mattered. The Hollywood landscape was littered with real couples who had no on-screen chemistry and just looked wrong for each other. Being perfect for each other didn't always show up when reflected back from the fun-house mirrors that were Hollywood.

"You look serious," Blue said.

"Well, you got us this far," Jodi said. "Now what?"

"Now it's up to you," Blue said. "He knows you, and knows your business. I'd say that his agent sent you."

She smiled. She hadn't thought of that. She hadn't thought of entry at all, which told her how much she was concentrating on the dark magic, and how little she was thinking about the practical things.

The elevator stopped, the doors opened, and Blue eased himself out of their clinch, moving forward at an odd angle. Then he extended his left hand, which she found weird, even though she took it. It wasn't until they reached the row of room doors that she realized what he was doing.

He was making their movements look natural to the manager down below, in case he was watching on camera. The doors to the rooms opened in such a way that Blue on Jodi's right would be almost invisible from the keyhole, and the person who opened the door wouldn't see Blue at all.

He did lead them to the door, and then he knocked, moving back just a bit.

"What?" came a deep masculine annoyed voice from inside.

Jodi glanced at Blue who nodded at her. Then she silently cursed herself for asking his permission to do this. (She could probably lie to herself and pretend that she was just acting that way for the security cameras, but she had a hunch she wouldn't convince herself.)

"Mr. Shea, it's Jodi Walters from Enchantment Management. May I come in and talk with you?"

She heard a rustling from behind the door and knew

that Shea had looked through the peephole. She felt her heart lift for a moment, and then he said, "Why the hell didn't you just call me?" and she knew things weren't going to be easy.

"I was at a business meeting at LAX, then I called your agent, and he said you were here. I just figured it was easier to stop than to drive all the way back to my office to call you and have you come see me."

"Look, I appreciate it," Shea said, "but I'm not really interested in work right now. I have a few personal issues to deal with."

Blue shifted from foot to foot. He clearly hadn't expected this. Jodi hadn't either, but she probably should have. Blue would have retreated in this instance, probably had retreated way back when. Part of her had assumed that Shea hadn't known he was the stalker. Apparently, he did. He called the stalker stuff personal issues. And he was scared. He probably didn't want to see women. She should have planned for that.

"Mr. Shea, it's an opportunity of a lifetime, and the moment I heard about the job, I thought of you." Jodi was rather amazed at how easily the lie came. Of course, she said things like this all the time to her clients, and generally only meant half of the sentence—and not always the same half. So the ease with which she lied about the whole sentence shouldn't have surprised her.

Shea didn't respond, which made Blue shift again but actually gave Jodi hope. If Shea had told them to go away immediately, they would have had to improvise something else. But this silence meant that he was actually considering what she had to say.

Then something thumped in the room, and Blue gave

her an alarmed look. But Jodi smiled at him reassuringly. She recognized that kind of thump. It was the thump of a man cleaning up the front room of his apartment.

"I'm not sure if I should accept work right now," Shea said, his voice sounding farther away.

"Believe me," Jodi said, "you'll regret it if you don't take this opportunity."

That, at least, was true enough. There was another moment of silence, followed by the slap of the security bar going back. Then the click of the lock.

He opened the door partway so that Jodi could only see part of his face. A waft of warm, stale air hit her, and she wondered how long he had been cooped up in there.

"Okay, talk," Shea said.

"I really don't want to discuss this in the hall," she said. She'd done this before too. "We don't know who is listening, and this is one of those deals…"

He sighed, closed his eye, and pressed his head against the door. Then he stepped back, pulling the door open wide.

Jodi walked in, followed by Blue.

"What the hell?" Shea said. "Who are you?"

"My new assistant," Jodi said. "Sadly, I've learned the hard way about the stupidity of going places alone."

Blue pushed the door closed.

The little two-room suite was nicely laid out, with a sofa, two comfortable chairs, even a small dining table near the kitchenette. The door to the bedroom was mostly closed, but a few stray socks prevented it from closing all the way.

Apparently, Shea had tossed everything in there to deal with later.

"Sorry," Shea mumbled. "I wasn't expecting anyone."

Clearly. He had stubble on his face, his eyes had bags as if he hadn't been getting much sleep, and his hair was newly combed but too long. He wore jeans that looked one size too big, his feet were bare, and he had a dress shirt over it that still had lines from the way it had been folded in its little plastic wrapper at the store.

"That's all right," Jodi said. "I knew I would be surprising you, so I didn't expect anything special. Just let me take a quick look at you if you don't mind."

He stood very still. "What do you want me to do?"

Poor man, he had no acting or modeling instincts. If she had told one of her more experienced clients to let her look, they would have preened, then asked if she wanted a runway walk or a pirouette or some kind of pose.

"What you're doing is just great," she said.

Blue had flanked her. He saw what she did—that this indeed was their man. Shea looked just like the police sketches. No wonder he hadn't left the suite. It was amazing he had let her in.

Jodi focused on him, concentrating on his aura. If he was a minor Charming—and she had noted that in his file—then she should have seen some blue in his aura. Maybe not as much as Blue's aura, but enough to make the aura bluish, like that light powder blue tuxedos had been made out of in the 1970s (thank heavens that era was over). But she didn't see anything except some faint amber, and lots and lots of sparks.

Whatever that spell was, it was dominating his magic. She wanted to say that the spell was eating his magic alive, but she doubted that was how it worked. Because if that happened, the spell would kill him, and it hadn't killed Blue.

Instead, she would guess, that the spell used up all the magic, then went dormant while the magic replenished itself. One of the ways that Blue had dominated the spell was to drink the charm away so that the magic really didn't replenish itself.

Charm was one of those interacting magicks that needed someone on the other side of it to function properly. A charming loner, in magical terms, was an impossibility.

Shea's aura looked broken and out of order, pieces of it jabbing out like badly shattered windshield glass. This was what she had hoped to see—although not in this bad a condition. But the damage to Shea's aura was similar to what was happening with Blue's, and Shea didn't have the magic that Blue did.

So she might be able to fix it.

"All right, Mr. Shea," she said, deliberately changing her tone. "I need to be up-front with you."

He froze in place. She blinked twice to make his aura recede.

She said, "We're here, not because of a job, but because we know who you are."

His eyes got wide and he actually bit his lower lip.

"I know you're the Fairy Tale Stalker," she said.

He let out a cry and backed up, hitting the table. If Blue hadn't been standing in the entry, Shea probably would have run to the door.

"And," she said louder, holding up her hand, hoping to keep him from panicking too badly, "I know it's not your fault."

Shea had caught the table with his hands. Now he was just braced against it, like a man who didn't know where to go.

"What?" he asked in a half whisper.

"It's a spell," she said. "A particularly nasty one. At first, I thought it was a curse, but it's more vicious than that."

"How can you possibly know that?" he asked.

She glanced at Blue. He gave her a small, almost invisible shrug. They were about to take a big risk, letting Shea know who Blue was. She tilted her head just a little—a question: *Should I tell him?*

"She knows it," Blue said, "because she's been working with me."

Shea gathered himself, letting go of the table. It looked like he was trying to pull the remaining bits of his dignity together.

"And am I supposed to know who you are?" he asked, as if he were a bouncer trying to prevent Blue from coming into a club.

Blue gave him a crooked smile. "Yeah, you're supposed to know who I am since you use my name often enough. I'm Bluebeard."

Chapter 42

SHEA SCREAMED.

It was a loud, piercing scream, filled with panic and dread. He backed up again, slammed the table against the wall, then ducked and tried to half run, half crawl to the bedroom.

Neither Jodi nor Blue moved. They watched him, Jodi with surprise. Then she glanced at Blue. He didn't look surprised at all. Just sad, and resigned.

How many people had reacted to him that way before? And he had always felt he deserved it.

She wondered if he felt like he deserved it now.

Shea reached the door of the bedroom, shoved it open, and launched himself inside. Only he couldn't get past the mounds of clothing. The clothing tumbled around him, and he fell, landing so hard that the floor shook.

"I'm not going to harm you," Blue said calmly. "In fact, if you believe my history, which is now in some doubt, but if you do, then you'd see that I only go after women. And attractive women at that. Jodi here should be afraid of me, not you."

She looked sideways at Blue. He still looked resigned, but she thought she might have seen something else. A bit of impatience? Anger?

If looked at in terms of the fairy tale, Shea was being ridiculous. But in terms of what had been happening to Shea, Jodi didn't entirely blame him. He'd been slowly turning into Bluebeard—warning all the women away from him before he hurt them, using Bluebeard's name—and now Bluebeard was confronting him in his own safe space.

"It's all right, really," Jodi said in her most soothing voice. This was where her magic came in. Soothe and comfort, guide and ease. "If it weren't for you, Gregory, we wouldn't know what was going on with Blue here."

"Me?" Shea said, his voice a raspy squeak. Apparently that scream had scraped his vocal chords. "What did I do?"

"Well, nothing, actually," Jodi said. "I know that's hard for you to believe, because you have fragments of memory in which you're stalking women—"

"I'm not stalking anyone. I haven't left this room in weeks. At least, that I know of." Shea looked up at both of them, a pleading expression on his face. "And that's me on the television, and if I fall asleep…"

"You know those women, right?" Blue said.

"In passing," Shea said. "I don't know where they live. I didn't even know the name of one of them until the TV mentioned it."

Blue nodded. "That's very familiar. It'll get worse unless we can slow the spell down."

"Reverse it," Jodi said firmly. She didn't want Shea to think that what she was about to do would fail. She had learned that the thought of failure, especially with magic, often guaranteed it.

"As we were investigating this," Blue said, "we initially thought it was a curse. But it's not. It's more complicated than that."

"It's a spell," Jodi said. "You're a Charming, right?"

Shea lowered his head, shaking it. "Not like the real Charmings. My family is hereditary royalty without the wealth. My father used to say everything was diluted from the money to the royal heritage to the magic. I might be able to make you smile, but I don't have that wowza ability that the real Charmings have."

Wowza ability. Jodi liked that phrase. It was accurate. It was how she had felt when she first saw Blue, and she had blamed it on the charm. And then she saw him turn the charm on, and she realized what she had felt had been minor compared with what he could actually do. Still, *wowza.* Wowza.

She didn't look at him at this moment. She didn't want Shea to see her personal reaction to Blue.

So she nodded instead. "But your magic, it's charm magic, right?" she asked.

"Yeah," Shea said. "Not much more. I thought I'd come here and actually have a better life in the Greater World. No worries about the fact that I'm seventy-second in line to the throne, which bugs the hell out of my dad, no refusing jobs because they were too demeaning for a Charming. I could be my own man here. You were really kind when I first got here. That's why I let you in. Because you were kind."

And Jodi didn't even remember him.

At least she had been kind. She always tried to be kind, but in Hollywood that was hard. This place called itself the Dream Factory, but it never explained what kind of factory it was. Some factories make things. Some crush things and make them into something else.

Hollywood was the second type. It crushed dreams and made them into something that seemed dreamlike, the cheesy kind, the kind that peeled around the edges. And for some people on the periphery of the Dream Factory, well, those people realized along the way that dreams weren't just fluffy and golden and beautiful. There was an entire other subset of dreams, and those were called nightmares.

That was what had captured Shea. Jodi had lost other clients to it, mostly in mundane, mortal ways. Never before had she had a client whose life was destroyed by a spell.

"I'll be honest with you," she said, still using her comfort magic. "I heard about what was happening to you, and I had to find you. I wanted to see if your aura had the same problems that Blue's does."

"Does it?" Shea asked, looking at her with complete fear.

"Yes." She decided not to tell him that his spell was weaker than Blue's because she had no idea if what she was going to do would hurt him or not. Again, she wanted to manage Shea's expectations.

"Did you fix his?" Shea asked.

Blue started to answer, but Jodi jumped in. Again, she had to handle this delicately, and she wasn't sure Blue could be delicate.

"Not yet," Jodi said. "His has a secondary issue. He has been under that spell for centuries."

"You mean he's still dangerous?" Shea squeaked.

Jodi couldn't imagine a less scary stalker. Whoever had chosen this guy to be the Fairy Tale Stalker must have done it as some kind of joke.

"I'm not dangerous," Blue said with more conviction than Jodi expected from him. "The spell is. But

I've neutralized it many times in the past, and it's under control now."

If he meant *now* as in right this instant, then he was right. It was under control. But if he meant *now* as in currently, as in this week, he was lying his ass off.

Either way, he sounded convincing.

"You fix him first, then me," Shea said.

"If only it were that easy," Jodi said. She pulled out one of the kitchen chairs and sat down. She had been uncomfortable standing. She wanted Shea to regain his balance, and she hoped this would help.

Shea watched her closely. Blue did not move away from his post near the door.

"I'm sure you remember your first Principles of Magic Course," she said.

Shea's eyes narrowed. The last thing she wanted him to tell her was that as a Charming, he had been exempted from school. She knew some of the royalty in some of the Kingdoms did that.

But he didn't say anything.

"One of the basic tenants of magic," she said, "one of the ones we get taught in the first weeks of class. The older the spell…"

He let out a gust of air. "…the stronger it is," he finished for her.

Thank God he remembered. That made her story believable. She didn't have to explain the weakness in his magic compared with Blue's.

"I needed to see your aura to see if the spell matched. It does, and it's engulfing your magic."

"What does that mean?" Shea said.

"I'm not exactly sure," Jodi said. "But it's also

ripping your aura apart, taking all the strength out of it by reshaping it. I believe I can organize your magic and pull the bad spell out."

Blue looked sharply at her, clearly surprised. Blue had some guile, but not a lot, and she had caught him off-guard.

"So let me ask you the most important question of all," she said, deliberately ignoring Blue. "How long have you been suffering under this spell?"

"I don't know," Shea moaned.

She was beginning to dislike him. She didn't like whiners. Was it possible to dislike a Charming? She hadn't liked Blue much when he was drinking, but then, she hadn't interacted with him. She had only watched him from afar. Still, she hadn't liked him. Was it the diminished charm or had it been the effects of the spell?

Or both?

"When did the symptoms first show up?" she asked, feeling her patience thin.

"What do you mean by symptoms?" he asked, his voice thick, like he was going to cry.

"When did women start being afraid of you?" Blue snapped. "Did it happen before you got here?"

Shea looked up at him, like he was looking at the Devil himself. Shea took a deep breath. "Well..." he said slowly, "my last girlfriend in the Kingdom told me I had gotten really creepy."

"Creepy how?" Blue asked.

Apparently he was getting through to Shea better than she was.

"She said she just didn't like the way I was treating

her," Shea said. "I didn't ask for clarification. She was starting to grate on me too."

"How long ago was that?" Jodi asked.

He leaned back, beginning to look relaxed for the first time since she arrived. If relaxed was the right word. Maybe… a bit more comfortable. Not as tense. A little less stressed.

"Just before I got here," he said.

"More than a year ago, right?" Jodi asked.

"Yeah," he said, sounding surprised that she knew.

"That's a much more recent spell than mine," Blue said.

Shea gave Jodi the most hopeful look she had seen from him. "You think you can fix this?"

"I can try," she said. "I know how to disentangle spells, and how to organize magic. Those are part of my magical skill set. However, if this turns out to be a curse, then I won't have done anything."

Shea clenched a hand into a fist, then loosened it again. Jodi recognized the movement. It was a relaxation technique taught by one of the full body coaches the studios liked. Then Shea rubbed that hand on his thigh, took a deep breath, and looked up at Blue.

"Would you let her do this?"

"I don't let her do anything," Blue said, and Jodi had to look down so that the involuntary smile didn't cross her face. That was a relationship answer, and Shea hadn't asked a relationship question.

"I mean, reorganize your magic? Would you let her do that to you?"

Blue paused. Jodi's heart started hammering. Was he going to ruin this? Was he going to get in the way?

"She has a point about the age of the spell," Blue said. "I think I'd want some magical backup if she tried to mess with my aura. It's been broken for a long, long time."

"But me, I'm a year or so in," Shea said softly. "So it'll be okay."

"That's what we're hoping," Jodi said. "I'm not going to give you any guarantees."

Shea let out a barking laugh. "That's exactly what you said to me when I told you that I wanted to make my name in Hollywood. You said there are no guarantees. And now I'm famous."

"But not with your name," Blue said.

Shea's smile faded, and he nodded once. "You're right. Not with my name."

"We can fix this," Jodi said. "Just let me try."

Shea stood up. He was shaking visibly. "Are you sure you don't want magical backup?"

Jodi tried to imagine Selda here or Tank or anyone else who might have the power to contain some of the magic she might unleash. The problem with her powerful friends was simple: they wanted to be in charge. They would argue with her over every point. She didn't need argument.

She needed practice. She needed a relatively painless first attempt.

And she didn't want to insult Shea by telling him that.

"I think we'll do fine without the backup," she said. "Besides, Blue will be here."

"You have other magic skills besides Charm?" Shea asked.

"You'd be surprised at what I can do," Blue said.

And, as Jodi stood to start her work on Shea, she realized that once again, Blue hadn't answered an important question directly.

Chapter 43

As Jodi stood up to help the Fairy Tale Stalker, Blue realized just how small she was. And fragile.

And precious.

He made himself take a deep breath. She knew what she was doing, or at least, that was what she said.

He had to trust her.

He hadn't trusted anyone for a very long time.

The stalker—Gregory. Shea. Jeez, Blue wished he knew the man's real name. His magical name. The name he was born with. The name that gave the person who knew it very real power.

All of this talk of magical backup made Blue very nervous. More nervous than he had been.

Although, if he was honest with himself, he had been nervous from the moment they had arrived in this hotel room/apartment/suite thingie. He recognized it as part of that downward slide. Only he had had his in the Kingdom, and then he had come here, continuing it. He couldn't quite remember how he had gone from crappy impersonal apartments to crappy impersonal hotel rooms to crappy impersonal patches of earth underneath bridges, but he had done all of that, hugging a bottle.

The stalker—Blue couldn't think of him as anything else—stood up. He weighed almost double what Jodi did. If he got physical as she tried to disentangle the evil spell from his aura, then he could do some real damage, maybe even before Blue got over there.

"One thing before you start," Blue said, amazed at the firmness in his own voice.

They both looked at him, almost as if they had forgotten he was there.

He didn't look at Jodi. He looked directly at the stalker.

"I need to know your real name," Blue said.

"Blue," Jodi said in that tone he was beginning to recognize as a reprimand. She had never really used it with him before.

"He wants magical backup. You *need* magical backup. We can't have it without knowing who this guy is. His *real* name, not the name he uses here."

The stalker swallowed hard. His eyes moved from side to side—shifty, untrustworthy—and then they settled on Jodi, and in them, Blue saw need. This guy was scared.

Blue hoped scared triumphed over all that training everyone got from babyhood on. *Keep your name secret. Don't tell anyone who you are. If someone you don't know asks your name, lie. Make something up.*

Blue wasn't even sure how he would know if the guy was lying. He could only hope that Jodi would figure it out.

"Gregor," the stalker said. "Young Gregor of Kent."

Kent. There was always a Kent. Every damn Kingdom had a Kent. It was like the name "Springfield" in America. Every state had a Springfield. Every Kingdom had a Kent.

"Which Kingdom?" Blue asked.

Young Gregor looked down. If he was a boy, he

might have scuffed the floor with his bare foot, kicking imaginary dirt. At that moment, Blue realized just how young this guy was.

He was a baby. He probably hadn't even hit his first century yet. And he was scared.

"The Fifty-Fifth Kingdom," Young Gregor said with a touch of shame. "I'm from the Fifty-Fifth Kingdom."

Blue felt a stab of pity. Not only was Young Gregor seventy-somethingth to the throne, but he was seventy-somethingth to the throne of an insignificant Kingdom. The Brothers Grimm only made it to the first fifteen Kingdoms, and the last five were one of those whirl-wind tours, filled with wine and food and probably dancing girls.

A couple of the other fairy tale writers had visited some of the Kingdoms with numbers up to twenty-five, and there were rumors that Oscar Wilde caused some real havoc in the sixty-ninth Kingdom, but for the most part, no one—no *mortal*—had been to the Kingdoms above twenty. Not well enough to write the Kingdom stories as fairy tales.

Not well enough to make them part of the mythos that had blended into the Greater World.

The stalker had to be telling the truth. No one from the Kingdoms admitted they were from the lesser Kingdoms unless they actually were.

"Satisfied now?" Young Gregor asked. The words were challenging, but the tone wasn't.

"Yes," Blue said.

He wasn't sure what he would do with the infor-mation. He really didn't have other magic besides his Charm. Except for the magic that everyone had. He had

the ability to send all of them to the Fates, which had the
benefit of freezing time enough to prevent a haphazard
death or some other catastrophe—unless the Fates themselves decided not to intervene.

Blue supposed that would have to do.

He would have to trust Jodi.

He didn't want to trust Jodi.

But he saw no other choice.

Chapter 44

JODI STOOD IN FRONT OF YOUNG GREGOR, NEAR THE half-closed door of the bedroom. To her right was the bathroom, and to her left, a closet. Behind her, the table and Blue. She wished she could see Blue, but she knew it was better not to see him.

He would distract her. She couldn't afford a distraction right now.

She didn't like the half-open door. She had no idea what she could conjure up in that back room or what Young Gregor had conjured up.

"Excuse me just a moment," she said and reached around him. The very movement made him jump. He scrambled away from her as if she frightened him.

She probably did.

She kicked the socks into the mound of clothing that looked (and smelled) like a live thing. Through the half-open door she could see drawn curtains, a faint light, and an unmade bed. The television was on low, sending its light across the tangled sheets.

She had a sense—and her senses were generally good—that no one else was in that room. (If they were, she had no idea how they could handle the smell of those clothes.)

She pulled the door closed all the way, then closed the bathroom and closet doors. Then she surveyed the area.

It was small and cramped, and it made her uncomfortable. It had been designed for the doors to stay open. With the doors closed, the suite's flow got compromised.

"Let's step into the living area," she said. "I'm not sure if I want to perform any kind of magic in a space this small."

Young Gregor almost hopped into the living area. Jodi looked down. The floor had the remains of pretzels and chips and half a dozen "meals" of dubious nutritious value.

She felt a similar pity for him that she had felt for Blue after she had met him but before she really knew him. The reality of Young Gregor's situation was that he had been heading the same way, into a lonely, confusing exile.

She wondered if it was even harder to survive this sort of thing for those with Charm. Their magic required interaction with others, which meant that on some level, they needed people (of course, on some level everyone needed people, but she suspected folks with Charm needed people more). Blue had mentioned suicide; she knew he had considered it. She wouldn't be surprised if the thought was lurking in the future for Young Gregor if she couldn't help him reverse this spell.

Young Gregor stood between the coffee table and the ugly industrial-strength couch, which bore an indent from his rather slender body. All around her, she saw examples of a life in hiding, a life filled with fear and confusion and hopelessness.

Maybe that was why he let her in. Because she had once represented hope to him. Certainly that was why he was letting her help him now. He probably saw it— rightly so—as his only chance.

Blue still stood near the door, his legs spread just a little as he braced himself. He seemed to believe that Young Gregor might try to leave, and it was pretty clear that if Gregor rushed Blue, Gregor wouldn't get anywhere.

In the past, Jodi had noticed how trim and well-muscled Blue was, but she had not realized until now how physically strong that made him. She kept seeing the possibilities on him, the possibilities for his future, and the lost opportunities of his past.

But she couldn't focus on Blue right now. She had to think of Young Gregor. Although she was grateful to Blue for getting Young Gregor's real name. Jodi didn't need it for the spell she was going to do, but if something went wrong, it was better to know who she had been working on than having to get help finding out his history.

"All right then," she said to Young Gregor. "You ready?"

He didn't look ready. He looked scared. And very young. She hoped that, at some point, Young Gregor would be able to drop the "young" from his name and live a real life. Maybe she could help with that.

"As ready as I'll ever be," he said with obvious bravado.

She smiled at him. "I'm not sure how this will feel. I suspect you'll have some kind of pain. I'm going to try to keep it at a minimum."

He nodded once, nervously. Then he swallowed, his prominent Adam's apple bobbing.

She focused her vision so she could see his aura again. It was dark amber now, with sparks flying off it, almost as if it knew what she was going to do.

Maybe it did. The aura was part of Young Gregor, and Young Gregor knew what she was about.

This evil spell was insidious. It apparently had some defensive as well as offensive capability.

She took a deep breath and raised her hands, touching the outside of his aura. It was hot and prickly, and whenever it sparked, it felt like she was trying to grab a Fourth of July sparkler.

But she didn't pull away. Instead, she brought her hands inward, compressing the aura a bit until the amber couldn't hold its defensive shape. Through it, strands of blue appeared, pale and faint, but visible.

With one hand, she took a strand of blue, and with the other, she grabbed some amber. Then she peeled them apart, the way you'd peel the protective layer off the sticky part of an envelope.

The amber felt like the sticky part. It tried to cling to everything. She had to concentrate hard to separate it out. As she did, she followed the threads of amber with her eyes. The threads led back to a gigantic fat thing sitting in the middle of Young Gregor's aura like a huge spider.

She let out a small sound of recognition. This explained the corporeal nature of the spell, and it also explained how the spell could disappear over time. And how that the spell could make defensive action.

The spell wasn't the amber threads. It was the little creature, which was a magically created representation of the spell. It had rudimentary thought processes, and it had a kind of life as well.

This spell was of a type called parasitic spells. Parasitic spells were particularly tricky to deal with, and very hard to see. Like so many real parasites, the spell could masquerade as many things just to remain alive.

But she had chatelaine magic, and that made her deadly to parasites. Because parasites—bugs of all types, really—made a homey environment impossible. So she had not just the magic to defeat them, but the magical knowledge.

She knew the worst thing she could do was grab the thing and pull. Her action might actually shred Young Gregor's aura, killing him.

Instead, she wrapped some of the blue of his aura around her wrist, so that she didn't lose her place, then made a pistol with her thumb and forefinger. She shot a magical dart, filled with the magical equivalent of pesticide, at the creature.

The dart hit the spider-thing directly in its underbelly. Eyes opened all over its body, dark, black eyes that she knew were not a part of the spider-thing at all. The spider-thing had amber eyes above some pincers. These black eyes looked at her, hard, and with complete fury.

Fear twisted her stomach, but she didn't move. Instead, she stared back at all of those eyes.

The poison from the dart threaded through the creature's body, bright green against its amber frame, illuminating all of the complex pieces of the spell. The green lasted only for a moment, then it turned black as parts of the spider-thing died off.

The amber strands collapsed, broke, and vanished. Then the spider-thing exploded, sending bits of magic all over the room.

Jodi ducked, but she felt some of it hit her. It burned, like some kind of toxic slime. The explosion sounded loud in the small room, but she wasn't sure if she was the only one who heard it because of her magic.

Then the black, the green, and the amber disappeared. Young Gregor's aura retreated, like injured auras did, and Jodi smiled.

Young Gregor's gaze met hers. It was glassy. His lower lip moved. Then his eyes rolled back, and he collapsed.

Chapter 45

FOR THE LONGEST TIME, JODI HAD STOOD WITH HER hands spread six inches away from Young Gregor's biceps. Then she had taken a step backward, tilted one hand, and raised the other, moving methodically.

Blue had watched, trying not to hold his breath, trying to be prepared for whatever was about to happen. He had no idea what he needed to do. He wouldn't know until he was needed. If he was needed.

Sometimes it was impossible to see magic, even if you were magical. When someone experienced was doing their job, you simply had to trust them, to believe that they knew what they were doing, even though there was no way to see the actual work.

Young Gregor had watched Jodi too, his body rigid. Beads of sweat had formed on his forehead and had started running down his face. He had grown pale. He was already shaking, but it seemed to Blue that the shaking had gotten worse.

He had clearly been in pain. Jodi had warned him that this might hurt, and it clearly did. Blue wasn't sure how long Young Gregor could stand there, absorbing the pain. Jodi didn't even seem to notice.

But she wasn't focused on Young Gregor. She was looking at his aura. She probably had no idea the effect her work was having on him.

She moved her hands like she was weaving or

conducting a very slow symphony. She was clearly working on something, and occasionally, little flashes of amber would appear.

The amber didn't look healthy to Blue. It looked… alive, almost. It felt malevolent. He had no idea how a color could be malevolent, but this one was.

Then Jodi had raised her right hand, and with her thumb and forefinger, she formed a small gun. She moved her hand as if she had fired a gun, and Blue thought he saw a tiny green bullet disappear into the area in front of Young Gregor. A hole, small and black and smoke-filled, appeared in the air where the bullet had disappeared.

Blue saw eyes in that hole, dozens of eyes, all glinting with that same malevolent blackness. They looked up as a unit, saw him, and a shiver ran through him.

He recognized those eyes.

He'd seen them in his sleep.

Then they vanished.

Young Gregor was twitching, his skin so pale that it had turned a bluish gray. Even his lips had turned blue.

Then something popped, and Jodi ducked, and shards of amber flew at Blue. He couldn't quite back away. They hit him like magical shrapnel, sending reverberations through him.

Only, they hadn't quite hit him. They hovered in front of him as if they were plastered against something. His aura? He didn't know, since he couldn't see auras.

The gobs of amber turned green, then black, and slowly slid off whatever it was that had kept them in the air. Some of them hit the floor before they had turned completely black, and in those spots, they left little smoky slime trails that seemed to be burning through the surface.

Jodi stood up slowly, looking at Young Gregor as if she was seeing him for the first time. Young Gregor couldn't even look at her. His eyelids fluttered, then his eyes rolled back, and he passed out.

At least, Blue hoped he had passed out.

Blue hurried across the floor to catch the poor kid, but he didn't get there in time. Young Gregor plummeted downward as his muscles failed him, his back and shoulders bouncing off the couch, his arms hitting the coffee table, his head landing with a thud on the floor.

Jodi had tried to catch him too. She bumped into Blue, nearly knocking him aside.

"Is he all right?" Blue asked.

"I don't know," Jodi said. "I hope I didn't kill him."

Then Blue understood why she had worked on Young Gregor first. She had been afraid that the power of the evil spell would kill whoever was hooked into it. Young Gregor's spell was new, and disarming it had done this.

What would disarming the spell enveloping Blue do?

He couldn't think about that. He moved the hair away from Young Gregor's forehead. Young Gregor's skin was clammy and he was shivering.

He was clearly alive.

"He's breathing," Blue said.

"Oh, thank the Powers." Jodi touched Young Gregor's face as well, then cupped his chin.

Blue eased Young Gregor upward, so that he wasn't crumpled between the couch and the coffee table. Blue braced Young Gregor's neck on the edge of the couch, then extended his legs outward. Young Gregor would be bruised and he probably would have a headache from his fall, but he would be all right.

At least, physically.

"Is he supposed to be out like this?" Blue asked.

"It's probably best," Jodi said. "I really messed with his aura."

"What exploded like that?" Blue asked. "I thought I saw eyes."

Jodi looked at him sideways. "You saw that?"

"Not much of it. Just a pile of eyes. And then a bunch of goo came at me. I think it's eating through the floor over there."

She looked behind him. The smoking continued near where he had been standing. She got up and peered down at it. Then she ran her hand over the floor, and the smoking stopped.

"This is one powerful spell," she said.

Blue could almost feel the weight of the spell gathering around him. He had been carrying something with *eyes* like that? For centuries? He didn't quite shudder.

She came back over and crouched beside him.

"The spell is dangerous and difficult," she said, putting her hand on Young Gregor's face, as if she could touch him back to consciousness, "and I could have killed him."

"But you didn't," Blue said. "You saved him."

"I hope so," she said. "His aura is so small right now."

"But no eyes in it, right?"

She gave him an odd look. "That's right," she said after a moment. "No eyes in it. I got everything. But what it did to him, I have no idea. I wish he would wake up."

Blue patted him on the face. He wanted Young Gregor to wake up too.

"C'mon, kid," he said. Because now, to him, Young Gregor wasn't a threat or even a stalker. Just a poor unfortunate who had a mild version of the evil thing that Blue had been living with. Blue wanted the kid to be all right. "Wake up."

Young Gregor moaned. Then he turned his head away from Blue's hand. Young Gregor's eyes blinked open, and Blue saw no amber, no weird eye reflection, nothing except fear.

"What happened?" Young Gregor asked. He put a hand to his face. Then he squinched his eyes shut as if they bothered him and opened them again. "Is it—did it work?"

He looked from Jodi to Blue.

"You tell me," Jodi said.

Young Gregor looked almost as if he was going to cry. "I don't know. I never could feel it in the first place, whatever it was. So I don't feel any different. Except I have a headache."

"You fell," Jodi said. "I didn't catch you in time."

"Then that's not it," Young Gregor said. "How am I supposed to know if you got it?"

Blue had an idea. He hadn't felt the spell either, but he knew its effects.

"Think for a minute," he said. "Think about those so-called attacks. Can you remember them?"

Young Gregor didn't even try. "I never could remember them," he said.

"Except for bits and pieces," Blue said, "flashes so real that you thought you had been there. After all, how could you know what those rooms looked like? And in one case, you told the woman at the last minute, you said if she didn't watch out, you would treat her like Bluebeard did."

Young Gregor's cheeks turned a light pink. It was the first color he had shown since Jodi started working on him.

"Yeah," he said.

"Access the memory," Blue said. "Is it there?"

He was asking with a bit too much hope. He wanted the memories gone more than anything. But he also knew that the memories were the only real tangible thing about the evil spell—tangible to him, at least.

Young Gregor was frowning. Then the frown grew deeper, and he let out a small sigh. "I—you—it's not the same," he said after a minute.

"What's different?" Blue asked.

"This is going to sound weird," Young Gregor said. "I remember having the memory. I even kinda remember the memory, like you do when someone tells you what happened. But I can't access the memory. At all."

"Try the others," Blue said.

Young Gregor kept frowning. He rubbed his temple. His head was clearly hurting him.

Jodi took his hand and pulled it down. "That's enough," she said. "You can't access it."

She sounded both convinced and relieved.

"What you did worked," Blue said to her.

"Yeah," she said.

"Why would the memories go?" Young Gregor asked, not like he wanted them back, but more like a man who couldn't believe his good fortune—a man who didn't want to believe his good fortune, not right yet, at least, in case he might be disappointed.

"They weren't yours to begin with," Jodi said. "They belonged to the spell."

That sentence chilled Blue. "How can a spell have a memory?"

"It's not a standard spell," Jodi said. "That's what we missed. It's a parasite spell."

Blue rocked back on his heels, nearly lost his balance, and had to sit down. A parasite spell. And he'd had the damn thing for centuries. How big was it? And how hard would it be to dislodge?

If it was anything like a physical parasite, the older they got, the stronger they got. And the more they had woven their way into their host. He knew of some physical parasites that, once they were in place, they couldn't be removed without killing the host.

No wonder Jodi had been worried.

She was watching him now. She understood exactly what he was thinking. She had probably been thinking the same thing.

"Did you know that before you tried this?" Blue asked.

She shook her head. Of course she didn't know. If she had known, she would probably not have tried.

"So, I had the spell's memories?" Young Gregor asked. "It was an actual thing?"

"It had a life of its own," Jodi said.

"What was that, then, that appeared to those women?" Young Gregor asked, his voice trembling. "Was it me under the influence of the parasite?"

"It was another part of the spell," Jodi said. "It had several forms. I'll have to look it up, but I suspect that it can exist in more than one level at once. And it uses some kind of raw emotion to go after the women."

She spoke so dispassionately, as if she wasn't one of the women it went after.

"And then creates what?" Blue asked. "Some kind of avatar?"

"I'm not exactly sure," Jodi said. "But what I saw—"

She was looking at Young Gregor now.

"—was spiderlike, sending little tendrils out around it, weaving them into your aura."

The description made Blue queasy. That was in him? Now? And had been for centuries?

"Some of the pieces of it got onto the floor there," Jodi said, nodding toward the kitchen area. "Maybe it could send out pieces of itself. I'm not sure. I seem to recall that some parasite spells can do that, send out little branches of themselves to enact the point of the spell."

"Oh, wow," Young Gregor said.

Oh, wow is right, Blue thought, *and not in a good way*.

Then Young Gregor looked at Blue with an expression filled with pity. "You still have yours."

Blue nodded.

"And it's centuries old."

Blue nodded again.

"Jeez," Young Gregor said. "No wonder you wanted to work on mine first. Getting rid of mine knocked me cold, and I've only had it for a year or two. What's going to happen to you?"

"I have no idea," Blue said. Then he took a deep breath, gathering all the strength that he had. "But I'm willing to find out."

Chapter 46

"Well, I'm not willing to find out," Jodi said. Blue had never seen her look quite this stubborn—or quite this scared.

She sat on her knees next to Young Gregor. He still had his head braced against the couch. The coffee table had moved out a little, probably from his fall, and some newspapers had fallen off onto the floor.

Jodi's green eyes were wide, her mouth in a thin line. She was breathing shallowly, and Blue could tell she was fighting back some emotion, but he couldn't tell what it was. Anger? Fear? A combination of both?

He wasn't certain.

"You're my only hope, Jodi," he said softly. "I suppose I could go back to drinking, but I don't think that'll stop this new round. I don't think that'll save you."

"What's that?" Young Gregor asked.

"Not important," Jodi said.

"Very important," Blue said. "She's in the cycle. This thing has targeted her now because of me, and I think she could die."

"No." Young Gregor grabbed her hand. "You can't die. What'll happen then?"

Jodi looked over at Blue. Her auburn hair fell so that it shielded her face from Young Gregor, and she rolled her eyes.

But Blue wasn't so dismissive. He understood exactly

how Young Gregor felt—with a huge dose of added guilt and a lot of fear.

"It's my call," Blue said, "and I'm willing to take the risk. Otherwise, neither of us has a life."

Jodi took a deep breath. "I'm not sure what we're facing," she said. "It could be just like Young Gregor's spell here, in which case we're dealing with something relatively small, or it could be the mother of all parasite spells, and we could all die."

Blue waited. Young Gregor was actually biting his lip.

"Let's take this to the Archetype Place, tell Selda what's happening, and have a team around us," Jodi said. "This is so big, she might not want to handle it either. She might send us to the Kingdoms—"

"I don't want to go back to the Kingdoms," Young Gregor said. "I got infected there."

Blue looked at him in complete shock. Young Gregor seemed oblivious to the look. He seemed oblivious to all of it. Apparently, he thought he was part of the team now.

And who could blame him, really? He had been the first step in all of this, the first experiment, the beginning of the end.

"You didn't get infected there," Jodi said a bit too dismissively. She was so scared she clearly wasn't tolerating any crap. "It's not like some Greater World parasite that you pick up from drinking bad water. It's a spell, an evil spell."

"That someone cast on me—cast on *us*—in the Kingdoms," Young Gregor said, waving his hand at himself and at Blue. "Whatever it is that caused this, it lives there, and it wants to hurt us, and I don't want to go near it."

"We'll keep you on assignment here," Blue said before Jodi could speak again. "It'll all work out."

Young Gregor let out a large sigh of relief. Then he gave Blue a puppy-doggish look. "You're a lot more courageous than I am."

"No," Blue said gently. "I'm a lot more desperate."

"I don't like this, Blue," Jodi said.

"I don't either," he said, "but what choice do I have?"

He deliberately didn't use the word "we," because he wanted to let Jodi off the hook. Selda probably knew other chatelaines who could do this work, and maybe there was other magic that was equally suited to taking on parasitical magic.

Jodi nodded, clearly distracted, and then she stood, wiping the dirt off the legs of her jeans. She extended a hand to Young Gregor.

"Let's see if you can stand," she said.

"I'm okay," he said and levered himself up slowly, like an old man, using the couch and the coffee table to steady himself. He paled as he got up.

"Dizzy?" Blue asked.

"No," Young Gregor said. "I'm just sore everywhere."

Blue half envied him. Blue wanted to feel the aftermath of ditching that parasitical spell. He wanted to be free.

Jodi had walked over to the kitchen chair where she had left her purse. She reached inside it. "I'll call Selda and let her know that we're on our way, and what I'm planning to do."

Then she looked at the phone: She pushed on it a few times and swore.

"Not working?" Blue asked.

"It looks like the magic in the room blew it out," Jodi said.

Blue glanced at the microwave. The digital clock/ timer didn't seem to be working. And there was no little light at the bottom of the flat-screen television set either.

"Looks like all the electronics are gone," Blue said.

"Oh," Young Gregor said, "the manager is going to hate that."

"Just pay the hotel for it," Blue said. "Offer double what everything's worth. They always listen to that."

"You sound like you know," Young Gregor said.

"You have no idea," Blue said, not wanting to think about everything he had ruined in the past.

Something thudded in the bedroom. Jodi whirled.

"Did you hear that?" she asked.

Blue nodded. He was the only one who hadn't stood yet, and he did so now, slowly, moving out of the way of the coffee table. Jodi headed toward the bedroom door.

"Don't," Blue said to her. Something felt off.

She stopped and looked over her shoulder. Young Gregor stood silently between them, like a scared bunny. His nose almost seemed to be twitching.

Then the bedroom door slammed open.

"How the hell does anyone stand that stench?" A thin man with a hooked nose stood on the pile of dirty cloth-ing. He kicked some of it aside so that he could walk out of the room into the living area.

Blue had never seen him before.

Or had he?

The eyes looked familiar. They were black with a bit of amber in them.

"Who are you?" Young Gregor asked, his voice trembling.

"Get back," Jodi said to him, as if Young Gregor had moved forward. He hadn't, of course. He wasn't that courageous.

"So you recognize me, do you, honey?" the thin man asked.

"Actually, no," Jodi said, somehow making herself look taller. "I've never met you, but I've been looking at your nasty little spells all day."

"They're not little, sweetheart. If they were little, you wouldn't be afraid of them." He smiled sideways.

Blue's heart was pounding. This was the man who had hurt him. This was the man who had destroyed his life.

And Blue didn't recognize him either.

"I'm not afraid of them," Jodi said.

"Who *are* you?" Young Gregor said again. Obviously, Young Gregor wasn't the brightest candle in the chandelier.

"Now I'm hurt," the man said. "Of all the people in this room, Young Gregor of Kent, you're the one who should recognize me. After all, you saw me the most recently."

"I don't—oh my God," Young Gregor said. "You're the bad guy."

The man shrugged. "If that's how you want to play it, then yes, I'm the 'bad' guy."

And Young Gregor started to scream.

Chapter 47

HE WASN'T OBVIOUSLY HURT, AND YET HE WAS SCREAM-ing. Jodi turned just enough so that she could see Young Gregor. He looked terrified. But Jodi didn't see anything wrong in his diminished aura, nor could she see any magic trailing from this horrible thin man in front of her to Young Gregor.

Young Gregor was a screamer, that was all. He had the courage of a gnat.

"You'd think that a princeling would have better manners," said the horrible thin man. "But he's always been a bit overly dramatic."

Jodi's gaze narrowed. The horrible thin man had high cheekbones, a hooked nose like a cartoon villain and very thin lips, which she assumed weren't natural. He had probably worn his lips down by pressing them together disapprovingly for so long.

He had an amber aura as well, but it wasn't that sickly color that she had seen in Young Gregor's aura. It was a deep amber, the color found in nature, rich and fine. It was also sparking with incredible energy.

This horrible thin guy was one of the most powerful mages she had ever seen—in the most traditional way. He could conjure up anything, whip up any spell he wanted, wave an arm and create something or destroy it.

She was terribly overmatched.

"So," Blue said from behind her. "You're the one."

Only Blue's tone wasn't nasty or sarcastic or even bitter. It was admiring.

Blue's voice shut down Young Gregor's scream. Young Gregor put a hand over his mouth, as if his own lack of control frightened him.

Jodi pivoted even more, careful not to turn her back on the bad guy, as Young Gregor so disingenuously called him. Yet she wanted to see Blue's expression.

It was warm and welcoming, and she wondered if that evil spell poisoning his aura had made him "like" this man in front of them.

"It depends on what you mean," the horrible thin man said. "Am I The One in the sense of *The Matrix*? The One and Only, out of fairy tales? The Chosen One that so many stories in this Greater World refer to? Then probably not. No one has ever considered me to be the romantic hero or the next in line to the throne or the one that the entire world has been waiting for."

"You're the one with all the magic," Blue said in that same admiring tone. He put an arm around Jodi's back and moved her aside, ever so carefully, and she grabbed at him. She didn't want him anywhere near that man.

"Oh," the horrible thin man said, "not *all* the magic. Just my own fair share."

"Still," Blue said, "those are some mighty impressive spells you've designed."

The horrible thin man smiled. The smile seemed genuine. He seemed flattered by all of the attention. "They are, aren't they?"

Blue had planted himself in front of Jodi. He was taller and wider, and she couldn't see around him without moving. She started to move, and that was when she figured out what Blue was doing.

He was charming the bugger so that she and Young Gregor could get away.

But she didn't want to get away. She wanted to stay beside Blue, to help him.

"I certainly didn't expect to meet you," Blue said. "At least not this way."

"Well, you found me out," the horrible thin man said, "so it was the least I could do."

But he should have come sooner. He should have stopped Jodi from getting anywhere near Blue. The horrible thin man should have defended himself after she destroyed his spell on Young Gregor.

Young Gregor had passed out when the spell shattered. Had the horrible thin man done the same? It was the only thing that made sense.

And now he was here to what? Stop her, probably. Blue had clearly figured that out already, and he was letting her escape.

Instead, she moved closer to him. She glanced at Young Gregor who appeared rooted in place, hand still over his mouth. She couldn't worry about him.

She slipped her dead phone in her pocket and focused her vision on Blue's aura.

The amber was sparking and reaching toward the horrible man, like a child wanting to be picked up. Some of Blue's dark blue charm was still visible, and she reached into it with her right hand.

Blue started, then remained still.

"You've been charming me, haven't you?" the horrible thin man said, with real menace in his voice. "You don't remember me at all, do you, because if you did, you'd realize how much I hate charm."

"I'm sorry," Blue said, with even more warmth. "I should have realized. It's a reflex, you know. It's how I operate when I meet someone I want to impress. I just ramp up the charm a bit. I'll ramp it down."

Jodi didn't want to touch the amber in Blue's aura, because that would let the horrible thin man know what she was about. She was searching, though, searching for the parasitical representative of the spell. It had to be easy to see, because it had to be huge.

She peered around the blueness and saw it. What she thought was a sea of amber was actually its big, fat, dominating body. It was huge, and killing it just might kill Blue.

But he had already told her he had wanted out, and if this horrible thin man got hurt when his magic got hurt, then he was already diminished a bit from what she had done to Young Gregor. She wouldn't get a better chance.

She wished she could tell Young Gregor to call for Selda or Tank or some kind of backup. But she couldn't. She was on her own.

They were on their own.

"You think you can charm me, don't you?" the horrible thin man said. "You think you can just talk your way out of this. Have you learned *nothing* these past several centuries?"

The horrible thin man was getting angry. The sparking in Blue's aura had grown worse.

"Oh, no," Blue said. "I've learned a lot, thanks to you. I realized that charm magic simply can't hold a candle to most other kinds of magic. We Charmings are dependent on everyone else for everything."

He was telling her to go ahead. She was shaking. She didn't want to do this.

But she had no choice.

She formed a pistol with her thumb and forefinger, imagined the biggest bullet she had ever seen, and fired.

Chapter 48

BLUE FELT SOMETHING BURROWING THROUGH HIS magic. He didn't know if it came from this malevolent being in front of him or from Jodi. He didn't want to focus on it or think about it any further. He needed all of his charm right now, and he hoped to whatever god he should believe in that Jodi had figured out what to do.

Because he couldn't hold off this guy for long.

"I know you!" Young Gregor shouted from behind Blue. "I remember you now!"

Blue let out a small sigh, trying to camouflage it as best he could. Young Gregor was a problem.

So was whatever Jodi was doing. It hurt. Rivulets of pain ran through him, taking all of his control to keep his body from shuddering.

"You!" Young Gregor said, stepping forward. He was pointing at the man in front of Blue.

"You don't need to shout," the man said calmly to Young Gregor.

Young Gregor gave Blue a panicked look, and Blue finally understood what Young Gregor was doing. He had gotten the message Blue had meant for Jodi. Young Gregor was doing his best to help Blue.

"Gregor," Blue said, "Why don't you do what we were talking about earlier?"

"I know who he is, though," Young Gregor said to

Blue. "He's that etiquette instructor my father hired. You're an odious little man!"

"Gregor!" Blue said. "Please. Leave. Now."

Young Gregor gave him a confused look.

"You're insulting our guest," Blue said, wishing he could be blunter, wishing he could tell Young Gregor that he had this under control.

"Well, the boy never had manners. He was one of those charming rebellious types, the kind that women fawned all over because they thought he would improve somehow." The man spoke with disdain. "He's completely ineffectual. If you've assigned him some task, he won't do it."

"I didn't assign him anything," Blue said, turning his attention away from Young Gregor. If Young Gregor had gotten the message about helping Blue, then he should have understood this one.

At least Blue hoped so. Because he couldn't do much more. Sweat was beginning to form along his torso. Something was happening all through him. He felt queasy and the pain was growing worse.

"I'm not staying here with him!" Young Gregor said, and Blue wanted to close his eyes. The kid would never be an actor, no matter how handsome he was, no matter how much he wanted it.

He certainly wasn't convincing Blue right now.

"I have to leave!" Young Gregor announced. And then he slammed out of the room.

To Blue's surprise, the man let him go.

"You know," Blue said to the man, trying to keep him distracted, "you've been such an influential part of my life, and I don't even know what to call you."

The amber in the man's eyes grew flinty. "The boy gave you a clue. You don't remember me at all?"

Blue caught his breath, as much from pain as from any kind of realization. "You're Mr. Danvers," he said, more breathlessly than he wanted to.

He was getting light-headed. He needed to continue to focus.

"Ah." Danvers smiled. "You do remember."

Blue remembered, all right. Danvers had been hired to teach Blue royal etiquette, how to behave in every circumstance from a ball to a private dinner. How to dress. How to hire a gentleman's gentleman. How to be a prince, as if Danvers—a lowly commoner—had known that.

He had been hired when Blue was very young and impulsive, and Blue had asked him at one point where his expertise came from.

Were you a prince? Blue had asked naively.

Of course not, Danvers had snapped. *But I have molded generations of them.*

And he had already become bitter. If Blue had done something wrong, Danvers pinched him, leaving little bruises everywhere. The bruises were what eventually got him fired. Not the verbal abuse, not his real lack of expertise.

Those little bruises that Blue's father could see.

A prince should not have discipline marks, his father had said and had fired Danvers.

"Yes, of course I remember," Blue said warmly. He was focusing as hard as he could on being pleasant, on being charming without being obvious about it. "I never understood why you left. I thought we were doing so very well. I never really did as well after that."

That last part, at least, wasn't a lie.

Danvers's mouth twisted. Blue actually remembered that expression. He hadn't remembered the man, but that nasty smile had remained locked in his memory for a very long time.

"Your father said I was no longer needed. He told me that you could handle any situation thrown at you." Danvers's eyes twinkled, the amber looking particularly threatening. "It took me years, but I eventually proved him wrong."

Blue swayed, then caught himself. He was feeling awful. He almost lost his composure at that moment, almost told Danvers that once Blue figured out what was going on—what he *believed* was going on, in any case—he had found a way to handle it. It hadn't been pretty, but it had saved lives.

"Don't bother to talk," Danvers said. "I know that your little girlfriend is doing her best to destroy my spell. She thinks it'll hurt me, when all it will do is murder you."

Blue should have felt afraid. He didn't. He also knew that Danvers was the one lying right now.

"I've had my fun with you and Young Gregor both," Danvers said, "and now I'm off to find new people to torment."

"You don't like charming men, do you?" Blue asked, keeping his voice level. He wished he was standing a bit closer to the table so he could brace himself. Hell, he wished he could see Jodi so that he could convince her to leave. He had no idea if she even knew this conversation was going on, not while she was trying to eradicate the parasitical spell.

"I think 'like' is one of those misleading terms," Danvers said. "I think the world, the worlds, really, the Greater World and the Kingdoms, are terribly unfair. There you are, born to power, with your pretty face and your ability to convince anyone of anything, no real talent to speak of, a man who has never worked at anything, and if you had followed your script, you would have gotten your pick of the women, and you would have remained rich and powerful."

But Danvers had gotten in the way of that. Blue was seeing sparks in front of his eyes. He didn't know if that was because he was about to pass out. He hoped not.

"But I have worked hard to become what I am, and because I am not rich and handsome and born into the right family, people ignore me. Even now, when I am more powerful than the rest of you put together."

He peered around Blue, clearly trying to get to Jodi.

Blue wanted to step sideways but couldn't.

"You two really aren't thinkers, are you?" Danvers asked. "Because, really, all I have to do is this."

He clenched one hand into a fist. Something (someone?) slammed into Blue's back. The pain was excruciating.

"And," Danvers said, raising his other arm. "If I do one more thing, you'll never find me. All I have to do is vanish."

He smiled that twisted smile again. Blue shuddered, trying to figure out what Danvers was doing.

"Because even if I pass out, you won't be able to trace the magic until it's too late." Then he chuckled. "What am I saying? Your friends won't be able to trace the magic. I'll be long gone—and you'll be long dead."

Gone. Blue's brain had become sluggish, but he got

that. He used the last of his strength to grab Danvers's arms and pulled him forward. That made the pain even worse, and Danvers struggled mightily.

But Danvers was trying to disappear. He was going to vanish as mysteriously as he arrived, and Blue couldn't allow that. He would stop it with his dying breath.

Danvers had the wrong kind of magic for this spell. He needed to move his arms to cast it. And Blue couldn't let him do that.

All Blue had to do was hang on.

Chapter 49

THE POISON BULLET WAS WORKING, BUT NOT FAST enough. Jodi could see the green of the poison filtering through the amber. The green actually outlined the complex system of tendrils and vessels and spider veins that made up this gigantic parasite spell.

She had never seen anything so huge, and she still hadn't found its head. She had felt the impact of the bullet, seen the amber actually cringe, watched the blue of Blue's aura grow for just a minute.

She made another pistol with her thumb and forefinger and shot a second bullet, as big as the first, but it didn't seem to have an impact either. She was swimming in blue and green and amber light. She pushed in closer, trying to find the head of this thing. It had to be huge.

It was centuries old. It had been alive, as a spell, as a parasite, longer than she had. She hoped she had enough power to defeat it.

She hoped she could defeat it without killing Blue.

But she couldn't let herself think of that right now. She didn't dare.

She was working hard to find its center, when suddenly, a spray of tentacles reached for her. She couldn't back away—she knew that was what it wanted—and she willed them back.

Only they burrowed right into her own aura, sending shocks through her. She nearly passed out.

The tentacles pulled her forward and she slammed against something. She couldn't see outside of the aura because she was so lost in it, but she had a hunch she had just rammed Blue in the back.

Then a voice said, *We have had you for days. You cannot escape us. Don't even try.*

It sounded almost like Blue, but it wasn't Blue. The accent was wrong.

She had heard the voice of the spell.

And somehow that made her feel stronger. The spell was right: it had its hooks in her, had since that day Blue looked at her. But she wouldn't let it defeat her.

She raised her hands, envisioned little needles on her fingertips, then put one finger on each tentacle. She sent more poison into this thing.

Green flooded the tentacles. They tried to peel off her, but she stuck her fingers in deeper.

This thing might kill her, but in doing so, it would kill itself as well.

Then she saw the head. It peered through the green-ish amber goo. Only one set of eyes this time, and all she could hope was that the other eyes—the eyes that belonged to that horrible thin man outside of this spell—were busy elsewhere.

These eyes, though, were bad enough. They were almost as big as her head. And the pincers they rose above were the size of Gunther's hand. The edges were sharp. The pincers had hair along the edges—or was that teeth?

A thread of fear started in her, and she tamped it down. Fear was her enemy, like this thing was her enemy.

But she finally understood how all the other women had lost their heads.

No tool had sliced it off. No man had stood over them with an ax, no one had cut through the carotid with a sharp blade.

These pincers, these giant pincers, had enveloped the head and then bit it off.

She unhooked her right hand from the tentacles, made one last pistol with her thumb and forefinger, and, as the pincers opened, she fired directly inside.

Chapter 50

SOMETHING SCREAMED.

Jodi couldn't tell if it came from inside or outside of this aura. The amber tentacles that she had let go of had wrapped themselves around her torso and were squeezing so hard, she couldn't catch her breath. But the tentacles were a dark green at the tips and pale green at the back. When they turned black, they would start dissolving, if they were anything like the things inside Young Gregor's aura.

But she wasn't looking at them. Even as she struggled for air, she watched that last bullet she fired travel inside the gigantic parasite thing. It went down a central core, as if there was one big tentacle (its neck?), heading down, down, down, until it hit large amber rock.

Only, she realized, that wasn't a rock.

That was the thing's heart. If this thing had a heart.

That was the foundation of whatever it was, its brain maybe, or maybe just the center of the spell.

The bullet hit, shattered, and splattered green everywhere.

Then the green extended outward, met some of the other green, and turned darker and darker.

She couldn't draw enough breath to warn Blue to duck. This explosion would hit the center of his back—his torso—sending all of that power, all of that goo, right into him.

The magical shrapnel from Young Gregor's spell had burned through the floor.

What would this do to Blue?

They were linked through this spell. Maybe she could communicate to him through it.

She willed him to hear her thoughts. *Duck! Get out of the way! Protect your back!*

And then the green dazzled, overtook everything, and she knew, she knew it was going to blow.

The tentacles slid off her, and she took a breath, about to scream a warning, when the gigantic parasite exploded.

She got hit in the face with magical goo. It spattered all over her, but it didn't burn. It smelled like mint.

Her own spell had hit her—protecting her? She wasn't sure—but she let her legs collapse beneath her, as much to get away from the rest of the explosion as anything.

But there wasn't just one explosion. There were several.

First the gigantic center of the creature. Then its exterior. Then the remaining amber tentacles. And then smaller explosions as the green destroyed the last of the amber.

She couldn't quite cover her head. She needed to see the blue return.

And it did, for just a moment, before vibrating like bad Jell-O, and then retreating.

She saw Blue's back, covered with black stuff, smoke coming off his shirt. But she couldn't see his aura any longer.

She grabbed the shirt and ripped it off him. His skin was red but not damaged, at least not yet.

He was still standing upright. She had expected him to collapse.

She touched him, and he toppled, and she tried to catch him.

Her hands hit something else, though, a different torso, too skinny by half.

A grayish green face rose over Blue's shoulder. That horrible thin man, eyes closed, expression malevolent, even though he was clearly unconscious.

Jodi tried to hold them both up and failed. Instead, she slipped down with them, flipping them enough to cushion Blue's body with her own.

His arms slipped off the horrible thin man, and that guy fell backward, hitting the bathroom door as he went down, head thumping against the doorknob, then sliding against the door frame, until his skull smacked hard on the floor.

If he had been partially conscious before, he had to be unconscious now.

And so was Blue.

Blue wasn't there at all. His body was dead weight.

Jodi clung to him for a moment, hugging him close, thinking *Please don't be dead. Please don't be dead*.

And then she realized how useless that was.

She had to try to save him.

Even though she didn't have that kind of skill.

It was the least she could do.

Chapter 51

THERE WAS NO SUCH THING AS MAGICAL 911 AND THAT, Jodi decided, had to be rectified. She would definitely remember to tell someone to set something up when she got out of this.

If she got out of it.

Blue was crammed in the small space near the table and the in-room refrigerator/counter/sink. On the other side was the horrible thin man, also crumpled, a bit of blood seeping from the back of his head across the floor.

Jodi wanted to get past him, get to Blue, get something done, but the two men were locked together, Blue's hands on a death grip around the horrible thin man's wrists.

Jodi couldn't separate them. She knew better than to try.

Or maybe she didn't know better. She just had to focus on Blue right now.

His skin was clammy, his color bluish—and not in a good way. It was as if all the blood had left his face. His eyes were closed and sunken into his skull.

He looked dead.

She hoped he wasn't dead.

She prayed he wasn't dead.

She put her hands flat on his chest and started CPR because she didn't know what else to do. He wasn't a building or a home, he couldn't be healed with her magic — any more than she already had.

The evil spell was gone, spattered all over the room. Amber goo dissolved into blackness, dripping off the walls, the light fixtures, the ceiling, smoking wherever it landed. But the creature itself was gone.

And so was Blue's aura.

She hoped it had retreated, like Young Gregor's had.

It had taken Young Gregor a while to wake up. But he hadn't looked like this, and his hands weren't locked in a death grip with someone so evil that Jodi didn't know how to deal with him.

She didn't know if the magic was still flowing between them. She couldn't tell.

She couldn't see it.

In fact, she couldn't see the horrible thin man's aura at all or his magic or the magical sparks she had seen before.

She needed to forget him, at least for the moment. She had to work on Blue.

Because she didn't know what else to do, she continued the CPR. What had Ramon taught her to do? Oh yeah. Press according to the beat of that awful Bee Gees song, "Stayin' Alive." Ironic, yes. But useful. Very useful.

Even if she didn't want that Chipmunk-like chorus of voices in her head right now.

Still. She pressed to a disco beat. She couldn't tell if it was working or not.

She was going to do the breath thing, even though Ramon told her that was discredited now, but she didn't know what else to do, how else to do it. She wasn't even sure the compression was necessary.

Yes, magic had a physical effect, but sometimes bad magic or bad magical reactions caused a stasis, and normal mortal methods wouldn't help. Even with Bee Gees music.

She leaned forward, and then, because she couldn't help herself, she kissed Blue, lightly at first, then putting all of herself into that kiss.

She had been so stupid. She should have done that before. When he was present. When he could feel it.

When he was *alive*.

His lips were still warm at least. Or maybe they were cooling off. She didn't know.

She had not pushed air into his lungs. She needed to do that. She had to hold his head a certain way, and she wasn't sure what that way was.

Why hadn't she learned this stuff? What was wrong with her? Too late to chastise herself now. She had to do everything she could to bring him back.

She'd do a few more chest compressions, then she'd try the breath thing, and she wouldn't forget herself.

She wouldn't kiss him.

She leaned back and took a deep breath, ready to start again. Okay, Bee Gees, let's get the rhythm. She put her hands flat on Blue's chest when his eyelashes fluttered.

He smiled, his eyes open, clear and blue.

"You could do that again, you know," he said, "and maybe this time I'll kiss you back."

Chapter 52

SHE LET OUT A LITTLE SHUDDERY BREATH OF SURPRISE and relief, and her eyes teared up and she felt a small bit of anger at that, because she wasn't a crier, never had been, never would be, but the relief was so great, she didn't know what else to do.

So she went for sarcasm, because she didn't want him to see how moved she was—not that he could miss it. A blind man couldn't miss it. Heck, people across the street couldn't miss it.

"*Maybe* you'll kiss me back?" she asked.

His smile was soft, and his eyes twinkled.

She hadn't realized how much she loved the twinkle in his eyes.

"Well," he said, "I can't let go of this doofus. If I release his arms, he can cast his spells, and that would be a bad thing."

Blue didn't even move his hands, but he did look down at them.

That reminder about the horrible thin man tamped down Jodi's relief just a bit. She glanced at the horrible thin man. He hadn't moved, and the blood was still seeping from behind his head.

"I think he's unconscious," she said.

"I'm sure that's what he wants you to think," Blue said. "He has a lot of power. He could make us see anything."

Okay, now she was frightened. She moved off Blue's chest—

"Hey!" he said. "You didn't have to move."

—and she smiled at him. "Let's take care of this guy first."

If nothing else, she would tie him up. She would wrap him in Young Gregor's dirty clothes, stick one of the smelly socks in the man's mouth, and drag him into the bathroom, locking him in there.

She toyed with calling the police—the real police—to see if they could come and arrest him, for what she didn't know.

But she needed someone to help, because she and Blue didn't have the ability to take this guy on alone.

Her phone was dead. She didn't know where Young Gregor's was. She picked up the hotel phone, heard the dial tone (at least that thing hadn't died—all this magic hadn't shorted out the entire hotel, which it very well could have), and followed the instructions on the face of the phone. She hit "8" for an outside line.

As she did, she felt a whoosh of air. She whirled, expecting to see the horrible thin man standing beside her, or hurting Blue or doing *something*.

Instead, Tank was fluttering a few inches from her face.

"You should have called for backup," Tank said. "What the hell were you thinking?"

"Don't yell at me," Jodi said. "Do something with that awful bad guy. Can you? Wrap him in fairy dust or something."

"Don't tell me how to do my job," Tank said, but she flew away from Jodi toward the horrible thin man. Jodi felt even more moving air, and then Tank's entire posse appeared, all of them wearing black goth lace dresses or Victorian topcoats and pants. Jodi counted at least fifty of them, and she wondered how Tank had assembled them on such short notice.

"You don't look so good, buddy," Tank said to Blue as she flew over him.

"Yeah, well, your magic still smells like baby powder," he said, and Jodi smiled. Apparently she wasn't the only one who had noticed that.

"Shut up or I won't help you," Tank said, but they all knew it was an idle threat. She was hovering over his hands as she spoke. The posse had gathered around the horrible thin man's face.

Jodi, for one, felt a lot calmer now that someone with useful magic was here—not that hers wasn't useful, not that she hadn't done something really good—but she was at her limit, and that thought made her knees wobble, and she sat down.

She was exhausted. When was the last time she had used that much magic all at once?

"Is he unconscious?" Tank asked the posse.

"Can't tell," someone said.

Tank cursed, creatively and powerfully, then said, "That tears it. We're not dealing with this jerkwad on our own. I need three of you."

Three members of the posse flew over to Tank. Blue was watching it all, his head still at that awkward angle. Jodi wasn't sure if he was staying that way because he was afraid to move or because he couldn't move.

"We need binders," Tank said. "And nothing gauzy. It has to be tough. Got that?"

The three fairies nodded, then went to work, flying around the horrible thin man's wrists. Eventually Blue's hands, the horrible thin man's hands, and the fairies themselves vanished in a flurry of fairy dust.

Blue looked over at Jodi and smiled. He hadn't stopped smiling. Did that mean he felt better, or was he just putting on a good show?

She didn't know. But she did know that her next task would be to put this room in order. Goo still dripped from every surface, sending little smoke clouds into the air. She would have to clear out the bad magic, just so this room would be habitable again.

But she couldn't quite bring herself to move. Not yet at least.

Then the door burst open, and Young Gregor tripped as he came in. He looked wobbly and still much too pale.

He saw Tank and said, "Oh, thank the Powers you're here. You vanished on me."

Tank ignored him. She was giving orders to the rest of her posse.

Young Gregor sank into the chair next to Jodi. "I got a hold of Selda. She sent Tank. But you know that."

"Thank you," Jodi said tiredly. She wasn't sure what they would have done without Tank.

"Selda's coming. She's bringing an army. She says you shouldn't worry about this place. She'll deal with it. She sees it as another magical crime scene."

"Because I killed two parasites?" Jodi asked.

"An extension of the other magical crime scenes," Young Gregor said. "And maybe a clue as to what happened centuries ago. There're a lot of unsolved deaths at the hands of Mr. Danvers over there."

Jodi looked sharply at him. "Danvers?"

"Yeah," Blue said.

"Was he *married*?" Jodi asked.

"Oh, yeah," Young Gregor said. "His wife was a chatelaine, but she was the meanest chatelaine I had ever met. She came to the Greater World long before I did."

"And worked for a friend of mine," Jodi said. "Died in a terrible fire that I'm pretty sure she set. Hitchcock made an Oscar-winning film about that whole incident. Minus the magic, of course."

In fact, Jodi had walked off that set when it became clear that Hitch was going to follow the novel rather than the actual events. For all his love of the macabre, Hitch wasn't much of a believer in magic, no matter what he witnessed—and he had witnessed a lot more than he was willing to admit.

"Okay," Tank said. "Blue, I think you can let go now."

Jodi leaned forward.

The smile had left Blue's face. "If I let go and you're wrong, we're all dead."

"I'm not wrong," Tank said.

Blue let out a small breath, then raised his hands toward his face. His hands looked cramped, only half-open.

The horrible thin man—Danvers—stirred, his eyes popped open, and he glared at Blue. "I'll make you pay, you son of a bitch. I'll—"

One of the posse dropped a dirty sock in Danvers's mouth, and then half the group covered it with fairy dust, holding it in place as effectively as duct-tape would have.

Jodi liked that the magical all seemed to think alike about this guy.

"You owe me," Tank said to Blue. Then she waved her little arms. "To the Fates!"

She vanished, along with her posse, and the horrible thin guy. Fairy dust floated in the air like dust motes. Blood still marked the floor.

"She hates the Fates," Jodi said. "She avoids them at all costs."

"She must have figured out this was the only way to deal with Danvers," Blue said. He still hadn't moved.

Then Tank popped back into the room.

"Sorry. Forgot something," she said, then flew over the Young Gregor and grabbed him by the ear. "I need your testimony."

She grinned at Blue, then waved her free arm. "To The Fates!" she said again.

Then she and Young Gregor disappeared.

Jodi let out a small sigh. Then she got up from the chair, went over to Blue, and crouched beside him. "Let me help you up."

"I'm not sure I want to move," he said.

"We can take you somewhere," she said. "I'm sure there's someone who can help you."

His hands were still crabbed. He slowly flattened them on the floor and winced, as if the very act of doing so hurt.

Then he levered himself upright, so he wasn't in that awkward position. He moved his head in a circle, and Jodi heard something in his neck pop.

"Well," he said, "I'm going to be bruised."

"You fell hard," Jodi said. "I'm amazed you managed to hang onto that Danvers character."

"That's all I could think about," Blue said.

"I'm amazed you were thinking at all," she said. "I thought you were a goner."

"Is that why you kissed me?" he asked.

She was going to say something snide, but she couldn't bring herself to do so. She smiled, and the very act of smiling brought tears to her eyes.

"I was going to do mouth-to-mouth," she said. "I got sidetracked. It's lucky you didn't need the CPR after all."

"You're right," he said. "It wasn't the CPR that saved me."

"I know," Jodi said. "You didn't need saving."

"You know, for someone who has lived in and worked on fairy tales all her life, you sometimes miss the obvious," Blue said.

She frowned. "What do you mean, the obvious?"

"There's a reason people wake up with a kiss in a fairy tale," he said.

"What's that?" she asked.

He smiled and slid a hand around her neck.

"Kisses," he said, gently pulling her head forward, "have a magic all their own."

Chapter 53

KISSES DID HAVE A MAGIC ALL THEIR OWN, AND SO DID Jodi. Her magic was subtle, difficult for others to notice, but oh so important when it wasn't there. She had used it to its limits all day, but she still had some left. Just enough, in fact.

She leaned against Blue, separating from the kiss. He reached for her, and she put her forefinger on his lips. He kissed it. She smiled.

"One second," she said.

She had to concentrate, a sign that she was tired. She leaned forward and with a wave of her hands, got rid of the goo. Then she stood, pushed open the bedroom door, and slapped her hands together several times as if she were playing the cymbals. The clothes disappeared. The windows opened for a brief moment, and a strong cool breeze—from somewhere else, not LA—filled the air.

She snapped her fingers at the sheets. They rose off the bed and vanished. New sheets, unused sheets from the laundry room in the basement of the motel, hovered over the bed, like sheets in a fabric commercial. Then they landed on the bed, the blankets on the floor. New pillows and towels arrived too, just a moment later.

Finally, she turned toward the main door and barred it. She knew Selda and the crime scene folks were coming. She didn't care. She left a magical do-not-disturb sign outside, although if she was honest with herself, it was more like she had taken a tie and knotted it around her dorm room door.

Then she extended a hand to Blue. "Your aura's coming back," she said.

"I didn't know it was missing," he said.

"For a few minutes there, when I thought you were gone," she said. She couldn't say dead. She didn't want to think dead anymore.

He took her hand and let her help him stand. He had color in his face. He looked stronger, maybe than he ever had.

And oh, the charm. He was lethally handsome, amazingly beautiful, and stunningly gorgeous.

Or maybe that wasn't charm at all. Maybe that was just him.

She kissed him.

He wrapped his arms around her and kissed her back, pulling her so close that she couldn't tell where she ended and he began.

Then he said, without taking his lips from hers, "You cleaned the room."

"I figured we needed some privacy," she said, "and I really didn't want to drive across LA again."

She could feel him smile. Then he kissed her, long and slow, his mouth opening, taking her in. She had never been kissed like this, not once in her long life. It felt like the very first time.

He paused and moved his head just enough to take his lips away. She felt the loss. He kissed her forehead, and it felt dismissive.

Then he sighed. "Do you know how long it's been since I've done this?"

"Made love?" she asked.

He half chuckled. "I actually meant kiss someone." He paused again, then said, "I've never made love."

"Never?" she asked.

"Not once," he said.

"You were married," she said.

"My wife died. Before…" And that sad look returned.

She hated that look. She could spend the rest of her life making sure that look never came back.

The rest of her life. She had never thought that before about anyone.

She was sure about it with Blue.

She stood on her toes so that she could find his mouth again. "We're going to have to fix that. You know, when we were young, the man was supposed to be the experienced one."

"I know," he said. "I'm sorry—"

"But," she said, speaking over him. "This is the Greater World. Women are liberated. Which means that we can lead sometimes."

She kissed him. He kissed back, his eyes half-closed, his body pressed against hers, his arousal obvious.

She slid her hand down his arm until she found his hand. "Come on, my handsome prince. Let me teach you a few things."

His cheeks were flushed, those miraculous blue eyes sparkling. "Only a few?" he asked a bit breathlessly.

"This time," she said. "I'll teach you more next time. In fact, I know a lifetime of things."

He swallowed visibly, and for a moment, she thought she had frightened him off.

"Jodi," he said, "a lifetime? That's not something to joke about."

Her fingers threaded through his. "I'm not joking."

"A lifetime, though," Blue said, his voice shaking. "You realize that I'm a recovering alcoholic, right?"

"You drank for a reason," Jodi said.

"Everyone drinks for a reason. I learned how to drink to excess. I'll be going to AA all my life. I'll probably have to do some outpatient work with Dr. Hargrove. I really need to learn this stuff this time."

Jodi pulled him close and kissed him again. "Hmm," she said as she broke the kiss for just a moment. "A man who cares enough to get better. That sounds wonderful to me."

"It's work," Blue said. "It's—"

"And maybe this is why you lack experience?" Jodi said. "Your propensity for conversation?"

He almost answered her, then stopped himself and grinned. "Point taken," he said and pushed the bedroom door open all the way. "I see clean sheets."

She pulled him into the room. "I promise you," she said. "They won't remain clean for long."

Read on for an excerpt from

Wickedly Charming

by Kristine Grayson

He's given up on happily-ever-after…

Cinderella's Prince Charming is divorced and at a dead end.
The new owner of a bookstore, Charming has given up on
women, royalty, and anything that smacks of a future. That is,
until he meets up with Mellie…

But she may be the key to happily-right-now…

Mellie is sick and tired of stepmothers being misunderstood.
Vampires have redeemed their reputation, why shouldn't
stepmothers do the same? Then she runs into the handsomest,
most charming man she's ever met and discovers she's going
about her mission all wrong…

"Grayson deftly nods to pop culture and offers clever
spins on classic legends and lore while adding unique
twists all her own."—*Booklist* starred review

"I love this take on an old story… Exceedingly endearing…"
—*Night Owl Reviews* Reviewer Top Pick

Available now from Sourcebooks Casablanca

Chapter 1

BOOK FAIR

The very words of the sign filled Mellie with loathing. Book Fair indeed. More like Book Unfair.

Every time people wrote something down, they got it wrong. She'd learned that in her exceptionally long life.

Not that she was old—not by any stretch. In fact, by the standards of her people, she was in early middle age. She'd been in early middle age, it seemed, for most of her adult life. Of course that wasn't true. She'd only been in early middle age for her life in the public eye— two very different things.

And now she was paying for it.

She stood in a huge but nearly empty parking lot in the bright morning sun. It was going to be hot— California, too-dry-to-tolerate hot, fifty-bottles-of-Gatorade hot—but it wasn't hot yet. Still, she hoped she had on enough sunscreen (even if it did make her smell like a weird, chemical coconut). She had her hands on her hips (which hadn't expanded [much] since she was a beautiful young girl, who caught the eye of every man) as she surveyed the stunningly large building in front of her, with the banner strung across its multitude of doors.

The Largest Book Fair in the World!, the banner proclaimed in bright red letters. The largest book fair with the largest number of publishers, writers, readers and moguls—movie and gaming and every other type of mogul the entertainment industry had come up with.

It probably should be called *Mogul Fair* (Mogul Unfair?). But people were pitching books, not pitching moguls (although someone probably should pitch moguls; it was her experience that anyone with a shred of power should be pitched across a room [or down a staircase] every now and then).

This season's books, next season's books, books for every race, creed, and constituency, large books, small books, and the all-important evergreen books which were not, as she once believed, books about evergreens, but books that never went out of style, like *Little Women* or anything by Jane Austen or, dammit, by that villain Hans Christian Andersen.

Not that Andersen started it all. He didn't. It was those Grimm brothers, two better named individuals she had never met.

It didn't matter that Mellie had set them straight. By then, their "tales" were already on the market, poisoning the well, so to speak. (Or the apple. Those boys did love their poisons. It would have been so much better for all concerned if they had turned their attention to crime fiction. They could have invented the entire category. But *noooo*. They had to focus on what they called "fairies," as misnamed as their little "tales.")

She made herself breathe. Even alone with her own thoughts, she couldn't help going on a bit of a rant about those creepy little men.

She made herself turn away from the gigantic building and walk to the back of her minivan. With the push of a button, the hatchback unlocked (now *that* was magic) and she pulled the thing open.

Fifty signs and placards leaned haphazardly against each other. Last time, she'd only needed twenty. She hoped she would use all fifty this time.

She glanced at her watch. One hour until the Book Unfair opened.

Half an hour until her group showed up.

Mellie glared at the building again. Sometimes she thought of these things like a maze she needed to thread her way through. But this was a fortress, one she needed to conquer. All those entrances intimidated her. It was impossible to tell where she'd get the most media exposure. Certainly not at the front doors, with the handicapped ramp blocking access along one side.

Once someone else arrived to help her hand out the placards, she could leave for a few minutes and reconnoiter.

She wanted the maximum amount of air time for the minimum amount of exposure. She'd learned long ago that if she gave the media too much time in the beginning, they'd distort everything she said.

Better to parcel out information bit by bit.

The Book Unfair was only her first salvo.

But she knew it would be the most important.

———

He parked his silver Mercedes at the far end of the massive parking lot. He did it not so that he wouldn't be recognized—he wouldn't be, anyway—but because he'd learned long ago that if he parked his Mercedes anywhere near the front, the car would either end up with door dings and key scratches, or would go missing.

He reached into the glove box and removed his prized purple bookseller's badge. He had worked for two years to acquire that thing. Not that he minded. It still amazed him that no one at the palace had thought of opening a bookstore on the grounds.

He could still hear his father's initial objection: *We are not shopkeepers!* He'd said it in that tone that meant shopkeepers were lower than scullery maids. In fact, shopkeepers had become his father's favorite epithet in the past few decades, scullery maid being both politically and familially incorrect.

It took some convincing—the resident scholars had to prove to his father's satisfaction that true shopkeepers made a living at what they did, and in no way would a bookstore on the palace grounds provide anyone's living—but the bookstore finally happened.

With it came myriad book catalogues and discounts and advance reading copies and a little bit of bookish swag.

He'd been in heaven. Particularly when he realized he could attend every single book fair in the Greater World and get free books.

Not that he couldn't pay for his own books—he could, as well as books for each person in the entire Third Kingdom (which he did last year, to much complaint: it seemed everyone thought they would be tested on the contents of said gift books. Not everyone loved reading as much as he did, more's the pity).

Books had been his retreat since boyhood. He loved hiding in imaginary worlds. Back then, books were harder to come by, often hidden in monasteries (and going to those had caused some consternation for his

parents until they realized he was reading, not practicing for his future profession). Once the printing press
caught on, he bought his own books—he now devoted
the entire winter palace to his collection—but it still
wasn't enough.

If he could, he would read every single book ever
written—or at least scan them, trying to get a sense of
them. Even with the unusually long life granted to people of the Third Kingdom, especially when compared
with people in the Greater World (the world that had
provided his Mercedes and this quite exciting book fair),
he would never achieve it. There were simply too many
existing books in too many languages, with too many
more being written all the time.

He felt overwhelmed when he thought of all the
books he hadn't read, all the books he wanted to read,
and all the books he would want to read. Not to mention
all the books that he hadn't heard of.

Those dismayed him the most.

Hence, the book fair.

He was told to come early. There was a breakfast for
booksellers—coffee and doughnuts, the website said, free
of charge. He loved this idea of free as an enticement. He
wondered if he could use it for anything back home.

The morning was clear, with the promise of great heat.
A smog bank had started to form over Los Angeles, and
he couldn't see the ocean, although the brochures assured
him it was somewhere nearby. The parking lot looked
like a city all by itself. It went on for blocks, delineated
only by signs that labeled the rows with double letters.

The only other car in this part of the lot wasn't a car at
all but one of those minivans built so that families could

take their possessions and their entertainment systems with them.

The attractive black-haired woman unloading a passel of signs from the van looked familiar to him, but he couldn't remember where he had seen her before.

He wasn't about to go ask her either. His divorce had left him feeling very insecure, especially around women. Whenever he saw a pretty woman, the words of his ex-wife rose in his head.

She had screamed them at him in that very last fight, the horrible, unforgettable fight when she took the glass slipper—the thing that defined all that was good and pure in their relationship—and heaved it against the wall above his head.

Not so charming now, are you, asshole? Nope, not charming at all.

He had to concede she had a point—although he never would have conceded it to her. Still, those formerly dulcet tones echoed in his brain whenever he looked in the mirror and saw not the square-jawed hero who saved her from a life of poverty, but a balding, paunchy middle-aged man who would never achieve his full potential—not without killing his father, and that was a different story entirely.

Charming squared his shoulders and pinned his precious name badge to his shirt. The name badge did not use his real name. It used his *nom de plume*—which sounded a lot more romantic than The Name He Used Because His Real Name Was Stupid.

He called himself Dave. Dave Encanto, for those who required last names. His family didn't even have a last name—that's how long they'd been around—and even though he knew Prince was now considered a last name, he couldn't bring himself to use it.

He couldn't bring himself to use any name, really. He still thought of himself as Charming even though he knew his ex was right—he wasn't "charming" anymore. Not that he didn't try. It was just that charming used to come easily to him, when he had a head full of black, black hair, and an unwrinkled face, and the squarest of square jaws.

Prince Charming was a young man's name, in truth, and then only the name of an arrogant young man. To use that name now would seem like wish fulfillment or a really bad joke. He couldn't go with P.C. because the initials had been usurped, and people would catch the double irony of a prince trying to be p.c. with his own name change.

And as for Prince—that name was overused. In addition to the musician, Princes abounded. People named their horses Prince, for heaven's sake, and their dogs, and their surrogate children. In other words, only the nutty named a human being Prince these days, and much as Charming resented his father, he couldn't put either of his parents in the nutty category.

So he told people to call him Dave, which was emphatically not a family name. Too many family names had been co-opted as well—Edward, George, Louis, Philippe, even Harry, not just by another prince, but by some very famous, very fictional, magical potter's kid.

Dave, not David, a man who could go anywhere incognito any time he liked. Gone were the days when people would do a double-take, and some would say, *Aren't you…?* or *You know you look just like that prince—whatsisname?—Charming.*

About the Author

Before turning to romance writing, award-winning author Kristine Kathryn Rusch edited the *Magazine of Fantasy & Science Fiction* and ran Pulphouse Publishing (which won her a World Fantasy Award). As Kristine Grayson she has published eight novels so far and has won the *RT Book Reviews* Reviewer's Choice Award for Best Paranormal Romance, and, under her real name, Kristine Kathryn Rusch, the prestigious Hugo award. She lives in Oregon with her own Prince Charming, writer Dean Wesley Smith (who is not old enough to be one of the originals, but he is handsome enough) as well as the obligatory writers' cats. www.kriswrites.com.

Utterly Charming

by Kristine Grayson

—∿∿—

He could be her own personal Prince Charming if only dreams did come true...

Mysterious, handsome wizard Aethelstan Blackstone hires beautiful, hardworking attorney Nora Barr to get a restraining order to protect Sleeping Beauty from her evil stepmother. But if Sleeping Beauty is supposed to be his soul mate, then how come he's becoming bewitched by Nora?

And when Nora finds herself baby-sitting a clueless maiden from the Middle Ages, avoiding a very wicked witch, and falling hard for a man whose magic she doesn't believe in, she begins to think that love itself is only a fairy tale...

—∿∿—

"Grayson uses smooth prose and humorous, human characters to create a delightful, breezy tale perfect for anyone who truly enjoys happy endings."—*Publishers Weekly*

"This is another fascinating tale! I love how Kristine Grayson adds twists to the fairy tales that we all know and love!"
—*Bitten by Books*

For more Kristine Grayson, visit:

www.sourcebooks.com

Thoroughly Kissed

by Kristine Grayson

Sleeping Beauty has sworn off kissing…

Emma awakens to an entirely different world than the one she lived in a thousand years ago, and although she's the real Sleeping Beauty, her life is no fairy tale. After parting ways with her supposed Prince Charming, she's determined to be a normal girl—she hides her magic and swears off kissing strange men.

But her gorgeous boss Michael knows there's something unusual about Emma, and he thinks she's as infuriating as she is beautiful. Now Emma needs to teach Michael a lesson, which means mastering her magic. She knows she's flirting with danger, but after one look at Michael's perfect lips, all she can think is, "What's another thousand years…?"

Welcome to the fractious fairy tale world of Kristine Grayson, where the bumpy road to happily ever after is paved with surprises…

For more Kristine Grayson, visit:

www.sourcebooks.com